WATER
BORNE

BOOK TEN

THE CIRCLE OF CERIDWEN SAGA

WATER BORNE

OCTAVIA RANDOLPH

PYEWACKET PRESS

Water Borne is the tenth book in
The Circle of Ceridwen Saga by Octavia Randolph

Copyright © 2023 Octavia Randolph
ISBN Softcover 978-1-942044-37-6
ISBN Hardcover 978-1-942044-39-0

Book cover design by DesignforBooks.com. Maps by Michael Rohani.
Photo credits: boat, Shutterstock © Seyhan Ahen; landscape,
Shutterstock © Mepstock; and dress, Shutterstock © Faestock.

Pyewacket Press

The Circle of Ceridwen Saga employs British spellings, alternate spellings,
archaic words, and oftentimes unusual verb to subject placement. This is
intentional. A Glossary of Terms will be found at the end of the novel.

CONTENTS

LIST OF CHARACTERS

Ceric, son of Ceridwen and Gyric,
grandson of Godwulf of Kilton

Dwynwen, a noble maid of Ceredigion, in Wales

Edgyth, Lady of Kilton, widow of Godwin,
mother by adoption to Edwin

Edwin, younger brother to Ceric,
and Lord of Kilton in Wessex

Worr, the horse-thegn of Kilton, pledged man of Ceric

Tegwedd, a Welsh slave

Mindred, a serving woman of Kilton

Dunnere, priest of Kilton

Alwin and **Wystan**, captains of Edwin's body-guard

Elidon, King of Ceredigion in Wales, uncle to Dwynwen

Gwydden, his priest

Luned, a woman of Wales

Garrulf, scop of Kilton

Dagmar, daughter of the late Guthrum,
King of the Danes in Angle-land

Ingigerd, a woman of Dane-mark

Jorild, a woman of Dane-mark

Ase, a brewer in Ribe

Thorlak and **Ulfkel**, wine-merchant sons of Ase

Ælfwyn, formerly Lady of Four Stones,
now wife to Raedwulf of Defenas

Raedwulf, Bailiff of Defenas in Wessex

Burginde, companion and nurse to Ælfwyn

Cerd, grandson to Ælfwyn

Blida and **Bettelin,** orphaned siblings of Defenas

Ealhswith, daughter of Ælfwyn and Sidroc

Indract and **Lioba**, married couple,
stewards of Raedwulf's hall

Hrald, son of Ælfwyn and Sidroc, Jarl of the
keep of Four Stones in South Lindisse

Pega of Mercia, wife to Hrald, and Lady of Four Stones

Ælfgiva, infant daughter of Pega and Hrald

Mealla, companion to Pega, a maid of Éireann

Yrling, son of Ceridwen and Sidroc

Kjeld, second in command at Four Stones

Jari, a warrior of Four Stones, chief body-guard to Hrald

Bork, a stable-boy and orphan under Hrald's care

Ælfred, King of Wessex

Asberg, brother-in-law to Ælfwyn, in
command at the fortress of Turcesig

Wulgan, a Saxon ship-master and trader

Fremund, a Saxon merchant

Ruddick, a Frisian ship-master and trader

Ceridwen, Mistress of the hall Tyrsborg on
the island of Gotland, wife to Sidroc

Sidroc the Dane, formerly Jarl of
Four Stones in South Lindisse

Tindr, a bow hunter

Rannveig, a brewster on Gotland, mother of Tindr

Eirian, daughter to Ceridwen and Sidroc

Rodiaud, youngest daughter of Ceridwen and Sidroc

Runulv, a Gotlandic ship-master and trader

WATER BORNE MAPS

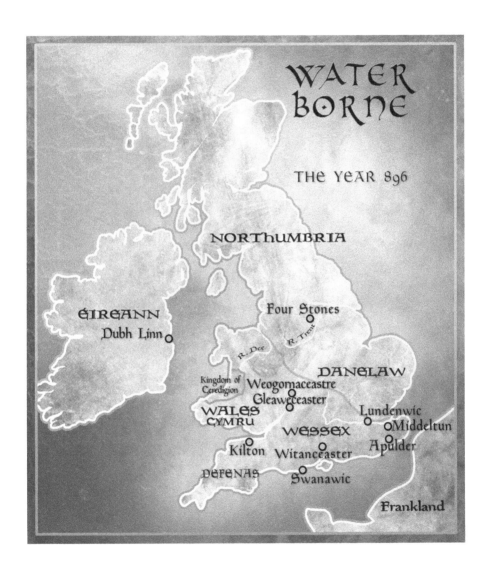

WATER BORNE

THE YEAR 896

NORThUMBRIA

ÉIREANN
Dubh Linn

Four Stones

R. Trent

R. Dee

DANELAW

Kingdom of
Ceredigion Weogomaceastre
Gleawecceaster

WALES
CYMRU

WESSEX

Kilton Witanceaster

DEFENAS Swanawic

Lundenwic
Middeltun
Apulder

Frankland

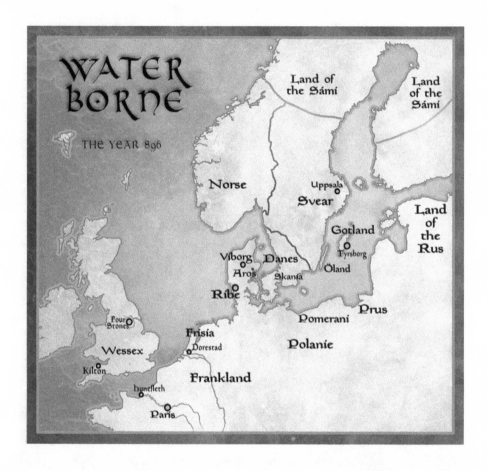

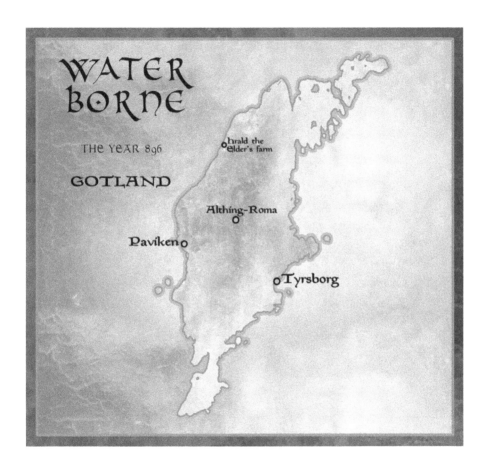

WATER
BORNE

THE YEAR 896

GOTLAND

Hrald the
Elder's farm

Althing-Roma

Pavíken

Tyrsborg

WATER BORNE

DWYNWEN
OF CEREDIGION

Kilton in Wessex

The Year 896

CERIC lowered the silver cup from his mouth. The water within was cool, as cool as the eyes of the Welsh girl who had offered it to him. He passed it back to Dwynwen, and she set it with care upon the table.

She sat down next him. The morning garden was quiet, but the steady roll of the sea against the cliffs of Kilton could be heard below. The eyes of both Ceric and Dwynwen rested upon the silver bridal-bowl before them.

Dwynwen lifted her hand and placed it on his forearm. It made him look at her. She slid her hand down to cover his own, lying there on the table. She clasped that hand.

"I will not leave you," she told him.

She knew his Lady-wife had been forced to leave; she was dead. But Dwynwen was here, alive, and at his side.

And she herself had been left. Her mother, as fiery as a grass-land blaze and just as unpredictable, sickened and

1

died when Dwynwen was but six years of age. Her father Dunwyd, Prince of Ceredigion, so serene, just, and temperate, brought the Lady Luned to his mountain hall the following year. Luned's warmth was of a different nature, but her interest in Dwynwen was unfeigned. At Dunwyd's death, when Dwynwen knew nine Summers, the two faced their future together. When Elidon claimed their hall for his son, go live with the King they must. Forest, crag, and cwm were lost to them; they would henceforth live at the sea's edge, with a scouring tide marking the passage of time. Of the girl's years there, one thing only was constant. The Lady Luned had been there half of Dwynwen's life, and became her whole world. It was a world that Lady schooled her in, and must school her to leave when Dwynwen grew old enough to wed.

Now Dwynwen brought her face closer to the ear of Ceric, and spoke again.

"I will not leave you."

He turned his hand under hers, so that their palms faced. His fingers threaded through hers, and he closed them in a firm clasp.

"I was sent to you," she told him. His curling coppery hair, Sun-streaked and tousled, framed his furrowed brow.

Sent to me, thought Ceric. Did Ashild send you, he asked himself. Or was it God.

"Who . . . sent you," he breathed.

"Lady Luned foretold my coming," she explained. "But she did not send me."

She remembered St Ninnoc in the stone chantry. "The saints, I think, called me here. St Ninnoc."

They sat alone, her words in the air. Their hands remained intertwined, in silent communion.

A figure appeared at the edge of the garden. Dwynwen saw her; it was the slave Tegwedd she had brought with her from Ceredigion. Tegwedd would not enter the garden, but stood at its margin, twisting her hands until she raised one of them to her mistress. Dwynwen did not respond. Tegwedd turned and left.

The lifting Sun was climbing higher in the garden. The roses smothering the trellis behind where they sat were filled with the droning of honeybees, the air alive with their low hum. Fat bumblebees were there as well, shaking the tender buds as they forced their way into the golden hearts. The hands of Ceric and Dwynwen remained clasped.

A second female appeared at the margin of the pleasure garden, a serving woman of Kilton. Lady Edgyth had given Dwynwen this servant upon her arrival yesterday. The Welsh girl understood that this woman, Mindred by name, would act not only to serve her, but as a kind of chaperone to her for as long as she remained unwed here at Kilton. As such, the Lady Edgyth had granted Mindred authority which Dwynwen must heed.

Dwynwen stood, her small hand still held by that of Ceric. "Lady Edgyth wants me." She imagined this was so, and therefore said it, though she could have spent the day sitting there at the side of this man.

He was loath to let go her hand; he must control the pressure of his fingers as she withdrew it. He looked up at her. She was being called from his side, so soon.

His eyes fell to the bridal-cup.

"It is in your keeping," she told him. She smiled then, and left with Mindred.

Lady Edgyth had indeed a full day planned for Dwynwen. If she was to be Edwin's bride, and Lady of the hall, there would be much with which she must acquaint herself. Edgyth wished the girl to begin to know some of it, and to be seen by those whom she might soon be in charge of.

They began at the hearths and fire-rings of the kitchen, that most needful operance. A hall's folk being fed depended on the good management of its Lady. The demand was greatest for the warriors of the hall; the first claim of all was they have meat and drink in sufficiency to train and fight. Food was ever the first recompense for service, from the highest to the lowest, and a shrunken belly the loudest claimant to disloyalty. The kitchens, bake-ovens, brew-house and storehouses of Kilton were as extensive as those housed at the royal estate of Elidon, King of Ceredigion, Dwynwen's uncle. Dwynwen and Luned had nothing to do with them; her step-mother had run the hall of Dwynwen's father Dunwyd, one far smaller. And Dwynwen had known but nine years of age when they left there. Today she was led about by Lady Edgyth, and saw the respectful greeting in the eyes of all who saw Kilton's Lady. Dwynwen bobbed her head to their bows and curtsies of welcome.

They moved then to the hall itself. Within was a storeroom, a kind of second treasure room, in which were kept the hammered salvers and stemmed cups of dark bronze most of the warriors used. This room also housed the silver salvers and silver cups used by those favoured to sit at the high table. The rest of the hall dined from platters of polished wood; these too were here. Edgyth took keys from her waist and opened the chests holding metal, showing Dwynwen the counting-sticks on which they were all numbered at the end of the evening meal, when they had been washed and wiped and made ready to be locked away another night.

"You will have help each night in doing so," Edgyth told her, "but it is ever good that you are here, attending as they are tallied."

Dwynwen nodded. Elidon had a steward who did much the same, protecting against loss of these costly items.

The hall's linens were stored in the treasure room, but Edgyth did not take her there today. It was the chamber in which her son slept, and too intimate a space in which to draw the girl now. She would see it later, when she had decided she would stay, and be Edwin's wife. Excepting this, Edgyth thought it best to treat Dwynwen as if they were already betrothed.

Lady Edgyth came to Ceric late in the afternoon. He had spent much of the day at the table in the pleasure garden, and Worr had come and sat with him as he could. Worr knew Ceric was exhausted in body and mind. It compelled him to remain still, to sit, to absorb what beauty and life he could. The day was fair and fine as a high Summer's day could be, but once alone the thoughts of Ceric travelled beyond the scented confines of the sheltered place. The Welsh girl was foremost in his mind, her lovely strangeness, the delicacy of her person, the quiet assurance of her soft voice.

Edgyth looked down at Ceric as he sat there. "Will you come to the hall tonight," she asked. Her tone was as kind as ever, but no ear could fail to hear the note of expectancy in her words.

He looked at her, this woman who had done so much for him and his brother, and all of Kilton.

He took a breath. "I will come," he said.

Her smile was warm and broad. "I am so glad," she answered, quickly enough to underscore the real gratitude she felt. "I am eager for you to meet the Welsh girl, Lady Dwynwen. She is a remarkable young woman."

He nodded; it was all he could do. He had already seen her rareness.

When Ceric went into his bower house to change, he drew out from his clothing chest one of his best tunics, one Edgyth had made. It was deep green. Onto the hem and collar she had sewn bands of highly coloured tablet weaving, the product also of her own hands.

He ran his hand through his hair, much of it now no longer than an extended finger. He took his comb and used it. Short as it was, the natural wave in it was unhindered, and it curled about his face and neck.

As he turned to go he saw on the window casement the small wooden bird which had been his toy as a child. Begu had brought it to him in the forest. It had helped recall him to an earlier, and happier self. He picked the bird up now. Under his fingers he could feel the marks of his teething upon the bird's rounded head. Begu's words came back to him, reminding him he had a son of his own, who needed him. He placed the bird back on the sill of the window, and went to the hall.

Ceric had to steel himself, entering. There was always a man stationed at the door, and he pulled it open for him with a nod of greeting. The noise of the gathering folk was an assault to his ears. This was the first time he had supped here at night since his return; he had come some days to break his fast only. Those who spotted him quieted. He moved to where Edgyth stood at the high table, a smile for him on her lips.

Dwynwen stood next her, and wore a gown of soft green this night, which oddly made her eyes of blue the richer. Ceric inclined his head to the girl as Edgyth presented her. He saw in those eyes tawny streaks of brown, and a rim of greenish grey about the iris as well. They were an odd shade, not quite blue, nor brown. Much resided there, he thought, and much lay behind them.

Dwynwen was placed between Ceric and his brother at table. Edwin, in the carved, high-backed chair of the Lord, was separate from them, for Dwynwen sat upon the cushioned bench next Ceric. He was most aware of the slight pressure of her slender thigh when she sat down, just touching his own.

They ate from their own salvers; only those wed shared one. They scarcely exchanged a word beyond their first greeting, but Ceric was mindful of Edwin as he spoke to their guest. Ceric left before the scop Garrulf began to sing; he feared the man would try to honour him with some favourite tale of his, or even sing of some exploit of his own.

He made hasty fare-well to Lady Edgyth, to Edwin, and their guest, and retreated into the dusk of the hall yard. Once at his bower house he began to undress, then stopped, and sat down at the small table not far from his bed.

The room fell into deeper shadow. He had lit a single beeswax taper when he entered, and as its light gathered against the growing dark his eye was drawn to the soft glow of the silver bowl set near it. She had brought him water in it, for a thirst he did not know he felt.

The gap in his closed wooden shutters had shown the black of night for some time when someone tapped at his door. It might be a serving man, asking if he needed ought for the night; yet he knew it to be late for that. He rose and went to the door.

Outside was Dwynwen. She was alone, with nothing in her hands. Her hair was loose, without even the slightest of ribbands to hold it. He stood there in his doorway, outlined by the small light of the taper behind him. He wore only his leggings, with his small gold cross upon his chest.

Dwynwen stepped forward into his arms, and held him to her.

He accepted her, lowered his head to hers, holding her to his chest. Her name arose on his lips.

"Dwynwen. Dwynwen, Dwynwen . . ." he repeated. A name like a spell, an incantation.

"I will not leave you," she said once more.

His hands came around from her back, and up to her face. He cupped that small face as he had the silver bridal-bowl she had brought him. Their eyes were fixed. He saw hers were glistening. She spoke again.

"I will not leave you. I will not leave you." It sounded as an urgent whisper, a promise, a vow. She pressed herself more closely to him. He bent his head; his lips touched hers, the lightest of kisses.

She drew breath. Her hand reached up upon his bare chest, and wrapped about the small gold cross there. She lifted it to her lips a moment and spoke.

"Under the eyes of God, the Holy Mother Mary, Ninnoc, and all the saints, I give myself to you."

He tried to pull back. He began to utter his next word, also a name. "Edwin . . ."

"You are my husband," she insisted. "It is you I came to wed."

Ceric shook his head, yet held onto her. He could not do otherwise. He stepped backward into the room with her and closed the door.

They turned. His bed was there, the four posts of it rising up above their heads, crowned with the opened mouths of dragons, tongues flicking.

Dwynwen's gasp was soft, yet deep.

"Fire-drakes," she uttered. It was confirmation of all, that she would be led to this bed, guarded by dragons.

He stripped off her gown and shift as they stood there. The little light of the taper flickered upon her nakedness. Her budding breasts and barely rounded hips shone ivory. Her fall of straight hair reached down her back nearly to her knees. He dropped to the floor, undid the silver toggles of her green shoes and drew them off, along with the low stockings clinging to her slender legs.

She was so young. Her body was almost that of a child; he knew this. Yet she had been sent to be his wife.

As if in answer to this thought, her hands came down to where he knelt, and touched his face, drawing him up. When he stood before her she pressed that tender body to his naked chest.

They moved almost as one to that space guarded by dragons, its thick feather-bed, the cushions and pillows of down, the sheets of creamy linen, nubby to the touch.

Ceric pulled off his leggings. He did not speak as Dwynwen lay down, nor when he climbed above her. Scarcely a sound came from his mouth as he kissed her face and lips. He could summon no words.

She awakened a thirst in him, as if that first sip of water she had offered from the silver bowl had but presaged a deeper yearning he was become aware of. Now he might drown in her, tangled in her hair, arms and legs locked. She gave of her small body with a fearlessness, rising to the urgency of his demand. Ceric felt himself drowning with her, or drowning in her. When he rooted his body within her own, her hands and arms clung to his back; they swam together in shared movement. The golden cross around his neck hung down and touched her breast, connecting them from heart to heart.

Their love-making was fierce, and infinitely tender. A gasping fish might struggle free in the hands of its captor, and landing in its watery element, once again draw freeing breath as it streaks away. This was akin to what Ceric felt; this fear, this struggle, then final bliss.

When it was over, Ceric did not pull fully away from her. He lay, looking at her, while Dwynwen, on her back, smiled at him. Her eyes went to the two fire-drakes, looking down at her from the foot of the bed.

He spoke, his words low, sombre, and yet tinged with a note of discovery.

"It is our wedding day. And you are my wife."

Past dawn a serving man knocked on the door. Ceric opened to him, and answered the man's unvoiced question of where, this day, Ceric would break his fast.

"Here, I thank you. Please to bring enough for two."

The man was surprised, but gratified. Since his return to the hall the elder son thereof had eaten so sparingly; today he must finally feel hungered. Then he noticed the bed. It was not empty. A figure lay there.

The serving man averted his eyes. He bowed his head, and left.

Ceric returned to the bed. He drew Dwynwen close, and held her. A vast change had been wrought in their lives in the last few hours, the effects of which would ripple out to many. He knew to some it would be no ripple, but tidal flood. Just now, when all was still sacred with private knowing, he must hold her.

All the serving folk of Kilton were now beginning their duties. Mindred knocked on the door of the bower given to Lady Dwynwen. She found only the slave girl there, distracted with worry, and for lack of a common speech, unable to expand on what the unused bed already revealed.

Mindred hastened to the side of Lady Edgyth with her finding. Edgyth sent her to the house of the horse-thegn, bidding him come. Worr listened to what little the Lady of Kilton knew, then went to the gate-keepers at the palisade walls, and questioned also those men who had been on the ramparts from dusk through dawn. None had passed through during the night.

Worr and Edgyth stood outside her bower, fast by the church, speaking of this. The Welsh slave was of no use; she could not speak to them, and by her copious tears showed she feared being blamed for the absence of her mistress. The eyes of both horse-thegn and Lady met over the girl's head as they considered their next step.

Edwin entered the pleasure garden, looking for Ceric. He wished to take Dwynwen out in one of the small boats later, and wanted his brother with him to help manage the craft.

He found Ceric, but he was not alone. Edwin came around the trellis work of the pavilion to see his brother, sitting at the table there, sharing a single bench with Dwynwen. Their hands were clasped upon the table before them.

Edwin was at first shocked into silence.

Ceric stood up, and Edwin took a step nearer. His eyes dropped to where the Lady Dwynwen of Ceredigion sat. His first words were for her.

"You were meant for me!"

Dwynwen took a moment before she answered.

"I was meant for Ceric."

Edwin looked accusingly at each of them in turn.

His brother spoke. "It is too late, Edwin."

"Too late!"

The girl had only arrived three days ago; Ceric had not even seen her that first day. It could not be too late. Edwin was about to speak again in protest of this judgement. The look on his brother's face stopped him.

"It is too late," Ceric repeated.

It could not be true. Ceric could not have taken this girl to his bed. Yet the steadiness of his brother's eyes on him said much.

"You mean – you have –" He could not say the rest aloud.

"She has given herself, yes," came the answer.

Edwin was staggered. He had been willing to wait a year for her. Now his brother had, on the second night of Dwynwen's arrival, robbed her from him.

"Given! You have taken her. Taken her from me!"

Dwynwen spoke again. "I came for Ceric," she asserted.

Edwin glared at her; glared and then dismissed her claim. He turned on his brother.

"You are my pledged man!"

Ceric said nothing, only stood looking steadily at his brother as Edwin's shock exploded into anger.

Edwin lunged at Ceric, throwing a punch at his jaw. It hit him squarely, nearly knocking him off his feet. Dwynwen, leaping up, gave a shriek of alarm.

Ceric had staggered under the blow, but did nothing to defend himself. The Lord of Kilton stood, staring at his brother. It enraged Edwin, the way he took that blow. Ceric's mouth was bleeding, yet all he did was step back.

Worr arrived at a run, and in time to see Edwin throw the second punch. A seam opened up along his brother's left eyebrow. Ceric staggered back once more, almost falling, but did not raise his fists to fight, nor even lift his hands to ward Edwin off.

Dwynwen screamed, and tried to move to Ceric. Edwin blocked her way.

Again, Ceric straightened up, without raising his arms to defend himself against his younger brother.

But Worr was there, with Lady Edgyth behind him. The horse-thegn grabbed Edwin, pinning his arms behind his back. Edwin was no match for Worr's strength. He struggled in vain against the hold, and against the older man's words.

"Edwin! He is not well."

"Not well? He is well enough to couple with my bride!"

It was not this startling claim that allowed Worr to release his hold, rather the new slackness in Edwin's body. He let go the arms he pinned, and Edwin, now freed, shrugged his pained shoulders. But he did not move again toward Ceric.

Confused horror was on Edgyth's face. "Dwynwen," she murmured.

"It was Ceric I came to wed," she said. Her eyes were fastened on Ceric, but then looked to all in turn. It was a quiet proclamation, but forceful in its steady surety.

Edgyth's hand lifted toward her breast. "Ceric? But – how did you know?"

"Luned told me. She told me long ago."

None of this made sense; the Lady Luned knew nothing of either brother before Edwin's journeying to Ceredigion.

The Welsh girl said the next not as threat, nor as offer. She spoke as if this were a simple telling of truth.

"If I am not welcome here, I will return to Ceredigion. If Ceric will come with me, Elidon will make of him a Prince."

Edwin was quick to answer. His words were for Ceric, not the Welsh girl.

"You would desert me?"

Ceric stood there, his lip and eye bleeding. As he gave his answer his eyes were fixed on Edwin, as if they were alone.

"I will never desert you."

Dwynwen saw this; understood the bond there, one of blood, yes, but of sworn loyalty unto death. She saw, and spoke to this bond, a voice quiet, almost light.

"Then I must stay here," she decided.

The shouting voices and Dwynwen's scream had brought a raft of warriors and serving folk to the margins of the garden. Foremost amongst them were Edwin's two chief body-guards, Alwin and Wystan. Yet with Worr and Lady Edgyth there, they must not intrude. Alwin gestured all back, and to their abandoned tasks.

Worr was the first to speak. They must be clear of public view, and he would talk to the brothers together. Worr looked about for a suitable space; they could not enter Ceric's bower house, the dragon bed of which Dwynwen had so lately left.

"Edwin, Ceric," he told them, as near to an order as he had given to either in many a year. "We will go into the hall."

Edgyth made gesture she would tend to the bloody face of Ceric. Worr shook this off. "I will do it." The three men turned and made for the hall.

Edgyth looked at her guest. "Let us go to my bower, Dwynwen," she invited.

Once inside Edgyth bade Dwynwen sit. It was at that small table covered with the watered green silk which Modwynn had laid there, a table which had been witness to many private moments between the two women. The table covering seemed almost to flow into the pale green of Dwynwen's gown.

Edgyth's first words were the hardest to utter.

"He did not – force you in any way." It was scarce above a whisper, so afraid was she to voice the question.

Dwynwen shook her head, her look of bewilderment saying much.

"I came to him," she said, almost as plea. "I came to his bower house."

She told the Lady of Kilton what she had told its oldest son. "I was sent to him."

"Sent to him . . ."

Edgyth shook her head, both hands rising to her temples as if to clear her thoughts. The union Dwynwen had been sent to make was not merely private marriage, but state-craft.

"But King Elidon – will he not be angered? You came to wed the Lord of Kilton. Edwin."

Edgyth could not speak her deepest fear, that the King would hear of this and think it rape, or at least, bride-theft.

Dwynwen was decided in her answer.

"My uncle wants silver. The jug he sent back, filled with it. And he wants a bond with your King, Ælfred. Ceric is the god-son of your King. Dunnere wrote this to Gwynedd, who told me. Elidon will think the bond the stronger, with the King's own god-son."

If it were true, she could not fault the girl's reasoning.

"And you are – quite well?" Edgyth hazarded.

Dwynwen dropped her eyes a moment. "Luned told me much of such matters," she said. Edgyth did not accept this simple claim as full answer, and with her eyes kept inquiring of the girl how she was. Dwynwen could not dissemble before such kindness. "In truth, I am sore, yes," she murmured. "Luned said it would be so."

"Did she tell you how to care for yourself, a bath in flowers of yellow centaury? I will make you such a bath," she offered. Edgyth smiled, and reached out her hand to the girl.

"You are kind, Lady. But Ceric is bleeding. I must make a compress of mallow and blackthorn for his eye."

Edgyth paused. These were the very herbs she would use to remedy the swelling. "We shall make it together," she told the girl.

The Lady of Kilton turned to the chest beneath the window. Within were pottery jars of Simples of every kind, culled from Kilton's gardens and woodland. She shook out the dried leaves of mallow and thin peelings of blackthorn root and almost filled a small linen bag with them.

"Sew it firmly shut," she instructed Dwynwen, "while I get hot water from the kitchen."

When the soaked compress had cooled, Edgyth carried it in a basin to Ceric. He was alone in his bower house. She would speak to Edwin soon, but felt she must know more from Ceric first.

When he answered her knock she winced at the look of his battered face. Ceric seemed almost unaware of it; his first words, rushed and near-desperate, proved this.

"I must wed her, Lady. Today. I will wed her. If Dunnere will not bless us we will ask God to."

"Ah, my boy, my boy," she murmured, deeply moved. She brushed a tear from her eye with her free hand. "I do not understand any of this. But I believe you. I believe you, Ceric. And I believe Dwynwen." Such surety could not be denied.

"I will make it so," she promised. "You will be truly wed today, and I shall witness."

She set down the basin. "Lie down," she instructed, gesturing to the bed. Ceric did so. She could see where Worr had wiped away the blood from the left eyebrow. The eye was closing, showing purple already, and the lower lip swollen where it had split. "Hold this compress on your hurt. Dwynwen and I prepared it together." She guided his hand as he lifted it to his face. She looked about her, and went on. "I must see your brother."

When Worr left with the brothers, they had gone to the treasure room. Edwin slept within, and therein was stored the armoury of the burh. Great treasure was there as well in ornaments of silver and gold, but much of the coinage had been buried within the hall precincts, as proof against raids. Edwin had been raised in this room, given as a babe to Godwin, Lord, and Edgyth, Lady.

Entering it now, the two brothers took up position at either end of the table. Worr came to stand in the middle.

"Ceric. Is this true, what your brother said? You have coupled with the Lady?"

He named drew breath. "It is true."

Edwin could scarce contain himself. "That is all you can say? You stole my wife from me!"

Worr raised his hand to caution Edwin from his anger. Edwin could not stay his words.

"Who are you," he demanded of the horse-thegn, "to bid me stop? I am Lord here." He glared at Ceric. "Not you."

Ceric had no response. The Welsh maid had been directed to him, and in the night he had thought her a gift divinely sent. Yet he knew the loss to Edwin was great. Ceric would never desert his brother, but now saw Edwin might cast him from the hall.

Before Edwin could say more he mastered himself. He turned his face from the two men before him, turned it in silent dismissal. Ceric and Worr left.

When his mother Edgyth came to him, Edwin was still standing, almost without motion, at the end of the table.

She walked to his side, and began in a low tone.

"Edwin, this was a blow indeed. An unlooked-for surprise –"

Great was his umbrage, and he could not hide it from his voice.

"Surprise? It is a treacherous theft. It is – rape."

His Lady-mother countered this, gently, but with certain firmness. All had happened with dizzying speed, but she recounted what she knew with calm attention.

"No, it is neither of those things. Dwynwen came, to see if Kilton could be her home. She wishes to stay. She has a strong calling to be here. She feels – directed to be here. It was foretold by her step-mother, the Lady Luned. Omens are powerful. This one must be true, or neither she nor Ceric would have acted as they did."

Edgyth recurred to the stipulation that Dwynwen see Kilton first. The girl had somehow known something else was in store for her, or she would have wed Edwin when she was still at her uncle's court in Ceredigion. This gave strength to Edgyth's reasoning, and her voice.

"It is not a question of your relinquishing her, my son. She was not yours, but you were the vital instrument of bringing her here. I would have peace between you and Ceric, those whom I love most on Earth.

"You heard your brother. Ceric will never desert you, never leave Kilton. But you could cast him out, a renegade. That would, I know, kill him; and do such harm to you that your life would be blighted ever more.

"Let her go. Let her go to Ceric." Her last words were spoken with solemn finality. "They are already wed."

Edwin squeezed his eyes shut, to keep the water forming there from spilling over.

"Yes," he conceded. "She is now his wife."

At the noon hour Edwin went to Ceric in his bower house. His brother was alone; his mother had told him that Dwynwen would stay with her until the ceremony later this day.

Ceric opened the door to his brother. Edwin could not help but look to the dragon bed, its broad expanse, the sheets and pillows in disarray. He saw the silver hand-fast bowl upon the table; the bowl he had carried to Ceredigion to act as a pledge if the girl were pleasing. Dwynwen had drunk from that bowl, but not with him; she had shared it with his brother.

Ceric was watching his brother's eyes, taking in the tumbled bedclothes which the dragon posts stood looking down upon, and then the silver bowl.

With his eyes still fastened on the bowl, Edwin spoke. "The bridal-cup."

Ceric made answer. The cup was the start of all, and he must tell of it. "Yes. She brought it to me, filled with water, and bade me drink. It was yesterday, in the morning."

Edwin stood silent.

"She has chosen you," he said at last.

Edwin sat down at the table. Ceric came and sat as well.

Ceric knew of the agreed-upon bride-price, and now spoke of it. It was his to render. "The wine jug – I will fill it with coins, and have it sent to her uncle."

Edwin nodded; there was nothing else he could do.

The Welsh girl had come into their lives and disrupted all. If Elidon would not be angered, did not feel himself cheated, that was some consolation to Edwin. He did not wish to deal with that. Yet he had not only lost a bride, but lost a prime chance to build alliance with a Kingdom which could help protect Kilton, and preserve Wessex. He had imagined Ælfred's approval at his union with the maid of Ceredigion. Now once again it was Ceric who claimed primacy.

He looked at his brother's face, the swollen lip, the blackening eye. It was horrible to hit a man who would not hit back; not even raise his hands in defence to ward off the oncoming blow. How much the worse when that man was your brother, who you have ever looked up to.

"Why did you let me hit you," was all Edwin could ask. It was voiced as quietly as was Ceric's answer.

"I cannot raise my hand against my Lord."

Edwin hung his head.

"It will not happen again," he muttered. He could not beg forgiveness. But at this moment he wished for Ceric and not he to be Lord of Kilton.

Ceric was older, a better warrior, the god-son of the King, and had, through the will of Dwynwen, or Fate, or God, or all three, been granted the Lord of Kilton's bride as his own. If Edwin could throw off that mantle of Lordship this instant he would have done so, and in a single beat of his heart.

His heart. Edwin remembered then whose blood coursed through that heart: that of his true father, Godwin of Kilton, Lord before him. This was his own Fate, and his birth-right. He must accept it, and forge the best way with it, as he could. He felt deep shame at striking Ceric, a doubled shame for doing so twice after his brother had made it clear he would not raise his hands against the blows. How terrible is my power as Lord, thought Edwin. Worr's voice came resounding back to him, comparing Edwin to his father, urging him to see this in his nature and curb its growth.

He reached his hand out to his brother's forearm, placed it there, and gave a squeeze.

After his brother left, Ceric walked to Dunnere's house. The man was seated at his writing-table, a book before him. He rose when his murmured word admitted Ceric. He startled at Ceric's face; he had been out in the village during the upset and had heard none of it.

Ceric at once began.

"Dunnere, I have wed Dwynwen of Ceredigion. I would have you bless us, today, in the chantry."

The priest leant forward, and set his fingertips onto the surface of the table, as if to steady his feet beneath him.

"Edwin has surrendered her," Ceric went on. "Lady Edgyth has blest it. I would have you bless the union as well."

Dunnere was nearly dumbstruck. He recovered himself enough to utter the next.

"Yes, yes," he answered. "I will do so, today." He looked about the room, prising his eyes away from Ceric. "Before the hall gathers to sup tonight."

The blessing of the sacrament of marriage would be conferred. The priest recollected himself to his pastoral duty. "Would you confess, my son?"

Ceric sank down upon his knees. "Only that I allowed this maid into my bed last night. But she named me husband, and after the act, I named her wife."

Dunnere listened. The pair were fully wed; there was no absolution he could grant. If things had been made right with the Lord of Kilton, well, that was forgiveness which was not Dunnere's to grant. But Edwin had done so.

He answered. "I see no sin. You are man and wife. I will speak to Lady Dwynwen, to see if there is ought she would say to me. And I will be there to bless you."

Before the priest visited the Lady Dwynwen, the shaken cleric must take a moment to compose himself. He and his brother priest Gwydden had laid out the means through which union of Kilton and Ceredigion could be accomplished; but the end achieved was of quite different effect. How this news would be received by Gwydden, Elidon, and the girl's step-mother Luned, he could not begin to compass.

He found the Welsh girl at the bower of Lady Edgyth, who opened to him. When she saw it was the priest, Edgyth excused herself, guessing what he had come for.

"Lady Dwynwen," he began, once they were alone. "Ceric has told me of . . . your changed estate. You have entered into Holy Matrimony with him. I will be there to give the blessing of the Church this afternoon, when we gather at the chantry."

The girl smiled at this, but said nothing. It forced Dunnere to go on.

"Would you make confession, my child, beforehand?" His naming of her had never been more apt. Dunnere was used to calling men and women older than he, "my son" or "my daughter"; it was the convention of pastoral care. But Dwynwen truly looked little more than a child.

Her answer was that of a thoughtful woman.

"I thank you, Father Dunnere. Gwydden taught that God's creation is perfect. If this be so, and I was unsullied, I have acted the role that God and Nature ordained for me. I have no sin to confess."

Dunnere blinked. It was not pertinacity, but inner composure welling from a source he could not guess.

He found himself nodding in agreement, and again assured her of his presence in the chantry.

Late in the afternoon Ceric went alone to the stone church. He would not make his vows at the threshold of the door, as was common, but rather wished to do so within the chantry itself.

Before any arrived he sought a quiet moment at the tomb of his grandmother, and spent time as well over that of his father, buried with his little sister, Ninnoc, at his side. The statue of that saint looked over at him, resplendent in her red gown in the sharp shaft of sunlight falling upon her. He went to it, and saw again the golden rings his parents had worn for the duration of their marriage, there at the statue's base.

Ceric thought of another stone church, far to the north-east. Under a ledger stone of pure white lay Ashild. She was wife to him, had given him a son as well. But Ashild had never named him husband. Dwynwen had, in one of the first utterances she had spoken to him. He turned his head, looking through the window glass, so filled with the light of the lowering Sun it seemed a burning veil through which he could see nothing beyond.

Did you send her, Ashild, he silently asked. His eyes, unable to withstand that light, shifted again to the serene face of St Ninnoc. Or was it you, Ninnoc, you of Wales, whose name my tiny sister also bore.

As he stood there the priest entered, wearing his white chasuble, that reserved for joyous occasions. The tomb of Godwulf and Modwynn lay before the altar, and Dunnere took up position there. Ceric stood, his feet just before the incised name of his grandmother.

Lady Edgyth came next, Dwynwen at her side, with Worr behind them. Worr turned his head as he entered, looking back as if he sought someone. He left the heavy oaken door open.

The three walked toward Ceric.

Dwynwen was attired in a gown darkly red. It was of silk, as all heard by its rustle, and saw by its soft sheen. On her head was pinned a fine veil of filmy stuff, cream-coloured, and held in place by two long hair pins of gold, affixed above her ears. She had upon her breast a round pin of silver, in which was worked a dragon, its red eyes garnets which flashed as she walked in the bright sunlight. Edgyth at her side was in a gown of even deeper red, nearly black, sewn with bands of grey at neckline, hem, and wrists, making a striking backdrop for Dwynwen's resplendence.

Ceric had donned a tunic of rich blue, one he found in his clothes chest and had never yet worn. With the hurt to his face, he looked a warrior lately come from the field of battle. Although he wore his gem-set seax belted across his belly, there was no sword at his side. That weapon had been left behind, hanging where it had been more than a year, in its carved scabbard, on a tooled belt by his bed in the bower.

There was meaning in this, great meaning, to those who saw him. Not all pledged couples came to their bridals with a tool emblematic of their role in life, which they would briefly exchange as part of their vows. Dwynwen was akin to a Princess. Yes, she would weave and sew as did all other high-born women, but she brought no shuttle with her. She was bringing her name, her royal blood, and her treasure to her husband. For a sword-bearing warrior it was tradition that he would hand the hilt to his bride a moment, emblem not only of his livelihood, but of his willingness to protect her and their offspring with its blade. Ceric stood before Dwynwen, not a warrior, but a man.

Dunnere began by blessing the assembled, asking that their ears might be opened to the vows they were about to hear, and that they forever aid the couple in helping them adhere to their promise. The pair then made their simple vows. The elder son of the hall began. He faced Dwynwen, and took up her hand in his own.

"I Ceric, son of Gyric of Kilton, grand-son of Godwulf, Lord of Kilton, affirm that you, Dwynwen of Ceredigion, are my true wife. I will honour you as long as God grants me space to tread upon this Earth."

This was voiced with utmost gravity, one echoed by his young bride.

"I Dwynwen, daughter of Prince Dunwyd, niece to Elidon, King of Ceredigion, join my hand with yours, Ceric of Kilton. You are ever my husband. Never shall I leave you. May our Kingdoms know peace, and our union be a blessing to both."

She wanted to say aloud that she hoped to be a blessing unto the hall. But seeing how she had so disordered it, she was content to say the next.

"I give thanks for the goodness of your noble hall, to which I have come."

Edgyth, Lady of Kilton, stepped forward. She had drawn from her sleeve a ribband of yellow, so deep it was like unto gold. Thirty years ago that ribband bound her own hand to that of Godwin of Kilton. She had saved it these long years, and would use it now, to show her welcome of this new pair. She took the ribband and wrapped it about their joined hands.

"I give this ribband into your care, Dwynwen," she told her. "May it herald the start of an unbreakable bond in your lives."

Neither Ceric nor Dwynwen had expected this, and the bride was so moved that a tear escaped her eye and fell upon it. Edgyth kissed the girl upon her brow, and then bestowed another upon the brow of Ceric.

After the final blessing by Dunnere, Edgyth embraced both man and wife, first together, and then in turn. Worr stepped forward, the only male supporter Ceric had, wrapped his arms about him, and made a bow to his bride.

They turned, and saw Edwin by the door. He had been standing outside, and when Ceric began his vow, had slipped in. Ceric was pledged to him. Now Edwin must accept that his brother had given another pledge, to this Welsh girl. She too had claim on him. Ceric was not hot-headed, nor rash. For all its suddenness it ran to the bone, that his brother had done this.

Edgyth's heart was made glad, seeing her son there, and she raised her hand to gesture him near. Edwin could not do so. He gave but a nod, and left.

The bridal party then walked to the priest's house. The record of Kilton's marriages, births, and deaths was kept by Dunnere. The priest had expected that he would sign the register for the bride; but no. Dwynwen took the quill in hand and wrote her name, in large and proud letters. It was her left hand in which she wielded it, significant, the priest thought. Those who favoured the left were often afflicted with wayward thinking.

Then Dwynwen held the quill more firmly, and dipping again, drew with it. It was a symbol she made, a glyph, a secret sign, a design turning in upon itself in spirals and a trailing tail; a sign of completion, but also new beginning.

"What mark is that?" Dunnere must ask.

"A kind of seal," she answered. And she smiled.

Later, in the hall, Edwin was crossing to the door of the treasure room. Alwin caught his eye. He knew the man had been standing there on alert at the edge of the garden, and had seen at least part of what had transpired between him and Ceric. Now, the hall filling, Edwin would come to the table without either his brother or his intended bride. He stood still, and with a slight nod of his head gestured Alwin forward.

As his captain neared, Edwin lifted his hand and brushed his hair away from his forehead. The hand was stiff and aching, even in a gesture as slight as this.

Alwin saw the skinned knuckles of Edwin's right hand, the sign of a punch connecting with something hard.

Edwin did not know how to couch the coming truth, and let the words tumble forth. "The Lady Dwynwen – she has wed Ceric. They will not be in the hall tonight."

Alwin's mouth opened. He and the rest of Edwin's picked men had made a long journey that their Lord might woo the girl. They had returned safely with her, and her dower, but she had turned away from being Lady of Kilton, and given her hand to Edwin's older brother.

There was to be no bridal-feast, not here at any rate; and the grimness of Edwin's face made clear there was nothing for him to celebrate. Edwin's skinned knuckles – he had used them against Ceric, that was clear to Alwin.

But the captain just nodded. It was not his place to make comment on so private a matter. Yet it was public as well, as Edwin's next words confirmed.

"Let it be known amongst the men. She has wed Ceric. That is the end of it."

※※※※※※※※※※

It was true the wedded pair did not venture to the hall, but retreated to the bower house of Ceric. Edgyth had a meal of delicacy brought to them, and a flagon of mead to lend the provender heady sweetness.

Edgyth had worked another surprise which awaited. While they were in the chantry, she had her serving women go to the bower. They carried fresh linens, newly made towels and sheets, and jugs of flowers. None were more sweet than the red rose petals they scattered over the coverlet of the dragon bed.

DWYNWEN OF KILTON

DURING that night Dwynwen awoke at the side of Ceric. She was not sure why she had awakened, but she was at once aware that Ceric was sitting up, his back against the cushions piled at the head of the dragon bed. No cresset nor taper yet burned, but there was owl-light enough, for through a slit in the shutters the waning Moon poured itself into the bower. It fell, a sharp beam upon the white coverlet she lay beneath. She sat up.

She could see his eyes were open, and staring ahead. Ceric sat perfectly still, and even when she moved to kneel at his side to face him, he did not respond. She waved her hand slowly before his open eyes. He did not blink. She then laid her hand on one of his where it sat upon the linen sheet. His flesh was cool.

Dwynwen sat back, looking at him, unable to control the pounding of her heart.

"Elf-shot," she breathed. "I think you are Elf-shot."

Such were beyond the reach of easy recall, and in so delicate a state that they might be deeply harmed if any violence was tried in attempt to break the spell.

Elf-shot could befall men or animals, making them dull-eyed and unable to act. It could come and go, but the shot must be returned from whence it came to effect a cure.

"Luned," she murmured. Her step-mother would know what to do; Dwynwen had heard from the hall folk that Luned had cured a youth struck thus, freeing him from the numbness which had possessed him. There was danger in doing so, not only to the afflicted but to the healer who used wort-cunning to free them.

She leant in, and just let her lips touch his. Those lips, which had been so hot upon her body a few hours ago, were now also cool. She felt fear then, fear for where he was, and how she might reclaim him. But she would not let herself cry out, such could harm him.

Dwynwen uncurled her legs and lowered herself to his side. She lay over his lap, holding him, as if she might keep him from further receding. She heard his steady, if shallow breath rise and fall, and by her own bodily heat hoped to warm him. She tried to pace her breathing to his own. By and by she fell asleep, to awaken sometime later. The room was lighter; dawn was nigh. Ceric was stroking her hair.

She sat up and looked at him, a rush of gladness flooding her at his action. But his eyes were not fully upon her; and when he spoke she heard the odd note of his voice, as if it were almost detached from his body.

"I have been mad, Lady," he whispered.

She paused before she spoke. "Soon you will be well," she answered. His eyes did not shift to her; she did not think he heard her.

Ceric fell into silence. She lay down next him, one arm about his waist, and tried to pull him down by her side. He came, but his eyes remained open; she saw this.

When she again awoke he was lying on his back next to her. Her arm was upon him, on his chest. She pushed herself up on one elbow. His eyes were still open, but now looking at her. He smiled, and pulled her atop him. His hands rose to the naked flesh of her waist, and moved upwards to rest lightly upon her breasts. They slid under the waterfall of her hair to her back, and pulled her close so he might kiss her. He winced when their lips met; she knew his own pained him. His left eye was mostly closed with the bruise that had arisen there. He did not let these slight hurts stop him. His want for her was great, and wasted though his body was, his muscled strength was foremost. He rolled with her to her back, splaying her legs open with his own, kissing her nipples, then running his tongue up her neck so that his mouth might fasten on her own. Despite his want for her body, his was no driven urgency. His movements were slow, his hands now warm and sure upon her. He whispered her name, again and again as they moved together, until his lips were closed by a pleasure which made him draw gasping breath. He lay then at her side, again pulling her close, kissing the top of her head as his breathing slowed.

Ceric had no memory of speaking with Dwynwen during the night. Now she was nestled under his arm, as he held her. The bliss of his body's needed release began to drain away. He became aware his face hurt; his left eye was swollen almost shut. His jaw ached from the blow it had taken. He had not felt it much the night before, but now the hurt had settled, and deepened. Still, he lowered his sore mouth to the hair of she at his side, and wrapped his arm about her in a kind of wonder.

Dwynwen had fallen into his ken like a thunderbolt. Her freshness, her youth, her innocent willingness as bedmate, the fact that she dwelt entirely outside the borders of his past, free of all taint and sorrow, all made her instantly and almost painfully precious to him. The sweetness of kissing her rosebud mouth, the tender liveliness with which she pressed him to her slight form, the ecstatic bodily expression he found therein; she seemed a salve for deep hurts, a way forward in the void. She had in the space of single day and night lit a taper, flickering deep within his darkness. He could follow her light.

All were revelations to him; his sensory response to her nearness, her warmth in his bed, her presence at his side. It had been more than three years since his single night with Ashild. He had known no woman since then. The deprivation he had visited upon his body during the year of his forest sojourn had heightened some senses yet starved others; driven them almost to extinction. Now he could not get enough of his young wife. He wanted her at all times.

They lay for a while, his mind turning, full of these thoughts, as he listened to her soft breathing. She may have fallen back into sleep; it was still early.

Then she lifted her head. Her eyes opened, golden-flecked, blue, and wide. He bent over her, his forearms framing her head, and spoke.

"When I first saw you, I thought you of the land of Faery."

She gave the slightest of smiles.

"What do you think now," she whispered back.

He looked at her fully and gave answer, a voice soft, but sure.

"That you are of the land of Faery."

"Come to steal your soul?" she asked. There was no playfulness in her voice as she asked this.

The pause that followed was filled with the way he looked at her.

"Come perhaps to return it."

He pulled back now, and looked down wonderingly at her youthful body.

"Are you . . . truly a woman," he finally asked.

She paused, unsure if he had recurred to his earlier conviction that she was fey. He said more, which gave her guidance.

"Your body . . . you are like a child," he said. "You are so young. I feel I am . . . doing wrong to you, that you are also a bride . . ."

She smiled now, her small half-smile, one that made her eyes shine the brighter.

"I am a woman, for close to two years," she assured him. "But yes, I will grow more. Luned told me."

He took this in. The name she had uttered fell strangely into his ear. "Luned," he breathed. "Who is this?"

"Lady Luned is my step-mother. It is she who foretold that you needed me."

He was silent a moment.

"Is she then a seer, or . . . a witch?"

Dwynwen's face clouded in concentration. She did not know this last word in the tongue of the Saxons. But Luned was far-seeing, that she could affirm.

"She sees much, yes. She is a wise-woman, if that is what a witch is."

He nodded once, and she went on.

"She knows many things, and has taught me some of them."

"But . . . even though you are still a child, you are fully woman?"

She gave a little laugh at his disbelief, but did not answer. She trusted she could bear a babe in due time. Her silence made him go on.

"You are my child-wife," he murmured, pulling her near.

When Lady Edgyth appeared in the pleasure garden the bridal pair had finished with the contents of the salver Mindred had carried to them. It was still early morning, but the days long enough that the Sun had risen hours before. Edgyth had come to the margins of the garden and caught glimpse of the couple earlier, but left, not wishing to disturb their shared repast. Now, seeing the salver set aside, she began to make her way to them.

She had not taken more than a few steps beyond the beech hedge when Dwynwen saw her. The girl fairly ran to her, a gladsome smile on her face. Edgyth could do nothing but return this, and open her arms to the girl, who kissed her cheek as the Lady of Kilton's arm came up around her slight form. Edgyth's smile, and returning kiss, were sincere; the girl's quick affection was both unexpected and endearing. There was truth to it as well; Edgyth did not think Dwynwen one to dissemble, least of all in matters of the heart.

Dwynwen took Edgyth by the hand and led her to the table, and into that circle she had briefly quitted. As they neared Ceric rose. The swelling of his lip had subsided, but his left eye was almost wholly closed. Edgyth felt doubly grateful that Kilton afforded so private a refuge as this, that Ceric might be away from its stir and din. In the hall proper his face would elicit comment; here he had the privacy of garden and bower and chantry, away from prying eyes.

Dwynwen sat down next to Ceric on the bench, and as Edgyth seated herself in one of the chairs, he sat as well. She watched his hand quickly return to that of his bride; she had seen he had been holding it when she appeared at the hedge.

Another thing she saw, and that was how little Ceric had eaten. Two loaves of bread were set upon that silver salver, two small pots of cheese. Those nearest Ceric were barely touched.

The droning of the honeybees in the roses around them prompted Edgyth's first words.

"Our bees do well this Summer," she told them. "Our yield for mead will be great." Indeed, the hives were just on the other side of the garden, and of honey and beeswax both these smallest of Kilton's workers made her proud.

Her mention of mead prompted a second thought, which she also shared with a smile.

"I have a wedding gift for you; it will be ready on the morrow."

"I thank you, Lady," Dwynwen answered.

Ceric had not spoken, and Edgyth addressed him directly now.

"Your eye, Ceric – would you like another compress for it?"

In truth, she knew the swelling must subside on its own, a compress now would do little good. But she must hear him speak.

He lifted his free hand toward the bruised eye. "It is better," he assured her.

"Opening more and more."

She considered the paucity of what he had eaten. Men on campaign and short on provender were forced to go on half-rations. This was the way Ceric was eating; the same sparing consumption he allowed himself in the greenwood. He was still at war.

"But Mindred did not bring food to your liking," she suggested.

The serving man who attended to the slight needs of Ceric had been supplanted by Mindred, a thoroughly capable, if severe, woman in her third decade. This morning Mindred had also brought Ceric two cups, one with warm broth, the second with the draught of crushed seed of wild celery, which Edgyth hoped would spur his appetite. He had drunk but a sip of this latter.

Ceric saw Edgyth's eye fall upon this, and his hand reached for the pottery cup holding the draught. He took a mouthful of it, and swallowed it down.

Edgyth nodded. Dutiful as his act was, he had drunk some. She went on with what she had come to say.

"I would like you both to spend as much time as you like at rest, and in peace. There is no need to come to the hall, until you are both ready, although of course you are greatly welcome there."

She was Lady, she could say this; though what emotions roiled in her son Edwin's breast she had yet to learn. "The pleasures of these private precincts are yours." She glanced at the sea, calm and with a light breeze blowing over it. She looked to Dwynwen.

"Ceric is skilled at sailing. He and Worr might take you out in one of our small boats."

Dwynwen smiled at once. "I would like that," she said, "riding the tossing mane of the sea."

Edgyth spoke to Ceric now. "When Worr comes to see you, you might ask him," she offered. Ceric gave a nod.

Edgyth felt it time to leave them again alone. Worr would decide if Ceric was up to such activity; all she could do was to affirm her love for this troubled young man.

"I will leave you now," she murmured. She rose, smiling, gracious, hiding her concern.

The Welsh girl stood, and with her free hand gestured to Edgyth. She smiled, but there was some little urgency in her voice. "Lady, may I come with you? I will take but a few moments of your time."

Edgyth could not help but see the quick way in which Ceric had more firmly clasped his bride's hand, unwilling to let her go.

Dwynwen was undaunted. She spoke gently, even playfully, to her husband. "I will not be long." She looked up at the blue and cloud-flecked sky. "The Sun will have hardly moved when I return." She pulled her hand from his, but gave his a pat. She turned and left with Edgyth.

It was all Dwynwen could do not to look back as she walked away from Ceric as he sat there. Being at the side of Lady Edgyth gave some firmness to her step, as did the hope that Lady could aid them both.

The two had scarce entered Edgyth's bower when Dwynwen turned to her. The girl reached for, and took, Edgyth's hand in her own.

"Ceric," she began. "Last night I awoke long before dawn. He was sitting up, staring into the dark. He could not see me. I watched him. He was bedazed. I think he was . . . Elf-shot."

Edgyth took this in, and gave a long and slow nod. The girl had knowledge of wort-cunning, she had already shown Edgyth this. She must believe Dwynwen knew of what she spoke. Yet this injury with no wound was amongst the most troubling of all ills. At the Abbey of Glastunburh there had been such cases.

"I know of nuns skilled in such conditions; the Abbot too," she murmured. She looked at the girl's searching face. "What happened, then?"

"I feared disturbing him. I lay across his lap, holding him. I fell asleep. Then he awakened me by stroking my hair. He spoke. He called me Lady, as if he did not know my name, nor who I was. He told me he had been mad. That was all he said. But he let me pull him down next to me, so we lay facing each other.

"When I awoke again, it was light. He smiled."

"And he seemed well?"

A flush mantled her round cheeks, and she glanced down a moment.

"Yes, more than well."

Edgyth understood what followed, and gave the briefest of nods.

She gestured they sit at the small table, and both did. Something of the table carried a strong presence of Modwynn about it, and sitting there gave Edgyth comfort.

The Lady of Kilton bethought herself. During her time spent at Glastunburh, she had copied out many healing recipes, also the thoughts and inquiries of the most skilled of the healers there amongst the nuns and monks. Amongst her gathered parchments she knew she had nothing for the condition known as Elf-shot. Yet she had heard tell of the method of treatment. She drew a long breath.

"Let me think." She closed her eyes, summoning what she had heard from the recesses of her memory. "Metals three. A blade of steel, its wooden haft held by copper nails; an iron key. Also, a silver coin, unmarred, one minted with a cross. The shield for the healer is wrought of words. The herb – a leaf of Lady's mantle plucked early, still holding the gazing ball of dawn – a drop of dew still held in its hand . . ."

Her voice trailed off as her forehead creased with the energy of her remembrance. "For an animal, these things tied into a bag, and hung about the neck of the beast.

"For man or woman, the same, but placed under the pillow."

Dwynwen remembered something she had heard of Luned's work. "The leech – he or she must sing the cure."

Edgyth recalled this as well. "Yes. You must order the point back from whence it came."

"Like a spear-point, or arrow head?" the girl asked. It must be some kind of unseen weapon, if one could be shot with it.

Edgyth nodded. "Imagine it as such," she counselled.

Dwynwen did not ask who sent a malevolent affliction such as this. Coming from the mountains as she did she knew those fey might prove both helpful and hurtful to man and beast. Elves were large and could be demanding, covetous of human happiness, envying mortals for those qualities which they lacked, or of joys and delights they could not understand nor partake of. Faeries were tiny, but could expand themselves as needed; dappering by nature, rarely malicious, and would often come to the aid of those lost in the woodland by showing them the way out through unseen means. But if a Faery felt betrayed after an act of kindness, or if one tried to capture it, evil could result.

Edgyth had additional words for the girl. "This journey may be a slow one, for both Ceric, and for you, dear Dwynwen. Madness has many faces. But he has made great strides. With you, he will make many more. I know this. I feel it," she ended. She could not help but smile at the young face studying her own.

"You – you must protect yourself, my child." No one was more suited to say the next than Edgyth herself. "You will wish to take on his griefs, to free him from them. You must never do so.

"You must stay strong and whole. This is the surest way for you to return him to his own wholeness."

Dwynwen had another question. "Dunnere – what does he know?"

Edgyth paused, and answered with care. "He knows of what he has read. Not of what he has used, and done, as you and I, or Lady Modwynn, the grandmother of Ceric, did." The Lady of Kilton let a moment pass, a reflective one. "Ours is the knowledge of use."

The girl nodded. "Still, Dunnere can help me, with the names of things, in your tongue. There are plants and trees I know to use, but do not know how to call them. He will help with that."

Edgyth endorsed this fully, both with a nod of her head, and in her response. "Yes. He will be greatly helpful with that." The priest must aid Dwynwen, and Edgyth told the girl so. "I will make sure he understands he is to extend every service to you."

Dwynwen's response was soft, but heartfelt. "I thank you, my Lady."

The Lady of Kilton beheld this girl, on whom a great deal rested. "Ceric being well again – it will mean so much. Kilton needs him. Edwin needs him." Edgyth could not express how deep was this need, that Edwin have his brother at his side. No one she thought, save herself and Worr, who had watched both boys from birth, could truly understand this dependence. Yet with the girl's strange power of perception, she may have already discerned this.

Edgyth went on. "I need him. And most dearly of all – you, his young and lovely wife."

The girl smiled then, a sweet smile, a child's smile.

"Ceric named me his child-wife," she admitted. Her smile did not fade, happy as she was to share so private an utterance with this woman who had taken their side.

Edgyth too must smile. "Yes, you are that," she answered. Regarding the girl, she could not help but say the next. "I would have liked for you to have waited another year to wed Ceric. Yet for his sake I am glad you did not."

It was difficult for Edgyth to say more. Dwynwen was so far from maturity that if she had decided to stay at Kilton and wed Edwin, Edgyth would have asked him to wait a year for her to grow. Dwynwen was not given that chance; or rather, she had seen the man she felt Fated for and acted upon her belief.

Right now they must both attend to the task at hand. Edgyth, so skilled at the ordering of a hall, set out their next steps.

"I will gather all needful for the charm," she told the girl, "but the leaf of Lady's mantle you must pick yourself. It grows in the garden, beneath the bay laurel, to the right of the pavilion. It must be done early, with the dew still upon it, so that you might see yourself, as if the drop it holds was a tiny gazing ball."

The girl nodded her head in understanding. "I will see myself in the drop before I pick it, and make sure the leaf does not touch the soil after I do." Such would rob the herb of its potency, Dwynwen knew.

Edgyth could help with this. "I will have the bag made up for you, and you need only place the leaf within," she offered.

Of a sudden the girl's face clouded. She seemed to hear Luned's voice in her ear.

"Nay," she said. "I must make all myself; gather all, sew the pouch, pluck the herb."

She paused a moment. "The archer makes his own shafts," she breathed.

Edgyth could not gainsay this. Any charm gained in potency through the work of a single hand. She would let the Welsh girl do all.

Dwynwen and Ceric spent much of that day in the garden. Ceric was content to sit at the pavilion table, but Dwynwen took his arm and made him walk about with her. She asked him of the roses, some of which were on wood thick and hoary with age. They stopped before such a bush, with blooms so richly red that Dwynwen thought they might be those scattered upon their bed last night.

She had picked up a few of those petals this morning, and placed them in a jar of silver she had.

"This one . . . I think has always been here; since I was a boy, perhaps," he told her. "My grandmother must have planted it."

"And its petals were strewn between the fire-drakes," she reminded. "I am glad it was planted by her." Dwynwen knew it meaningful that Ceric had chosen to stand upon the Lady Modwynn's ledger stone to proclaim his vow to her, as if to invoke his grandmother's blessing.

"She would like you," he said now.

Dwynwen smiled, and he spoke again.

"Your spirit would gladden her."

Dwynwen gave a little laugh at this, her small mouth upturning in a way that forced Ceric to bend his head to hers and kiss her. The sunlight striking his hair gave a golden cast to it, and she closed one of her hands about the curls at his neck, as if to hold them a moment. There was a seeming ease in how he spoke, and in his manner too, one Dwynwen saw when Ceric spoke of times long past; his own boyhood, for instance.

They walked on a while. She thought of what Lady Edgyth had said, that Worr would be coming to check on Ceric.

It made her look up at him. "Who is Worr?" she asked.

She had on her arrival at the hall been introduced to this man, and had heard his title, horse-thegn of Kilton. She had met his wife Wilgyfu, and later that night seen their three small boys. It was the way Worr had entered and taken command of the terrible confrontation between the brothers that made her wish to know more.

"He is our horse-thegn; he has the care and breeding of all our beasts in his hands. And Worr is our best tracker."

No one else but Worr could have found Ceric in that wood, and he knew it.

Dwynwen listened with care, and then spoke again. "And he is a friend to you."

"Yes," he said. Worr was closer to Ceric than anyone at Kilton, and knew him best.

"Your companion," she offered.

"Yes," he answered. "He was so to my father as well, who returned, blinded by Danes, to Kilton."

Dwynwen's lips parted in dismay, but she did not interrupt.

Ceric had turned his head to the sea as he spoke. "He was held captive, and brought back by the maid Ceridwen, who became my mother." He looked down at Dwynwen. "She was not much older than you."

This fact took on new resonance now, and it took him a moment to continue.

"My father could no longer fight. Worr was young, but a thegn. He was made my father's companion, and body-guard. I was raised with him, almost as if he were an uncle."

Dwynwen took this in.

"It is a blessing to have such a man."

"Yes. He has been at my side through nearly all." Ceric looked about at the garden, and went on. "Since I – returned to the hall, he spends part of every day with me."

This all held great meaning to her. She squeezed his arm, and was about to speak when the horse-thegn appeared at the edge of the garden. Dwynwen raised her hand, in a gesture of welcome. Worr seemed at first hesitant to intrude, but by her smile and a nod of her head she bade him approach.

The three walked together back to the pavilion. They sat down, she and Ceric next each other on a bench, and Worr in the same chair Edgyth had earlier used. Dwynwen met the horse-thegn's eyes.

"Ceric told me you have been with him his whole life," she offered.

Her voice fell, high-pitched but soft, into Worr's ears; a voice, he thought, very much that of a child. Yet there was a careful precision in the way she formed her words, revealing that this was not her native tongue. It added a kind of charm to all she said.

"And with his father, who you also companioned, you spent much time," she went on.

Worr nodded his head. He gave thought to these truths. His service to Gyric had not been an easy one, but doing so may have been what kept Worr alive. In those early years he continued his training in arms, yet was not exposed to the many dangers of actual fighting. He must be at the side of Gyric to help keep the man from falling into despair at his blindness, rendered unfit to defend Kilton.

"And you and Ceric have . . . known much together," Dwynwen went on.

"Since he was a boy," Worr admitted. "I taught him to ride, and to track. We have ridden together on every campaign for Eadward." Worr's face became more thoughtful "Yes, we have seen much."

Dwynwen let a moment pass. She placed her hand over the top of her husband's own. She looked up into the face of the horse-thegn and spoke.

"What hurt has Ceric suffered, Worr? I must know, so that I may search this wound. Tell me, both if you can, or you alone, Worr, if Ceric can not. Tell me what hurt is this."

Worr looked to Ceric. He gave no sign of forbidding Worr to speak, and in fact, if he could recount the outline of the story aloud, it might help Ceric in more deeply accepting the truth of it. Worr took a breath and began.

"In Lindisse, in Anglia, past that line of Danelaw decreed by Ælfred and Guthrum when they made their Peace of Wedmore, there is a hall. It is known as Four Stones. The Jarl thereof, Hrald by name, is young, two or three years younger than Ceric. The two of them have been friends since boyhood, for their mothers were close friends.

"Hrald was not first-born, but the oldest child was a girl. Her name was Ashild."

Worr was speaking, but Dwynwen's eyes were fixed on Ceric. She saw his eyelids begin to lower, and the movement, almost imperceptible, but there, of his eyes beneath those shrouded lids. The tenseness of his jaw relaxed. He looked as though he was being drawn deep into his thoughts; a portal through which he must venture. Just now she could not keep him from that crossing; he must go there.

Worr went on.

"Ceric and she did not often see each other. I was there when they did. We journeyed once some years ago to spend a Summer at Four Stones, and then later a far briefer trip.

"On that second visit Ceric and Ashild became man and wife. Then he and I must return to Wessex."

Worr took pause there, mindful of what he would next tell, and the words he used.

"Ceric fights in the train of Eadward, the son of Ælfred. In his service he was away for many months, far longer than the standard tour of duty. Danes were ranging throughout Anglia, those who had done much damage to Wessex. Eadward trailed them.

"Also trailing these Danes was Hrald. Battle was joined: the Danes, the warriors of Four Stones, and then the men of Wessex under Eadward's command. Many men fell on all sides. An old thegn from Kilton was there as well, one respected by all, and a life-long friend to Lady Modwynn, the grandmother of Ceric. Cadmar was his name. He was killed. Ceric was setting stones upon the body when he saw a Dane, carrying a battle-flag. The figure had its back to him."

Here Worr slowed even more. "Ceric could see nothing except the Dane, and the enemy flag. He ran after the man, and threw a spear. It hit the figure in the back.

"Ceric went to the figure, and saw it was Ashild. She was on the field, searching for her brother, Hrald. She died at once, in an instant."

Even though Ceric had bowed his head, both could see the tears flowing down his face at these words.

"We rode all night with the body," Worr went on, "taking her back to Four Stones. Ashild was buried in the nearby Abbey of Oundle, in its church.

"Then we left. When we returned to Kilton, there was a memorial for the lost Cadmar. Lady Modwynn led Kilton after the death of her sons, waiting for Edwin's sword-bearing. She and Ceric were very close. Lady Modwynn was now old; she had guided Kilton through many challenges. She died that night. At her funeral Mass Ceric walked from the chantry. He kept walking, out through the gates. He vanished into the forest.

"He was in that wood for a year. I would bring supplies, of which Ceric took a small portion. He ended living in a shallow cave, over Winter.

"Seven nights before you arrived Ceric returned to the hall."

In just a few lines Worr had covered years of their lives. Dwynwen's eyes did not close at this telling. The shutting of her eyes would have granted her no distance from these sorrowful truths. Despite the recounting of loss after loss suffered by her husband, they only opened the wider, taking them in. Yet within her breast she felt a wrenching in her heart.

The silence that followed ended when Ceric raised his tear-streaked face and looked to the man. His voice was just above a whisper.

"I have been mad, Worr," he said. "I have been mad."

"Yes," Worr returned, his voice as hushed as if he soothed his young sons. "Now you grow better. Now you are wed. And your Lady will help you. As will I."

Ceric nodded at him, but said no more. Worr watched him carefully, keeping his own silence as he did so. At last Worr rose, and addressed Dwynwen in a low tone.

"Lady Edgyth spoke of our going out in one of the boats." Worr scanned the sky above the gently rolling waves, noting the clarity of the horizon line. "If all is well with Ceric, we could go tomorrow, in the morning, when the sea is calmest." There was one constant at Kilton; he had no fear of a lack of wind riffling the sea below them. "There is always breeze enough to fill our sails."

"I thank you," Dwynwen said. "And also, for what you have just shared, I thank you."

She offered that quick smile of hers. Worr gave another nod, and left them.

Ceric emerged from his stupor, gradually, and in his own time. Dwynwen sat at his side. He looked wonderingly at her, and then around.

"Worr is gone," she told him. "He will be back in the morning, and we three will go sailing." Her lips bowed in gladness. "I will like that."

He must smile at her, for the pleasure she seemed to be taking in this thought. "Now you will lie down and rest," she invited. She stood and led him to the bower house, with the same promise she had made to him in the morning. "I must see Lady Edgyth, but will not be long."

Indeed, the action of his tears and the swift distance he had travelled while Elf-shot had caused a great weariness to come over him. He lay upon the dragon bed, and after being granted a kiss from his young wife, let her leave.

Lady Edgyth was ready for her. First Dwynwen must make report, one that Edgyth was not surprised to hear.

"The Elf-shot pierced him again. Worr was just with us, and it happened before him as well."

The older Lady's brow furrowed, but Dwynwen's next words brought some comfort.

"It did not pierce him deeply. I asked Worr to tell me of the hurt Ceric had suffered. Ceric wept silent tears as Worr told me of the mishap of his Lady-wife's death, and the loss of his honoured grandmother." The girl took a moment to reflect before continuing. "Worr left, and Ceric returned to me. I left him resting in the bower."

Edgyth fought the water forming in her eyes. She drew breath, and turned to the task at hand. She could not but take heart at Dwynwen's resolve. This child's body housed a large spirit, and a mind capable of encompassing much.

She gave Dwynwen a small basket, and together they began to collect all needful for the charm. For the newly-minted coin of silver, Edgyth opened a small chest which had been that of Modwynn. Within were perfect coins of Wessex, whole, unclipped, and bearing the cross upon them. Modwynn had selected them herself for use as special alms. Dwynwen hovered her hand above the gleaming pieces, then plucked out one. Now that she knew how Ceric had loved his grandmother, choosing a coin from her store gave the unmarred silver added worth.

They went next to the kitchen yard, and found there a knife, of small but lethal sharpness. It offered a plain haft of wood, into which Dwynwen could drive the three small brads of copper. These they asked of one of the joiners in his work shed.

"The treasure room now," Edgyth told her, as they made their way to the hall. She knew Edwin was out sparring with his body-guard; they would not be disturbed. This storehouse had once been her own private domain, when Godwin was Lord of Kilton. Into it she had brought Edwin as a babe, the day Ceridwen and Gyric surrendered him to them. As Edgyth turned the key in the massive box lock she remembered that just two days earlier she had decided the Welsh girl should not see the interior of Edwin's chamber until their betrothal. Everything had changed so quickly, and she had no reluctance to bring her in now.

They crossed to one corner of the room, where upon a stepped series of larger chests, sat one of blackened wood, quite small. Edgyth carried it to the table and lifted the lid for her. "Old keys," she said. "None know what they once opened."

"Yes," breathed Dwynwen. "Their use is lost. Such look for something to unlock." She gazed at Edgyth, lips parted in wonder. "I thank you for thinking of this," she added.

Again, Dwynwen held her hand above the mass of keys, large and small, which lay in a jumble within the box. She closed her eyes and let her searching fingers pick one.

She looked at that which she had found. It was the length of her pointing finger, with a lobed head, and three teeth. She laid it in the basket with the other items.

They turned to leave. Done with the room, they both took it in. A great wall loom, long unused, was set against a wall, awaiting new hands to warp it, and with thread-charged shuttle to build up growing rows of woollen stuff. Edwin's bed was there, one Lord Godwulf had built for him and Modwynn when she was his bride. Its honey-coloured wood had darkened to deep brown, but the solidness of its head and foot boards was testament to its soundness. Against another wall were ranged armaments, neatly stacked and hung, and numberless chests and casks, concealing their contents from view.

Dwynwen thought of the bower house of Ceric. He gave me fire-drakes, she said to herself. She felt a flush of heat within her, like the flicking tongues of those fabled beasts. And he gave me himself. I have all I shall ever want.

They parted then, but not before Dwynwen bestowed a kiss upon Edgyth. "I will make the pouch from my own clothing, that which I have worn next to my skin," she told her. "And at dawn I will rise and pick the Lady's mantle, after I have seen my reflection in the gazing ball it holds."

Edgyth nodded. All solemnness was in her next words. "Do not forget the shield. As you place the charm beneath his pillow, you must arm yourself with it."

Dwynwen drew breath. Though the shield be beyond the sight of man, its protection was needed. "I will summon the shield," she promised. "And sing the cure."

When Dwynwen returned to the bower Ceric was still asleep. Her clothing and goods had been set in the large chest next to that which held those of Ceric. She took from it now a shift of linen, one Luned had made for her, and the sewing box her father Dunwyd had given her in her eighth Summer. The box was built of a framework of silver, inset with panels of rosewood, and precious enough to hold gems. Dwynwen still recalled his delight at her astonishment in receiving it, and opening it to find the tiny gold-chased shears, the slender leathern packet holding a score of steel needles of unparalleled smoothness, and the many bone thread holders charged with silk thread. All would be part of the spell-bag she would cut and sew; Luned who had made the shift from which it would be formed, her father who gave her shears and needles; and she herself in the making of it. The bag need not be large, and in fact she sized it to match the length of her own small hand. This was long enough to hold the knife, and all else she would place within.

Dwynwen bent over her work, sitting at the table there, upon which sat the silver bridal-cup. With the linen folded in half, she need stitch only two sides now. She could just hear Ceric breathing as he slept, and let first the action of her shears and then her threaded needle flow in movement to that soft sound. He began to stir just as she had completed stitching the second side of the pouch. She turned it right side out, and laid it back into the basket Edgyth had given her. On the morrow she would pluck the herb, place all within, and stitch the final side. She set the basket with her sewing box atop her clothes chest. Then under the never-sleeping eyes of the fire-drakes, she went to her husband and kissed his lips.

His eyelids blinked open, and his arm came up around her. "Dwynwen," he murmured. Ceric awakened, not to pain and loss, but to her sweetness. She was here, encircled in his arm. He kissed her again, then pressed her strongly to his chest. He embraced her without words, feeling the rise and fall of her own breath. He bethought himself of the great gift he held. They were wed, in Nature, in law, and in the eyes of God. She could not be taken from him. Only death could take her, and God would not be so cruel. He had taken much from Ceric, but would grant Dwynwen to him. He could not live without her.

Dawn had just cast its first light through the chink in the wooden shutters when Dwynwen arose. She and Ceric had taken their supper in the garden, and stayed late within its leafy confines, listening to the fluting melody of a song thrush. He still slept, deeply, and seemingly untroubled, as she pulled on gown and night shoes of wool, and, basket in hand, stepped outside. No one was afoot at this early hour; only the night-guards in the last hour of their watch, and the kitchen folk who stoked and fed the bread-ovens, would be up.

She made for the beech hedge and what lay beyond it. All was still grey; only when she lifted her face to the horizon did Dwynwen spy a faint stain of pink upon the water, reflected from the Sun arising beyond the buildings and walls of Kilton. She went to the bed where the bay laurel tree grew. There fronting it were the broad and spreading leaves of Lady's mantle. She set down her basket, and took up the pouch of linen in her right hand. All needful was within, save the knife and the dew-bearing leaf. The knife she must fix next. She would drive the three brads of copper into its wooden haft. Of the metal elements it seemed the most vital of all, an act to awaken the power of the iron in the blade, and so she saved it for last.

Dwynwen fingered each brad in turn, holding in thought the task she asked of it, to direct the aim of the steel knife. She drove the copper brads into the smooth wood with the flat of her weaving sword. All was ready.

She let her knees drop to the round stones of the path, and lowered her face to the plant. Every deep green leaf was veined to its stem, a green hand making a hollow where a single drop of dew might rest. In the dim but growing light she saw each leaf held one. As the fingers of sunlight began to stretch across the garden, she determined to let the leaf she should choose reveal itself to her.

"Lady," she whispered. "Lead me to that gazing ball you mean for me."

She bent lower, nearing leaves of richer or paler green, and greater or smaller size. Then she saw it, or rather saw herself, reflected in the dew drop one offered. The drop, of crystal clarity, was no larger than a pea, and her visage in it smaller still. Staring at her minikin reflection, she spoke aloud.

"I give you myself, Ceric," she murmured, "that I might heal you."

Then she kept silence, looking at herself, held in that hand of green.

Dwynwen let out the breath she had been holding, then grasped the stem with the fingers of her left hand, snapping it. She carried it to the pouch and set it within, letting the single drop of dew upon the broad leaf run from its green confines and fall amongst the contents of that bag, anointing them. She was part of all of that she had made. The pouch was of her clothing, the coin, knife, and key, of her choosing. She had spied her own face in the tiny gazing ball formed by the orb of dew held in the leaf.

When she opened the door of the bower, Ceric lay asleep. She had threaded needle ready in her sewing box, and with nimble fingers made the final stitches in the spell-bag. She would not set the spell until tonight, but all was now ready. She laid the pouch into her silver and rosewood sewing box. Then she pulled off her clothing and went to his side.

TWO CUPS
BEARING FOUR NAMES

THE morning was as fair as Worr promised. Not long after the serving woman Mindred had cleared away the couple's salver, the horse-thegn presented himself in the pleasure garden. All three turned to look across to the sea. The sky was fast becoming a rich and ready blue, with thin clouds scudding ribband-like along the horizon. The smallest of whitecaps tipped the dark water, frothing under the breeze. Though the day promised more warmth, they had each at hand a short cloak to ward off unwanted chill. Worr had also a pottery flask filled with water should any grow athirst under the wind and Sun.

Edgyth arrived to see them off. She smiled to see Dwynwen's excitement, and was further heartened at the prospect that such an outing would gladden Ceric. She walked with them to the edge of the cliff, where the steps cut sideways into the stone began, and found herself lifting her hands in a kind of benediction as the three began their descent. No setting out upon the water was without danger, but the pleasure doing so had brought Ceric in the past was foremost in her mind. They vanished from sight, and her own thoughts were carried back to her bride-hood. She remembered the steep walk down, her hand held fast in that of Godwin, on the many times they went out together in her first few months at Kilton.

As the boating party stepped from the final hewed stone they were not unwatched. When the three gained the narrow strip of shingled beach, four thegns of Ceric stood ready by a second vessel. They would go out with their own boat and stay at alert, scanning the horizon, there if needed to call out alarm or supply aid in case of distress.

This was unusual, a precaution Worr had arranged. He was not certain how Ceric might react to being on the water, nor how, in the event of some misadventure he might respond. There were, as always, men stationed on the next bluff, scanning the waters, horns at the ready to sound an alarm should strange ships appear. But this boat manned with a few thegns at the ready lent further assurance to this first outing.

As the group approached them, the four men bowed their heads in greeting to Ceric. His blackened eye was there for all to see. Ceric did not speak to the men, but paused, took them in, and gave to each of them a returning nod. There was natural, and always good-natured, rivalry between the followers of the two brothers. But at this point Ceric's men knew, as did every warrior in the hall, that Edwin had punched his brother, and more than once, judging by the way the serving man, and others, had reported the look of his face. And here was the proof.

The boat Ceric, Dwynwen, and Worr would sail in was before them. It was a stout little craft, broad-beamed enough to remain stable in rolling waves, and large enough to afford the dropping of a small net should fish be wanted. It had been dragged up on the shingle beach so that only the end of the keel was wet. The short mast was already set upright in the mast lock, the linen and wool sail furled upon its spar. Both Dwynwen and Worr could see the interest Ceric had as they approached it. He went to one side of the stern at once, as Worr did to the other, and together they heaved it forward over the pebbles. The scraping of the stones as they were dislodged under its hull was preamble to its freeing. Then Ceric turned to Dwynwen, and grinning, picked her up by her waist to hoist her over the gunwale on the starboard side. As he did so she lifted her heels backwards in the air, as a little girl might, and laughed in glee. There were three boards upon which to sit, one at the stern, one behind the mast, and the shortest of all in the prow. Dwynwen made for the foremost, clambering with a cat's agility over the ribs to the seat.

They pushed the prow out into free water. Ceric swung in and took up position at the sail. Worr gave a final push to clear the hull from the beach, then jumped in, placing himself at the steering-oar.

The thegns kept their silence about their leader's bruised face until the three they were here to guard pushed off. Glances fraught with meaning were exchanged. They would not speak aloud, even to each other, against the Lord of Kilton, yet they had a right to their own thoughts. One of them muttered, "So it is true." Then they readied to push off themselves.

"Hold fast," Ceric called out to Dwynwen. She turned her smiling face back to him, then grasped the gunwale edges with her hands. His warning was well given.

As soon as the prow hit the first oncoming wave, it rose high into the air. If Dwynwen had not been holding on she may well have been knocked backwards off her seat and on to the bottom of the boat. Instead she gave a delighted whoop of surprise. She had been sprayed with droplets of sea water, and only laughed the more at this. At Edgyth's suggestion she had plaited her hair and tied it up in a short kerchief, so she had nothing to obscure her view or tangle in the cross-wise breezes.

Once past the waves raking the shore, Ceric let loose the lines and unfurled the sail, heaving it up. The heavy fabric caught at once, billowing to harness the ever-freshening wind. The boat took off, surging forward. Dwynwen, clinging onto the gunwales, pressed herself forward over the low curved prow, as if she were the eyes of the boat. Her laughter streamed in pealing snatches into the ears of both men as they worked sail and oar.

Worr, standing at the steering-beam, looked back at the second boat bearing the thegns. They had cleared the surf, had raised their own sail, and were gaining on them. Once free of the surf's pull they trimmed their sail to trail them at a distance. They were far enough out to have good view both up and down the coast.

Dwynwen too was aware of the small boat that flanked them; its purpose to guard them was clear. She thought little of it, save for the fact that the current was swift, and that sea raiders had visited these shores. At Elidon's fortress in Ceredigion she had been but lightly guarded, and at her father, Prince Dunwyd's mountain hall, scarcely at all. But Kilton was different, she saw; Ceric had such importance that he must be protected whenever possible.

Worr headed on a south-westerly path, Ceric manning the sail and tacking in response to the demands of the wind. They flew by the coast to their left, an expanse of brown rock face, towering trees clothed in every hue of green, and shaded inlets deep-seeming and mysterious. The water they ploughed through parted under their speed, frothing up against the prow, creaming in bubbles behind the stern. In her wonder, and with the wind blowing in her face, Dwynwen almost did not know where to look. On they went, a white-maned stallion cantering heedless of hindrance, with no seeming bar to how fast or far they might fly. A black-headed gull swooped down near Dwynwen's head, close enough for her to see the brown of its eye, and her own freedom seemed almost to match that it had been born to.

She stood, hanging on, a small figure in the prow, unable to sit for excitement, laughing and crying aloud in sheer joyance at their movement through sea and air.

When Worr called out to Ceric that they would head back, Dwynwen turned round to them. Her view of both was imperfect due to the tacking of the sail, but the wide loop they began to make was unmistakable. Both men caught sight of her. The small face, so wreathed in smiles, fell in momentary disappointment. Then Ceric smiled back, struck at the breathless elation she had found here, out on the water. There was an ardent winsomeness in her pleasure, and it gave him pleasure of his own to see her thus.

The day had held unexpected delight. Ceric's response to being again behind a sail was all Edgyth and Worr could have hoped for, and it was clear that Dwynwen's so deeply entering into this small adventure vested him more fully into the new sphere her arrival presented him.

"I watched you, looking at the waves, as if you welcomed them," he told her when they lay abed. It had been her first time at sea, something she had already confessed.

The half-smile that so often bowed her lips did so again. "I did welcome them," she answered. Her smile broadened. "It is my name. Dwynwen means 'wave.'"

A hushed cry of astonishment passed his lips. Water again. She had brought him water, and her very name meant water as well. How much had she already brought him. It made his breath catch in his throat.

"I welcome all you give me," he whispered.

He had at dawn been awakened by her movement in the bed; she was smiling at him. He had no response but to clasp her naked body to him and again caress her. Now he felt driven to do so again. It was not only his own want of her, but the offering she made of herself which drove him. It was the honeyed yielding of her clinging mouth, the youthful strength in her slender limbs, her lack of any shyness or reserve in how she touched him, and wordlessly invited him to touch her. She seemed a well of unique and untapped passion, responsive to all he did, a sea bird yet new-fledged, but fully capable of strong flight.

Dwynwen, young as she was, had done more than gain entry into a woman's estate. For her to lie between the watchful fire-drakes in the arms of this man seemed full discovery, of him, and of herself. Luned, she thought. You knew what awaited me. You were right.

After his final kiss to her Ceric fell into sleep. It dropped upon him like a thick blanket after the exertion of the sail, the surfeit of fresh air and Sun, and then the passion spent with her.

His bride slipped from the bed in the dark and went to her rosewood sewing box. She drew forth the linen pouch and returned to stand at his side.

The pillows of the dragon bed were large ones; she could slide the pouch beneath that upon which his head rested with no disturbance to his slumber. Ceric scarce moved, so profound did his sleep appear.

Dwynwen let go the breath she had been holding. She had formed the pouch and placed all within with high intent; she must trust that it would affect the good she sought. Next she must set the shield in place. She moved her hand before her, as if describing the outline of a great protective disc. Her uttered words, though low, still thrilled with urgency.

"I stand behind linden wood, behind alder, behind willow, behind a wall of oak! I stand protected, casting out the point that troubles thee!"

Now she began to sing, a song meant not for human ears, but for the wound.

"I send the spear back, I send the point back, back from whence it came. It harms no one, not even the sender, for it falls in pure water which dissolves all blame."

The words fell, almost effortlessly from her lips. She had not planned the spell out beforehand, but had trusted she would be guided in her working of it. She sang it first in the tongue of Angle-land, then in that of Cymru. The words came from her mouth and fell into her own ears, and felt right. She repeated the spell in both tongues, and used the third telling to set it.

Then she fell, exhausted, next to him.

In the morning Dwynwen opened her eyes to the pearly light of a new day. Though he had been restless at dawn, Ceric lay asleep next her. His face was now calm, the brow untroubled. The swelling of his blackened eye had further receded. Lying there looking upon him, she thought of something else.

She need calculate how long the spell-bag should remain under his pillow. If it were true the charm held healing power, would a single night suffice? She bit her small lip, asking herself this. Perhaps Lady Edgyth would know; she might recall. Then Dwynwen stopped herself. Nay, she must know this, within herself.

She quieted her own breathing. The distress was in her husband's head. He had lain that troubled head upon a pillow, beneath which her spell-bag was set. A single night was not enough for so deep a distress. Three nights, perhaps, she wondered. In three nights the Moon travelled a great distance across the sky; much could be accomplished. This too Dwynwen dismissed, with a shake of her head. Nay, it must be a full seven, the same span God had used to create all.

She counted upon the charm to give her grace, if not to utterly cure her husband, to effect more good upon his health, to strengthen him to overcome the bolt with which he had been shot. His eyes blinked open then, saw her looking at him, and he smiled.

As they were dressing Ceric picked up his round silver looking-disc. The face therein was gaunt, but his own. There was reassurance in this, but something in it had changed forever. He knew he had been mad, been in and out of a cruel and scathing delirium which had taxed him to his limit. But he lived; he had been called back.

"I have been mad," he told Dwynwen.

It was not the first time he had uttered these words to her, but he did not recall that first utterance. There was a new directness now. He spoke slowly, but as if stating a fact.

She set down her comb and came to him. "Luned told me that those mad are closest to the mouth of God," she answered.

"Luned," he mused aloud. "I would like to meet that Lady, yet am almost afraid to." He thought a moment before going on. "She seems to know much of me."

It made Dwynwen think, as well. She had not understood why Luned had so changed her mind about Edwin of Kilton. First she had told Dwynwen that she could dismiss this suitor after little more than a glance at him. Then she let it be known that she would approve of her going to Wessex with him. The Lady had been right; her Fate did lay here at Kilton.

"She promised I would see her face again," she repeated. "And I feel she wishes to see yours."

When Lady Edgyth came to them in the garden that morning she bore a wooden box with a hinged lid.

"Your bridal gift," she told them, with a smile.

Dwynwen looked to Ceric, who, with a nod, bid her be the one to open it. Within were two paired silver cups, with gold rims. Cut into those rims on one was the name CERIC, and on the other, DWYNWEN.

Dwynwen gave a gasp of delight at the sight of them.

Ceric knew these cups, though he had not seen them for a long time. His eyes lifted to those of Edgyth. She smiled and nodded.

He reached for the cup inscribed with his name, and turning it, saw his father's name, GYRIC, engraved there.

"My parents' cups," he said. He again lifted his eyes to Lady Edgyth.

It was clear this gift held great meaning to him, and Edgyth felt her throat narrow in response. The boy had been deprived of both, so young.

Ceric looked now to his bride, his smile an encouragement to pick up the second cup. She ran her fingers across the bold lettering cut there, DWYNWEN, and then turned the rim. CERIDWEN it read, a name of Cymru, a name in length and ending like her own.

If any gift could affirm their union, or bind her more fully into the family of Kilton, this was it.

In Edgyth's mind there had never been any question which of the two brothers should receive these vessels. Kilton had a worker in both silver and gold. Modwynn and Godwulf had the man fashion the cups for Gyric and presented them at his symbel, his sword-bearing, with his name engraved thereon the first of them. The second cup was left unadorned, awaiting the name of the woman he would wed. After Ceridwen arrived Kilton, her name had been cut into that cup. Ceric was their firstborn, and these cups should descend through his father to him.

The ribband of golden yellow Edgyth had wrapped about their wrists in the chantry was a different matter. None witnessing that act knew it was that which had been wrapped around her own wrist, and that of Godwin, the day they wed. She could have saved that ribband for her son Edwin. Yet she had been moved to draw it forth from the small box in which resided the most cherished artefacts of her union with Godwin. Ceric needed it more, she felt, as did Dwynwen. It was her commitment in acknowledging their union, as sudden and disruptive as it had been.

The three sat a moment, looking upon the cups which stood together side by side.

These were cherished heirlooms, which had been given the bridal pair, cups made now equally theirs by the bearing of their names.

Edgyth let her eyes meet those of Dwynwen.

"Let us take them into the bower, until they are ready to be brought to the hall," Edgyth offered. This slight pretense to be alone with the girl was enough. Dwynwen stood, placed the cups into the box, and with a smile at Ceric, turned with Edgyth to do just this.

"No ill effect?" Lady Edgyth questioned, as soon as they were within.

Dwynwen shook her head. "Toward dawn I was awakened by his restlessness. I placed my hand on his brow. His skin was again cool, almost cold, the way it had felt the first night I found him Elf-shot. I lay across him, to warm him, and it awakened him enough so that he fell into peaceful sleep again."

"Ah. Perhaps a sign of the charm working," Edgyth offered. "And you, my girl – no ill effect on you?"

"None. I was greatly tired when I finished, and fell into heavy sleep of my own."

Edgyth took her hand. "Indeed. It must have been huge effort."

Dwynwen thought of something else. Mindred had not yet taken away their salver, one from which Ceric had eaten far too little. Dwynwen had seen Edgyth's eyes fall upon it as she approached.

"How to make him eat more?" the girl asked.

"Wild celery," Edgyth answered. "I have tried to get him to drink some."

"Yes, wild celery," she agreed. "I have heard of that. Lady Luned has used it. Also Gwydden, our priest, on those who were failing."

"Mindred will keep bringing it. Try to make him drink a cupful each day. Make of it a game. He will do as you ask," she suggested.

Dwynwen did not wait for the morning salver and its draught of the brew. That evening when their supper was brought them, she made a point to praise the aroma of the barley browis, and make much of the carrots glistening under a glaze of butter. Ceric looked at the food with attention as well, enjoying her own interest there. But after three or four bites he seemed sated, and ready to stop.

"You are eating less than your child-wife," she teased. The spoon in her hand was one of silver, brought from Ceredigion, and she wagged it playfully at him. But her tone took on a more serious note in her next words. "You must eat, to grow strong again. You must match me, spoon for spoon, and bite for bite."

She pressed this challenge, smiling as she dipped up the savoury mix, not placing it in her mouth until he had done the same with his own spoonful. He took several more spoons than would have been his wont this way, and when he faltered, took a last when Dwynwen laughingly cried out, "But I am still hungry!" and took a final spoon herself. She was well pleased, as he had eaten more than at any prior meal, and with seeming relish.

There was still bright light in the sky when they finished; they supped well before the hall gathered each night. Dwynwen had another thought.

"You have not seen my dower," she said. Her eyes were twinkling as she said this, and her voice carried the gladsome note now natural to her when she spoke. Yet Ceric knew her first words uttered to his face would forever sound within him. The sombre tone of Dwynwen's promising she would never leave him had been followed by the heart-stilling gravity of her sacred vow, one offered at his own threshold as she gave herself to him. Those words seemed a portal that once passed through, blocked out an unhappy past for Ceric, and opened the brightest of futures for Dwynwen. Her joy in him and their shared present was foremost.

It was true, Ceric had not glimpsed her treasure. But he responded with a start. He had made Dwynwen of Ceredigion his wife, and not paid her bride-price. That very word came to his lips now, and not without a thrill of urgency.

"Your bride-price – I must fulfil it."

She gave a small and carefree laugh. "King Elidon does not know we are wed; I could be here for weeks, and not make up my mind. There is no cause for haste."

Yet Dwynwen could see that Ceric was of a sudden troubled by this. Both wife and goods were here, and Kilton had made no move to uphold its end of the agreement. When he spoke next she did not jest about his concern.

"The wine jug," he told her. "I must fill it before I see your dowry." There was such earnestness in his face that she did not smile as he said this. "It is only fitting," he added.

Her small hands opened in a gesture of acceptance. Anything which would give his mind ease she would endorse.

"I have great store of silver in coins," he went on. "My mother left me over 3,000 pieces, much of what my grandsire Godwulf gave to her. I have not touched it. Lady Edgyth has told me that my grandmother also left a treasure in silver to me; it has been in her keeping, but is mine. But my mother's I have here, in the bower."

Dwynwen considered this. He could use treasure granted by his own mother to buy her hand. It was fitting indeed, as Luned had provided for her.

"Let me fill it," she asked, "from your mother's legacy." Her eyes, blue and tawny, were dancing as she said this.

His lips parted in surprise. Brides had no part in the selecting and packing up of the treasure exchanged for them; indeed, many never wholly knew what that price had been. Dwynwen not only had full knowledge of that sum she had been traded for, but wished to take active part in fulfilling it.

"I want to," she went on. "The silver is that left you by your mother; this has great meaning to me."

Watching her face, seeing her excitement, he was caught up in her own fervency, and must assent. And this put the silver to a high use, one he felt both mother and grandsire would approve.

"We will fill it together," he answered.

Dwynwen went straightaway to Mindred, for her help. The woman well knew the wine jug the bride asked after; it stood with the bronze and silver tableware in the locked hall storeroom, but Lady Edgyth readily gave access. It did not take long for a serving man to appear at the bower house door, pulling the wine jug behind him in a small hand wain. With it were the two grain scoops Dwynwen had asked for, lest they be needed.

Ceric thanked the man, and after he vanished, pulled the wain over the low wooden threshold and into the house. It must be filled where it lay, in the wain, as soon it would be too heavy for a single man to move.

Ceric crossed to the wall where stood the heavy cradle. The silver was there, buried beneath the three broad planks whereon it sat. He pushed the cradle aside. So cleverly had the spot been concealed that even the nail heads matched those of the rest of the floor; yet these had been cut short, and attached to nothing.

He lifted the first plank. It revealed what looked to be a second floor beneath, for a flat surface of grey stone greeted them. He lifted the second plank, and then the third. What had seemed a stone floor was actually several slabs fitted together, but free of any mortar. There was a finger's distance between them, and Ceric pulled them up, one by one, and stacked them on the wooden floor. Beneath lay the treasure. It was housed in an array of crockery and bronze crocks and jars. Each was sealed with a wooden stopper.

"It is in two layers," Ceric told her. "The smaller pots on top."

Dwynwen dropped on her knees beside the hole, and with a smile Ceric gestured that she choose the first pot to pull up. Her hands went to a jar of dull red clay. Its mouth was not wide, but she was surprised at its heft, and needed both hands to pull it forth. She set it on top of the stones he had stacked. He nodded again. She lifted the wooden stopper. There they were, filled to the top of the neck of the squat jar, what looked to be hundreds and hundreds of small silver coins. She took the jar in both hands, lifted it to the mouth of the wine jug, and began to pour them in. The coins rained down inside, a bright tinkling as they fell against each other, a muffled clanging din as they struck the fired clay bottom.

They took turns drawing out the stored silver, and pouring the coins into the receiving wine jug. After the fourth crock had been emptied out, Dwynwen bent over the wine jug and reached her arm in. She could just feel the mounded coins within.

She looked up at Ceric, her arm still within the wine jug. "Oof! I am costing you a great fortune," she cried. She was smiling as she said it, but felt it the truth.

"You are worth any fortune," he assured her. His smile said as much as his words.

They had removed enough of the smaller crocks to reveal one much larger, seated on a bed of gravel beneath them. Ceric squatted down and wrapped his hands about it. He hauled it out upon the floor. Dwynwen was ready with one of the scoops, and he let her lift any number of glittering scoopfuls from it, which she carefully carried to the wine jug. A few coins escaped her, dropping and rolling across the broad floor boards, and she ran after them, though a few dropped deep within the cracks between the boards, beyond sight and reach. She shrugged her shoulders and laughed. "Now there will always be silver in this house, even if we empty this secret store."

Ceric then picked up the still-heavy crock and emptied it. It brought the coinage up to the tapering shoulders of the jug.

"One more," he gauged, and Dwynwen reached for another of the smaller jars. She was glad to be allowed to pour the final coins in, and beamed at him when she had done so. They spent a shared moment looking at the shining discs, filling the wine jug brimful. Then Ceric used his fist to pound the wooden stopper back in. The jug, wain and all, would reside here until he could send it to King Elidon, but it marked a needed fulfilment. This treasure, having been designated and set aside, now allowed him to view her dowry.

Dwynwen was eager to show it. "Now, the treasure Lady Luned has given me. It is in that chest." She pointed to a chest of mid-size, one newly-made, delicately carved with tracery of dragons set into the wood on either end, and strapped with black iron bands. "Also here," she added, removing a stout lidded jug from her clothes chest. She lifted the lid of the jug, and offered it, as she had seen Luned do back at Ceredigion. Ceric bent over it, and did not need his bride's next words to know its contents; they proclaimed themselves by scent.

"Peppercorns," she announced. They were from islands at the furthest reaches of Middle Earth; all knew this. One could almost ransom a Prince with this jar.

Somehow Ceric was not surprised at Dwynwen's next words. "I will give the peppercorns to Lady Edgyth. She will make the best use of them."

For answer he only planted a kiss on her head.

"This is the greater part of what Luned gave," she went on, pushing back the lid of the carved chest. The door to the bower was still open, the casement too, and the lowering Sun streamed through. There could have been no better light under which to view the bolts of fabric Dwynwen pulled, one by one, from that chest.

"She gave me silk," Dwynwen said, lifting her smiling face to Ceric.

"There is much of it. We can clothe ourselves, make gifts of it, and save some for later. Even trade for it if you like, as Luned did to gather it all for me."

"Are you pleased," she asked, making of her question a winsome demand.

"Most pleased," he told her. "But not as much as with she who brings such treasure."

Ceric had missed one more benchmark of his newly-wedded state. He had something in reserve to present, something of high value. None knew he had planned to one day give it to Ashild of Four Stones; he had told no one this. Ashild was far beyond such concerns, and just as his mother's silver seemed the highest use for his wife's bride-price, this granting, once meant for his first wife, should go now to Dwynwen.

"I have a piece of land, well-tenanted, awarded me by Prince Eadward. It is a place called Iglea. I would like to make it yours, as your morgen-gyfu."

"Land," she repeated. She clapped her hands together in delight. "I thank you."

"It is two days' journey from here. We will go to view it."

He said this, knowing the last time he had passed that granting it had been upon his return to Kilton following Ashild's death. As fragile as was his state of mind he had been aware of how close he was to something which he hoped would bring his bride pleasure. It had been another wrenching reminder of his act. Yet, even above that raw and worked silver which was his, the holding at Iglea was by far the most valuable of all his possessions he could give, and he rightly wanted to honour his new wife by bestowing it upon her. God or St Ninnoc or Ashild had sent Dwynwen to him; he must honour the gift with one of this magnitude.

They slept that night feeling the richer for what they had partook. The wine jug of silver and the bolts of silk were there, handled, admired, and exchanged for the shared life they would build.

When the Lady of Kilton came to them in the morning, Ceric was more than prepared to speak of it.

"Dwynwen's bride-price – it is now ready to go to Ceredigion," he told her.

The three of them stepped through the bower-house door. The hand wain with its iron-rimmed wheels stood there, not far from the cradle. Edgyth was not surprised to see the jug within.

Dwynwen gestured to the table, upon which sat three large linen sacks, the contents showing from the opened ends.

"And here is my silk, Lady, which Luned gave to me. Forty ells worth, in red, blue, and green." Dwynwen shook out each resplendent bolt in turn from its sack. Her smile was as warm and open as were her hands, lifting to them. "Please to make yourself free of it, for yourself, and . . . for Edwin."

Edgyth was at first taken aback at the sheer abundance of material. Dwynwen's unstinting liberality concerning it was equally surprising. It said much of how the girl had been raised, and what she had been taught to value. Or was it in fact that Dwynwen, by her self-same nature, cared little or nothing for such riches? Whatever its source, Edgyth must spend a moment, looking upon it all. She considered the lustrous folds before her, their hues intense, their sheen almost as if sunlight itself had been woven with the fine filaments. It was wonderful stuff, wonderfully offered. Modwynn had left her silk gowns, yet these were rarely worn. And silk for Edwin . . . she gave her head the smallest of shakes. It would be difficult for him to wear any from this store. Dwynwen was perhaps too young to see this. She only nodded at the girl's kindness.

Still, the opulence of this treasure was meant to be enjoyed, and Dwynwen's expectant face demanded answer.

"You wear it, my girl," she answered, with deep sincerity and warmth. "You and Ceric. I will help you with a special tunic for him, if you have not made such clothes."

Dwynwen had in fact never fashioned clothing for a man, and her eager nod of acceptance gladdened Edgyth.

Ceric spoke now. "My men will carry Dwynwen's bride-price to Elidon," he began. "I will ask Worr to choose those to do so."

Edgyth murmured her approval. She was glad that Ceric had not suggested Worr himself should go. He was of far too vital use here, at Kilton, and with Ceric.

"And I must send a message to Lady Luned," Dwynwen offered. "And Elidon," she added.

Edgyth nodded in agreement. She and Dunnere had already been conferring on how best to frame the news to be sent. She left the pair soon after, to return to her own duties.

The day was not a fair one; a slight drisk had begun to fall as the couple broke their fast in the pleasure garden, and the grey sky was now pattering rain. There would be no sitting out in the garden until it passed. Edgyth had earlier brought them one of Kilton's books, King Ælfred's translation of Boethius' *Consolations*, and Ceric had begun reading it aloud to Dwynwen. The musings of this long-dead wise man as he awaited execution were filled with sober beauty, one which the King had embellished and made the more pertinent by transposing it to the tongue of the Saxons, and adding impressions of his own.

Dwynwen took great pleasure in Ceric's skill, and listened with care. She was not at all abashed to tell him she could read and write only a few names in the tongue of Cymru, and he kissed her for her simple admission, and kissed her again when she wondered aloud if she might herself learn this art. "It is easier to read than to write," he told her. "But you are so young, and clever, I think you might learn both, and soon. Lady Edgyth will teach you; Dunnere too, and I will help."

The drumming of the rain increased, and the sky darkened with the clouds that bore it. By and by Ceric yawned; he had been reading a good while, and they had reached the end of Book One, and fully met the kind but stern woman who was Philosophy, come to comfort the Roman in his cell. Dwynwen placed her hands on the leathern binding, and took it from him. Ceric seemed more tired than on prior days; was it her leech-craft at work, she wondered.

"Let us lie down together," she invited. "To rest," she added, with a shy smile. No healing could be achieved without sleep, and Ceric had been ragged for months with lack of it.

He nodded. Dwynwen closed the wooden shutters, summoning dusk in as short a time as it took for her to do so. Ceric pulled off his boots. He lay down upon the coverlet. She did the same.

He fell into ready sleep. Dwynwen dozed as well, and as it happened, awakened first. They had not slept over-long; the rain fell, still steady upon their pointed roof. She swung her legs down, and went to the waiting ewer for a sip of water, which she poured into her new silver cup.

As Dwynwen drank, Ceric awoke. He was lying on his side, facing her. As he began to push himself up, he slid his hand beneath his pillow. He felt something there, something hard. Dwynwen went to his side as he lifted himself and pulled the pillow away. A small bag of plain linen lay there.

He did not touch it, but looked first at it and then to her. He knew it to be purposeful, and a charm of some kind. Dwynwen looked alert, but not at all alarmed.

"What . . . what charm is this," he asked her. Spells and charms could be of any nature, and his concern was there upon his brow. Then before she could answer, he asked a second question, in more hopeful tone. "You made this, did you not?"

She nodded, and his face cleared.

"Lady Edgyth helped me; she knew the parts it must contain." She paused a moment. "But I made, and set the spell. It is one of healing."

He listened, looking from the linen bag to her as she spoke.

"You have suffered Elf-shot."

Ceric knew of this condition, but had never seen anyone struck with it.

Dwynwen paused before she went on; she had given much thought to the cause. "We do not know who sent it, but now that I am your wife I have a guess.

"Perhaps some Elfin Queen had spied you during your time in the forest, and wanted you for her own. When you came out from the wood, she sent a dart, which struck you, and tried to pull you back." She gave her quick half-smile then. "But she cannot have you."

Ceric attended to this with rapt attention. Nothing seemed fanciful at this point; he had been through too much to discount any explanation.

"Why did the Elf Queen come for me?" he now asked.

Dwynwen's eyes dropped a moment, before she raised them to his own. "Luned told me such can lust after human men.

"And . . . I think she saw the great emptiness within you."

He reached his hand to hers.

"It is being filled," he said, as he clasped it. "You have filled it."

She thought of something now, and surprised him with her question. "The land you have given me – Iglea. Does that lie near the forest in which you sheltered?"

He shook his head, wondering at the connection she had formed. "It is far from it. Iglea is to the south-east."

She nodded, but the small face was still grave. "That is good," she answered. "For you should not venture into that wood again. Lest the Elf Queen find you."

Ceric pondered this, and slowly asked, "Could she harm you?"

Dwynwen knew the answer, and gave it, with calm firmness. "She could not. One must be in the line of sight for an Elf to cast a spell. I did not enter your forest." She raised her head to the bower house walls. "Nor can Elves tread land which has felt the plough, nor enter within walls built by men." Her smile, and her next words, were resolute. "I am quite safe."

"What will this charm do, if it works?" he next asked.

"Return the bolt from whence it came. Not to harm they who sent it. I fixed the spell to fall into water, to dissolve all ill doing."

He took this in. "You are wise," he told her. "How know you all this?"

She considered a moment before she answered. Certain things had been taught her. Dwynwen was only in her sixth Summer when her birth mother died. But she still had memory of the woman, or if not memory, the sensation of being in her presence. It was she who had first told her of the Elves. Later it was Luned who had shared far more with her. But other knowledge she held, without understanding how.

"There are different ways of knowing," Dwynwen finally answered. "Luned taught me. That, and what I feel when I think upon such things."

Ceric could only nod. This girl had depths he could not guess at, but believed.

He glanced again at the small linen bag. As plain as it looked, he believed that it might aid him. "How long must the spell-bag remain there?"

"Seven nights," Dwynwen announced. "Then I will release it, to the waves below."

She had before considered this, and felt this end the safest and most respectful for the bag.

"Have I disturbed the charm, by learning about it?" he next wanted to know.

"Nay," she assured him. "I think not. You wish to grow well. Those who do, help themselves in their healing. By welcoming this charm you further seek wholeness."

His eyes brimmed with sudden tears. "You will not leave me, Dwynwen," he said.

She leant forward and kissed those eyes, tasting the salt.

"I will never leave you. We have shared a sacred cup. I am in you, and you are in me."

"I love you, Dwynwen. More than myself, more than my own life, I love you."

THE HALL OF KILTON

OVER the next few days Edwin's wretchedness descended to new depths. All in hall and village knew he had gone to seek a bride, and saw him return with one. Suddenly, by his own order, it was known the Welsh girl had instead wed his brother. Edwin had not been good enough for the niece of the King of Ceredigion. He felt that, strongly, piercingly; and also outrage at the contradicting truth, that she had been snatched from him, by a man who knew her even less than he did. The girl had wrought this, he knew; but Ceric had accepted her act, had allowed it.

All his men knew it. The prattle of the serving folk or crofters concerned him not; it was his men he cared about. Alwin, the captain of his body-guard, had arrived too late to see him punch Ceric; but Worr had seen it. And Edwin knew Alwin had discerned what had happened; the girl's screams, his own raised voice, the fact that though Ceric had stayed largely out of sight, it was well known that his eye was black. And he was sure Alwin had seen his skinned knuckles. His men knew the Lord of Kilton had struck one of his own men, a man who could not strike back. And that man happened to be the elder son of the hall, who rode with Prince Eadward and was honoured by Ælfred.

The shame of this – of a Lord striking one of his own men – was at times too much for Edwin to embrace. In his head he must constantly revert to the fact that he had struck his brother. As terrible as this was, it was easier to accept than the crime of striking a pledged man. Yet the fact that Ceric responded as his man, defended himself not, allowed himself to be hurt, gave the lie to this.

Almost as bad as this was the fact that Worr had witnessed this abuse. Edwin had discredited himself before Kilton's horse-thegn, a man esteemed by all. As a result Edwin could not allow himself to be in Worr's company. That Worr had seen him throw that second punch, and had then overpowered him as if he were yet a boy, only added to his shame.

His mother had seen that second blow as well. Such was her generous heart that Edwin assumed himself forgiven in her eyes. Yet how poorly his action showed compared to those of the prior Lords of Kilton.

Hardest of all to consider was Ceric himself. Edwin could not untangle which was stronger in his breast – his shame at having struck his brother, or his anger at him. It was true that later that day he had gone to see Ceric, and had laid his hand upon his arm. In his shock and anger it was all he could do. He had scarce seen either Ceric or Dwynwen since he had stood, reluctant witness, at their hand-fast.

Since that day Edwin felt what he read as sudden estrangement between himself and the followers of Ceric. As thegns of Kilton, Edwin was of course their over-Lord; yet it was common and even encouraged for the pledged thegns of second or third sons to be rigorously devoted to that man. Since being named Lord, Edwin commanded their respect and was always greeted with a nod of deference. Now these same men appeared to be looking away at his approach, or at least not meeting his eyes. It was subtle, yet their eyes were seemingly elsewhere and engaged when he neared. He felt shunned, and it hurt him; a silent, deep, even profound chasm riven now between the men of Ceric and the Lord of Kilton. And it extended to his own men – he felt he had lost their full respect.

He had no one to speak to of this, and must bear it alone. Cadmar was dead, his grandmother as well; and Edwin could not think of the horse-thegn without the blush of shame mantling his cheek. It left only his mother, who, while always mild and kind to him, had, he felt, fully taken up the union of the Welsh girl to his brother. Her care and attention were directed to his brother, not to him.

He had not even the woman Begu to retreat to. She had gone, abandoned him without fare-well, left Kilton to wed far from here. It was galling that it was she who reclaimed Ceric from that wood; Begu had done that which no other of them could. He had kept his jealousy of her prior arrangement with Ceric under check by acknowledging a few simple facts. Ceric, believing himself already wed in spirit, had determined to see the woman no more. He had offered Edwin his place in Begu's life, and in her bed, and she had accepted. Yet Edwin never felt himself adequate replacement for his older brother. He could not, at times when in her bed, help imagining Ceric having been there before him. Edwin knew Begu was the first woman Ceric had known, just as she was for him. Edwin knew himself clumsy at first, despite her

welcoming gestures. As he grew more sure this sense
receded, though at times he felt she looked for more
than he knew how to give. It made him wonder if there
were some other heights known to Ceric and she, heights
denied him by his awkwardness or unwillingness to ask
her access to them. As final blow, she had left no message for Edwin, no fare-well. Begu's thoughts, like those
of Lady Edgyth, seemed all for Ceric.

So it was that the young Lord of Kilton suffered the
seething turmoil of loss, shame, anger, and frustration.

It was no effort for Edwin to avoid seeing the bridal
pair. The Lord of Kilton had never need to enter the plea-
sure-garden; he lived in the hall, set just behind the palisade gates. The only time he neared the garden or the
bower of Ceric was when he entered the stone church,
and even then the pleasure garden, still in its Summer fullness, was largely screened from view by the beech hedge.

Ceric had been gone from Kilton a full year, then
taken meat in the hall a single night. Few had seen him
since. But a fortnight into his new marriage, Ceric determined to come to the hall with his bride. His blackened
eye had subsided, the swelling gone, the orbit of the eye
just showing a greenish yellow at this point. He must
begin to resume his duties, and part of this was his presence at his brother's side in the hall each night.

Ceric had told Edgyth in advance, and she had taken
their silver cups. It was the appearance of these cups
upon the table that alerted Edwin that his brother and
wife would be joining them. He watched the man who
served as steward of the high table place them there,
before Edgyth could even bring him the news, for she
had returned to her own bower for a more festive gown.

Edwin approached the table, saw the names cut into the cups, and retreated to the treasure room. When she tapped on the door thereof, where Edwin was as usual just before the commencement of the evening meal, he did not answer.

The hall was largely filled when Ceric and Dwynwen appeared. They came through the side door, that closest to the private precincts, and nearest to the high table. Dwynwen wore the gown of red she had arrived Kilton in, and Ceric the tunic of blue he had worn at their hand-fast. About the brows of both was a thin fillet of gold. These also had been his parents', and before they left the bower Ceric had placed that of his mother upon Dwynwen's brow. He wished tonight to present her as she was, daughter of a Prince, niece to a King, and his beloved wife, worthy of all treasure he could bestow.

As they were noticed the noise of the place fell away. Edwin was not yet at table, but Edgyth was standing next her chair, and opened her hands to them in a gesture of welcome, her pale eyes lit from within by her pleasure. Worr, already seated at the high table, stood. The pledged men of Ceric, thirty strong, sat at their own table. As the first of them saw Ceric he leapt to his feet, mouth open. A moment later every one of them stood, raising their arms in acclamation, calling out Ceric's name. They had served long and hard duty under his command in service to Prince Eadward, months of rough sleeping, little and poor rations, bloody and thankless skirmishes. Ceric had shared every privation with them, and taken on a doubled tour of duty while those wed amongst them returned home. The hardships and hunger they had suffered might have broken lesser warriors, or those under a lesser man.

Yet they had been part of actions which had wrought a costly and victor-less battle at Middeltun, routed the Danes at Fearnhamme, and resulted in the capture of Haesten's wife and sons. Under the leadership of Ceric they had been commended by that Prince and rewarded in silver. Now they rose, all thirty, full-throated in their praise, greeting their war-chief and his bride.

The two captains of Edwin, the chief of his body-guards Alwin and Wystan, sat at the high table with their Lord, as did his most favoured warriors. The balance of Edwin's fifty men sat throughout the hall, with wives and children if they were wed. These all remained silent for the long moments of bellowing acclamation greeting Ceric. Edwin was not here, but Alwin, captain of his guard, must react.

Despite the personal allegiance to Ceric, all the warriors of the hall were bound to its Lord, and that was Edwin. Alwin must encourage their unity. He stood as well, raising his arm and lifting his voice in acclamation to Ceric. All stood with him, a deafening roar of welcome issuing from their throats.

Edwin, still within the treasure room, heard first the cheers of a small number of men, their exclamations and shouts, indistinct but strongly voiced. He heard his brother's name called out. The accolade grew. It was joined a long moment later by what sounded like the entire hall, a thronging chorus, heartily voiced, shouting out honoured acclaim. He took a breath and stepped out to this. All the folk therein were on their feet, greeting Ceric and his wife, who still stood before the table, arrested in their action of reaching their seats. Edwin raised his head and nodded, forcing a smile that felt a grimace. He too lifted his hand in welcome; it was as much as he could do.

As Edwin approached his chair the noise quieted. It gave Ceric a long moment to face the hall, and give to all a silent nod of acknowledgement. Then he made his way to the bench on which he sat. This was at his brother's right, as always. But this night, and every night thereafter, Dwynwen sat not between them, but at the right of Ceric.

The next day Ceric went to see his brother. He walked from the private confines of the family of Kilton to which he had so long kept himself, and into the bustle of the working burh. He came early, just after the hall had broken its fast, yet before Edwin might be heading out to spar. The young Lord was thus back in the treasure room, donning the heavy leathern tunic he would wear to protect against errant blows. Ceric stood outside the door, rapped upon its solid planks, and called his brother's name. Edwin opened, almost at once.

The two spent a moment regarding the other. Ceric saw the wariness on Edwin's face, but his brother gave a nod of assent. Ceric began.

"The wine jug – it has been filled. I will send half of my men with it. I come to ask if you can spare one or two of your own who had gone to Ceredigion, to act as guides."

Edwin had not thought of this. It would of course speed the trip, make it both safer and surer, to have along two who had so recently made the journey.

"Yes," Edwin answered, then made a further decision. "Wystan is a good tracker. He will be one of them."

This was generous. Offering his second captain was more than what Ceric expected.

"I thank you," he returned.

The silence that ensued was awkward for both. Yet Ceric had more to say.

"Your mother and Dunnere are each writing letters to go with it. You are welcome to read either."

Edwin had almost to laugh, but if he had it would have been one without a trace of mirth. Both the priest and the Lady of Kilton were skilled in quiet diplomacy, which both had long practice in, and he could be assured that all involved parties would be cast in the best possible light.

"I have no need of that," he answered, giving his head a single shake. "They will say that which is needed."

Ceric gave a nod. "I trust that they will." It was clear he had no desire to read such a missive, either.

After another moment it seemed that neither had more to say. Ceric made a gesture of his head, as if to leave. It prompted Edwin to open his mouth.

"It was good to have you in the hall last night."

Ceric took a slow breath. Dwynwen had enjoyed each moment there, and after eating had spent much time walking about with Edgyth, meeting this or that woman of the hall, greeting the thegns' wives and children, and as any observing could see, quickly winning the approval of all to whom she turned her bright eyes and quick smile. Edwin had watched her, his chest constricting. Dwynwen was like a pretty child, one so captivating that approval could not be withheld. But he had seen how self-directed she was, had felt the force of her decision-making.

"It pleased Dwynwen to be there," Ceric said. He took another slow breath before finishing. "As it did, me."

Dwynwen had asked Edgyth to write a letter to be read to Luned. The girl knew Dunnere was writing a formal one, addressed to Elidon, King of Ceredigion, but wished the Lady of Kilton to speak directly to her step-mother. That afternoon while Worr was with Ceric they began it.

"Gwydden will read it, just as you write it; he is an honest man," she told Edgyth. The girl's assessment of the priest's character brought a smile to Edgyth's lips, but she understood. Gwydden must have proven himself unswerving in his past services to Lady Luned, and this Dwynwen relied upon.

"Luned wishes to know all about Ceridwen, the mother of Ceric," the girl went on. They were in Edgyth's bower, Edgyth seated at that small table to which she had brought Dwynwen after her first night spent with Ceric. All the Lady's writing implements were upon it, fresh goose quills, blade, scraper, ruling board and pins; also a small pot of newly-made ink, and several pieces of squared parchment. The table cover of watered green silk had been folded and set aside, to spare it from spatter. Edgyth sat there alone, for Dwynwen walked to and fro as she spoke, her excitement growing as she thought upon what her step-mother wished to hear.

Edgyth was in secret glad to have been asked to per-form this task, as it spared Dunnere from details which Dwynwen's step-mother would have certain interest in.

And Dwynwen herself was so definite in what she wished to relate to Lady Luned that Edgyth felt the priest would hardly have the patience to do so.

Before they began, Edgyth had her own question to ask. "Tell me of Lady Luned," she invited.

Dwynwen's mouth creased into a wide grin. "She is a wise-woman. She knows of plants, and of stars, of the ways of water and trees, and of dreams. And Luned knows much of men. Everything, I think," the girl decided, looking back on all that Lady had told her. "She knows everything of the act of love. How it is with a youth, his first time to bed with a woman. How it is with a man who is old, who wishes pleasure with you, but whose body needs help to respond. And she knows which herbs to use to open the womb so that a woman might bear a babe the quicker. How when a woman is got with child and wishes to rid herself of it, she should proceed. Also, what herbs to pick, and brews to make, to help the sudden heat that older women feel, when their wombs contract and wisdom comes upon them."

Edgyth, modest by nature, found herself dropping her eyelids at this report. This slip of a girl had heard much from her step-mother.

Dwynwen, nothing abashed, picked up her own thread.

"Please to tell all you know of Lady Ceridwen."

The Lady sighed, but it was one that ended in a smile.

"I was not here when Ceridwen arrived with Gyric. I was wed to his older brother, Godwin, and their father Godwulf was still alive. But I, having lost many babes, was at the Abbey of Glastunburh.

"Worr was here," she remembered. "He was quite young, just made a thegn. But he will recall much of what he witnessed, and what he heard. I know she took Gyric from a cellar where he had been left to die."

Her listener nodded her head. "That was the keep of Four Stones, where Ceric's friend Hrald is Jarl," Dwynwen offered. She saw the surprise on Edgyth's face and answered it. "Ceric told me of their friendship, as did Worr."

"Yes," she allowed. "It is a great fortress; Ceridwen had gone there with her friend, Lady Ælfwyn. Ceridwen had help from the kitchen folk there, and Ælfwyn, and she rode off with Gyric. They travelled many weeks and survived high danger to reach here."

Edgyth paused again, as if walking back across the decades. Again, the shadow of a smile graced her lips.

"But I can tell you, and Lady Luned, of the young woman I knew. When I returned to Kilton Ceridwen had brought forth a babe. It was Ceric."

Both smiled at this, and Edgyth went on. "She knew I could not bear one myself, and was generous in allowing me time with the child. We came to the bower house – your bower house. Ceridwen was quite young when she arrived here, just a year more than you."

Dwynwen broke in here. "That was what Ceric told me," she exclaimed. "Please to tell Luned this; she wishes to learn all about her as a girl."

Edgyth nodded; she would omit none of what she had just told, nor of Modwynn's astonishment at Ceridwen's actions; that Lady had written to her at Glastunburh. "All honoured her courage; her bringing Gyric back alive was proof of it. But in her innocence, it was a bravery she did not even recognise or admit."

Edgyth spent a moment looking at the girl before her and thinking, just as you do not know your own courage.

"But the men here did. I will let Worr tell you of that part; for again, he was here. Gyric told the story in detail, I know." It was hard for Edgyth to travel down this path, knowing that the story of the maiming of Gyric led her husband Godwin to terrible acts of vengeance. She closed her eyes a moment to clear her vision, and went on.

"Luned may wish to know that Lady Modwynn welcomed Ceridwen from the start, naming her daughter that first day. She had, it seemed to all, brought Gyric back from the dead; the hall was in deep mourning for him when they arrived. Though cruelly blinded they rejoiced to have him return."

Dwynwen's mind too skipped over some of this; it was too much to compass, how a young man raised as a warrior would not himself have gone mad, or even ended his life, having been rendered so unfit for his role in the hall. And it was too close to what might have been the Fate of Ceric, as well. It was the maid Ceridwen she fastened upon. Dwynwen said the first thing that came into her mind.

"Her love for Gyric must have been strong, to keep him alive."

"It was. Most strong. He told me once she was the greatest blessing of his life."

Like Ceric and me, Dwynwen thought. It was Ceridwen's Fate to save a man, and she did. Just as I was sent to Ceric.

It drew a line, sudden but inviolable, from Ceridwen to her. This thrill of realisation was so great, she must squeeze her eyes shut at it.

Edgyth was speaking again; Dwynwen could and would return to this revelation later, and savour the sensations arising from it.

"And none could deny that Ceridwen proved to be a blessing to all of Kilton, for she produced two sons. Not only Ceric, but then Edwin, whom she gave to Godwin and me."

"And Godwin was Lord then," Dwynwen offered.

"He was. Godwulf had died some years earlier. And we had no child. Ceridwen giving Edwin to us meant I could remain his wife, for I had resolved to have our union sundered, so he might marry again, and sire an heir."

Ceridwen held Kilton together, Dwynwen thought. Luned will wish to know this, of her great value to this rich burh.

She asked a searching question, one without judgement or blame. "But where is she now? Why did she leave?"

Luned had not told Dwynwen the scant details she had heard from the lips of Edwin. She had wanted the girl to find things out herself, and from those older who could best recall the sequence of events. Edgyth recounted what she knew, promising to commit it in outline to the parchment before her. Her lips pursed in a rueful smile. She would need more than the three squared pieces before her.

All Edgyth related seemed to be of great interest to the girl, but Dwynwen had one further request. "And please to tell Luned these words from me, written large: 'It was the older brother, Ceric, who was foretold.'"

"And then, as only you can, tell all of Ceric, and also how he came to live in your forest, and of the Elf-shot we are curing."

Dwynwen's hapless scribe only nodded her head at the ever-growing task. Yet Edgyth could regret none of it. Dwynwen was utterly disarming. Despite the initial upset to the hall, the girl had brought nothing but good to Ceric. She recalled the day of Ceric's return to the hall, and her trusting that Divine Providence would send him what he needed for his healing. God had sent this Welsh girl, now his wife. Edgyth saw each day the good she was doing him.

Ceric was gaining flesh, showed more interest in life about him, and his bride said he suffered Elf-shot less and less. And Dwynwen's youthful cheerfulness was being felt in every quarter. Such was her engaging appeal that few could look upon the girl without a smile.

Even more, here, in Modwynn's bower, sitting in what had been her chair, it was easy for Edgyth to imagine how strongly her mother-in-law would have taken to Dwynwen. It would have been, she felt, a deep endorsement, one welling from the heart; the sincerest approval of the girl and her character. This assurance, that Modwynn would have felt the same, served to validate her own feelings for the girl.

When Edgyth had finished, Dwynwen looked carefully at the many lines of script, covering the front and reverse of six pieces of parchment. She could not know the warmth with which the Lady of Kilton closed her letter, her words of praise for Dwynwen, nor glean that Edgyth had ended with an earnest invitation that the Lady Luned should visit Kilton, and see for herself the man her step-daughter had wed, and the blessings her presence had already bestowed.

⌘⌘⌘⌘⌘⌘⌘⌘⌘⌘

Dunnere had complete freedom in what he would pen in his own letter. His brother priest Gwydden was the only one at Elidon's court who possessed the art of reading. Gwydden could read most of the missive aloud, omitting those parts meant for his ears only. Dunnere thus resolved that the first paragraph, and then every other, would be indented, with those written such intended for Elidon's priest.

Kilton's priest had been told that neither Edwin nor Ceric wished to be privy to what he wrote. And Lady Edgyth had inked her own letter, intended for Lady Luned, and had entrusted Dunnere with expressing the outcome of the Welsh girl's arrival. This gave the priest full license in both tone and choice of words.

Dunnere was thus surprised when Lady Edgyth and Dwynwen presented themselves at his small house, with the request that the Welsh girl be allowed to append her own message to his. As request it was not unreasonable, and he could not gainsay it. Both letters were to be sealed and delivered in one package, and that written by Dunnere was thus still sitting upon his writing table. The Lady of Kilton saw it, and made a silent gesture of inquiry if she might avail herself of its contents. Again, Dunnere could not refuse, and by the opening of his hands toward the lengthy missive granted access.

Edgyth picked it up, and quickly saw the message covered both sides. She had no qualms in reading it. This was not private conversation; Dunnere was writing as an envoy of Kilton, and Edgyth, as its Lady, had a right to know how it was being presented. Her eyes scanned the lines.

It was seemingly impossible for Dunnere to construct a simple salutation. Perhaps in this case the news the letter bore demanded his effusion.

TO ELIDON, GREAT KING OF CEREDIGION IN CYMRU, NOBLE PATRON OF THE HOLY CHURCH; AND TO THE FAITHFUL SERVANT OF CHURCH AND KING, GWYDDEN, GREETINGS AND GOOD TIDINGS FROM DUNNERE, HUMBLE PRIEST OF KILTON

> Gwydden, what I am to speak may arouse concern in the breast of your noble King, and in that of the Lady Luned. Therefore I pray you to attend to every segment of this missive in which I have curtailed its sprawl; these are private words for the eyes of my Brother in Christ. Those of normal width are to be read aloud to your King, and all others concerned.

I, Dunnere, send glad tidings for the King and country of Ceredigion. After a journey of no hardship Lady Dwynwen and her escort arrived Kilton, to be met with honour by the Lady thereof, Edgyth. Through the beneficence of God, who sees and knows all, and whose wisdom surpasseth understanding, she is now happily and honourably wed to Ceric, renowned warrior of Wessex, elder son of the burh of Kilton, and god-son of King Ælfred himself, who has ever shown royal favour to this young man, one of unspotted character. Edwin,

Lord of Kilton, was there to witness their union, one blest by me here in the chantry of Kilton, and one to which Lady Edgyth gave her full and open consent.

> Gwydden, brother; this was as unforeseen as a thunder-clap in a sky of blue. It was the maid herself who made her choice. I need not tell you Lady Dwynwen is of singular character, and of uncommon and determined mind. By the grace of God the attraction was mutual, and Ceric took her to wife.

Elidon, King, will be, I trust, gratified to learn of how favourably this union will be viewed by the royal house of Wessex, and by that also of Mercia, whose honourable Lady Æthelflaed, being daughter to King Ælfred, serves the interests of both countries. King Ælfred will, I am assured, travel soon to Kilton to welcome Lady Dwynwen, for as stated above, Ceric is indeed the King's beloved and favoured god-son. This is, I might confide to your Lordship's ear, a match even more desirable than that which had first been entertained. Ceric is possessed of great riches, and will be heir to far more. When the contents of the wine-jug are overturned, I trust as well his Lordship will be equally gratified to see therein many thousands of coins entire, none snipped nor cut, sent with all good wishes from Ceric of Kilton.

> Gwydden, I was but helpless to guide the girl; all was accomplished with such speed and finality.

Finally, gracious Elidon, Lady Luned, know that all folk of Kilton rejoice in Lady Dwynwen, be assured.

Gwydden, this last is true.

Yours in the blood of Christ,

Dunnere, Servant of God

Dunnere was watching her as she read, and Edgyth kept all expression from her face as she did so. She was not overly surprised at the manner in which he had constructed his letter. It underscored the art needed, and duplicity possible, to those who read and wrote. Written thus, how easy a thing it was, to omit or alter details in the reading. It was both a private and a public telling in one document.

Such tidings must almost of necessity be so. The priest had understandably expressed his astonishment at the sudden turn of events, and at the utter coolness of the maid. He had, in effect, been forced to see them wed. Edgyth took satisfaction in his last line, confirming how welcome Dwynwen was here. As confounding as it was, the girl's quicksilver nature was part of her high attraction.

When Edgyth finished she looked over the parchment to the priest. Her lips under her pale eyes wore a slight smile. "Well expressed, as always," she said.

Lady Dwynwen had been watching with care, and now smiled as well at the Lady's opinion. The girl gestured to a metal tray upon the table, one holding discarded quills, rumpled scraps of linen blotted with ink, and quire trimmings.

"Please, Father Dunnere, may I have a quill of no use to you?"

There were any number in the tray, quills now either too brittle to be re-cut, or too short to properly hold in the hand.

"You may have your pick, Lady," he answered.

She chose one, laid it on the cutting board, and with his sharp blade snipped out a segment of feather near the rounded top. Then she sliced through the tubular quill itself, and slid it down over the narrow segment of feather, leaving a tip of exposed plume. She dipped this in the pot of ink and pulled it out, a fine brush with which to draw.

At the bottom of Dunnere's letter she described a series of lines, dashes, circles and spirals, some with other symbols drawn through them. The signs were large and filled almost all the remainder of the sheet.

"I thank you," she told the priest, when she had finished her work. The ink was glistening and would need some time to dry, but she was pleased with what she had drawn.

Dunnere did not ask as to the meaning of the young Lady's work. They were not runes, but fanciful symbols of the girl's devising. It was some magical signatory, he felt, but as it was intended for Gwydden's eyes as well, must not be of any malicious nature. He merely blinked at what she had done.

"It is for my step-mother. Gwydden will know this, and show it her," she assured the priest.

They left, and once outside Dwynwen threaded her arm through that of Edgyth. She tilted up her chin and smiled at her.

"I wrote, 'I will save his life.'"

Letters and wine jug were carried off two days hence, escorted by fifteen men from Ceric, and two from Edwin. The send-off for the thegns was as quiet as Ceric could keep it. Unwarranted pomp would be unseemly given the circumstances, yet the families of the men riding out to accomplish this errand must be present, the parting cup of ale presented, and Dunnere's blessing upon the endeavour conferred. When a war-leader was sending his men without him, it was custom for him to address them as a group, to hearten and exhort them to the coming task. His own female kin would remain with the families being left behind, to cheer them. But Ceric walked arm in arm with his bride as he spoke a word or two to each of the men. Dwynwen said little, but gave her own affirming nod of thanks, or ready smile to the men who rode to deliver her bride-price. In size Dwynwen might be almost the young daughter of Ceric, clinging to her father's arm. But none looking on the faces of the pair could ascribe a familial mien to either, but rather one of shared and ardent love.

Edwin must be there as well for this leave-taking, and stood at the hall door, Edgyth at his side. He stayed only as long as was meet, then vanished into the recesses of the hall and to the treasure room. Its confines gave him what little comfort he could find. He fell into rumination about the Welsh girl, a path his thoughts had often trod since the shock of her bonding with his brother.

Dwynwen was quickly become everyone's pet, the beguiling lambkin none could say no to. Other than her noble origins, she was, Edwin now realised, almost entirely unsuited to the role he had chosen her for. For one thing, she lacked decorum. His future wife, the Lady of Kilton, must be possessed of prudent good judgement and be worthy of – nay – command, respect. Edwin now thought Dwynwen temperamentally incapable of such behaviour. He had seen Dwynwen at the side of Lady Edgyth as they crossed the forecourt one noon. Several of the thegns' children were there, playing at hoop rolling. When the errant hoop ran past Dwynwen, close enough to startle his mother, Dwynwen not only sprang forward to catch it, but turned it with a merry laugh and gave it a solid forward thrust to wheel it skittering back to those boys who had sent it. The Lord of Kilton could summon several other examples of similar laxity in judgement.

Edwin, thinking on the Welsh girl, found himself enumerating those traits he might once have been entranced by, but now saw as flaws. These began with her extreme youth, included her use of her left hand with which to feed herself, her tendency to break into a skipping step as she walked alone, to clap her hands when pleased, to break into peals of laughter, and many other girlish attributes. She was, he thought, of no use to his mother. To his eyes it was almost as if Lady Edgyth had a new child to look after.

And it disconcerted Edwin, the way she flashed her cheerful smile at him, as if nothing had happened. In one particular only was this Welsh girl ideally suited to her spurned role: the folk of Kilton already loved her. And in fairness he must admit that Dwynwen seemed devout, attended carefully at Mass, and appeared to pray most fervently. But this was not enough. She made Edwin, not yet in his twentieth year, feel far older, and somehow stern. None of this was comfortable for him, but it was what he must use to help himself over her loss.

Edwin knew, in the recesses of his mind, what he was doing. He was possessed of natural intelligence, and had not spent his life surrounded by the thoughtful considerations of the likes of Lady Modwynn, Cadmar, and his own mother without their examples having presented him with a set of keys with which to unlock his own motivations. By finding fault in Dwynwen he helped to shift her to a further remove from his own hopes and aspirations. It was the best, and only thing, he could do.

The bride he would find – well, she would be a woman, not a girl; a woman of stateliness and bearing. He felt certain of that. His mind returned more than once to Lady Pega of Mercia. She had likely wed the man she had been reserved for months ago. He could not help but wonder who was that Lord who had won her. She was out of Edwin's reach, but there would be others, perhaps equally far afield as Lady Pega or Dwynwen. Thinking on this, for the first time he was struck by a new possibility. A disordered Anglia must have any number of war-chiefs seeking union with Wessex. Perhaps of their daughters there was a well-born woman of the Danes.

After the thegns rode away, Dwynwen and Ceric returned to their bower house. Dwynwen perched on a small stool not far from the cradle. Her thoughts were fixed on the silver which had been laid by beneath that cradle, and of that large portion now beginning its journey to Ceredigion. She jumped up and went to the cradle itself, and lay her hand upon it so it gave a gentle list. It was old, one which had soothed many babes, and its wood was smooth to the touch. Ceric was seated at the table, looking over the Boethius, but she pictured him as a babe, being rocked by Ceridwen.

One day we might have a babe to lay within this, she thought. Her thoughts did not dwell there, for now her eyes went to the small wooden bird on the casement. It seemed to call to her. She walked to it, and picked it up, rubbing her fingers over the burnished surface.

"This little bird," she began. "Did you carve it?"

Ceric lifted his eyes to where she stood. "My father did, for me, when I was very small."

Her bright round eyes grew the rounder. "He carved it . . . while blind?"

"Yes. Just by feel, I imagine, the shaping guided by his hands."

She regarded it even more carefully now, and with true tenderness. "Someone has been chewing on it. Are these your teeth marks, as a babe?"

Ceric had to smile. "They are."

He watched her as she held the piece, and saw with what regard she studied it.

"Do you know I have a son?" he asked of a sudden. "Did Edgyth tell you?"

"Nay," she answered, clearly surprised. "With your first Lady-wife?" she asked, for of course Ceric might have fathered a child on another woman, as well.

"Yes. His mother was Ashild of Four Stones." His brow creased then, as if in remembrance. "Worr, I think, spoke of her to you."

"He did, yes. Your marriage was brief, he said."

A long moment passed before Ceric could respond.

"Of time together, yes. We had but one night."

Dwynwen took this in, with all seriousness. "Yet she bore your babe. Mother Mary favoured her, to grant this gift."

Ceric had almost to smile. He would not tell Dwynwen now that Ashild, though baptised, was no confirmed Christian. He felt her to have been a doubter, but still a seeker.

"Your little boy – how old is he? Please to tell of him."

"His name is Cerd. It is the name of my mother's father. The elder Cerd was a war-chief, with a keep by the River Dee."

"Ah," she said, with a nod.

"Cerd has nearly three years. He lives with Ashild's mother, the Lady Ælfwyn, a Saxon who wed a powerful Dane. He conquered Four Stones, and was Ashild's father."

"So Cerd is with your best friend Hrald, and his mother," she summed.

"Yes."

"He must be greatly cherished," Dwynwen offered.

"I know he is. I met him once . . ."

Ceric could not continue, not revisit that event at which he had seen and held his child.

As the daughter of a royal house Dwynwen had full knowledge of the importance of the offspring thereof. It prompted her to ask the next.

"You are his father," she began. "Will Cerd remain there, with the Lady of the hall, and your friend Hrald?"

Ceric shook his head.

"I do not know." The pain this was causing him was clear, and Dwynwen regretted the question. Yet Ceric looked as though he must speak.

"He is all they have left of Ashild, whose life I took."

His staring eyes now burned as he went on. "To take him from Four Stones . . . It is another cruelty."

"Perhaps he does not need to be taken," she offered. She set down the toy, and went to his side and placed her hand on his. "Perhaps when he is older he can be fostered here, so you might know your own boy." She warmed to this idea. "I will always welcome him."

Since Ceric had returned to the hall he had ridden out two or three times with Worr. With the advent of Dwynwen in his life, he bethought him that she might enjoy such an outing. He spoke to Worr about a good mount for her.

Worr had to pause. A mount suitable for one Dwynwen's size would be a pony. Yet a Lady of her rank must have a horse of elegance, even if small. Kilton's herd had few candidates. Several ponies were kept for the children of thegns, but they were shaggy, short-legged little beasts.

"I will do what I can," he promised. As it turned out no effort by the horse-thegn was needed. When Ceric made his offer to her, Dwynwen demurred, as prettily as she ever did when she voiced a contrary view. His young wife preferred to enjoy horses from a distance. She did not ride, she told Ceric, as she thought it unkind.

"If I were a horse I know I should not like it," she said with her quick smile. "Why should I bear the weight of another, when he has two perfectly good legs of his own?"

In case Ceric was about to object to this logic, Dwynwen was ready with a second answer, her reasoning just as sound.

"To draw a waggon, yes; for those are goods too heavy for us."

Ceric must smile back at her. She wished horses to be as free and unfettered as she herself was.

Yet Dwynwen was more than happy to walk with Ceric to the stable, and watch him and Worr saddle their chosen mounts. Worr had a young stallion he was train-ing, a black shading with age to dappled grey. As he and Ceric would be alone, and Worr need not concern him-self with the supervision of a young, and possibly untried rider, Worr saddled him. Ceric owned three horses, but had much of Kilton's horse-flesh at his disposal; still he had asked for his trusted bay stallion, that which Hrald had given him, to be brought. Dwynwen waved them through the gates, mouth and eyes smiling at both. Then she turned and walked back to the private precincts of the hall.

Edgyth was there, at one end of the pleasure garden, bent over her Simples, collecting the seed heads of poppy and thorn-apple. Mindred and the Welsh slave Tegwedd were with her, holding shears and basket. Thus it was all three of them saw Dwynwen as she entered the garden and approached the cliff face. Edgyth thought the girl was come to admire the sea view. The sea this morning was of stilly calmness, nearly flat as it rippled into shore. The breeze however was picking up, enough to lift Dwynwen's long hair and ruffle it under her kerchief. The girl did not pause at the edge. She went straight to where the stone steps leading down had been carved along the side of the cliff face. Dwynwen picked up her skirts, bunching them in one hand, and vanished so quickly from view that Edgyth could not help but feel a slight thrill of alarm for the girl's safety. The Lady of Kilton straightened up fully and walked to the edge. By the time Edgyth was close enough to peer over it, she saw Dwynwen, already on the stony beach below. Edgyth lifted her eyes to the expanse of empty sea. Ceric must have neglected to tell his bride not to descend to the shore alone. Then the Lady's eyes scanned the bluff to the right. There were always two men there, secreted in a kind of blind, keeping watch upon the waters. Sure enough, within moments one of the men appeared, from behind a sheltering copse. He craned his neck and looked down upon the girl. Edgyth raised her arm and waved it, to catch the guard's attention, and let him know she saw the girl there as well.

The Lady of Kilton felt torn between at once sending Tegwedd after Dwynwen, to bid her to return, and allowing the girl to have this private visit. She let her eyes drop. Dwynwen stood on a small hillock of stones mounded from the last tide, and lifted her hands, palms down, in front of her toward the water. She stood perfectly still; almost as if she were at prayer; but Edgyth had seen Dwynwen at prayer in the church, her small hands folded before her, or clasped at her bosom. This gesture was new. Dwynwen held this pose a long moment. Then the girl lowered her arms, and looked left and right. She took a few steps and bent to retrieve a piece of driftwood, walked on with it a few steps, and began poking at a tangle of brown seaweed heaped at the water's edge.

Edgyth shifted her eyes back to the bluff; the watchman was also eyeing the girl. Edgyth lifted her arms and waved them before her to the man, in a symbol of all clear. Even as she did so, she questioned herself. There was about Dwynwen something that made it possible, and even natural, to accept her actions, even if they be counter to custom. She must let her be. Yet the watchman knew Dwynwen was there, and would keep an eye on her. The guard waved back at Edgyth. They knew the young wife of Ceric was down there and alone, and would hold close watch.

The boat Ceric and Worr had taken her sailing in was beached to one side, pulled high from the suck of the tide, its open hull overlaid by oiled tarpaulins. Edgyth watched Dwynwen pull back the smallest of them, that covering the prow, climb over the side, and take her seat there behind its curved stem.

The day after this Ceric went out with Worr to walk about the burh, to see his men, and most of all, to be seen. It was true that now each night he and Dwynwen sat at table in the hall, but this ramble at the side of the horse-thegn allowed more private encounters for Ceric and those pledged to him, and so expanded the range of his interaction here at Kilton. It gave his men a chance to speak to him, to show him in word or gesture how they welcomed his return. And it gave Ceric opportunity to thank them for past service, to recall some action in which a certain man had distinguished himself, or to comment on the birth of a new son or daughter. It proved a welcome undertaking for Ceric, as did the voiced approbation he was met with concerning his bride.

On his return he went first to the pleasure garden, thinking he might find Dwynwen there. She was not, but when he approached his bower he saw the door was open. He stepped inside. Dwynwen was standing there, by the dragon bed, and wearing his sword.

There was no way to fasten the buckle properly around her slender middle; she had pulled the broad belt about her waist, then tucked the long tail of it behind itself, and pulled it snug. The weapon was so long on her that the golden chape tipping the scabbard rested upon the wooden floor.

His startle was at once overcome by her shining face as she looked to him. "It is so heavy!"

He had to laugh.

"It is the scabbard," he explained. "Pull out the sword. It is much lighter in the hand than you think."

She did so, carefully, almost reverently. She held the blade before her, eyes skimming from pommel to tip, and back to the grip.

"All the gold. It is so pretty." She lowered it, and looked at Ceric.

"Was it your father's?"

The sword of Gyric had been taken from him the day of his capture, never to be reclaimed. Ceric let this pass, and gave of his head a shake.

"It was that of my grandsire Godwulf, Ealdorman and Lord here. But before that it had belonged to King Æthelwulf of Wessex, who gave it him.

"It is," he went on, more slowly, "the sword of Offa, the great King of Mercia."

Dwynwen gave a delighted laugh. "He who built the dyke, to keep we Cymry out. Or in."

She grew serious, and considered. "Then it is very old."

"Yes."

"And precious, with this gold, and memory of those who have owned it."

"Yes."

"And it is yours."

Ceric nodded.

"I had already been born when Godwulf died, though I was a small babe. When he was laid out before his burial, his weapons were upon him and at his side. Garrulf, our scop, told me of his war-splendour, and that my mother held me up in her arms that I might see him. Before Godwulf was lowered into the chantry his widow, Lady Modwynn, my grandmother, set aside his war-kit. She gave it to me at my sword-bearing, when I was fifteen."

"Ah," she breathed. "If I had known this I would have asked Lady Edgyth to write that part to Luned as well." She bit her lip a moment. "But it does not matter. Luned does not care for weapons. But Elidon will like this story. We will make sure he hears it one day. Perhaps he will laugh as well, at it being the sword of Offa."

Ceric had a sudden thought of his own. It was hard to think of Dwynwen as a mother, so young was she, but when she did bear a child, and a son, this sword would rightly be left to him, a boy half-Welsh.

He came to her now, guided the sword back into its scabbard, and freed her from its belt. He hung it up on its wall peg, but she placed her hand back upon the scabbard.

"Such a sword may hold great power," she said. It was almost a private utterance, voiced as she pressed her hand against the weapon, as if she sensed that power living now. "A bit left from every man who has used it," she added, turning her head to look at her husband. "One can work magic with such a blade."

Ceric only nodded. Iron and steel were part of many charms, bringing the vital force of the Earth to bear, and the skill of men to forge with fire.

She let drop her hand and turned to face him fully.

"Will you fight again?" she asked of a sudden. The nearest Ceric had seen to fear was now in her eyes.

He paused, lifting his own eyes up, and through the open door at all that was Kilton beyond its frame. His answer was sombre admission.

"I must. That is my role. One of only two open to men of my estate."

"And the second?" she wished to know.

"The Church, of course, to profess as a monk, or even go as a priest." A moment passed before he went on. "But one needs a true calling for that.

"The only other path is that I was born to. To defend Kilton. And Wessex."

Dwynwen's next words were a hopeful offering. "Perhaps we will have peace, and no more fighting will be needed."

"Yes," he answered, just above his breath.

He gestured her forward to embrace her. She came so readily to his arms.

⁂

Worr had been thinking similar thoughts. Ælfred had no need to call up the fyrd these recent months, but at any point Kilton, and thus Ceric, could be called to duty. Ceric must return to service. Worr wished to spar with him, so he could gauge his fitness. And, Worr decided, they must be alone, and unobserved.

The horse-thegn went to Alwin. He was pushing the limits of his authority in doing so; he was the Lord of Kilton's first captain, and no one else could command him. Yet Worr's standing here was such that he could make request, and he did so.

"I will be sparring with Ceric soon; perhaps on the morrow. No one should watch us." It was a statement, not an order, but Alwin, looking at Worr's face, nodded.

"No one will be there," he assured him. "You will have the ground to yourself."

The next day when Worr came to Ceric in the garden, he spent some little time regarding him. His face was fully healed, and he had gained flesh. Worr would hazard his next words.

"I thought we might train later today," he began, referring to weapons practice.

Ceric's lips parted, and he lowered his eyes.

"Just you and me," Worr went on. "Swords, only."

He must add this last; he felt it might be some time before Ceric would take up a spear again.

"Swords only," the horse-thegn repeated.

Ceric knew he must. He did not tell Dwynwen of this, only that he would be with Worr. The fact that she was with Lady Edgyth meant he could retrieve his war-kit and arm himself unobserved. The very act of pulling on the quilted linen tunic, and over this, one of hardened leather, felt as foreign as the first time Ceric had ever donned them. Yet he did so. He belted on his sword, and carried his helmet in his hand.

Worr was awaiting him at the practice ground. It was, as promised, deserted. Worr had ready the leathern sheaths to slide over their sharp blades as protection. The two dropped their helmets over their heads, and took up position. Worr drew his sword, and Ceric, his.

Worr took the lead. The result was worse than the horse-thegn had envisioned. Facing Ceric was like facing a man without resolve. It was almost as if he did not inhabit his own body. Ceric returned, blow for blow, thrust for thrust, the movement of Worr's sword and shield. Ceric was in his twenty-fifth year and in strength and speed at the peak of his fighting years. Yet he took no initiative, exhibited no drive, pulled no feints which caught the horse-thegn off guard.

At the end of it Worr's eyes fell on that bench where Cadmar was wont to sit and watch, calling out commands and hurling taunts, along with, when earned, a few words of praise. Worr imagined Cadmar here now. The old man's spirit seemed to hover about them; or perhaps it was the fact that the sword in Worr's hand had been that long held in Cadmar's marred right. He could see the warrior-monk shaking his head over Ceric's performance, and thought he knew the words which would issue from the old warrior's mouth.

"He is a battle-shade," Cadmar would have judged. A shadow of his warrior self.

Such a man would not live long in pitched battle. His body lived but he was dead to fighting.

After they pulled off their helmets Ceric looked to Worr. The horse-thegn could not read Ceric's face, was not sure if he looked for a word of approval.

Worr just nodded. "It is a good start," he said. In truth, it was merely a start.

⸜⸝⸜⸝⸜⸝⸜⸝⸜⸝

Edgyth had a second letter to write, one she did alone, and without consulting he who it most concerned. Edwin must have a wife. Dunnere had tried his best to help the young Lord to one of Wales. Edgyth did not wish to lower a second bucket into that well. Her new missive was to none less than King Ælfred. In it she asked that the King give thought to a suitable wife for Edwin. As great a boon as Dwynwen's arrival at Kilton had been for Ceric, Edwin was left ever further from his goal of a fitting help-meet for himself. Edgyth suspected that the upheaval of the Welsh girl's arrival had caused him to reconsider the very standards by which he might adjudge a suitable wife. Mother and son had not directly spoken of this, but Edgyth knew her boy so well that she could guess Edwin might now prefer a woman of settled and mild disposition, or possibly even a young widow.

Her written request was couched in that direct and warm humility which her long acquaintanceship with the King allowed. She could almost picture the thoughtful gravity of Ælfred's expression as he read it, and the slight upturning of his mouth at a jest she made. Most of all she trusted that the King, regardless of the state of his health, would make of this a signal effort, resulting in a considered choice to grace the hall of Kilton.

She told no one of this letter save Worr. The horse-thegn would use the chance to send word to his father-in-law Raedwulf, telling him of the return of Ceric, and subsequent marriage to Dwynwen of Ceredigion, once intended for the young Lord of Kilton. The bailiff of Defenas would thus be the bearer of this news to the King of Wessex.

CEREDIGION

THOSE men bearing Lady Dwynwen's bride-price to King Elidon knew to say nothing on their own. They carried a packet of paired letters, and the tall wine jug. They were to deliver these to the King of Ceredigion with due respect. All queries were to be referred to the letters they bore. Their role was to deliver both, and say nothing more.

Elidon sent the men to his kitchen yard. He had his hall cleared of his own folk; his priest Gwydden was already at his side. Lady Luned was called for, and appeared, gowned as was her wont in white, her snowy hair twisted and looped above her pale brow. She had dreamt the night before of standing on the windy beach, watching the steady approach of a ship toward her, one with a billowing sail. The ship proved free of any guiding hand when the keel crunched into the shingle, yet the empty vessel still carried with it the pleasure of a safe landing. Luned was thus prepared.

The King readied to accept his niece's bride-price with no more than his priest, his sister-in-law, and two of his picked men before him. These were now stationed standing with the wine jug on the floor between them.

The letters must come first. They were encased in a packet formed of parchment, elegantly shaped and laced closed with silken cord. Dunnere had laboured over this enveloping packet and its closure, sign that much should be justly made of its contents.

Gwydden untied the large round knot, unlaced the silken cord. The use of knife point or shears would be akin to sacrilege for such an effort. He began the reading of his brother priest Dunnere's letter to the King.

Luned, standing at the side of Gwydden, listened without expression, yet with keen attention. Elidon, suddenly befuddled by what he was hearing, raised his hand and asked Gwydden to repeat the line about just who his niece had wed. He had followed through without difficulty until the beneficence of God had been invoked, and the warning that His wisdom surpassed all understanding, and then Elidon thought Gwydden said his niece had wed the older brother.

Gwydden, torn between scanning ahead in the private notes from Dunnere and the official message, kept admirably cool, and did so, repeating the announcement that an even more desirable match had been made, one with Ceric. If the King noticed the frantic movement of his priest's eyes, he ascribed it only to the difficulty of the art of reading. Luned, also watching the man's face, kept to her accustomed silence.

At the end of the reading, which Gwydden delivered in a tone fairly trumpeting with congratulations, the priest paused. The letter, penned in Dunnere's small and precise script, terminated in large freely drawn glyphs, graceful in their own way. It was the alphabet Lady Luned shared with the girl, one which he could himself not decipher.

He held the parchment aslant; Luned's eyes fell upon the symbols.

I will save his life, they read.

Elidon, understanding the formal communication was at an end, sat upright in his carved chair. His brow creased deeply in thought, and counter to the scar that ran there. Then he looked to where Gwydden and Luned stood.

"The god-son of the King of Wessex," he cried in triumph. He slapped the arms of his chair with both hands. "The jug, the jug," he called, gesturing his men forward with it. It was hoisted upon the table, but far too heavy to be slid toward him. He must go to it, and was more than eager to do so. The wooden stopper, now devoid of its sealing wax, had been pounded in by the strong hand of Ceric, and the King drew his own knife to pry it out.

There they lay, brimful; thousands of tiny silver coins, newly minted, crisp-featured, all bearing the likeness of the King whose god-son his niece had wed. Given the circumstances they felt almost gift of the King himself.

He looked over to Luned. She had largely made the girl what she was, and he would give the woman her due. "I am made happy. My brother Dunwyd would be made happy."

Luned inclined her head, smiled, and gave a nod. And I am made happy, she thought. She lifted her eyes and looked pointedly at Gwydden. She had guessed the second packet lying there upon the table was for her, and fastening her eyes more steadily upon it, saw one of the two words inscribed there to be her own name.

"There is a second letter, for the Lady Luned, which I must now read to her," Gwydden told the King, in way of excusing them both.

"Yes," Elidon agreed, "Go, go."

Luned and Gwydden passed through the hall door, their goal the priest's house. As soon as they stepped outside, he placed the letter into Luned's hand. "My Lady," he said.

She felt the heft of it, and smiled to herself. It would be, she knew, almost as if the girl herself was here, speaking to her. They gained his neat house, and Gwydden waited for her to break the seal upon the outer parchment enfolding the thick missive. He sat, while Luned stood looking over the priest's shoulder as he read to her. She relished every word about Ceridwen. She listened with more than a mother's attention; it was also that of a seeker who had yearned to hear the continuation of a story cut short in the telling.

Gwydden used his finger to point out the words as he spoke them. Luned could not help but fasten her eyes upon a single line written far larger than the others.

"This is direct instruction from Lady Dwynwen; Lady Edgyth states so." His forefinger went to the first word of the enlarged script, and he went on.

"It was the older brother, Ceric, who was foretold," Gwydden repeated.

The words meant nothing to him, but prophecy it was, and he reported it with the same gravity of purpose as he did the rest.

Luned had clear memory of asking of the older son, the one who Edwin said most favoured their mother. It was yet another satisfaction for her.

She heard Lady Edgyth tell of Ceric, of his nature and attributes, his devoutness as well as his prowess in war. She heard of his wealth. Edgyth was unsparing of his madness as well; the great sorrows at its root, and his reclamation by a gentle villager who had served as his woman. Last, and in greatest detail, was the great good Dwynwen had affected in him. She spoke much of their happiness.

Luned listened. A rent in the weft of her life was being healed, the warp strings pulled close, stitched together, and new thread laid down. This end was highest and best for her girl; that was clear.

The letter closed with Lady Edgyth's warm invitation to visit them at Kilton, where she might herself see the affection Edgyth bore for Dwynwen, and witness Ceric's deep love and commitment to his young bride.

Something more was in the letter, folded in the final sheet. Edgyth had included a small gift, encased in a pouch of linen, its drawstring closure pulled tight. Luned opened it to find an open-work silver pin. It was a slender crescent Moon, encircled by a ring of silver; the New Moon being held in the arms of the old.

It signified both older women, Luned thought, looking after and nurturing one so rare as was Dwynwen.

As soon as the men returned to Kilton, Wystan presented a gift to the Lady thereof.

"From the Lady Luned," he told Edgyth, passing into her hands a large oval case of hardened leather. Its shape proclaimed what lay within; it could only be a harp. Ceric helped her with the laced fastening, so she might draw it out. The harp was of certain antiquity, with a red crackled finish, and though smaller than the harps Edgyth had before seen, was eye-catching in its colouration and delicacy. Such an instrument might have been played by generations of the bards of Cymru. Yet it was newly-strung, and the tuning pins whole and firmly seated. Edgyth could not help but smile, though it be one of wonderment. She turned to Dwynwen, whose delight was clear in her shining eyes.

"I know this. It is from my father's hall. Our old harper there."

Edgyth at once tried to press the harp on the girl, with the gentlest but truest of protests. "It is then a family heirloom. And rightfully yours."

Dwynwen smiled the deeper. "Nay, Lady. Luned sent it to you, to do as you see fit. To play it yourself if you like."

Edgyth looked down at the harp. "I do not play," she said in apology.

Dwynwen's smile did not falter. "Sometimes they play themselves," she offered.

Wystan had turned back to the supply waggon to retrieve a lidded basket, and nodded at Lady Dwynwen, indicating it bore something for her. The careful way in which he handled it told them all he had been apprised of its fragility.

"We will take it to the bower," Dwynwen decided. She and Ceric left with it, Dwynwen holding the basket herself, hugging it to her bosom. Once within their house she lifted the lid and parted the packing straw. She first lifted out a small, sealed pottery jug, fired of dark clay, and incised with glyphs unknown to the eyes of Ceric. This she set to one side, and with both hands lifted out what the jug had been nestled in.

It was a second glass bowl, which Dwynwen had not known Luned owned. Like that which sat upon the table in her step-mother's bower, it had three short legs of glass, and had been formed of clear glass with tiny bubbles ever floating in its walls.

"This is for me, yes," she breathed. She turned to Ceric.

"The jug will have water from the well she draws from."

She saw from the uncertain movement of his mouth that he did not know their purpose, other than the fact of the value of the glass bowl.

Dwynwen smiled at him. "The water she has sent me – it is for clarity of sight. I will pour it into the bowl, and look therein."

Ceric gave a nod of understanding. He could not, however, help his next thought. "But the water she has given you will not last. It will vanish into the air, over time."

"Any drawn water will serve," she assured him.

It was after all the eyes of the gazer that mattered, and not the source of the water.

"And it is her way of again telling me, You will see my face; I will see yours."

When Edgyth took the red harp to Garrulf, the scop respectfully drew it from its case. His eyes ran over it, but his fingers did not come close to the strings.

"There are many songs within, my Lady," he told Edgyth. "All in a tongue unknown to me."

Edgyth hesitated to say the next. Yet Garrulf was as trusted a member of the hall as any thegn. And as a singer of songs he had access to a well of knowledge beyond the ken of ordinary men.

"Lady Dwynwen told me . . . that such harps might play, unaided by human hands."

Garrulf bowed his head in agreement. "I have heard such, if they are present when spirits walk."

The Lady before him had straightened the more, and the scop feared he had alarmed her.

"The Welsh bride, my Lady. In her hands it will speak."

Garrulf was not certain he had allayed Edgyth's fears, and so said the next in heartier tone.

"I wager hers is a merry voice."

DANE-MARK

DAGMAR had finished in the bathing shed of the fortress when she heard the cries of the approaching rider. She had been here at Viborg for nearly eighteen months. She and Vigmund had left Angle-land in a cold Spring, and arrived here after arduous travelling nearly three weeks later. Now, with another Summer over, the birch tree leaves were yellowing beyond the grain fields outside the palisade walls.

The encampment had been quiet in the past four days. Vigmund was off with King Heligo and the rest of his body-guard, a full complement of his thirty best men. Harvest had followed a prolonged spell of heat and drought, which left the grain small and parched. What the garrison's thralls grew surrounding the palisade would not keep Viborg over Winter. Heligo and his men need ride out and collect what they could from the farms that lay about them, by force if need be. The Danish King had gone himself, for there had also been word of a potential usurper active in the north, almost at the very tip of the peninsula of Jutland, and Heligo would learn more if he could.

Dagmar's hair was still wet under her head-wrap as she left the bathing shed. Her damp towels and the soiled clothes she had been wearing were in a bag slung over her shoulder. She heard the cries of the rider, saw men and women appear from the various long houses, and a few emerge as well, barely dressed, from the bathing shed behind her. A few whistles and shouts were heard. The originator of the cries came into view. It was Hemming, one of Heligo's body-guard, kicking a horse heavily lathered and heaving for breath. He jerked the beast to a halt in front of Heligo's own hall, that in which Dagmar and Vigmund also slept. Hemming had ridden out with Heligo and Vigmund, and was back alone. Dagmar grasped her skirts in her hands and ran after the man, through the open hall door.

Hemming got as far inside as the cold fire-pit and shouted out his tidings.

"Heligo is dead! Heligo is dead!"

The outcry was immediate. The men and women within the hall were quickly joined by those who followed the messenger in. Hemming went on, breathless with the force of his news.

"An ambush, by Haldane and his men." Haldane was the rival to Heligo. He had found his quarry, and taken it.

Hemming grabbed at a cup left upon a bench, and drank down whatever it held. Dagmar had come up from behind the man, to stand with other of the body-guards' wives. Hemming drew his tunic sleeve across his face, wiping his damp brow. He looked in their faces one by one, shaking his head at nearly all, affirming their fears about the Fate of their husbands. The women's eyes were frantic, darting between him and the open door, where they hoped their men might rush in at any moment. He looked at Dagmar almost last; looked at her and again shook his head.

Hemming was not done. He spoke not only to the women, but to those men who had crowded inside.

"Haldane will be riding now. He will gather more men, and come here and take possession. Stay and take your chances with him and his warriors, or gather your silver, and go. That is what I am doing."

Some of the women shrieked. Others of them sank down on any nearby bench or stool, unable to stand upright under these tidings. The men amongst them bellowed. A few men turned and left at once, hastening back to their long houses to pack; others stood in twos and threes, brows knit, weighing whether to stay or go.

The first to make decision was Heligo's chief wife. She alone had the second key to Heligo's private chamber. She rushed to it, and as quickly as her thick fingers could move, locked herself within. The act drove several of Heligo's warriors to order her to come out, demanding their share of the treasure within. Most others, men and women both, ran to their alcoves to retrieve their own goods.

Dagmar's eyes were open, but scarcely seeing any of this. Her sight seemed to have stopped at Hemming's eyes, looking at her face, then shaking his head, affirming the death of Vigmund.

Her ears were open, though, and now filled with the shrill whistles of men and whinnying of horses outside the open door. Two more men staggered in, both of Heligo's body-guard. Hemming looked to them, and they shook their heads. One of them was wed, and his wife now reached for him, ashen-faced.

Dagmar looked upon the two latecomers. Now she must believe Hemming. All the rest were dead. If Hemming had been mistaken, if Vigmund still lived, she might be guilty of unwittingly running from Viborg with all the treasure he had worked so hard to win.

The second of these two survivors would allow no doubt. He looked about him, pointing to this or that woman in turn. His words were cruelly simple. "Dead," he told them of their men. He pointed to the wives of nearly all who had ridden. "Dead. Dead, dead," went his harsh tally. Dagmar was one who heard Vigmund dismissed this way.

Hemming and the other two survivors turned to their alcoves. Men with wives and children began gathering all they owned, hurling things into leathern bags, hurrying to make flight.

Dagmar and the other women looked at each other. Their husbands were dead. Those who had slain them were riding here, to claim all. The noise of wailing women and crying children was joined by the hurled oaths of men left suddenly King-less. Outside Heligo's chamber, his warriors were now come with axes and were taking turns hacking at the oaken door, unwilling to surrender its treasure to the conquerors. Dagmar could hear the shrieking imprecations of the King's first wife, within.

Dagmar turned to go to Vigmund's alcove. She clenched her hands so hard her fingernails, short as they were, cut into her palms. She must think if she were to live.

Vigmund owned two horses, and his first was already forfeit to his killer. She would take the second. Dagmar dropped on her knees on the planked floor before their box bed and fished out their hide bags. She stood and began stuffing them with her clothing. There was little she owned. She had but one more gown than those she arrived with, one she had sewn here, from a length of wool she had bartered from another woman. Vigmund had far more clothing, for he had taken it as battle-gain and as plunder from halls and farms he had overcome. But Dagmar took none of his. Even to look at his leggings and tunics tightened her throat so she could scarce draw breath. She spurred herself on.

From the tail of her eye she spotted Heligo's fourth and youngest wife, wailing babe in her arms, standing alone by the high table, tears spilling down her face. The child she held was a boy. Heligo's third wife came to the girl, and hustled her away.

Dagmar drew breath and forced herself to think. Of what she must take, most vital was the box of silver, both coinage and hack-silver, kept under their box bed. The wooden box was of good size, and Vigmund carried the only key. She could just fit it into her largest bag, and could smash it open later. There was also a small pouch of ready silver for use upon the road. Vigmund's sword and knife held true value, but they were now in the hands of the man who killed him. She could not think of that, nor of the moment nor manner of his death. Her tears must wait; she must now save herself, and grieve later.

"Where are you going?" called the woman from the next alcove, busy, as was Dagmar, in gathering as much as she could for her flight.

"I – I do not know," Dagmar admitted. She knew no one in Dane-mark save for those here at the fortress.

Another woman looked up from her own hasty packing and spoke to Dagmar.

"You should stay. You are beautiful, and Guthrum's daughter. Their leader Haldane – he who will be King – will want you as a wife." Indeed, Dagmar was alone in having no home to flee to.

Haldane's warriors would come brandishing their battle-gain. Dagmar thought of watching some strange man dumping out what he had won upon a trestle; and seeing there Vigmund's sword. She could not bear it.

Dagmar shook her head in answer. She looked to her right. A woman two alcoves down caught her eye and spoke.

"My people live at Aros. I am heading there." This trading town was on Jutland's eastern coast.

Another woman behind her now addressed Dagmar. "My father is still alive. He is near Ribe. I will go to him. I cannot stay."

This was Ingigerd, Heligo's second wife. The woman made wordless gesture to her son at her side, a boy of about six years. Dagmar understood; his mother need say nothing. As soon as it was learnt that this was Heligo's son, the boy would be killed, to keep him from growing and exacting revenge for the death of his father.

Ingigerd spoke again. "Come with me, if you want."

Ribe – or Aros, thought Dagmar. Both were here on Jutland, but Aros was to the east. Ribe lay on Danemark's western coast. She and Vigmund had ridden up from Ribe; the journey had taken three days.

"I will ride with you," Dagmar told Ingigerd. "And I thank you."

Other women, and many men, were still considering if they ought to stay, or go, choices forced amongst confusion and panic. None could guess what might await them as the result of their decision.

"They are coming from the north; we should be safe, heading south," Ingigerd told her. "And I know the roads."

Heligo's second wife was a woman a few years older than Dagmar, one with yellow hair of a coppery cast. She was even-featured and not without comeliness, but her eyes had hardened into fixed wariness from the life she had been forced to lead. Ingigerd had hardly spoken to Dagmar before this, but the haste in which all resolved to flee or stay made quick confederates.

Ingigerd left her then, to pack her own belongings. She had a few fine dresses, but no chest of coins and hack-silver as Vigmund had left to Dagmar. Ingigerd could have no share in anything laid by in Heligo's chamber. All her wealth was in the bronze and silver bracelets, pins, and necklaces Heligo had given her. She took nearly all of them off, secreting them in her clothing bag. Her boy was speechless and wide-eyed as he followed his mother to her own curtained bed, then back to Vigmund's alcove, where Dagmar was pinning on her mantle.

Behind the high table the men armed with axes had reduced the door of Heligo's chamber to splinters. The iron bar across the inside still stood, but one ducked beneath it, shot it back and vanished within with several of his brethren. A moment later Heligo's chief wife was pushed through the shattered opening, screaming and clawing at the men who expelled her.

The panicked actions at the front of the hall were but a foretaste of all across Viborg. Men and women, desperate to leave, packed their possessions with careless haste, and there were those amongst them not above taking the goods of others, slow or never to get there. When Dagmar and Ingigerd emerged from the hall, they saw the kitchen-yard swarmed with those seeking provisions for the road. Likewise at the stables and paddocks, as men recovered their horses for the trek ahead. Those who resolved to stay attempted to keep order, and were ignored, threat-ened, and even struck down for their efforts.

Still, nearly half the men of Viborg determined to stand fast and await Haldane. They would greet him as their new King. For most of them it was not the first time they had joined the war-band of one who had killed their leader. The strongest held sway, always. Haldane had proved his fitness, and Viborg was too fine a fortress to forfeit. When those who were fleeing had gone, they would open both gates wide, and stand just within, in welcome to their new war-chief.

No one challenged the two women as they made their way to the smaller stable and paddock housing the horses of the King and his picked men. Here was one of Heligo's widows, and that of one of his body-guards, come to claim what was rightly theirs. The stable-men were all thralls, and Ingigerd set two of them to work. Her boy had a pony given by his father, which was brought and saddled first, and the child placed upon its broad back.

"I am taking a third horse," Ingigerd told Dagmar, turning away from the slave she was ordering. "Take another for yourself."

"Vigmund owns only two," Dagmar replied.

"But there are so many," returned Ingigerd. Nothing had ever been given her freely, and without penalty. Now she would help herself, and urge Vigmund's widow to do so as well.

"Horse-theft," uttered Dagmar, almost to herself. Though her circumstances were desperate, this was a crime punishable by death. "Nej. Not for me," she answered. She thought of another reason not to so burden herself. "I may take ship at Ribe." She had seen how crowded that harbour was with ships.

As they rode through the gate neither woman looked back. The portal faced south, onto the road which led to Ribe, and they began at a canter to build distance between themselves and the fortress they had quit. When Viborg was no more than the dust they kicked up, they slowed. The boy was whimpering as he hung on, and they must save their horses for the journey ahead.

Others passed them as they left, riding even harder than they were, some pounding down the road. Many veered off onto side-tracks, and vanished into the trees. Soon they were alone, two women and a boy heading south. As they paced on they began to meet others. Coming slowly toward them, driven by weather-hardened men and women all unaware that yet a new King was about to rule them, came waggons and wains filled with baskets of squawking hens, black-smeared casks of pitch, and pallets heaped with newly pulled root vegetables. Dagmar and Ingigerd rode by without word or expression. They passed cattle drovers and their lowing charges, and then two aged women, long sticks in hand, driving honking geese, hemmed in by a black and white dog whose blueish eyes looked blind, but still fit for such service.

It had been almost mid-day when Hemming arrived. They rode on until the Sun crouched low in the sky. When they spotted a small farm across a broad meadowland, they followed the track to it. A dog barked at their approach, then trotted out to meet them. A woman came around from the back, a babe on her hip, followed by a man who had been in one of the work sheds. He was wiping his hands on his leggings as he neared. The three on horseback remained so. The two women exchanged a few words with the couple, gauging what kind of folk were these. Satisfied with their answers, Ingigerd leant from her saddle with a piece of silver coin for the woman, and asked for provender for the road, and their silence should they be later questioned.

When they again picked up their southward track they had bread and cheese and apples to get them through to morning. The woman had brought Ingigerd's son a piece of honeycomb while they had waited, a kindness the boy's mother did not expect.

When the shadows grew long they passed a small beck of free-flowing water, which coiled close to the road. They entered the trees there and made camp for the night, where they and their horses could drink. The air was rapidly cooling. They did not wish to strike a fire, and though they would be colder without one, their fear of discovery was great. The women had but a blanket each from their beds. They shook one out upon the ground, placed the boy between them, and pulled the second over them all.

It was then, lying on that hard ground under the gathering dusk, that Dagmar finally began to weep. An admixture of shock, grief, and fear rose in tumultuous and churning spasms. Vigmund was dead, and she was on the road fleeing his killer. And this lawless land, so strange to her, would never be home. Even Vigmund had wished to quit it. Now she would never live with him in some peaceful place, where they might truly build a life together. She felt utterly bereft.

Her tears were as links in a chain, joining every loss she had ever known, each to the next. All was connected, and all was lost. Her sobs did not awaken the boy sleeping between her and his mother; Dagmar saw this and felt it just, that her tears went unheard.

Ingigerd was silent until Dagmar's breath quieted. Then she spoke through the slight space between them. Her words were as hushed as the night now falling around them.

"You wonder why I do not weep for Heligo," she began. "I am glad to be free. It was never my choice to wed him. He collected me, as he collected many other women. I have my son, and my silver. That is enough."

This was life, Dagmar thought. We have few choices, and whatever we value can be snatched away at any moment. Her thoughts swept her back to the mingled shock and joy of seeing Vigmund alive, and at Four Stones. She squeezed her eyes closed so tightly that the tears beaded on her lashes wet her cheeks anew. And we might unwittingly throw away that which is most precious to us . . .

Ingigerd went on, a new strength in her voice. "On the overmorrow we will reach Ribe. My father will be glad. He did not wish to surrender me, but had no choice. Now I return with silver, and with my boy. I can start life anew."

Start life anew, Dagmar silently repeated. That is what I must do, as well.

The two women were up at dawn. Dagmar had never fully combed out her wet hair, and it was tangled into knots under her head-wrap; she would have to unpick it later. Just now she and Ingigerd were grateful for the sustenance of the hard bread and salty cheese. They saddled their horses. Ingigerd's sleepy son, clutching his apple, began to cry as his mother helped him onto his mount, and was quickly shushed with promises of the better life they rode to.

The morning was grey-skied and chilly. As the road became more heavily travelled, Ingigerd guided them along tracks and back trails, lest they meet brigands. They had no way to know how quickly the news of Heligo's death might travel, and could expect increased lawlessness until Haldane could prove himself secure from immediate challenge by lesser rivals.

So it was, as they wended along minor tracks late in the afternoon, they began to look for a place to spend their final night. They had passed a few farms carved out of the pine barrens, but it had been too early to stop. As the Sun was lowering they were relieved to spot a woman collecting firewood with her small children. The woman, a crofter at some nearby farm, was burdened with a great pile of faggots lashed upon her back, and the four young ones she led had their arms full of dried sticks and pine cones. Ingigerd and Dagmar reined in their horses. The crofter, bent as she was under the weight she bore, looked up at them with darting eyes. Her children stared, pop-eyed, at the boy on his pony.

Ingigerd made her request, in the same assured tone she would use with a serving woman. "Can you shelter us for the night?"

The crofter would not wait for an offer of silver. It was clear she wanted nothing to do with these errant women, well-dressed, but possibly on stolen animals. In answer she returned Ingigerd's coolness. "I have nothing to share." Yet her head turned, getting her bearings. She jabbed her finger up a side trail "Woman up there. She feeds everyone."

With a nod of their heads Ingigerd and Dagmar turned their horses back to the side trail. It was narrow, one used by nothing larger than a hand wain, and they must ride single file. But it opened to a croft of several rude buildings. A number of small children were about, and two of them were standing with an old woman behind a low wattle fence, helping her as she pulled broad beans from a rough trellis work of lashed-together sticks. As they rode in the woman raised her hand to shield her eyes from the setting Sun, which had emerged from beneath a wall of cloud. Two younger women worked behind her, both at the cooking ring. The old woman was nearest, and it was she Ingigerd addressed.

"Can you shelter us for the night?"

Before she could refuse Dagmar spoke. "We will give you silver," she added.

The woman was tall and gaunt, her wisps of grey hair barely caught by her faded head-wrap. The corners of her mouth drew back, showing she had still most of her teeth. She extended her hand through the air toward the visitors.

"I need no silver to feed those who travel. You are all welcome."

"We thank you," Dagmar answered, with as much gratitude as she felt.

A man in his third decade appeared, and the old woman gestured him to help Dagmar with the horses while Ingigerd attended to her boy. The croft children came over to him by ones and twos, and nodded their greeting.

Once the horses had been unsaddled they were turned out in the small pasture where lay the farm's two milk cows. Not long after, the folk of the croft and their guests sat down upon the benches in the kitchen-yard and supped. The pottage ladled from the cauldron was thin on grain, but a surfeit of turnips and the plump broad beans made it filling. There was the bread the old woman had baked that morning, and thanks to the two cows, yellow butter to smear upon the hard crusts.

They ate in near silence, the crofters not wishing to ask why these three were on the road. Their good horses, clothing, and the touches of silver visible under the women's mantles said much of their wealth. It was ever safer for all who granted hospitality not to know too much about those they sheltered. Yet as the younger women of the place gathered up the fragments of the meal, and Ingigerd went off with her boy and the croft's children, Dagmar rose and sat down nearer the old woman.

"Are these your children?" she asked, inclining her head to the women and sole man.

The old woman gave her head a shake. "Nej. My nieces, and their own young."

Dagmar was moved to ask the next. "You had none of your own?"

The woman lifted watery eyes to Dagmar's face. "I gave birth to a son, some forty years ago. The joy of my life. But the mistress of the farm sent me away, when my boy was weaned."

"His father raised him?"

"Já, já.

"The father, Hrald, could not keep me there."

Dagmar's chin lifted in sudden movement. "His name was Hrald?"

She gave her head a small shake; as a name it was far from rare, yet to hear it now startled her.

"Já. A good man he was, too. Far better than what his wife deserved."

A slight smile crossed the woman's thin lips, summoning a distant memory.

"I saw my boy once, as a man. It was at Ribe. I think he was taking ship, away from here, I hope. At least he and his friend were amongst outfitters."

Dagmar found herself asking the next. "Do you know if he still lives?"

The woman closed her eyes and brought her fingers to her bony breast. "I feel he still does. Where, I do not know, but I feel he does live."

Dagmar regarded her; this old woman still had deep feeling for her lost son.

"That is much, then," Dagmar returned.

The woman did not answer this, but it prompted her guest to ask more. "Your son – what did you name him?"

The woman smiled. "The boy's father let me name him. I chose Sidroc, after a Jarl I once heard tell of."

Dagmar stood up so quickly that the old woman looked as startled as she. This name was rare.

"Sidroc," she repeated.

Dagmar's lips next formed a question, a gentle one. "What is your own name?"

"Jorild."

"I will tell you this, Jorild. Your son became a Jarl. Not here, but in Angle-land. And his son, as well. Sidroc named him Hrald."

The old woman gaped.

Dagmar went on. "They both still live, as far as I know."

"How know you this?"

Dagmar gave a decided bob of her head. "I have lived in Anglia, and I know."

It was all she would allow herself to say. Dagmar, on the cusp of a new life, could not retreat once, let alone twice, to an earlier existence, so briefly her own. These tidings, confirmation of Jorild's youthful hopes, must be enough.

"Take comfort in that," she added. Jorild looked up at her, and slowly nodded her head.

Dagmar returned to the bench. Jorild studied her a moment, then asked a question. "You have no child of your own?"

Her guest's answer was soft, but firm. "None." Her eyes met those of Jorild, then glanced over to where Ingigerd sat with her son. She would tell more of the truth of her own life. "And our husbands are newly dead."

Jorild's claw-like hand reached out and touched Dagmar's forearm in comfort. The old woman had a runny eye, and after a moment she brushed away the salt water from it. This fine lady had lost her man, and yet she herself, born a thrall, took comfort in an inner assurance that her own son still lived, and was well. And if what her guest had said was true, her Sidroc had lived up to the name she had given him.

The visitors slept that night in alcoves vacated by the children, who huddled together with their parents. The house was no more than a hut, low-roofed and earthen-floored. Yet Dagmar, surrounded not by warriors but simple country folk, slept sounder than she had in many a month. For a few hours the grief and fear of the past two days had been laid by, and entering Jorild's world had connected Dagmar to her own larger past, with hope of a brighter future. Yet she had no one to share this knowledge with, and must suffer a pang knowing she had met the woman who remained nameless to Hrald.

By morning she had resolved to ask the husband of Jorild's niece for his aid. The man had helped her unsaddle their horses, and had dutifully hauled all their traps into the house before they supped. He knew the weight of one of Dagmar's leathern packs. The chest within was heavy and awkward, an unwanted burden to her and her horse. With Jorild at her side she pulled it out before the man. The thing was strapped over with iron bands, and the lock a black mass of iron.

"Have you a chisel, and hammer?" she asked the man, for to pick such a lock took skill and time. "If you can break the lock, I will give you the chest, and some silver as well."

There was always risk in exposing a treasure, but these folk had proven their goodness, and Dagmar did not know when she might again come upon their like. And she would reward Jorild for her trusting welcome with silver, just as she had already given the gift of the knowledge that her son and grandson had thriven.

The man carried the chest out into the bright glare of morning and to a work shed. There, with Jorild at Dagmar's side, he gave the box lock four sharp blows, holding the chisel at its borders and snapping the holding rod within. He stepped back, and let Dagmar lift the lid.

She bit her lip to keep the tears from springing to her eyes. This was what Vigmund had fought long years for, and now died for. His widow had seen the contents of this chest only once, so carefully did Vigmund protect it from the covetous eyes of his fellow warriors.

What lay within was mostly hack-silver, flattened silver arm rings, broken sections of bracelets, coils of silver rod, and several finger-long ingots of the precious stuff. There were a few large and fine round pins of bronze, such as to fasten a mantle with; one missing its sharp and pointed pin. There were women's shoulder brooches in bronze as well, enough pairs so that Dagmar wondered why Vigmund had never offered her them. He liked to see her wear her pearl-set pair, she knew, but a second, less eye-catching pair would have been welcome. And there were silver coins. These were whole and in pieces, nestled amongst the hack, sifting through the pins and covering the bottom of the chest.

Dagmar reached in. This was all she had, going forward. Yet it had all been wrenched from others, and she felt compelled to do the next. She plucked at a pair of shoulder brooches, and handed them to Jorild. Such was her poverty the straps of her gown were fastened at the shoulders by smoothed oval pieces of wood.

Then Dagmar took a fistful of silver, whatever her hand closed about. She gestured that the open-mouthed Jorild pass the brooches to the man, and open her own hands to receive what Dagmar grasped. Into those blue-veined hands she dropped a small mound of silver chain, broken jewellery bits, and shining silver coins.

"The grandson you never met would want you to have this," Dagmar said.

They took their leave, Dagmar's treasure distributed between her three leathern packs. Ridding herself and her horse of the bulky chest was a needful freeing of the past. Vigmund's hard-won battle-gain was now become his legacy, and wholly hers. That evening the three made their camp amongst the trees, with provender given them by a grateful Jorild and her kin. Dagmar did not weep that night. She listened to Ingigerd tell her son of the farm that awaited them on the morrow, whispering to the fretful child that their journeying was nearly at an end.

They reached the farm after noon. It was one in a cluster of three crofts, all prosperous, with flocks of woolly black-faced sheep and many milking cows. Ingigerd's father, Orm by name, had never visited his daughter at Viborg, and she had only been able to return to the farm once in the years of her marriage. He was startled, even alarmed, to see her. Ingigerd's two brothers had been small boys when she had ridden off with Heligo; they were now stripling youths who blinked up at her. A woman too young to be Ingigerd's mother stood with them, but readily embraced her husband's returning daughter. Orm was choked with emotion, which made Ingigerd's own eyes wet. A serving girl brought ale, and the family sat together by the cooking ring. Ingigerd grasped her pottery cup and gave her news.

"Heligo is dead," she began. "He was attacked north of Viborg. There is a new King, who killed him. A man named Haldane. I know nothing of him, but many men at Viborg were willing to stay and join him."

Heligo had gone from successful raider to local war-chief to toppling the then-King. Now he himself had been overthrown.

All were silent for a moment. Then her father nodded.

"Nothing will change," was all he said.

Orm turned his attention to his little grandson, whom he had met only once, when the child was a small babe. The boy was shy but approached at his mother's coaxing. Once the child was upon Orm's knee, Ingigerd turned to Dagmar.

"Stay with us a night or two."

Dagmar took thought. The farm was snug, Ingigerd and her father, welcoming. Yet she felt a pressing urge to continue on to Ribe.

"Haldane," was how she answered. "Soon it will be known that Heligo is dead. What if Haldane stops, or slows the flow of shipping, as he establishes himself?"

Ingigerd thought a moment, then nodded.

"Já. He will be sending his own men to collect the tolls. Beyond that I do not know what might happen." She paused a moment, glancing to her father. "Perhaps nothing," she echoed.

"I will go now," Dagmar decided. "But thank you for all."

"Where will you head?"

"I do not know."

She would learn her choices soon enough; traders from much of the known world stopped at Ribe.

"The land of the Franks," Ingigerd suggested. "You might go to Paris. I have not been, but Heligo had seen it, a city of stone, on its own island in the midst of a broad river." Ingigerd looked fully at she whom she counselled. "There are rich men there. You will find a husband.

"But you cannot travel alone," she went on. Women travelling thus were subject to every form of violation, even death.

"If you cannot find a ship with the wives of some of the men aboard it, then you must attach yourself to one of the men going aboard, just for the journey."

Dagmar could not think of this, not yet. She gave a slight shake of her head. It made Ingigerd question her further.

"Where will you stay, until you find a ship?"

Dagmar's lips parted. She had not been able to think this far ahead.

Ingigerd went on. "There is a brew-house, just inside the northern toll-gate. It is run by Ase and his family. At times they can offer an alcove in their house. Tell them you are a friend of Ingigerd, daughter of Orm. If they do not recall me, they will still know my father. They might help you."

Dagmar then asked a question of Ingigerd. "What will you do?"

Ingigerd was returned home, but she was still young, and comely. She gave a short laugh, then looked about at the croft. "I will wed again. As you must."

Dagmar felt herself alone as soon as her horse trotted out the wattle gate Ingigerd held open for her. She looked back once, raising her hand to the woman, then made for the well-worn track leading to the Ribe road. She fixed her eyes on the way ahead. Others were upon that road, headed in both directions, on foot, driving ox-carts, and a few riding. Not an hour had passed when the stockade fence of Ribe appeared.

The north toll gate was the one before her. She passed through after a word to the tolls man stating she bore nothing to sell, and was here to take ship. Her lack of goods abetted her story, and she passed within.

The brew-house stood to the left. It was low-slung but long, a timber building with a planked wooden roof, recently renewed. Before it was ranged a number of tables and benches, at this hour peopled with folk draining pottery and wooden cups. Griddle cakes were also on offer, and serving women passed amongst the tables with trays of them, crisp-edged and still steaming from the fire. There was a mounting block by the toll house, and Dagmar used it, then led her horse to where the nearest woman balanced her tray.

Dagmar's request for Ase was met by the woman turning her head and bellowing out the name. A man, tall and slight and of some five decades, came out from the building's dim interior. He squinted in the sunlight.

He wore a long linen apron stained with splotches of greenish yellow. A squat woman, similarly garbed, was just behind him, and came to stand at his side. They had about them the smell of herbs.

The uncertain furrow between Ase's eyes smoothed when he saw Dagmar. He smiled. Here was no impoverished traveller, begging free drink of him. This handsome woman did have request, though.

"Can you help me? I am a friend of Ingigerd, daughter of Orm. I need safe passage to Frankland."

Dagmar hesitated a moment; Frankland was huge, its long coast dotted with trading posts and fortified towns. "Paris, perhaps," she went on. The couple said nothing, but seemed surprised at her indecision.

Ase answered first, with a question of his own. "Ingigerd – she who is one of Heligo's wives?"

"Já. I have just left her at her father's farm." She said the next with more firmness.

"If you will arrange my passage, and provision me for the journey, I will give you my horse."

The brewer looked from Dagmar to the horse, a good chestnut gelding, with a broad chest and two white stockings.

"The animal – it is truly yours?"

Dagmar nodded. "It was one of two owned by my dead husband. He was one of Heligo's men. Heligo and most of his body-guard were killed days ago, up north, past Viborg. If you have not heard this, now you know."

The brewer stood still. The news was sometimes not instantly spread, when a new man arose, calling himself King. A succeeding leader might wait days, and sometimes weeks, to consolidate his own forces. Still, the brewer stepped forward into the road, looking at the two men who staffed the toll-house. They were the same collectors he saw each day.

"Já." Dagmar said, in understanding. "Expect new men at the toll-gate."

The brewer heaved a deep breath. He looked to his wife, who gave a slight nod of approval. His eyes then rose to the animal. It bore no brands nor earmarks to identify it. And this woman, handsome as she was, carried her sorrow about her. He must believe her.

"We will help you," he agreed. "Our sons are heading to Paris in a few days, to buy wine. You can travel with them."

Dagmar must close her eyes a moment in gratitude. "I truly thank you," she murmured.

"Come around to the back," Ase next said. "We have a stable."

Ase's sons were two men nearing thirty years of age, tall and wiry of stature, with light brown hair, blue eyes, and the welcoming smile of their trade. The elder was Thorlak, and his brother, Ulfkel. They had made the journey to Paris several times. That evening in a quiet corner within the brew-house they described the route to her. The ship would be coasting the entire way, stopping each night at trading posts or sheltered beaches before continuing on. It would be lengthy, but far less arduous than the open water crossing she had suffered with Vigmund.

"The knorr we will take comes from Aros, around the tip of Jutland. When we leave here, we will head due south, stopping at one or two small trading posts," Thorlak began. "Then we will coast on a westerly path to the mouth of the Seine. We will land there, at the trading town Hunefleth, then begin the sail downriver to Paris. Unless Paris is your goal, there are other towns all along the coast of Francia, large trading posts as well."

"Please to tell me of my choices," Dagmar asked. She was utterly ignorant of Frankland, save that Danes had raided there almost as successfully as they had in Angle-land.

The younger brother, Ulfkel, grinned. "The best wine passes through Paris; that is why we go there."

"What tongue do they speak?" she asked.

"In Paris, Franceis, but through much of the land Gaulish as well. Frankish in the eastern reaches. Some trading posts have been taken over by Danes, and you will hear our speech there."

She had not considered that in Paris neither the tongue of Angle-land nor Dane-mark would be spoken. No matter; she would learn the speech of Paris; she would have to.

Now Thorlak spoke. "There are certain families we know, in Paris; those we have traded with. We will make you known to them. When we leave you there, you will not be friendless."

"I thank you more than you can know," she murmured.

Dagmar spent the next two days with Ase and his family, living in their dwelling behind the brew-house, sleeping in an alcove Ase's wife made ready for her. On the evening of the second day Thorlak came to her with the news that their ship had landed. It had only to take on fresh supplies, and they would be off on the early tide next morning.

She felt it none too soon. That same day a clamour arose outside the brew-house. A number of heavily armed horsemen clattered up, proclaiming that Haldane was now King. The men at the toll gate, who had taken up arms at their approach, were ordered to give up their posts, safe-boxes, keys, and all. Dagmar watched the arriving warriors from the shadows of the brew-house, her heart pounding. Any one of these men might have killed Vigmund. And she felt herself a fugitive, though all she had taken was lawfully hers. Ase's wife came and placed an arm about her shoulders, in support.

That night in her alcove sleep took long to come. All afternoon the brew-house had been alive with folk, gathering at the news of yet another King. Heligo's toll keepers, who had ringed Ribe, had to a man joined with the warriors of Haldane, and Ase told her their quick capitulation won them the chance to stay on in the rich trading town. During all this Dagmar had kept to the confines of house and stable yard, packed and repacked her goods, and then drew the heavy wadmal curtain of her alcove and hoped for sleep.

The face and form of Vigmund kept arising, and her tears with them. She fought to keep the moment of his death from her mind. He had ridden off and not returned; he had vanished. Yet she knew his body lay somewhere, bloody and despoiled. She could not picture this; his beauty, so compelling, must be inviolate. Now he was a corpse, unwashed, unwatched, subject to ravening dogs and carrion birds. He is in Asgard, she told herself, in Odin's high-roofed hall. Or in the interminable Purgatory of the Christians, languishing for his violent ignorance. Let him be granted Asgard, she found herself mouthing, daring to risk apostasy for his sake.

These past few months had not been easy ones between them. Dagmar was impatient with life at Viborg. Vigmund wanted time to gather additional booty, even as Heligo faced diminished chances to win more from a resistant and intractable folk. And Vigmund had questioned her, almost mocked her, over the fact that she was still not with child. It angered him, as if it reflected on his manhood. There had been bitter words and bitterer thoughts, none of which she could retract.

As the months unfolded as his wife, Dagmar had come to a sombre realisation. She had loved the image of Vigmund more than the man himself.

Now she was fleeing, to a future she could not even guess. I have nothing to trade on, she whispered to herself in the dark, except my face, and this silver in my packs. Even my blood avails me not. What good is being the daughter of a dead King, if I can bring forth no child in whom that blood flows?

She thought now of Ingigerd, one of the vaunted Heligo's wives, now back at her father's farm, where she had begun. That was how it ended, with her running to save the life of her boy.

A grey dawn found Dagmar at the harbour. The knorr, a broad-beamed merchant ship, was more commodious than that of her first crossing, providing much room to accommodate goods and the folk who travelled with them. The brewer Ase had spared no effort in his arrangements for Dagmar. Ase's wife walked her to where the knorr was tied; her sons had gone ahead with their father and the task of provisioning. When Dagmar arrived she saw behind the mast, on the port side near the stern, a small tent made of tanned cowhides. It was for Dagmar and her alone, a place where she might sleep in private and relieve herself into the bucket provided. Ase's wife had given her bedding, a broad sheet of linen for her bed, a feather-filled pillow, and a second woollen blanket. She also gave Dagmar another linen towel, a welcome addition to her small store. The brothers Thorlak and Ulfkel had pulled a hand wain with them, and were loading provisions to sustain all three of them. There was a smoked ham, some dozens of boiled eggs, bags of hazelnuts, apples and pears, bread loaves, cured cheeses, and a small cask of their own good ale. As they would be coasting, fresh provisions and water would be available at almost every land-fall.

Ase had already brought a roll of straw from his stable to cushion the wooden planking of the deck, and on his knees in her tent he unfurled Dagmar's bedding upon it. Then he grasped her packs and stowed them within. When he stood he grinned at her, proud of the accommodation they had made for their guest. "You will arrive Paris like a Queen," he told her.

As soon as she was aboard, Dagmar felt freer. She did not look forward to the sea-sickness she feared would come, but to leave Dane-mark was what she most wanted. She had landed here in Ribe with Vigmund, numb from exhaustion and weak with hard travelling. Still, having forfeited so much, she had hope then for their lives together. Now she had nothing but his silver.

As the men cast off she shook her head, an effort to banish such memories. She stood in the stern behind her low tent, and lifted her hand a final time in thanks to the brewer and his wife. The steers-man, on the starboard side, was standing at the steering-beam, its rudder-like oar not yet lowered. The portside crew pushed off with their oars, and the knorr glided past the end of the wooden pier. A number of spears lay secured by the keelson, reminder that these brawny men might need to defend their ship. Dagmar sank down on a bench, and turned her back to the receding town.

The knorr had a crew of twelve, more than enough to set and trim the ochre-dyed sail, but fully needed for defence. Of passengers Dagmar was one of five, two of whom had come from Aros and were heading on. There were no other women aboard on this opening leg, but at their first stop, a minor trading post, an older woman with a quantity of baskets came on for a single day. The sailing was mercifully smooth. They met two solid days of drizzle, which kept Dagmar much in her tent, save for those snatches of time she must walk about despite it. Many trading posts had wash houses in which she could clean herself and her linen; other times they dropped anchor overnight in coves.

The tedium of the sail felt a welcome salve to Dagmar's raw nerves. They stopped at this trading town, or that; took on and lost certain goods or folk. The constant was Thorlak and Ulfkel, well known to the steers-man and crew.

On the tenth day out they reached Hunefleth at the mouth of the Seine. There had been long beaches of pale

brown sand, and then towering cliffs of brilliant whiteness, which the brothers told her were chalk. Their last
three stops had been trading posts where the speech of the
Danes could still be heard, along with the far stranger notes
of the Gaulish and Frankish tongues. Now in Hunefleth
Dagmar heard Franceis as well; Thorlak, walking with her
by the stalls fronting the sea, told her which of the three
new tongues met their ears. The town was of no great size,
but growing in importance. The brothers described which
workshops, stalls, and brew-houses had arisen since their
trip last year. The knorr would take on fresh water, deposit
goods which had reached their destination, and ready for
the final sail down to the island of Paris.

She and the brothers sat down at one of the tables
fronting the largest of the brew-houses. The offered ale
was unlike any Dagmar had ever tasted, mild in flavour
but strong in smell. The benches were crowded with folk,
the sounds of their speech as unfamiliar as was this brew.
A group of men rose, wealthy merchants from the cut of
their dress. Beyond them Dagmar was surprised to see a
cluster of nuns and monks, seven or eight of them, in the
dark habits of the Benedictines. Thorlak and Ulfkel had
earlier told her Paris had a great cathedral, a structure
well worth seeing, and that all folk there were Christian.
Dagmar was close enough that snatches of conversation
came to her ears. Instead of a tongue foreign to her, she
heard the distinct cadence and accents of Angle-land. She
fell quiet, listening. It seemed these nuns and monks had
been to Paris, on pilgrimage to a church there; perchance
that which the brothers had mentioned. Now they were
homeward bound, to their abbey in Angle-land.

THE BAILIFF'S LADY

Defenas, Wessex Late Spring 896

THE promise of her new home drove her irresistibly on. That, and the presence of the man she would share it with. Ælfwyn's first glimpse of Raedwulf's dwelling was of a wall. It was of pale stone, showing almost golden in the morning light, and of obvious antiquity. Centuries had compromised it, the wall being higher in some places and lower in others; suggestive to Ælfwyn's eye as the ridged spine of some great and slumbering beast, and with the warm sunlight falling upon it, self-fortified, and safe unto itself. Where sections of the stone had fallen a timber palisade had been built up to it, completing, she guessed, the circuit about the hall and its immediate confines. Yet here, on their approach, the stone wall was mostly intact, the opening for the wooden gates set within stone piers slightly taller than the walls themselves. It made for an impressive approach for the bailiff's new Lady, and the young in her care. No cloistered holding could offer a sense of greater safekeeping, no fold more secure for herself, nor her sheep.

"The wall," Ælfwyn exclaimed.

Raedwulf looked down at her where she sat upon the waggon board. He had slowed the pacing of his black mare so that the waggon bearing his bride might approach at a rate allowing her to fully take in her new home.

He gave a short laugh. "I had neglected to mention it in the inventory of the hall's assets," he confessed. "It is ungainly in parts, I admit, but not, I hope, too taxing to the eyes."

She moved her gaze from his face back to the stone and timber wall. There was in the enclosing arms of it more than a declaration of strength and protection. It comprised a melding of two materials, stone, and wood, standing side by side, an emblem of a couple meeting life together.

"I find it wonderful," is how she answered this.

Ælfwyn was not alone in this assessment. Little Cerd, seated between her and Burginde, leapt up at seeing something he should like to climb so much as that golden stone. He would have scrambled down from the waggon if not restrained by the nurse. Ealhswith, seated on a bench behind the board, also exclaimed over the imposing boundary.

The long transit from Four Stones was at an end. Here was the hall of Raedwulf, north of Exanceaster, and the new home of Ælfwyn of Cirenceaster, lately Lady of Four Stones. The bailiff had fronted a train of some four waggons, bringing his bride home. The relative peace across the Kingdom of Wessex allowed him to ride with an escort of only twelve warriors, but they were picked for this duty from Ælfred's best men.

Besides the females and small boy in the lead conveyance, Ælfwyn was arriving with a large waggon stacked
full with her personal household goods, clothing, and the
loom she favoured. Also within were the chattels of her
daughter Ealhswith, and those far slighter of Burginde.
This was pulled by a doubled team of horses, and hooped
over with tarpaulins to protect its contents.

Perhaps just as dear to Ælfwyn's heart and interests
was the contents of a second, open waggon. This bore
three curly-horned rams prized by her, and with which
she hoped to build up a flock with the local Defenas ewes.
Nor were they her only livestock. As a parting gift Hrald
had presented a string of horses. Two were fillies whose
sire was that great white stallion of Ashild's, and three
were colts, all from the line of Sidroc's legendary bay.

The bailiff had sent one of the escort ahead to warn of
their near arrival, and the man now stood off to one side,
a grin on his face, as the procession turned in through the
opened palisade gates. The steward so long entrusted to
care for the place during Raedwulf's prolonged absences
stood in welcome with his wife and four children. A
number of other folk, serving men and women, grounds-
men and stablemen, stood to one side, the youngest of
them standing on tiptoe in excitement as they craned
their necks at the arrivals. Many of these folk were but
newly arrived themselves; the hall had formerly operated
with but a skeletal staff, so slight had been Raedwulf's
needs. The family kept two curly-coated hounds as watch
dogs, and these were both sitting at the heels of a lad at
the end of the line.

The steward Indract and his wife Lioba were the first
presented to she who would be Lady of the hall. Indract

was a former warrior, a thegn who had served alongside Raedwulf. His proven loyalty on the field of battle continued in his role as steward to the bailiff's holding. Now he and Lioba, after a decade in residence, might see that holding achieve its rightful potential.

Once within the hall yard the outbuildings revealed themselves. Stable, paddocks, barn, fowl houses, storehouses and workshops; all needful for the support of a family of Raedwulf's standing. None of the structures were overly large, but all were solidly built, with an eye to coming generations. For Ælfwyn to stand at the side of Raedwulf as she took this in was itself the fulfilment of a dream, as her smile made clear to all.

The door to the hall proper yawned open behind those who had lined up to greet them. The hall was of peeled oak trunks and of a solidness which would have been forbidding, were it not for the banner flying gaily aloft from the mossy roof. It was the golden dragon of Wessex that soared upon that linen, depicted on this flag as a beast with long body outstretched, like a pouncing cat.

Cerd had scampered over to the hounds, for the youth in charge of the animals had brought them nearer, and the boy was now making friends with them. As Burginde came to collect Cerd, a young girl of perhaps ten years came up to her, and dropped a quick but deep curtsy before her. Burginde spluttered at the mistake the girl had made, and gestured instead to Ælfwyn. But the girl spoke.

"No, Mistress Burginde, I am your help. My name is Blida."

The nurse could hardly close her astonished mouth. She looked from Ælfwyn to Raedwulf. The former looked nearly as surprised as was Burginde herself, but also highly pleased.

Raedwulf smiled. "Blida and her brother are fairly new to the hall," he explained. He had told them on the road that the Danish attack on Defenas had left many children outside the walls of Exanceaster orphaned, and both women understood these must be two of them. The bailiff raised his hand to a boy of about fourteen, standing with the dogs at his feet. Both youngsters had round faces and yellow hair, though the boy was growing into a youth; his Adam's apple showed as he nodded and swallowed. "Bettelin has been working about the grounds, work he is good at." Raedwulf looked now at his bride. "He will be a ready and useful help in your garden work.

"But Blida is to aid you, Burginde," he ended, his smile deepening.

It was true that growing years, and if truth be told, a growing girth, were slowing Burginde's nimbleness. Little Cerd was brimming with energy, from the hour he sprang from his bed in the morning to that moment when his eyes finally dropped shut at night. Here was a young, and to judge by her smile, eager girl, to help with him, and to fetch and carry whenever Burginde needed another set of hands.

Burginde had never encountered this, a serving woman being given a serving girl. But Burginde had ever enjoyed a special status in the life of she to whom she had dedicated her every waking hour. She had acted as Ælfwyn's wet-nurse, and been part of her every day, as inseparable from her as her shadow. She had been privy to all secrets, celebrated every gain, shared all privations. Born a cottar girl, Burginde now dressed as a sober aunt to her former charge, and her collection of silver pins and necklaces given by Ælfwyn over the years meant she never lacked adornment at feasts and high holidays. Yet it took a man who stood a distance from all this to provide her with the one thing she lacked, a greater measure of ease in her every-day life. Raedwulf felt Burginde had so well assisted his aim in wooing the Lady of Four Stones that this seemed a fitting way to reward her.

Burginde could not speak her thanks, for fear of tears flowing. But the vigourous nod of her head to the bailiff said much, that and her first words to Blida.

"This be Cerd, Blida, a boy born to run the live-long day. 'Twas ever true he will not touch his browis, and will steal every bread loaf from your salver and from that two salvers down. 'Tis climbing and horses he loves best, and he must be kept three times a day from breaking his sweet neck."

The cheerful way in which she delivered this warning made the boy crow with delight. As if to underscore her words, Cerd had a bump on his forehead from having flung himself off the waggon earlier that day. But Blida smiled, and stepped forward to him.

"There is a new foal in the paddock; would you like to see?"

Cerd's head bobbed so rapidly that Blida laughed. But she had a condition. "You must take my hand, to go there," she instructed. She could not risk any harm coming to the boy this first day, and having a firm grip on the small hand would ensure this. Cerd thrust out his hand, then began pulling the girl in the direction of the stable.

The paddocks and stable were soon to admit the many more horses arrived with the party from Four

Stones. But Ælfwyn herself stood by as the three snowy rams were guided down the ramp from the back of their waggon. They would be penned here in the hall yards until she selected the ewes she would buy. After this she must decide on the best pasturage for them on Raedwulf's land, and the right woman or man to shepherd them. The thought of these tasks filled her with happy anticipation, and Raedwulf, seeing this, must himself smile as he watched her face.

Then it was time to enter the hall for the welcome ale. Blida and Cerd had rejoined the family, the boy chattering away to Burginde of the little red foal he had seen, but happy enough to explore the high-peaked hall before them. The bailiff led his bride through the door, and all followed. The long, rock-edged fire-pit in the centre had a small fire burning at either end, enough to ward off the late Spring chill that hangs within such tall buildings. Alcoves numbering twenty lined the long walls, most awaiting curtains and bedding. The side door was open, and there were two windows, fitted with glass casements, a luxury Ælfwyn did not expect. But nothing made the hall as bright as did the coat of lime-wash upon timber walls and roof. The lime-wash was fresh; she could see that. It was free from any smudge of smoke. She turned and smiled at her husband.

"Yes. I have just done it," Raedwulf admitted. "I spent so little time here that I gave no thought to the dimness within."

Lioba had brewed the ale, of savour such that Ælfwyn could praise it honestly.

At the far end of the hall was a timber partition, set with two doors. As their massed goods were being carried into the hall, and Burginde and Ealhswith choosing their alcoves, Raedwulf walked his wife to one of the doors set therein. Both were heavily strapped with iron over planks of oak.

"The second is a store-room, nearly empty now, but of use for linens and table-ware," he told her, as he pressed the black key into the box lock of the main door. She heard the inner workings of the lock, and then its final click. "This one is our chamber." Raedwulf pressed open the door and revealed it.

This room too had been recently lime-washed for brightness. It had a window, high in the gable peak, giving light. There were three or four chests of goods, his clothing certainly, she thought, and the treasure he had acquired. He had moved nearly everything from his lodgings at Witanceaster here. There was a bank of shelves, and many pegs set into the wall from which to hang things.

The bed, broad and of unscarred wood, was newly built; she could see that. It had four square posts arising from its corners, with depictions of puff-cheeked faces topping them. She went to them at once to see them better.

"The four winds," Raedwulf told her.

Ælfwyn studied each in turn. Each face was distinct, and two were women, and two men. Winter was easy to pick out, for the blowing cheeks of the man were ragged with an ice-coated beard. But Spring was a young girl, a child, almost, who blew what seemed a mysterious whistle with her lips. Summer was also a woman, one in the prime of life, with cheeks barely rounded with wind, so gentle was the zephyr she blew. Autumn was a lusty fellow, with one eye open, and one shut. It was as if he looked both across to the woman of Summer, but shut his eye against the old man of coming Winter. Nevertheless it was a blast of wind he looked ready to unleash from his pursed lips.

"How grand," she cried, turning to him. "Did some artisan in Exanceaster make them for you?" She had yet to see this large town, built by the men of Caesar and fortified ever since. He had told her of the large range of goods to be found there.

He gave a laugh. "An artisan rather more local. I carved the heads."

As a man who had been out in every weather, and only rarely under cover, Raedwulf had captured the seasons perfectly. "I wanted our bed to give you pleasure every time you looked upon it."

She came to him then. "You have made a fine start," she murmured.

There, with his arm about her, she looked again at the carved heads. "I had no idea you had such ability," she added.

He gave another dismissive laugh. "It has served to while away long evening hours," he explained. But he was truly gifted, she could see that. There was so much they did not yet know about the other; so much to discover, and prize.

Their marriage bed was new, yet in the hall proper the long trestles of the tables were not. While hardly abused, they showed the sign of use through two generations, and now were set to welcome another. All of them had been freshly waxed; Ælfwyn could see this, and even smell the new beeswax, as she neared to sit that night. This first meal, with all assembled within, was another notable event in a day filled with them. Yet it gladdened Ælfwyn that they were so few that all could sit at one table. She had unwrapped her silver bird-shaped ewer, and it was with no little ceremony that all eyes fastened upon the new Lady of the hall as she moved about, filling every cup. Raedwulf had seen her handle it so many times at Four Stones that to see her use it here had deep meaning. She had brought it with her from Cirenceaster; it had been her mother's, and her mother's before that; and now to pour Lioba's good ale from it into the waiting cups held before her was the start of another ritual of her rich new life.

Raedwulf told her more about her new home.

"King Æthelwulf built it," he explained, as they sat side by side on the broad bench. "The remaining stone walls must have made him do so."

He went on to tell her that the men of Rome had built the walls as they established a foothold amongst the native folk, those fierce Britons whose tribes had once covered all this land. Ælfwyn had seen a fair measure of what remained of Roman work, and had just travelled part of the way here on their good stone roads.

"For Æthelwulf it was a hall in which to stay, outside Exanceaster," Raedwulf went on. "But I doubt he spent much time here. He never established a village, so it was little more than a place to camp on his way through Defenas."

"And his son Ælfred gave it you," she noted.

"Yes. Years ago. My parents were of Exanceaster. The King gauged that when I was not with him at Witanceaster I might choose the peace and seclusion of my native countryside."

He hoped to find a broader version of just that, now. He glanced about. Oil cressets on the table gave a cheering glow, and all looked to be savouring the meal. Ealhswith sat on Ælfwyn's left, next to Burginde. Cerd, standing on the bench yet hemmed in between Burginde and Blida, had a hunk of bread in each hand, just as foretold.

Raedwulf brought his eyes back to his wife, and went on.

"The hall is as yet unnamed," he said, in way of apology of this oversight. "One of many things it has always lacked." His smile told her a mistress was the greatest of these. "If you think of a suitable name, I will be glad to hear it."

She gave her gentle laugh. "That which sprang to my mind at first sight. It is so modest I hesitate to share it, yet approaching as we did with my rams, and knowing that henceforth this would be my new home, my refuge – my all – two words rose to my mind, emblem of true safe-keeping to me and mine: The Fold."

The walls of golden limestone were indeed the greater part of what distinguished the hall from others. And she felt halls should perhaps have a part in their own naming. Four Stones rested upon a foundation of rock, and Raedwulf's fine hall was encircled by protective walls, making of it shelter, refuge, and happy destination.

"The Fold," Raedwulf repeated. "Yes. Our hall shall henceforth be known as that."

Ealhswith, sitting on the bench between her mother and Burginde, gave thought to her place in this new hall. Her mother was deep in converse with the bailiff, her smile signalling her happiness at his table. Burginde was busy with a bobbing and stomping Cerd, talking across the boy to a laughing Blida, recounting the child's many antics. Ealhswith turned her head. The steward Indract and his wife Lioba sat at the other side of Raedwulf. From the reception granted the new arrivals, Ealhswith knew her mother would regard this couple as more than able, and they seemed gratified to have the bailiff in residence at last. Lioba had certainly shown ready concern for Ealhswith, suggesting to her an alcove far from the draught of either door when opened in Winter, and then hanging it with heavy woollen curtains. These were twill-woven in two 'shades of blue, which, after the girl had praised them, Lioba admitted were the work of her loom.

Ealhswith had never slept in a hall proper. She had spent her nights up in the weaving room, and sometimes in her mother's bower. Now she had a deep alcove, private enough, but surrounded by other folk. So much would be new. Ealhswith was not sorry she had come, but she had not been able to at once tell her mother she was glad at the prospect of removing to Defenas. Her hesitation was couched in the fact that she alone had been privileged with the single choice whether to go with her mother, or remain with her brother at Four Stones.

Neither had aided her. Her mother was perhaps most helpful when she told Ealhswith that no decision was final; if she accompanied her mother she could return later to Four Stones, and if she stayed on with Hrald she could be sent to Defenas. But she was left to make the choice herself.

She had in private wished that Hrald had asked her to stay. That would have been a proof of her importance to him.

Ashild had been important to Hrald. She and Hrald were much together; they were close in age, and though Hrald was a boy, Ealhswith always felt he had looked up to Ashild. Ashild was older, yes, but it was more than that; there was always something definite about her; as if she knew herself so well. Ealhswith, though she could never hope that Hrald would hold her in such high regard, still yearned for that kind of closeness with him.

Hrald was as a hero to Ealhswith. Ashild and Hrald had been boy and girl together, playmates. She had not had that with Hrald. When he took their father's seat at the high table, hanging Sidroc's shield upon the wall, Ealhswith was but a small child. For years Hrald had been a man, in a sphere so unlike her own. And he was Jarl.

When they left Four Stones Hrald himself had fronted the escort leading to the borders of Anglia, to see them off. Up to the last moment Ealhswith hoped he would ask her to stay. He did not.

Though Hrald did not ask his little sister to remain, Ealhswith knew one reason to stay at Four Stones. It was as simple and profound as her dead sister's desire never to leave. Ashild had been Ealhswith's idol; even when she wished Ashild could be different, and did not understand the choices she made, she honoured the fact that her older sister would not, or could not, conform to the hopes and desires of others. This inner rebelliousness was something Ealhswith in secret admired, more than she would ever admit. Ealhswith's own nature was tuned to the sense of duty, tractability, and sacrifice all admired in their mother. Ashild was a source of vexation to many, yet Ealhswith wished she had the daring to be the same.

She glanced over to her mother, smiling at something Raedwulf was saying in her ear. Ealhswith knew she resembled her mother. Many had told her this. She had a clear memory of Ashild, whose word she most trusted, telling her this.

It had happened the Summer Ceric had come to stay with them. Ealhswith was nearing twelve years, and had gained in height. She was in her mother's bower house. Burginde had washed Ealhswith's hair over the basin there, and was now combing it out for her. Ashild walked in, seeking another comb to help pick out the bits of hay tangled in her own hair. She carried the scent of hay and horses about her, as she generally did. Burginde found the proper, wide-toothed comb for her, tutting as she often did at the state of Ashild's hair and dress. Nothing deterred, Ashild began tugging the comb through her knotted hair, as Burginde returned to the near-silken locks of her little sister.

"You are just like mother," Ashild told her, comb in hand. From her sister's lips it sounded an almost grudging admission. "You have her loveliness, and will have men flocking."

Ealhswith remembered smiling at this prediction, even delivered as it was in a tone of exasperation. Ashild went on.

"And you will wed a Prince or even a King. Whereas I could be mistaken for one of Mul's sons."

Mul was the head stableman of the yard, and his sons still gawky youths. The quip was fantastic enough to be a jest, and more proof Ashild could always make Ealhswith laugh.

"'Tis not as bad as all that," Burginde offered, taking the comparison seriously. "What you lack in the face, you make up in spirit. And the grand hall of Kilton has marked your worth none the less." This consolation delivered, Burginde now re-busied herself with Ealhswith's hair. "That young Ceric must want a handful," she muttered.

Back then Ealhswith had no idea that it would be her mother who would leave Four Stones. She knew she herself must, one day, when she was wed; but like her brother, Ealhswith had never countenanced another, fuller life for their mother.

Her mother had wed Raedwulf in Winter; in late Spring he would return to collect her. Weeks passed and Ealhswith had not made up her mind. Her mother had questioned her – would a short stay at Oundle help her decide? And Ealhswith felt in that question a further, deeper one: did she feel a calling to a life there? She could not answer her mother just then, but the girl, recalling this suggestion, hazarded something to Hrald one day when they were alone.

"I may go to Oundle . . ."

He had looked up at her, his surprise clear, but she was not certain if she read dismay as well. If Ashild had lived and gone to Kilton, that alliance would have greatly benefited Four Stones and perchance all of Lindisse. But

Ashild was dead, and Ealhswith was all Hrald had left with which to barter for peace.

"You would go as a nun?"

She did not answer at once. A maid had but two choices. To wed to benefit her family, or to profess at a nunnery. Ealhswith felt ready for neither. With her natural reticence, she thought living as a consecrated nun should appeal to her. Yet she also hoped for affection in her life, and feared that spiritual love would not be enough.

"Perhaps just to think . . ." she countered. This not knowing her own mind was a weakness she deplored in herself.

He had nodded his head at her. "Sigewif – and grandmother – they will help you in your decision."

Ealhswith had almost cried aloud in protest at this. It would be a loss to Four Stones, her being there, but if she had a higher calling he would always honour that. Instead she wanted him to ask her to stay, tell her of her importance to him, stress that he needed her to forge alliance with another great hall.

She wished to be to Hrald what Ashild refused to be. This was, she thought, the greatest chance she had to rise to the level of her sister, and even exceed her. Both Hrald and their mother wanted Ashild to wed Ceric, and go to Kilton. To watch Ashild disappoint so many was an unspoken misery for Ealhswith. She would wed any man Hrald selected to fulfil her role as daughter of Four Stones.

It did not end there of course, she knew. Marriage had pitfalls as sudden and deadly as that animal trap. Dagmar and Hrald had looked as though blest with happiness. Then Dagmar had disgraced herself by being found with another man. She had betrayed all of them, Ealhswith knew, or at least that was how Ashild, in her anger, had summed it. Ashild's reaction had shocked her younger sister more than Dagmar's offence. I am too soft, Ealhswith had told herself then; no good can come of misplaced tenderness. What had been more difficult about Ashild's condemnation was that in Ealhswith's mind the two women were somehow alike. Dagmar, like Ashild, was exceptional. Ealhswith might be, as she was so often told, lovely; but she thought she would never be exceptional. Now both women were lost to Four Stones.

Ealhswith too had left, forsaking the only home she had known. She bid fare-well to Hrald, the hero who asked nothing of her, though she yearned that he do so; and the tomb of Ashild, her love of whom had turned into a form of reverence.

She had amongst the thegns' daughters friends with whom she was sad to part. And she knew she would miss her Aunt Eanflad, as quiet as she was. Her steady presence in the weaving room and in the corner of their lives had been a life-long comfort to Ealhswith. Eanflad would ever be standing at her loom, content, self-contained, and with no expectation that she be or do ought beyond this. At times Ealhswith almost envied her that life, as narrow as it looked to others.

Then there was the parting from Oundle. Grandmother was there, and Ashild. The abbey could be reached in a few short hours by waggon. They did not often travel thence, but each visit was a reassurance and often a refreshment, even those more recent times when she had wept at the tomb of her sister. Parting from Abbess Sigewif was another matter. Sigewif almost frightened Ealhswith, so forbidding was she in her excellence and wisdom. Yet Ealhswith knew Pega looked forward to every hour spent in the presence of the abbess.

Ealhswith's lips parted in a sigh, inaudible in the noise of the table. Ealhswith could not but like Pega, even though, caring for Dagmar as she had, it was awkward to admit. But as kind as her brother's bride had been to Ealhswith, there was gulf between the two, despite their closeness in age. Pega had known much greater exposure in the world, and known far more loss. Pega had been graced with the honour of fulfilling the wishes of the royal leaders of two lands, Wessex and Mercia, and the further honour of being selected by Hrald to share his life. Ealhswith knew her mother had in good conscience surrendered her keys to such as Pega.

There was a second way Ealhswith was much like Ælfwyn. She knew herself to be more acted upon than acting. None could dispute that to serve well in that position was wholly admirable. Ealhswith could hope to emulate her mother in a way that she could never resemble Ashild. She could justly aspire to become a capable, resourceful, and kind mistress of a hall and household. Her mother had done it at Four Stones, and now would do so here at the hall of Raedwulf. Ealhswith hoped she could do the same. It was the best path open to her.

Hrald had not asked her to stay, and without that higher end, she could not watch her mother ride away from her. She would forsake all at Four Stones and Oundle to be with her. She felt she must. If Hrald had no real use for her, if she could not become the peace-weaver for him she aspired to be, she must stay at her mother's side.

Without her as guide Ealhswith did not know how she could move forward into any, lesser marriage.

This alone made her cast her lot. She determined to go to Defenas. The decision by itself brought little satisfaction. She must question herself, lest it was a choice made solely out of disappointment, and fear.

Ælfwyn's initial acts as Lady of The Fold filled her with satisfaction. The first was the task of establishing her own flock, the second the pleasure of planning and planting a garden. Their own source of wool was what she first turned her attention to. She had three fine rams and would begin with two or three score of the best young ewes she could buy. A farmer of known industry had holdings just south of the hall, and Raedwulf, knowing that his new wife would be in mind of starting her own flock, had prepared him for their visit.

The two had the pleasure of riding side-by-side on this errand. In these latter years Ælfwyn had not often ridden, but it was a skill she wished to maintain, and when Raedwulf proposed he saddle his own black mare for her she readily agreed. As soon as she was astride she felt closer to Ashild. She did not voice this, but Cerd was there in the stable yard with Burginde, and at once begged to be lifted up to her.

Raedwulf laughed, but then spoke seriously to the boy. "You cannot join us today, but I will find you a pony, Cerd," he promised. He followed this with quick reassurance to his wife and her nurse. "He is young, it is true, but Bettelin will walk at the pony's head, and Blida at the saddle, holding Cerd on, making sure he does not tumble." It was enough to make the boy squeal with joy, though the look exchanged by the two women was given voice by Burginde.

"Then you must find one no bigger than the hound Frost, if you please, Sir."

Happily Bettelin appeared with the dogs, distracting Cerd enough to permit the riders to depart.

The landscape they paced through held the same beauty Ælfwyn had exclaimed over upon entering Defenas. Gently rolling hills, verdant and lush, rose above sheltered small valleys. The greens of hedgerows and woodland, shading from near-yellow to almost black, were made all the more striking against the red soil of roads and ploughed fields. The valley depths, deeply shadowed in the early Sun, were shrouded in a delicate and rising mist, a smoking veil of silver tossed over the dark ribbands of growing verdure.

The Lady of The Fold began assessing the sheep even before reaching the farm. They dotted the meadowland fronting it, some lying at rest in the shade of its elms, others standing in the shallow stream which wove through the pasture. Most were white fleeced, white-legged as well, with broad heads and compact bodies. As they reined their horses down the long trackway to the house, several ewes lifted their heads, thoughtfully chewing tufts of long grass as they watched the arrival of the two riders.

The farmer was little daunted to find so discerning a buyer as Ælfwyn, and kenned the Lady's sharp eye almost at once. Her father's flocks had been the pride of

Cirenceaster, and her own pride. The night she had defiantly stood in the hall of Four Stones, picked up a plate crafted of precious metal and held it before Yrling and proclaimed that this treasure she had brought was nothing more than fleece turned to gold had perhaps left a deeper mark on her than on her war-chief husband.

Ælfwyn did more than value sheep. She loved them, and just as she had built from scratch a fine flock at Four Stones, she would do so here. This time she enjoyed an advantage she lacked long years ago. A good ram was half the flock, and she had arrived with three of them, fruit of her long efforts to improve the scattered stock driven out of the forests surrounding Four Stones. Those she brought with her were long-fleeced, well-muscled, with broad and strong forelegs. They were off-white, with the proclivity to throw white or cream-coloured lambs, the fleece most valued for dyeing. Each had been born either twinned, or one of triplets, and so carried the trait to sire multiple lambs in their blood. Now she needed ewes of Defenas to make her start.

Within minutes she and the farmer were walking amongst his offerings. A pailful of carrot tops and other treats offered by the man brought even the more skittish ewes to them. One of his boys tailed along, a pot of ruddy wet clay and a broad stick in hand, so he might daub the selected animals with a touch of red upon the withers and so mark them. The bailiff walked with them, holding to silence, but his chest expanding with pride as Ælfwyn accepted or dismissed this or that offering. As the farmer held the animals she gently parted their lips with her fingers to check the length and number of their teeth. She sought a mix of mature ewes and yearlings.

The older animals would be better mothers, be more likely to birth multiple lambs, and produce more milk for cheese-making after weaning. The yearlings would offer many fertile years ahead. The older ewes, having been recently sheared, were not yet in their deepest wool, but the farmer had brought out rolled fleeces representative of the flock for her to examine. The long staple of the wool was indicative of their spun quality. The Lady ran a long-fingered hand up the breast bone of a few ewes swirling about them, her palm slicked with rich lanolin when she pulled it from the curling fleece. Every ewe she had daubed possessed the densest of fleece, and as even a length over the entire body as was possible. Such would be a pleasure to spin and weave.

At the end of their inspection Ælfwyn had selected no fewer than fifty ewes, now smit with red. The chosen animals would be driven up to The Fold the third day hence. She had rejected more than twice this number, and on the way to the house to take refreshment and settle the bill the farmer, now walking side by side with the bailiff, met Raedwulf's eye. The man then cast a knowing look in the direction of Raedwulf's wife, one filled with admiration.

The start on what would become the pleasure garden brought Ælfwyn gladsome days of absorbing work. The area granted to her, behind the hall and to the left of the kitchen yard, had formerly served as part of a small pasture for the dairy cows. With a greater staff, these could now be taken outside the walls each day, and only returned to the milking shed morning and late afternoon.

A broad and flat ground, improved by years of the cows having enriched it by their presence, awaited her. An orchard of apple, plum, walnuts, and medlars would be planted, and the rest become her herb and flower garden. There were two fine old trees in the pasture, a spreading copper beech and a majestic ash. She claimed the beech to reside within her new garden. Young Bettelin lived up to Raedwulf's trust in his interest, and paced off the area with long strides, pausing to pound a stake in when Ælfwyn called out to him.

"Enclosure first," she decided, when she greeted the boy the first morning of their work. "First we will make a wattle fence surrounding the space to become the garden. This harvest tide we will collect the beech-nuts, and sprout them for Spring. They will become in just a few years a hedge for us."

The copper beech to provide the seedlings would sit at the centre of the garden. Under its canopy she would place ferns and other woodland plants which crave shade. The rest of the space would be given up to herbs and flowers which flourished in the long sunny southern days Defenas offered. In echo of the spreading reach of the beech boughs, the enclosure described a large and undulating circle, holding the many planting beds within. These would unfold in sinuous curves, with winding pathways to lead both eye and footfall onward. The paths would be gravel-set, that one might walk dry-shod in the wettest weather. Ælfwyn had saved seed from favoured flowers and herbs from year to year, and had a store of them, especially the yellow cowslips and blue cornflowers she loved. She looked forward as well to walking meadows and woodland, to search out what was native to Defenas, and happiest here.

Raedwulf came to check on their progress later that first day. Bettelin stood wide-eyed at Ælfwyn's side as she described her imaginings for the garden. Her enthusiasm and belief were such that Raedwulf must grin. This was part of what he had ever hoped for, that this place might be taken in hand by one ready to invest of herself in bringing it to a higher form. He readily joined in. The hall had always bought its grain from Exanceaster, and for now would continue to do so, but he looked forward to an expanded effort for their foodstuffs here on their own land.

"We will grow more ourselves, now that we are here," he agreed. The orchard trees would take years to fruit, with some yield in the foreseeable future, but one always planted trees for the next generation. Beginning now they would treble the area in which Indract and Lioba grew pot vegetables. "Another fowl house – three or four more cows so we might make more cheese," Raedwulf went on.

"And we will have my milking ewes," she added with a smile. He had complimented her on the quality of the sheep's cheese at Four Stones; now he might have that here as well.

He looked over the expanse of the future garden, now marked by little more than the few stakes the boy had pounded in.

"We will build a bower house in its centre, just as you had at Four Stones."

Ælfwyn had to smile. She had asked that the bower-house at Four Stones be built when Hrald was born. He had a fretful teething, and to spare Sidroc his tears she and Burginde and the babe began to sleep there, until the tiny teeth had pushed through. Ealhswith had been born in the bower-house, and she had used it often between times, and moved there for good after Sidroc and Ceridwen had been abducted.

Now a new bower could be built for her, one she could hope she might use if she were again blest with a babe.

Perhaps the bailiff's hopes did not extend to this height, yet he turned to her with his next, grateful words. "Many are the thegns who wished for respite enough to tend to their holdings. Now I can do just that."

He could not embrace her, much as he would like; not in front of the boy. He let his eyes and tone convey this, as he smiled on her. "As I now have such greater cause."

Ælfwyn had shrugged off much in wedding Raedwulf. Even in the undertaking of her new tasks of flock building and garden making, she almost revelled in the peace, quiet, and leisure she had gained in her new estate. Ælfwyn had never known indulgence, or thought herself selfish, not before this, and now found herself feeling so. She had left with Sigewif's urging, yet the many she had left behind tugged at her heart and mind.

She was no longer directing a large hall and addressing its many wants. It was not only the ceaseless responsibility to decently feed and clothe so many, with its vital supervision of stores, and consultation with kitchen yard and cooks. The cottars and crofters had wants, difficulties, and hardships she must try to allay, just as she must encourage them to be as productive as they were able so that the hall had yearly sufficiency of vegetables and surplus of grain. There was overseeing the care of her flocks, and the daily tasks of weaving, or at least spinning, for the clothing and linen needs of her own family, and the hall proper.

It was her charge to settle disputes between fractious serving folk, to visit and care for the sick of both hall and village; to help the young of both spheres to good matches. She was mindful always of any child who might show interest and aptitude in reading or writing, and took time from her too-full days to do just that, and give them what instruction she could.

Recounting this last she felt a pang, about one child in particular, Bork. When parting she had taken leave of the boy by bending her head to kiss him on his cheek. That cheek flamed in response, but the murmur from his lips and the quick tears which rushed into his eye spoke for him.

Another boy, nearly Bork's age, rose in her mind: Yrling. She had meant to part last with him, and to kiss him as well. But he had witnessed her parting from Bork, and when she came to Ceridwen's boy, he rocked back from her in an unmistakable signal of diffidence. She was left smiling at him, bidding him well in words, and no more. She had already assigned to Hrald a letter which Yrling would carry with him when he returned to Gotland. Yrling must stay at Four Stones with his brother, but he and Pega would now be left with his management, as well as a new babe. Ælfwyn must have faith that Hrald and Jari would keep him in line, and fight against the fear that she was abandoning the boy her friend had entrusted her with.

Bork was another, more subtle challenge. She had spoken to her son about him, a mere suggestion she let drop, to see if it might be taken up. "There is always Sigewif," was what she said. "And the shelter and opportunity of Oundle."

She said no more than this, but it held a world of meaning. Bork was bright, no one might doubt it, and hard-working almost to a fault. He had already displayed a true interest and aptitude for the scribal arts. Because Hrald and Ælfwyn had taken time with him, teaching him his letters, he had been the butt of other boys' teasing and even taunts, for being their cosset. His position amongst the youths of Four Stones was an awkward one. Of friends he had only Mul's own sons. Yrling did not like him, and Bork knew it and wished it were otherwise, as did Hrald and his mother.

Bork was also unusually devout for a boy. Hrald had told her he had glimpsed Bork at the modest mound covering his father, hands pressed together, praying over the man's lost soul. Yet none could mistake that the boy was fixed on the way of the warrior. He trained as hard as any of the boys, harder in fact, as if he knew himself a foundling, and far worse than that, guilty of being the son of a man who had killed one of Hrald's own warriors. He thus had more to prove.

Despite the rapid improvements about the hall, there was a way in which The Fold could never become wholly self-sufficient. Without a village it would never be large enough to support a priest. The family must keep to private devotions, and plan to go once a month to Exanceaster to be shriven and receive the sacrament. That stone-walled fortress, built above the River Exe, had been an old Roman stronghold, and was still impressive in every way.

Raedwulf, so often upon the road, was used to weeks without the rituals of Mass. Ælfred travelled with a priest when possible, and before the destruction by the Danes of so many foundations, they might seek shelter in a monastery or abbey, where every spiritual need could be attended to. Still, an organised and formal observance had been a rarity. The bailiff's faith was strong, yet self-contained.

Ælfwyn missed the presence of the priest Wilgot perhaps less than she would like to admit. For years she had been diligent in her daily prayers, and having the psaltery Ælfred had commissioned for her meant that the beauty of the songs of David were always at hand. As devout as she was, she had never handled the golden æstal the bailiff had also presented her with without remembering the morning in her garden when he admitted he had seen her as a maid at her parents' hall. She wished, but had been unable, to recover a memory of the young Raedwulf; her whole attention had been given to the second son of Kilton. But using the golden pointer to aid her reading somehow returned her to those youthful days. Her life's path had carried her far from her early desires, and taken her down long and arduous roads. The same was true for Raedwulf, yet here they were, united, steadfast, and possessed of blissful and mutual contentment.

Ælfwyn felt almost a girl again, but with greater happiness ever granted to her then. This wellspring was not alone the joy of a love fully met and returned, but also that sense of discovery which delights the newly paired.

For Raedwulf too, some years had rolled away. Ælfwyn's beauty had ever formed his womanly ideal, and to find it coupled with the bodily passion his bride expressed far exceeded his imaginings. There was another way in which the bailiff was returned to his youth. He felt of a sudden a father once more, in a way he had not since Wilgyfu's marriage to Worr. Ælfwyn's daughter must be guided to an advantageous and compatible union, and her little grandson Cerd was an endless source of mirth. And if they should be blest with a child of their own, his thankfulness would know no bounds.

The first interruption in the unfolding of their new union took place just past High Summer's Day.

It was at the feast day of Saints Peter and Paul, and the family of The Fold basked in the grasp of a warm and dry Summer. A messenger from Witanceaster arrived. The bailiff and his bride were out in the nascent garden with Cerd and Blida. At Raedwulf's request, one of the serving men had made a small table and two benches, so that one might sit under the shade of the beech, as he and Ælfwyn were now doing. The messenger was shown to them, one of Ælfred's riders known to the bailiff. Raedwulf was on extended leave, and as the man handed him the hardened leathern tube signifying a letter within, Ælfwyn feared her husband might be called back. Lioba had brought the man to them, and now led him back to the hall, to needed drink.

The bailiff and his Lady were left alone with the girl and her charge. Ælfwyn watched her husband's face as he unfurled the parchment. She could see the writing was of no great length, and stood there, searching his face, awaiting his response.

The message deeply surprised her.

"The King summons Ealhswith to Witanceaster on St Mary's Day, for a matter pertaining to her future. A message has also been sent to Hrald, Jarl of Four Stones."

The girl's mother found herself unable to speak, and was thankful when Raedwulf lowered the parchment and looked at her. It was not her husband who had been summoned, but her daughter.

There was but one conclusion to draw, and the bailiff offered it.

"He has, perchance, found a potential match for her."

Ælfwyn was nearly unaware she had been holding her breath, until she exhaled in gratitude.

"It is – it is wonderous news," she pondered aloud. "But why now? And why at Witanceaster? Perhaps, as he knows we have wed, and Ealhswith is here with us, in Wessex?"

The letter offered no details; all must be inferred by his request that Ealhswith be brought. Raedwulf considered this. Bringing her there would allow her to see, and be seen, by more than one potential mate. And the King himself had never beheld the girl. Raedwulf shared what the request suggested to him.

"He may have more than one suitor in mind."

He thought a moment before continuing. "And he has always been aware of the girl, my love. He has asked after her. Perhaps there was some event, which brought her more clearly to mind. Some immediate request, or need."

"St Mary's Day," she echoed. This was a time of great harvest. It was fully six weeks away.

He looked at her. "Though the trip be a long one, I know you wish to be with her."

She said the next as confirmation. "And Cerd must come with us," she added, looking over to where Cerd squatted next to Blida. The boy was prising up a flat rock with his fingertips to see what might be crawling beneath. Ælfwyn would not leave the child behind, and not only to spare him, at such a tender age, from the wrench of separation from her and Burginde. She said the next with quiet resolve.

"Young as he is, I want him to meet his King."

She raised her voice enough for Blida to hear.

"Please to fetch Ealhswith, Blida," she instructed. The girl straightened up and turned to leave, and Cerd went pattering after her. She stopped to allow him to catch up.

Ealhswith and Burginde were in the storeroom next to the sleeping chamber of the newlywed pair, taking in hand the ordering of the hall's existing supply of cups, salvers, and bowls, and those of the private store of Ælfwyn which had come from Four Stones. Ealhswith was numbering all the bronze ware on a tally stick, and began a separate one to keep track of those few of silver. She made a careful, neat notch for each one in the stick designated for them.

The locked room was also used as linen storage. Burginde was sorting through and measuring, by the arm-length, the linens kept there, and adding to them a number which she, Ælfwyn, Eanflad, and Ealhswith had spun and woven over the years. Amongst these were a few pieces Burginde knew Ashild had spun for; the lumpiness of the girl's thread told her so. These few she laid aside, too precious for daily use.

A short time after being sent, Blida and Cerd returned with Ealhswith. Burginde brought up the rear, as expectant a look on her face as was on Ealhswith's. They all faced the bailiff, who still held the parchment in hand. His smile could not help but strike a twinkle in his dark blue eyes.

"The King of Wessex would like to meet you, Ealhswith," he said.

She gave a start, and a soft gasp issued from her lips. Her mother beamed at her, which made the girl draw breath, and regain a measure of composure.

Though Ealhswith had yet to speak, Ælfwyn could guess what her daughter's first question would be.

"We know little more than that," she offered. "But he has asked for you to come to Witanceaster, at the feast of St Mary. Hrald should be there, as well."

Ealhswith's hopeful look forced Ælfwyn to hazard a guess. "The letter speaks only of a matter pertaining to your future. Perchance he has identified a worthy match for you, my girl."

A man selected for me, by the King of Wessex himself, thought Ealhswith. She could scarce get past this initial thought, now taking form.

Nor could the girl's step-father discount the importance of the summons. Raedwulf was bound to Ælfred until the King's death – or his own. As much as Raedwulf disliked thinking on it, he felt that Ælfred, exhausted by war and taxed by his chronic bleeding disease, might

soon be called to his greater reward. Ælfred had readily taken up the idea of Hrald wedding Lady Pega of
Mercia. Assuring a good match for the sister of that Jarl
would deepen the bond so forcefully taking root between
erstwhile enemies. To that end Raedwulf would aid the
King in every way, for the sake of Wessex, the fortress of
Four Stones, and most poignantly of all, the Lady lately
removed from that hall to his own, and whose happiness
meant most to him. The bailiff could not guess which
suitor Ælfred had identified, but stood ready to endorse
the match and do all he could to further it.

For Ælfwyn the moment was almost bittersweet.
They had but recently removed to Defenas, had not begun
to fully settle in, and the prospect of her youngest leaving
her forever had of a sudden arisen. The King of Wessex
– who Ælfwyn had never stopped regarding as her own
King – had taken interest in the girl. Her excitement at the
high honour conferred on Ealhswith was coupled with a
more subtle but still deep pleasure; the prospect of again
meeting Ælfred. She could date the last time she stood in
his presence to a signal occasion. Ælfred had then been
Prince, his older brother King, and Ælfred, a number of
young thegns with him, had stopped at Cirenceaster to
solicit help from her father. Amongst his followers was
one from the hall of Kilton, and one from Defenas . . .

Burginde was remembering much the same, and
was first to give voice to the sensation invoked by this
news. What might come of Ealhswith and any suitor was
beyond conjecture. One thing only was now assured. She
turned to Ælfwyn and burst into astonished tears.

"We will see the King again," was all she said.

IN THE HALL
OF THE KING

Four Stones in Lindisse

HRALD had received much the same summons. Four of his men had ridden in with the two Saxons who had carried it from distant Witanceaster. It was growing near dusk; the messengers would stay the night, resting themselves and their mounts, before starting back south at dawn with the Jarl's response.

Hrald had taken the leathern tube into the treasure room. He opened it before Pega, who sat at the table, suckling their babe. Her companion Mealla stood nearby, spinning, and when Hrald entered she lifted her eyes to him to see if she should leave. He nodded that she stay. Hrald had been raised with Burginde at his mother's side nearly every moment, and Mealla was likewise privy to all that occurred in Pega's sphere.

The riders had already told Hrald the message was from Ælfred. The letter was two lines only, the first bidding Hrald to appear at Witanceaster for St Mary's Day. The second line was of equal interest.

"Matters pertaining to the interests of your sister, Ealhswith of Four Stones," he read aloud.

Pega gasped, and Mealla gave a low but cheering laugh.

"He has found someone for her to wed," Hrald summed. "I wonder who."

He looked over to his wife. Little Ælfgiva, a Spring babe, was not yet six months old. His Aunt Æthelthryth was still living here at Four Stones to help Pega manage the hall. He must leave both wife and babe behind for this trip.

"I will be gone as few days as I can," he assured her.

Pega smiled, filled with bright hope. "And what news you shall return with," she offered. "You must kiss Ealhswith for me, and wish her every happiness for my sake." She paused a moment, to look down at the babe latched to her breast. "If she has half of that granted to me, she shall be content indeed."

Hrald studied the letter again. It was the product of two hands. The first, perhaps a monk, had inked the main body of the message, in a compact, rounded scribal hand. The large yet precise signature of the King, "Ælfred" was distinct, telling Hrald he had penned it himself. Beneath this the first hand had added, "King of the West Saxons".

He took the parchment to Pega and held it before her so she might see it. Mealla leant in to look as well. Hrald had never held a letter titled to him, sent by a royal hand. Pega, having spent years amidst the royal courts of the King's daughter and son-in-law, must have handled many such missives. He would tell the riders he would be there at Witanceaster as requested. The parchment he would take with him, to use as a safe-conduct when he entered Wessex, should his progress be challenged. It was a letter he knew he would preserve, and one which might presage enduring good.

Outside the treasure room door the glad barking of a hound could be heard, along with the sharp clicking of its nails as it ran over the stone floor. A moment later a fist gave a loud rap on the oak planks of the door. Hrald could hear his brother Yrling as he spoke, laughing, to the dog, and then delivered his news, his mouth at the box lock opening.

"Kjeld is back from Jorvik – with a dog!"

Ælfgiva was now sound asleep, and Pega handed the babe to Mealla as she fastened up her gown. They all followed Yrling and Frost out to the forecourt.

Hrald had sent his second in command to find the best breeding animal he could, a task Kjeld accepted with relish. Once in that great trading centre he had inquired after such hounds, and had travelled inland overnight to a farm where fine dogs were bred. That he chose was a young bitch, not yet a twelve-month old, nearly as tall at the shoulder as was Frost, her intended mate; but with a head more delicate, and the eyes even larger and more lustrous above her narrow muzzle. Her name was Myrkri, or darkness, fitting for her deep charcoal shade, one which would lighten somewhat as she grew older. She had known success in the field already, and her keeper had taught Kjeld how to continue that training.

Pega exclaimed over Myrkri; it was impossible not to. Despite her size, and the breadth of her black paws, there was true elegance to her, and young as she was, a frisking playfulness as well. Kjeld too was pleased with his selection, and as Frost and the new animal sniffed at each other, tails lashing, he told more.

"He said to bring back a pup or two next year, and he will give us another female, from a different sire, so we might build up our kennel."

Hrald considered. A kennel would allow them to breed enough to give the animals as fine gifts. He glanced to a laughing Pega, who had bent over to place a hand on both dogs' heads. "We will do that," he agreed.

Mealla was still holding Pega's babe as her mistress welcomed the new animal, and as Pega and Hrald patted the dogs, Kjeld found a moment to come closer to the black-haired girl's ear.

"I brought back something for you, as well."

Mealla gave a prim smile. "I am certain the dog carries enough fleas, without those carried back by you."

At this point Kjeld was almost used to the sting of the maid's jibes. He took a moment, as if he considered.

"My gift is larger than a flea, and of far more worth. Now I will give it to Thora, who will not chide me for a rich gift."

Thora was a the daughter of an older warrior, and quite a pretty girl. She was now of an age that many of Hrald's men had noticed her.

Mealla stiffened. This was the first time Kjeld had mentioned another maid. And Mealla knew Thora had noticed Kjeld. The girl could hardly do otherwise; he was second in command. If the girl stayed at Four Stones it was the best match she could make.

Kjeld gave a slight shrug of his shoulders and went on. "Give it to Thora I will. But I doubt you will be happy to see a pin of Éireann worn by a maid of the Danes."

"A pin of Éireann?"

Mealla's tone betrayed her interest, and she gave herself a little shake in self-reprimand. She made a single,
chuffing sound to dismiss this piece of news.

Kjeld kept his own silence, and did not move away.
At last Mealla must speak again.

"No doubt stolen from some honest woman of Dubh
Linn," she judged.

"Far from it, my raven-haired one. I bought it from a
woman of Éireann, there in Jorvik. She wed a Dane, long
years ago, and they trade goods from Dubh Linn."

Kjeld lingered long enough to open the pouch at
his belt. He lifted something out and held it in his palm
before Mealla.

"This she unpinned from her own shawl."

Mealla could not hold silence upon seeing it. A sigh,
almost a low whistle, escaped from between her teeth.

The pin was of a coiled bird, its long wings wrapped
up and around it so as to form a near circle. It was fashioned of pierced metal, so that the fabric upon which it
was pinned might show through, and the metal it was
wrought from was shining silver. The eye of the bird was a
milky, swirled white gem, a small Moonstone. The whole
was beautifully formed, and was of Dubh Linn.

"Ahh," she must say.

Mealla's arms were full of the sleeping Ælfgiva; she
could not touch the pin if she wanted to. She forced her
eyes from it and looked in Kjeld's good-natured face.

"And what does the giving of it signify?" she
demanded.

It was his turn to stiffen. Every time Kjeld tried to
chaff her back she won the skirmish. He decided to hew
to a win of the larger battle.

"Only that beauty deserves beauty."

It was so simply said, so unaffected in tone, that Mealla, after a pause, gave a puff of impatience. But there was no strength in her protest.

She peeled her palm away from the back of the sleeping babe. Kjeld wordlessly placed the pin there. Mealla flattened her hand against the child's back, and gave a bob of her head.

"Do not give yourself airs if you see me wearing it," she warned. Yet her tone softened, and her next words might as well have been spoken about Kjeld himself. "But I do like it."

***

Hrald's leave-taking was high-hearted; next to his travelling to Mercia to meet the ward of Lady Æthelflaed he had never reason to ride with such hopeful purpose. The King of Wessex conferred honour upon Four Stones in his considerations, and Hrald felt nearly as eager to learn who the proposed suitor was as Ealhswith must be. A bond between halls – and Hrald could not but think it must be between Kingdoms as well – should have great and lasting impact upon both houses. Much on both sides would be invested in its success.

Hrald regretted Pega could not attend, as it was a chance to show his pretty wife off to many of importance in Wessex. In the same measure the royal family of the same would see her happiness in her new estate, and the fine child she had already brought forth. But Pega, so reasonable and understanding, had just concern for little Ælfgiva. A babe's initial year was fraught with danger from sudden fevers and violent agues, and so precious was this first born that Pega was just as glad to remain home with her.

Pega and Mealla packed Hrald's clothing, selecting his finest tunics and leggings, including two of each from Pega's own hand. He would be a guest of the royal house of Wessex, in attendance on its King. Festive attire would be called for, each and every night in the hall. Hrald would not take the gold torc; its value made him uneasy. But he gladly packed the gold cuff for his wrist that had been his father's.

Pega made jest of this, as she rolled his tunics, and Mealla placed his best pair of boots into a linen bag.

"You are not the lucky man, this time, and should not outshine he who is."

He laughed as well. A marriage might be struck while he was present, just as suddenly as their own had been. Hrald could have some grave bargaining before him, for his little sister's hand. Whatever the dower was, he would have to send it on later. This thought gave rise to that of the bride-price. As Ælfred was making the match, Hrald might expect a vast amount of treasure in return.

A long-ago moment rose up in his mind, that of sitting in this room with Thorfast, and that chief of Turcesig proclaiming he would pay Ashild's weight in silver for her hand. It had been a startling, even crude, offer, and he and his mother had been taken aback by both its nature and its worth. Yet in its boldness it had been somehow fitting for Ashild. Hrald gave a slight shake of his head. He could not imagine Ealhswith inspiring such an offer. It would offend her, even frighten her, he thought.

His young wife roused him from these thoughts with her next words. "I will miss the chance to see your mother. But with her and Raedwulf at your side, I know Ealhswith will be in the best of hands."

She smiled up at him. "And it was Raedwulf and Ælfred who approved you, for me. I hope Ealhswith is so richly favoured."

Almost the final task for Hrald was the handing of the treasure room key to Kjeld. Pega held the other, but in the Jarl's absence his second in command must be granted ready access to the weaponry and treasure within. This was one of only a handful of times Hrald had taken the key from his belt and passed it to Kjeld. The small piece of iron held great significance, and Hrald had never done so without a moment of solemnity. For Kjeld too, the holding of it signalled a changed, if temporary, estate. All the men of Four Stones were charged to obey him for the duration of their Jarl's absence. Kjeld must keep order, and if it came to that, defend the fortress to the utmost. The dependent hall of Geornaham had been lately attacked, an event that Hrald had determined to avenge. He had ended by killing Haesten, and ridding three lands of the scourge of his predations. But Hrald had a smaller battle in mind as he passed the key to Kjeld.

The man had been trying with little success to court Mealla, who was proving as obdurate as Kjeld was persistent. Pega had told Hrald that she did not want her companion to wed solely because all around her felt Kjeld a good match, but because Mealla herself wanted him. And she suspected that her friend was in secret harbouring increasing interest in one who had so single-mindedly pursued her since the day of their arrival. Yet such was her pride that the maid of Éireann seemed loath to present Kjeld with the slightest encouragement.

Hrald and Kjeld stood in the stable yard, Bork holding the reins of the Jarl's bay. Yrling held Frost and Myrkri, who yawned and snapped at the air, whining to be let off their leads and join the riders. Hrald had given thought to taking both boys along with him. Such a trip would be good for his restless brother, and Bork relished any opportunity to be of service. But the seriousness of the trip made him wary of the boyish disputes that might arise. And the thought of the orphan lodging in the stable, while Yrling lived as Hrald did, put him off from having either.

Most of Hrald's body-guard were already mounted, with Jari astride his big grey gelding, which had its ears pricked forward, as if toward the open road. Pega stood smiling, holding her babe. Mealla, last to arrive, came through the side door of the hall to stand by her. She had a shawl of dark green draped over her shoulders, and wore at the breast the silver bird pin Kjeld gave her. It was the first time she had done so. Mealla stood as straight and proud as she ever did, and the bright metal of her new ornament shone in the morning light. Both men saw it. It seemed a hopeful sign, and was enough to prompt Hrald's words to the man.

Hrald took a step nearer Kjeld, so he might be unheard by the two women. He grinned as he handed him the treasure room key. "This at your belt should give you confidence."

Hrald and Jari fronted ten men, and five packhorses. So small an escort was all the better for speed and nimbleness. Fewer men attracted less attention, and had fewer needs upon the road. They would ride due south to the safety of Wessex. With Haesten dead, there were extended periods of peace, or at least marauding parties were small, and their threat no more than the random brigands who had ever plagued the roads. Given this, all who rode were fully armed.

They were aided in their journeying by the weather, for the most part fair and dry. The straight roads of stone built by the Caesars furthered their progress, for one ran south from the heart of Lindisse. Certain such roads had been lost in forest growth, but where they were still traceable Hrald made use of them. Much of the top layers of tiny pebbles and clay of the road beds had worn away, but they served well for waggons, and horses could be ridden alongside, hewing to the direct route so afforded. Between the paved roads and the fair weather they made good time, arriving Witanceaster on the sixth day out. Hrald had need to show the King's letter but once, past the stone cairns marking the border into Wessex. Once approaching the burh itself, the ward-men had been alerted, and Hrald had only need to speak his name.

Witanceaster had been of old one of the cities of the Caesars, and though it had been abandoned and then reclaimed, a fair measure of that grandeur remained. The imposing walls of fitted stone work had been augmented by those of timber, to extend its area. To aid in its defence, a doubled ditch had been trenched without. When the place had been resettled a cathedral of stone had been built, and the bishops thereof had gathered priests, nuns, and monks, so that it became for a while a centre of learning. The roads within were mostly new, laid out by Ælfred and formed upon a grid. Most of all Witanceaster had been the seat of the recent Kings of Wessex, that place where the Witan, the King's advisors, assembled. Ælfred had further distinguished the burh by the founding of a royal mint. It was true that the King and his young family had been driven from the fortress by a surprise Winter attack over Yule-tide by Guthrum's forces years ago. This had been the lowest ebb of both King and royal settlement. Witanceaster had rebounded, as Ælfred had. It was now impressive in every right, combining the utility of a military garrison with a multitude of structures for every needful facet of royal life.

The hundreds of folk living within its sheltering walls provided all necessities, and many luxuries. Weapon-smiths were there, silver and gold workers as well. Ælfred's minting works was kept fired, coining silver of purer quality than the King could ever before provide in his long reign. Amongst the women of his wife were those who spent all day at rich embroidery, embellishing the vestments of priests and bishops, and the sacred linens used in the offices of the holy sacraments. These needle-workers were just as able in the ornamentation of gowns and tunics, and the decoration of cushions and bed curtains. Some too were skilled in fine leatherwork, making dainty shoes of thin leather for feast day revelry, or purses, stamped and dyed in blue, green, or red, destined to hold the jingling silver and gold pieces of the fortunate.

Hrald's party would lodge in the King's own hall, and after the horses were surrendered, the men were shown their alcoves. Jari's was at the foot of Hrald's, running along the wall. Once under that high roof Hrald could compare it to the hall of the Lord and Lady of Mercia. Ælfred's hall was just as lofty, and even longer. There was no rafter nor wooden post which had not known the knife of a carver, who had left them adorned with twisting animals, twining vines, and mischievous heads, gaped-mouthed or grinning down on those who sat within.

It was late in the day when they arrived, and it was made known that Ælfred would greet Hrald when the hall gathered to sup. It left time for a needed visit to the wash house, and for Hrald to dress himself with the care the occasion demanded. He unpacked his gold cuff, but after picking it up in his hand, determined not to wear it this first night. There was as of yet nothing to celebrate, and unwanted show of wealth might prompt his sister's suitor to expect even more in the form of her dower than Hrald knew he must supply.

All were summoned to the hall by the clanging of an immense bronze gong. It hung in the forecourt, and was struck three times in alert. Folk were already streaming toward the opened doors when the gong sounded. Hrald walked in, Jari at his side, their ten men behind them. Jari and the rest of the escort were shown to a long table set to the left of the high table. The hall was quickly filling, and the men from Four Stones found themselves sharing benches with Ælfred's warriors. Hrald was led forward to the high table, where Ælfred had just appeared. The King made his way to the high-backed chair of oak set at the centre point of the long trestle. His wife took her place on one side, his Welsh priest Asser on his other. The King's keen eye fell on the approaching Hrald, and with a nod he gestured his guest forward. Hrald could hardly be more gratified by the King's opening words to him.

"I thank you for coming, my friend. Raedwulf, Lady Ælfwyn, and your sister will be arriving soon, tomorrow, I should think."

This was all he said; the swirl of activity as others took their places, and the many arriving serving folk bearing food and drink made further converse impossible. Hrald understood his murmured word of thanks was all the acknowledgment required. There would come time, and soon, when all parties were in attendance for full discourse. He let himself be led past the King, to a bench several seats down and to his left.

Though it was barely dusk outside, the hall was dim within. Oil cressets were set upon the trestles to lend light, and from every other upright post a torch flared. The eye accommodated to growing dimness, yet given the crush of folk, much was indistinct. The noise of their speech, the bright ringing of metal and the duller clatter of wood told of hearty fare and high spirits. Yet Hrald sat almost alone in it. There were several clergy at the King's table; he was flanked by one of them, while at his right was an older warrior he judged to be one of Ælfred's body-guards. Both greeted Hrald, as he did them, but after these brief exchanges little more was said. Hrald contented himself with his eyes, taking all in.

For the first time Hrald had the pleasure of a King's wife filling his cup. The Lady, discreet, modest, and quietly welcoming, yet gave the young Jarl the favour of meeting his eyes as she poured mead from her ewer into his lifted cup. That cup was of silver, and a quick glance to right and left served to tell Hrald that likely all at Ælfred's table drank thus.

It was a stout bronze cup Jari and every other man lifted at their tables. Serving men and women came forward in haste so that all cups were filled almost at once. Cups were raised, and as old safeguard against treachery, eyes locked with those who sat nearest. Salvers were brought, as heaped with food as the near-harvest season allowed. The men of Four Stones were hungry for all unobtainable while on the road. Here before them was fresh bread, sweet butter, formed pies filled with minced vegetables and meats and made pungent with juniper berries, egg puddings, and of course the good and strong mead. The warriors they sat amongst, long accustomed to supping with the men of other halls, were good-natured with their guests, and traded convivial banter between mouthfuls of food.

Jari, after some initial drinking of health to these fellows, and some friendly if pointed boasting as to who amongst the table-mates could drink the most without ill effect, recurred to his primary role. The Tyr-hand never entered the hall of another war-chief without a thorough scan of the place, its doors, walls, and window openings as well as those folk that filled it. As he moved to take his place his eyes glanced from table to table, taking in the many warriors whose seax hilts glinted in the light, as did the silver and gold gleaming from wrists, arms and necks. Pretty women too filled his eyes, those at the high table as well as at others, but he let his eye rest on them just enough to allow one corner of his mouth lift in private acknowledgment of their manifold charms.

Another guest had arrived that day, even later than Hrald. Edwin of Kilton had time only to don clean clothes before he was escorted to the King's table, to a bench a few places to his right. A royal introduction would have to wait, and the man Edwin was seated next to, a reeve of Wessex, assured him it would come upon the morrow. The Lord of Kilton was there in response to a letter delivered to him some weeks ago, one he read in the presence of his mother.

"King Ælfred requests that Edwin, Lord of Kilton come to Witanceaster, for St Mary's Day," he read to Lady Edgyth. "A light escort is all that will be needed." Edwin had looked up at his mother at this. "So it is not the threat of war."

Edgyth could not help but hope this invitation pertained directly to her entreaty to the King. She said nothing to give herself away, but smiled and mused aloud that her boy would at last see Witanceaster. Yet Edwin himself wondered if Ælfred had some woman in mind for him. It must be known that he needed one. To wed a maid chosen for him by the King – this was honour almost beyond measuring. Now Edwin was here, in a crowded hall, and wondering which of the many women about him might be she Ælfred wished him to wed.

Hrald had torn his bread loaf, and was lifting another piece of it when his eye was caught by the movement of one just entering the hall from the side door. There was, across the fire-pit that ran nearly the length of the hall, a women's table, one reserved for widows and unwed maids. Hrald watched a woman approach the far end of it. She was tall, and moved with slow and almost solemn dignity. Hrald saw the thick and glossy fall of dark hair from her head-wrap. As she paused a moment before she took to her bench, he saw her fully.

It was Dagmar.

Hrald gave a start. It was enough so that the priest beside glanced at him, but Hrald was unaware of all but she his eyes fell upon. He felt his heart turn in his breast, as if it had been clenched by an unseen hand and wrenched sideways. Here was Dagmar. His wife.

She was not dressed in the way of the Danes, but rather as a woman of Angle-land, in a long-sleeved gown of some deep but brilliant hue. In the dimness he could not see if it were blue or green.

She did not mark him, he thought. She sat, and said a word or two to the women about her, and when her salver was brought, picked up her spoon.

Hrald sat, staring, his chin slightly lowered but his eyes unwavering.

Dagmar had taken a spoon or two of food, then lowered her eyes to take up her own loaf. As she lifted her gaze her eyes travelled across the width of the King's hall to the high table. Then she froze.

She lowered her hand. The bread dropped into her salver. Hrald sat there, gazing upon her. He looked stricken, as stricken as she herself felt.

Dagmar felt the blood drain from her face; she feared she might faint. With effort she pressed herself up from the bench.

It was when she stood that Jari spotted her. Jari had not marked the female who had so recently seated herself at the end of the women's table. His eye had travelled but lightly over such groups. It was only when she stood he truly saw her. The abruptness of her doing so caught the tail of his eye. The expression of her face was almost blank, but her lips were parted enough to register her shock. Her height, the dark hair; Jari understood her for who she was. She turned and vanished into the gloom behind her.

Jari craned his head to the King's table. He saw Hrald, transfixed, staring at the retreating Dagmar. The Tyr-hand uttered a low but grave oath.

The rest of the meal was a kind of silent but sharp torture for Hrald. He felt he had taken a wound, one he could neither speak of nor seek healing for. He could not leave the table until the King and his Lady did. He must sit there as more food was brought, food he left untouched, and serving women filled and refilled his cup as he sought to slake the sudden dryness of his mouth. When the salvers were at last cleared away a scop appeared, harp in hand, and began to play.

It was only when the King rose that those who supped at his table might also do so. Hrald stood, bowed his head to Ælfred and his Lady, gave another bow to his two companions, and left. His numbness was such he scarce felt his feet. Yet they obeyed him, taking him out through the door he had entered and into a night cool and dark.

He had not made three steps when a boy came up, walking as if to pass him, but then pausing at Hrald's shoulder.

"The daughter of Guthrum will be at the east watch tower," the boy hissed. Then he passed into the hall. He left so quickly Hrald had no time to respond, nor even react.

All the air had fled Hrald's lungs. He had never wanted to see Dagmar again, and never thought it possible he would see her. And now they had been brought together under the roof of the King of Wessex. A rush of desperation washed over him. He no longer could judge what he wanted. His urge to flee was just as strong as his desire to see her. He dropped his eyes to the darkness of the pounded soil of the ground and let out a long, low breath.

Hrald lifted his gaze to the large man there before him, walking slowly toward where he stood, dumbstruck. It was Jari. Hrald saw from his body-guard's face that he had also seen Dagmar. The Tyr-hand stood before him without speaking.

Hrald too could say nothing. But the older man discerned much from the glittering, almost feverish cast of Hrald's eyes. His words to the young Jarl were slow and deliberate.

"I am here to safeguard your body," Jari told him. "More than that I cannot do."

The Tyr-hand said it all. Hrald's heart, his soul, these were his own purview.

Hrald could do no more than nod. He passed by Jari, leaving the hall behind him. Each time the door was opened, it threw a block of light onto the ground he trod. Soon he was beyond its reach, and the reach too of the noise escaping that door.

The east watch tower. The gate they had ridden through faced north. Hrald walked, skirting outbuildings and workshops, and reached the perimeter of the timber palisade. Above his head flared fire, held in iron baskets set on poles spaced at even intervals. A wooden tower had been built marking each direction. At some points along the palisade small buildings adjoined it, but there were long runs of wall with no encroachment. He reached the east tower and stepped back into its shadow.

Dagmar had been waiting. She had fled the hall, gone to her tiny house, and walked the floor in fitful hesitation. At last she resolved to send a message. Now Hrald was come. She stepped out from the side of the storehouse she had stood by and began to walk. She followed the line of torches to where she had seen him vanish. As she passed each one, her shadow, dark and mantled as she was, came up around from behind her and walked at her side a step or two before moving ahead, where she was bound to follow. Her shadow grew long, then faded as the thrown light dimmed. When she reached the next pool of torch light, it appeared again, coming around her left shoulder, leading her on.

Hrald watched her coming, illuminated in the light cast by the fires held aloft. She was hooded and wearing a long cloak. He moved away from the tower base. She came toward him with the graceful and remembered cadence of her gait.

He felt a further tightening of his constricted chest. When she was a man's length away, she stopped, as if fearing to approach too near. She spoke, in a voice both soft and sorrowful.

"My Jarl," were her first words. "May I speak to you," she asked, as if they had never met. Her tone, low and calm, was hers alone. It filled his ears.

Hrald stood there, meeting her eyes, so near, and yet with an unbridgeable gulf between them. It closed his throat. He said nothing, gave no sign of assent, but his remaining before her was enough for her to go on.

Dagmar's hands rose to her hood and she pushed it back, revealing the fall of dark hair framing her face.

"Have I leave to speak?" It was true plea, a petition, which might be easily refused.

They stood in a pool of light, yet one circumscribed enough that a single step would hide either one of them.

He did not answer this, but instead flogged himself to action. The words he forced from his mouth came out a hoarse whisper.

"Why are you here, in Witanceaster?"

The ghost of a smile played for one moment upon her lips.

"I sought shelter. Ælfred and his wife provided it. I do not know why. He knew of our parting, yet he welcomed me. He has, for all his skill in war, the soul of a priest. He seeks, I think, redemption for others. Surely I needed that. So perhaps it was charity, and the sense that here I could do little mischief, having done so much in Anglia."

Her eyebrows, dark and arched, lifted a moment in question. "Perhaps he took me in, not for my own sake, but for that of my father."

He said nothing, only continued to look at her. She felt she must go on, explaining her presence here.

"At first I lodged in the women's hall. Now I have a small house I have built, no more than a hut, but snug. I have been here some months."

She must now turn the question to him.

"Why – why are you here?"

His answer was so low that she must take a step nearer to hear him.

"Ælfred summoned me. He has a match for Ealhswith. Who, I do not know."

Hrald's next question was more forcefully put.

"Where is he?"

There was no need to append a name. Dagmar knew he meant Vigmund.

"He is dead. He died fighting by the side of Heligo, the King of Dane-mark. They were killed in an ambush, by he who became the new King."

The words, so softly and simply stated, were yet another blow to Hrald.

Dagmar looked beyond him a moment, into the darkness surrounding them. "I was forced to flee; all we women did. There was nought but war in Dane-mark. I had silver, and thought I would go to Frankland, to Paris. I was nearly there when I met a group of nuns and monks, returning here to Wessex from pilgrimage they had made. I came with them."

"There is war still here," Hrald said.

She nodded. "But I hear all grows better. And when the King dies, his son Eadward will rule. He is, I think, harder than his father, and will strike peace, a lasting one, now that Haesten is gone." She paused a moment. "It has been said you killed him."

He must answer this. "I did." He offered a rare oath, one heartfelt for all the harm that man had done. "Christ damn him."

She drew breath. "I know about – Ashild," she murmured.

He said nothing, and she went on.

"And . . . I heard that you had wed." She gave a small and dismissive laugh at herself. "The chatter of the court women brims with such tidings. Also nuns, when you befriend them, often know much."

Hrald could not answer this, could not summon Pega's name here.

"And you are free to wed," he said in return. He must say it. It was the only certain route for her, yet the words cost him dearly.

"Yes," she answered, in little more than a whisper.

The silence about them thickened. A burning brand in the basket over their heads crackled and shifted, and she spoke of something she felt bound to share.

"When I left Heligo's fortress I met your father's mother, outside Ribe."

Hrald shook his head, baffled by this. "How did you know her as such?"

"We spoke, as women do, of our lives. She told me of her son, whom she named Sidroc, after a great Jarl. And she told me the boy's father. His name was Hrald."

He could scarce compass these tidings, on top of the shock of again seeing her.

"Outside Ribe . . ."

"Yes. She is a poor cotter. She is also honest, and kind. Her name is Jorild. She lives with her nieces and their children."

A moment passed as Dagmar recalled the worn face.

"I gave her silver, in your name, and for her help to me."

Jorild was the name Hrald's grandfather used when speaking of the woman. It was too much for Hrald to absorb; he could not keep up with his own feelings.

Dagmar was watching his face, saw it cloud, and the brow furrow in distress.

"Forgive me," she said hastily. She shook her head at herself. "I could spend the rest of my days repeating those two words to you, and it would not be enough."

He struggled to say the next.

"What is done, is done."

"Is it done?" she whispered.

She spoke with true earnestness now. "The hurt I caused you – and to your family – has been a shame I have borne each and every day."

Dagmar drew a shallow breath, enough to fuel her next words. She would never have chance again to tell him what she most yearned for him to know.

"Whatever you thought of me is likely true, but this one thing you do not know. I was ready to send him away forever when you stepped into that room. I swear this to you, and would do so before God to my dying day."

She looked him fully in the eyes. He held her gaze a moment, then must close his own.

If he had not returned to the hall when he had, he would have never known it happened. He could have gone on in his happy life with her.

Though he was stunned almost senseless by her quiet declaration, Hrald could not but believe her. As shattered as he had been by her apparent betrayal, this was a greater cruelty. His entire life had been altered, and he had lost the woman he loved, in returning for that forgotten spear. Hrald's lips parted as he took this in. He rocked back on his heels, into the support of the timber wall. He could not have stood without it. The blow was too great.

It was crushing to bear, yet looking at her, hearing her speak, he could do nothing but accept her sworn

words. Hrald felt anew the anguished heat of that day of
discovery. The warrior Vigmund had appeared at Four
Stones to steal Hrald's wife. The man had goaded Hrald,
saying Dagmar had told him she loved him, words she
had not yet spoken to Hrald. Hrald had never considered
it a possibility that she would then drive Vigmund away.

Her crime that morning had been two-fold, the
betrayal of being found in the arms of another, and the
lesser, but still stinging pain of her earlier dissembling.

Dagmar had been guilty of an unspoken deceit, of a
crime of omission, but Hrald knew she had not lied to
him. He had never asked before they wed if she were
yet a maid; doing such was out of the question, for he
had assumed maid she was. He could not blame her
for not offering news which would dismay many men,
and for some, even cause them to withdraw their offer
of marriage. Hrald had not asked, and she had not lied.

She could bear his silence no longer, and must go on.

"The few months of being your wife – I hardly knew
how to accept what you gave me. What you wished to
give me. I lived in shame you would hear of my drunken
mother, of the fact that too young to choose wisely, I gave
myself to one such as Vigmund. And I bore the added
shame of my father – King of the Danes in Anglia! – leaving me nothing. I had nothing to give, nothing to offer a
man such as you.

"To live in shame, and fear of discovery, when you
and your mother had treated me so kindly – and then,
knowing that I had begun to love you, to allow Vigmund
within the hall – none can know how I curse myself for
such weakness. Yet I would have sent him away."

Dagmar's eyes had dropped. Her head hung in despair. Her next words were uttered from the well of her sorrow.

"Instead all was snatched from me." Her eyes lifted to his own, fastened upon her. "From us."

The entire landscape of Hrald's life had changed. He could not accept it. He could not give voice to this fresh grief, deeper even than that of betrayal. The raw hurt of the penalty exacted staggered him.

"I – I cannot . . ."

Dagmar, watching the pain in his face, spoke through her tears.

"Do not grieve, Hrald. Do not grieve. I wish only to speak the truth. To make what feeble amends are left to me. Nothing more.

"There is a second truth you do not know. You would have been forced to put me away. It seems I am barren. I cannot bring you the sons you deserve, nor even daughters to barter with."

The voice issuing from Hrald's throat rose from his core, spilling up from a deep reservoir of loss, so aggrieved was it. An urgent strength powered his next words.

"I would never have put you away."

At Dagmar's first visit to Four Stones she had teased his imagination by saying that if they wed, their offspring would be like giants. As forward as it was, that remark was a hint of the future intimacy to come. It ignited his desire. That desire was still there, and lodging with it, a profound pity for their blighted hopes.

He raised his eyes and looked into her face. He could not hold his gaze there for long, and shifted it upward to the glare of the fire.

Dagmar made a soft sound, one of despair.

"Weakness, and then barrenness. Either way I would have lost you."

It felt another wound to Hrald's breast. He looked about, casting his eyes as if for his next words, the desperate plea he feared speaking but was compelled to utter.

"I would never have put you away. Never," he repeated, lost in hopeless grief. "We would have found a son, a daughter too. Sigewif takes in foundlings. Or a cottar's child. We would have made a family."

It was terrible to hear himself say this, to project ahead to a time he was denied ever knowing. And it was admission of how much he loved her.

She shook her head at his claim. Tears ran from her eyes. "The child would not be of your blood. Nor your father's, who also ruled Four Stones."

Blood of Kings was the only thing Dagmar had ever possessed in her own right. A fostered child would ever be at a disadvantage. Yet he stood before her, vowing that they would have overcome the lack of a blood heir.

Dagmar's next words were voiced as gently as a prayer. "You love me still?"

She would offer now what she could not before. "For I love you, Hrald."

Dagmar must say it, now that he knew all. She heard the sudden intake of his breath, saw him again rock back on his heels, as if her whispered words were an assault.

Once again she had underestimated his heart.

Hrald must rebel, or succumb. To admit he loved her was a fatal act. His voice was strained, coming from a narrowed throat.

"I am wed. My wife is dear to me. She has given me a daughter."

Dagmar closed her eyes. The three words he had spoken to her every day would not again drop from his mouth. Hrald had lifted his new life as shield to protect himself.

Nothing was left but for her to answer in grave composure. "I am sure she is both lovely, and loved."

"She is of Mercia," Hrald found himself saying. "The ward of Lady Æthelflaed."

"Tell me of her," Dagmar invited. If the woman was made more real, it might keep her from her longing to hear him say he loved her still.

Hrald tried to describe Pega, small and yellow-haired.

"Like Inkera," she offered.

Yes, he thought, your half-sister Inkera, who smiled at me so gaily. And then I saw you.

Dagmar pictured another in her place at Four Stones, one devout, accomplished, and with the ample riches Hrald deserved. She must do so. As he had told her, all was over and done.

They heard a sound, and turned their heads to see a man with a hand-wain, steadily working his way from light basket to basket, replenishing the burning brands with fresh wood. Each flared up in turn with new fuel. It prompted Dagmar's next words.

"I would ask for one thing only." Her pause was long, considered, as if she steeled herself.

"A kiss of Peace, as Wilgot often named it."

He did not expect her to say this, to conjure the words of the priest of Four Stones when he asked the family thereof to greet each other with a holy kiss after receiving the sacrament. It was an act of openness, and also one of forgiveness.

Dagmar asked for this now, from him.

Hrald was struck. Even Christ was betrayed by a single kiss.

His face spoke what his tongue could not. He shook his head. It would be a kiss of torment. Hrald could not grant her this.

It felt the greatest of blows to Dagmar. She had only debased herself further. She clutched at what she could.

The man with the wain was nearing. Both knew they must part.

"Again, I ask your forgiveness," she breathed. She felt close to collapse, yet drew herself up enough to say the next.

"I will not return to the hall as long as you are here. You need not fear seeing me again."

She paused, unable to stop the next.

"If you want me, send message by the boy Ultan. He lives in the King's stable."

NO GOOD END

HRALD lay awake within his alcove for hours after his parting with Dagmar. She was here, widowed, and had wished to see him. She had at last told him she loved him. Hrald thought his torment could be no greater.

He could think only of his father, and what he would do. Sidroc had told his son enough about his long pursuit of Ceridwen that Hrald felt assured of one thing – if at any point on their arduous journey to Gotland she had welcomed him, his father would not have hesitated. Hrald understood – all men did if they were honest – the difference between wanting and being wanted. His father had waited long years to be wanted by the woman who would be his wife. Here was Hrald with the woman he had ever loved before him, wanting him.

It was a snare richly baited. After the initial satisfaction of yielding, nothing but heartbreak and shame could result. It would lodge in his own breast, and rear up and taint his whole existence. It could destroy any chance of Dagmar moving toward a fuller life. Yet the thought that they might have one night together granted him no rest. Dagmar was a lodestone to whom he was irresistibly drawn.

Oddly, he found himself thinking also of Ashild. Ashild knew what she wanted, and would seize it with both hands, as she had seized the single night she had spent with Ceric. Both Ceric and Hrald had thought that night commitment in itself, and that Ashild would surely wed Ceric. Both were wrong. She had given herself for the sake of the giving, to gain knowledge of herself and of Ceric, and had been ready to accept the good or ill which might flow from that event. Hrald did not think it possible for him to do the same. If he resolved to spend a single night with Dagmar, there would be no end of it. He would want more.

Hrald's mother too came to mind, her reminding him that the heart could hold more than one love. But she did not mean it in the fullest sense, of his being ready to act now; yet her understanding of his feelings toward his first wife could almost be read as encouragement.

Lying in the gloom of the hall, staring up into the darkness of the timber roof, Hrald found no respite from his tortured imaginings. He would not act on this desire. He must not.

⚬⚬⚬⚬⚬⚬⚬⚬⚬⚬

Hours later the Jarl of Four Stones was only dimly aware of the bell, tolling for Sabbath Mass. Hrald was drained from inner turmoil and lack of sleep and would not appear; he could not muster the needed fortitude to show himself. It was early on St Mary's Day; he heard the sounds of men around him stirring.

One visitor who passed through the cathedral door that morning was Edwin of Kilton. The stone church was high-roofed, with round-topped casements of glass and brightly painted statues within. If Edwin could expand the chantry of Kilton five-fold, this would be it. Edwin knew the King and his Lady and many of the royal retainers were already within; he had stood a respectful distance and watched them arrive. Large as it was, the edifice was full, and Edwin assumed a second service would be offered by the preaching cross outside the palisade. Edwin saw the reeve he had supped with last night. The reeve greeted him with a nod, and Edwin took a place next the man, near the back. Two priests robed in green moved across the altar, the incense swung by one of them hanging blue in the air. The women of Witanceaster stood in loose rows on the left, its men on the right.

Edwin attended to the Mass, while allowing his eyes to at times sweep over those assembled. One caught and held his attention. On the women's side, a few rows up from where he stood, was a woman Edwin had seen hastily rise and hurry from the King's hall last night. She stood out for her height, and the lustrous deep brown of her hair.

At the end of the Mass, following the benediction, all turned to watch Ælfred and his family leave, followed by his picked men and their wives who had also stood near the altar. The dark-haired woman was now turned toward Edwin. He saw a grave face, but one of striking mien. Others of Ælfred's household were now leaving, the married men going to meet their wives, that they might process from the church together. None seemed to be moving toward the tall woman. Edwin looked to the reeve at his side.

"The woman in dark blue – do you know of her?"

"That is a daughter of Guthrum," the man decided. "Her name is Dagmar. She has lived here at the King's behest for several months."

Edwin took this in. The woman before him was no less than the daughter of the dead King of the Danes in Angle-land, and a woman who had found favour enough with Ælfred to reside here as his guest. That was a pairing worthy of the Lord of Kilton.

"She is not wed?" Edwin posed. She was ready to turn and leave the church, alone.

"She is widowed – or her union was sundered; I am not certain. But she was raised in Anglia, at her father's hall, at Headleage."

"I thank you."

Edwin's interest was further heightened. A King's daughter, one of high and unusual looks, and one likely more than capable of running a hall such as Kilton.

***

After he had risen Hrald moved through the royal hall, intent on the stable where he knew his horse had been taken. The hall was nearly deserted, but serving folk were at work, for after the conclusion of the Mass all would return and break their fast here. Hrald wanted nothing so much as air and distance. He had nearly gained the opened door when Jari stood up from a bench on the inside wall. In the glare cast by the morning Sun Hrald had not seen him.

"I am going for a ride," Hrald said.

Jari nodded. "Me as well."

Within a few moments they were at the stable gate. Hrald's whistle brought his bay, head nodding, to him. As the stallion crossed the paddock, Jari's grey, as alert as was his master, followed in his wake with lifted head. The two men shrugged off the stable-boys' offers of help, and saddled their horses themselves. Hrald gave thought to Bork, back at Four Stones, then shifted his mind to the road leading out of the inner palisade gates, and then that leading through the arched opening of the old Roman wall.

They rode in near silence, first making a circuit of the confines of the burh, then striking out past orchards and grapevines on a road heading south. Hrald felt he must see that which he had not seen before, something fresh and new to engage his troubled senses. When at last they turned back the Sun was no longer overhead, but had begun its western decline.

They rode in, hungry and thirsty both, to find Raedwulf at the stable doors. A waggon, from which the horses had already been freed, stood nearby, and the bailiff was standing with four other men, handing over their saddle horses to the care of the boys there.

The bailiff's face broke into a smile, seeing Hrald. "Your mother and sister are in the third bower," he told him, gesturing to a range of buildings fanning out beyond the King's hall. "I will be along presently."

Hrald and Jari surrendered their own horses, and Hrald sent Jari off to the kitchen yard to forage for himself. The door to the bower stood open, and Hrald had not stepped over the threshold when he heard Ealhswith's happy cry. In a moment he was being held by both women.

Cerd was at their feet, screeching in joy at the sight of his uncle, growling his name and jumping in the air to be picked up. If any one thing could force a smile to Hrald's face, it was this, and he hoisted the boy into his arms.

They had been parted less than three months, but to Hrald's eyes Ealhswith seemed to have grown, not in stature, but in seriousness. Still, she clung to her brother with girlish ardour. It was Ælfwyn who saw the change in her son. She turned to Ealhswith.

"As Burginde has gone to the kitchen-yard, would you take Cerd there, and get for him an oat or honey cake?" The girl obliged, taking the boy by the hand with the promise of sweets to come.

When alone, Ælfwyn turned to her son. Hrald did not keep her in suspense.

"I have seen Dagmar. She is here, living in Witan-ceaster, guest of Ælfred."

His mother's face spoke more than her faltering words could. "What – how – "

"The Dane she rode off with, Guthrum's body-guard, is dead. So is the King he followed, in Dane-mark. Dagmar was able to flee with silver, before the victors arrived. She was headed to the court of Paris, but met nuns and monks returning to Wessex. She joined them, and ended here."

Ælfwyn had braced herself enough to voice a single soft word, a question on which all hung.

"And . . . ?"

Hrald lifted his head to the rafters over their heads.

"And I want her.

"As she wants me."

His mother's hands came to her face a moment, but nothing could shield her from the awe-fulness of these truths. She lowered her hands. She could not give way to either her shock or sorrow, not yet.

Her son's voice took on heightened strength as he went on. "When I discovered her there in the treasure room, she was about to send him away. Had I not come back when I did, she would still be my wife. Despite her love for him, she had committed to stay with me. She was learning to love me."

Now Ælfwyn must give way to her grief. Her hand lifted to her face as tears sprang to her eyes. This mischance, this trick of Fate, this single slip by Dagmar, had destroyed her boy's happiness, and his marriage. And it need not have been.

Foremost in the thoughts that followed in Ælfwyn's mind was Pega, awaiting Hrald's return, and the sweetness of their little babe. He must resist, at whatever cost to himself, or to Dagmar. Those innocent of any wrongdoing could not be laid upon the sacrificial altar; the pain of denying their love must be born by Hrald and Dagmar.

She could have smote herself for these pious judgements. How could she tell Hrald to be strong, to resist, when she would have given herself in a moment to Gyric if he had asked her? Her goodness, her piety, her restraint, all had been acquired over years. These traits had been ascribed to her, and not all had been fully deserved. There had been times when she knew them a mockery, and a sham. She had not earned such virtues; they had been forced upon her.

Still, she must do what she could to guide her son upon the upright path.

"There is no good end, Hrald." This truth was meant as warning, but she could scarce do more than whisper it.

She saw the pain in his face as he acknowledged this. "I know.

"But we have seen each other, and I have heard the truth."

"Then that must be the good that comes from it," his mother urged. "Cling to that."

Ælfred sat within his private chamber with the Bailiff of Defenas. Raedwulf had reported not to the great hall, but to the separate and substantial foursquare house of timber where Ælfred read, wrote, and deliberated. As if to indicate the importance to the King of such work, sentries were always positioned without, whether or not Ælfred was within.

The structure was brightened by three windows, as befit its role as a writing and working chamber. It was sparsely furnished, even monastic in its tone, with two tables, and a simple cot for the rare daytime rest in which Ælfred indulged. The King met here with trusted advisors, and others of those not requiring the ceremonial surroundings of the royal hall itself. For those outside the King's immediate circle, being called within this far more intimate space was thus regarded as an honour.

To Raedwulf's relief, the King's vigour while walking or standing seemed to have suffered no readily discernable diminution in his three month absence. Yet the pallor of Ælfred's face was such that his light blue eyes stood out in even more contrast. It told Raedwulf the King must be bleeding again. There was a slackness to the skin of cheeks and chin, and the dark orbits under those light eyes were more dusky than ever. With a glance Raedwulf took in the state of the writing table, covered with half-written parchments. Metal and pottery trays held small knives, scrapers, and fresh and spent quills. A cloth spotted and stained with ink lay crumpled at the right, where it had dropped from the King's hand, and two books were held open with small lead weights. Stubs of beeswax tapers in bronze holders ringed the active surface of the table. The bailiff recognised the larger of the volumes, a Latin text, which Ælfred used in his translations of philosophical works as he laboured to transcribe them into the tongue of Angle-land. The King of Wessex was working too hard, too late into the nights, pressing himself on every front in a race against failing health and utter exhaustion.

"It is Edwin, Lord of Kilton I have in mind for Ealhswith," the King said.

Raedwulf was more surprised than he showed.

"My Lord does my Lady-wife and her daughter honour," is what he said.

Ælfred lifted his hand in dismissal of this. "The girl is now your stepdaughter. I would not presume upon a friendship as old and warm as ours to promise her to any without your, and her mother's, fullest consent."

Raedwulf uttered a few words of thanks, then fell into silence as he considered the proposed union. The King had worked one greatly desired alliance, that of Pega of Mercia with Hrald of Lindisse. But with the death of the Jarl's sister Ashild, the long-awaited coupling of Kilton and Four Stones had been thwarted through the most tragic of circumstances. The King's godson Ceric was now wed to the royal blood of Wales. Yet each of the two great halls had a younger sibling to fulfil the earlier, and deferred dream.

Raedwulf's response was both slow and thoughtful. "It bridges the breach, yes."

"Certainly your marriage to Lady Ælfwyn has done much," Ælfred suggested. "You have brought the girl to Wessex. And her mother is of Cirenceaster. Ealhswith is a child of both Guthrum's Danelaw and here."

And she is also the daughter of the Dane Sidroc, Raedwulf thought; a most formidable foe. But he recalled his long-ago meeting with Lady Modwynn, and of how she had asked after the girl.

"Edwin is being brought to me now," Ælfred went on. "If all goes well, you will return to Lady Ælfwyn and her daughter with glad tidings."

When Edwin was admitted two serving men followed him in. One bore a tray bearing three stemmed cups, two of silver, and the King's own cup of gold. The second carried a ewer of hammered silver, from which he poured mead almost as yellow as the vessel Ælfred took up. When the serving men had left, Edwin gave his bow, first to his King, and then to the bailiff.

The young Lord had arrayed himself with care for this meeting. His tunic was of bright green, shot with silver thread about neck, hem, and wrist. Edwin's right wrist bore a heavy bracelet of braided red and yellow gold. He knew that his mother Ceridwen had presented it to him at his christening. It was the horse-thegn Worr who had told him it was the greatest treasure Godwin owned, and that he had years earlier given it to Ceridwen as reward for the return of his brother Gyric. Edwin knew nothing more than this, but it was enough to grant the piece special significance, not only for its surpassing worth, but for how, and to whom it had been given. Wearing it now with all his finery before the King could only add to its lustre. Young as he was, he felt equal to any task that might be asked of him.

The three took up their cups, lifted them as they let their eyes meet, then took a draught. Ælfred gestured both to sit at the small and empty table used for such meetings.

The King began, and with considerable formality. "I have had word through Worr, the son-in-law of the Bailiff of Defenas, that Ceric has returned to the hall. The tidings were welcome; that Ceric is gaining in health, and is now wed to a princess of Ceredigion."

Edwin had briefly closed his eyes at this recounting, a gesture subtle, but not unnoticed by either King or bailiff. Though it took Edwin a moment to affirm this, he answered steadily enough.

"This is all true, my Lord."

The King nodded, disposing of Edwin's discomfiture in a single, slight gesture.

"It is on the subject of another young woman that I have called you hence. There is a maid, well known to the bailiff, to serve as more than fitting wife to the Lord of Kilton."

Edwin's eyes shifted from the face of the King to that of Raedwulf. Having been handed the reins, the bailiff now took the lead.

"She is indeed well known to me, Edwin, as is her family. I have seen her grow over time, though she has only seventeen years. And I can vouch for her character, calmness of nature, devoutness, and increasing skill."

"Is she here?"

"She has just arrived with me and her mother, my new wife, Lady Ælfwyn, born of Cirenceaster, lately of Four Stones. The maid of whom we speak is the younger sister of Jarl Hrald of that fortress."

Edwin's lips parted, and he lowered his gaze. This was startling enough; Four Stones was the hall of which Ceric had tried to wed the older daughter. But Ashild was the half-sister of Hrald.

Fearful that his face had given away his startle, Edwin forced himself to pause. Raedwulf had been friend and confidante to his grandmother Modwynn, with, Edwin believed, that Lady's interests at heart. But now he had wed the Lady of Four Stones. It seemed to Edwin that the bailiff now had a foot on the back of twinned horses and must attempt to ride them side by side.

It took the Lord of Kilton a moment to fully understand the parentage of this younger girl. His head lifted in a start.

Edwin could not follow his first instinct and blurt out the words forming in his mouth: You are asking me to wed the daughter of the man who killed my father.

He swallowed his outrage as best he could. He drew a breath, and allowed it to carry the bulk of his anger out with it, without colouring his answer. Edwin did not look at the bailiff; what he must say would be addressed to the King.

He couched his response indirectly, and voiced it as coolly as he could, given his shock. "The suggestion is that I should wed the daughter of the man who killed the Lord of Kilton."

Ælfred gauged the depth of this response. The young man's face had flushed red, and his eyes had widened. The King answered in a low tone.

"Concessions must be made, for peace."

Edwin could give answer to this. This time there was rising energy in his words.

"My Lord, I will give my life for you, and Wessex. I trust my loyalty will never be held in doubt. But to take to wife such a woman – "

He need not defend himself; the King had raised his hand in acceptance, and Edwin fell into discomfited silence.

In truth, Edwin felt stifled. The expectation struck him as nothing short of monstrous. The girl was innocent, yet had sprung from the loins of one who had felled his closest kin. Edwin would be somehow demeaned in taking her to wife. All he could compare it to was those few sorry instances in which a ravished maid had been forced to wed her despoiler. What kind of marital bonds of trust and fidelity could be forged under such circumstances, one could ask.

The bailiff stood in perfect silence, his face betraying no emotion.

The King too was silent. Many were the times when the man who killed the father of a maid then went on to take that daughter as wife. Women were forced to accommodate themselves to such circumstances. It was far more rare that a man, aggrieved by the loss of his own kin, should then wed the daughter of the man whose hand had caused that loss. Ælfred was asking more than Edwin could give. The King had been baulked; the slight squaring of his shoulders told Raedwulf of his disappointment. Yet Wessex needed the unwavering loyalty of Kilton.

The silence extended long moments. Edwin felt he must speak, to spare himself from the charge of petulance.

It was Raedwulf who came to his aid. It was ever his task to reframe questions of difficulty, provide a path for retraction of hastily uttered words, and help all reach, if not an amiable conclusion, then one least harmful to future interests. He began by restating the kernel of Edwin's reaction. The bailiff's tone was calm, even mild, and spoken without a trace of displeasure.

"It is then your preference, to not meet the young woman?"

Despite the mildness of the query, Edwin felt how terrible was his position. To refuse to meet the girl was to slight the efforts of King and bailiff on his behalf. The former had favoured Edwin by proposing the maid, the latter was now step-father to the girl. In his aversion to the pairing, he risked direct insult. Yet he could not brazen his way through such an interview; he knew he could not.

"Would it not be unkind to do so," he hazarded, "when I know such a match is not possible?"

The bailiff's eyes met those of his King. If Edwin was this decided, yes, nothing could be gained, and much lost. Beyond this, it took courage to utter such words, and both Ælfred and Raedwulf, as sorry as they were to hear them, must admire him for doing so.

Ælfred finished it. "We will consider the question closed."

Edwin's murmured response was heartfelt. "I thank you, my Lord."

Some air seemed to have gone out of the room, its atmosphere rendered awkward and flat. The young Lord of Kilton could not end the conversation like this. He had spurned the King's offer, and would show his willingness to be aided by him nonetheless.

"It is my great regret that my bond to my adopted mother, Lady Edgyth, keeps me from accepting the maid you propose for me."

This carried its own gravity; Edgyth was admired by both men, and it was her Lord and husband who had been struck down by the Dane who was Ealhswith's father.

"I hope in near future to be worthy of your further consideration, my Lord."

It was the best he could do. Edwin gave a deep bow of his head. Ælfred nodded and uttered words of dismissal.

The bailiff would leave with Edwin. Raedwulf guessed how unnerved the young Lord might be after the fraught discussion. A few words might do much to reassure Edwin that his response had been no affront.

As soon as they were outside the chamber door, Raedwulf paused. There was a bench not far away where they would not be overheard, and with a movement of his hand he gestured that Edwin sit with him. To the bailiff's surprise, Edwin seemed more than eager to do so.

The Lord of Kilton recurred to the image which had been playing in his mind since yesternight.

"May I speak freely, Raedwulf?"

"Of course."

"I have seen a woman here. First last night in the hall, and then at Mass this morning."

Raedwulf watched the hopeful brightening of Edwin's countenance. The bailiff's face, alert, listening, spurred Edwin on.

"I was told she is a daughter of Guthrum, Dagmar. And that she is a widow."

It was Raedwulf's turn to be startled. "Dagmar," he muttered. Ælfred had months earlier mentioned her presence in the royal burh, and though the woman had been pointed out to the bailiff, they had never met.

The young Lord had singularly bad fortune.

"She may be widowed now," the bailiff offered. "But she was Jarl Hrald's first wife. He was forced to put her away three years ago when she was found with another man."

Edwin turned his head sharply away from this news. Despite the honied sweetness of the mead he had just drunk a taste as of bile came into his mouth. Dagmar was doubly tainted. The very woman he had marked had been discarded by Hrald of Four Stones, son of his father's killer. That hall cast a long shadow.

Edwin's attempt to scoff at himself lacked heartiness. "I thank you," he said, through teeth nearly clenched. "You have done me a service, Sir."

He looked ready to excuse himself, and ready too to flee Witanceaster. Raedwulf would stay him, with the only words of encouragement he could, in honesty, offer.

"I will be speaking with the King about your prospects. I will have news for you, later today or on the morrow. Do not leave until then."

Despite his urge to leave, Edwin drew breath. "I will not. And again, I thank you for your effort."

Hopes had been dashed on both sides. Yet the bailiff sought a way to redeem the unhappy meeting. The Lord of Kilton had just related something of importance, something to perhaps build upon.

"But such a woman as Guthrum's daughter," Raedwulf offered, "perhaps a young widow, one experienced in the running of a hall, would be to your taste?"

All Edwin could say was the next. "Yes, if this is possible."

His questioner gave a rueful laugh. "It is more than possible. With all the losses we have suffered these past years, Wessex has many young widows."

Edwin grasped at this new prospect. His next words were spoken with certainty, as if after long deliberation. "I hope for a woman both steady and stable. One who can take over Kilton. Not an untried girl."

"Ah." The bailiff's thoughtful release of breath was followed by his silence, as he studied the young Lord. Edwin's request was an unusually mature one, one far-thinking, and he did not expect it from the young man. It impressed the bailiff. And it opened up further possibilities, those with utmost benefit to Wessex.

"Would a foreign bride suit? Frankland is immense, with many small Princely holdings. Carolingians, the Danish holdings, the house of Paris. Such seek closer alignment with Wessex. Could one of their women suit?"

He paused a moment trying to read the young man's puzzled face as Edwin considered this.

"I will be glad to hear of any such," Edwin affirmed.

"I will speak to the King," Raedwulf promised.

Not an hour later Hrald was called to the same foursquare timber house. With the guards ever at attention Hrald had thought it perhaps some kind of treasure room, but was quickly disabused of this upon entering. It was the chamber of a scholar. The main feature of the room was its two tables. One was crowded with the detritus of writing, while the second held a green-glazed pottery jug and two flared tumblers of clear glass. At the end of this second, smaller table sat a sword in a tooled scabbard. Ælfred was already standing when Hrald was shown in. Hrald moved to the centre of the small room and inclined his head to his host.

Having been greeted as warmly as he had in the hall, Hrald was not prepared for the new gravity of the King's expression.

"Jarl Hrald, I regret the match I had intended for your sister Ealhswith cannot be accomplished. I had thought to unite the halls of Kilton and Four Stones. He intended was Edwin, Lord of Kilton."

Ælfred placed some little stress on the next, lest it be thought that Ealhswith's person was wanting. "His objection was solely over the girl's father."

Hrald worked to keep his face from showing his surprise.

The King went on, just as soberly. "I know your father killed Godwin, Lord of Kilton, under just cause. Worr was witness; he told me."

That bloody contest would never be forgotten. Hrald's answer was no more than a quiet reminder. "I was witness as well. As was Ceric. We were boys."

Hrald went on, in a low voice, addressing the union Ælfred had planned. "I would not have thought of this pairing."

Ælfred gave a slow nod. War ever made strange bed-fellows, and it was his charge to attempt to unite feuding factions through any reasonable means. "It was perhaps a step too far," he admitted. "However, the matter is closed. I regret I have brought your mother and sister so great a distance, only to be disappointed in their hope."

Hrald must deflect this. "They are gladdened to be here. And it has given me a chance to see them, after their recent removal to Defenas."

"I will ask them to stay a few days," the King went on, "that Ealhswith may be seen by others. She need not know of the failed effort."

Hrald thought his little sister might be crushed if she learnt she had been spurned, especially by a Lord of such wealth and rank as Edwin. She must be protected from this truth.

"I thank you. Of course Ealhswith will be guided by her mother in her choice, and I stand ready to provide a handsome dower."

"I know you shall. And the girl is young; she has time."

"Another matter," Ælfred said next. The King's tone changed as abruptly as the subject. He turned to the table and pulled the wooden stopper from the spout of the green jug. He poured a pale gold and creaming liquid into the two tumblers.

"Ale made by our monks. Mead is potent, and wine, if not well-watered, lethal to the head. But good ale is ever welcome, and a refreshment at all times. To share it with you is a pleasure."

He took up one of the cups and handed it to Hrald.

A King's wife has filled my cup with mead, and now the King himself pours out ale to share with me, Hrald thought.

"Toasted wheat and barley both," noted Ælfred, after Hrald both tasted and praised the brew.

The tumblers were small and the men drained them almost in a single draught. The King set his down upon the table, in his action inviting his guest to do the same.

"Haesten," Ælfred began. "Raedwulf has told me of your singular accomplishment."

To Hrald the act was one so wholly justified as to defy enlarging upon.

The King's next words suggested he agreed. "My son Eadward, having chased him so long, would have liked to have been the one to spill that blood. But Haesten was on your land. And no one had greater direct cause than you."

Needless to say, a few questions were asked of Hrald, forcing him to live through the duel at a distance. Ælfred listened with almost acute care, as if he garnered some kernels of information from even the simplest aspects of Hrald's telling.

"His sword?" the King asked, after a long silence.

"It has been destroyed."

Ælfred would ask no more on this; for a victor to destroy a sword of such renown and undoubted value spoke its own tale. He moved on to another remembered aspect of the account.

"Raedwulf said his sons had survived."

"They were but boys."

"Just so." Ælfred's eyes dropped a moment, but his sigh was audible. "And one of them, my godson."

He looked up to Hrald.

"We will hope that Frankland provides them with safe and sure harbour, and that they walk the path of righteousness."

Ælfred now turned back to the table. He took up the sheathed sword in both hands, and extended it before him to his guest.

"Your act of skill and courage has rid a scourge from every Kingdom Haesten touched. From myself and Wessex I present you with this sword, Jarl Hrald."

Hrald had no reason to expect such a reward, but accepted it in the manner it was presented. He bowed his head again. The scabbard itself was a work of considerable labour, its dark brown face crafted by one whose skill in leather work revealed itself through the intricate carving, stamping, and stitching affixed to the wooden backing. The grip of the weapon was of brown swirled horn, the guard and pommel of blued steel.

Ælfred gestured that Hrald free the blade. Permission to draw a weapon must always be granted when before a King, and Ælfred did so now.

Hrald held the fleece-lined scabbard by its mouth and pulled the sword out. Everything about the blade spoke to its quality. The steel, with its central fuller running the length of it, had been freshly polished. It emerged in his hand akin to a living thing, a glimmering water snake. It had been hammered of more layers of iron than any sword Hrald had ever beheld, and carried its rippling movement along its shining length.

"It was owned by my older brother King Æthelred, King before me," Ælfred explained. "It is, as you see, of Danish make, and a fine one. He would be greatly surprised, but glad to know it was now placed into the hands of such a Jarl as yourself."

It was a sword claimed by a King. From whose hand did it fall, Hrald wondered.

Such a rich gift, given by a royal hand, made it easy for Hrald to say the next.

"I will wear it henceforth."

SSSSSSSSSSS

It was Raedwulf's unhappy task to tell his bride that Ælfred had been thwarted in his nuptial plans for Ealhswith. Between the bustle of their arrival in the royal burh, the bailiff's having been called almost straightway to the King, and the requisite settling in, they had scarce a moment alone together. Burginde, Ealhswith, and Cerd would lodge in a separate bower, and as the time to ready themselves for the evening meal neared, Raedwulf found himself at last alone with Ælfwyn in their own.

For this first night at the King's table Ælfwyn had drawn on the rose pink gown she had worn at her recent wedding. Raedwulf dropped a chain of gold, gift of the King, over his head, to rest upon the dark brown of his tunic. Soon they must leave and call for her daughter. He must tell her, yet saw her own distraction.

"There is much on your mind, my love."

Ælfwyn could not, so soon after learning of it herself, share with Raedwulf her son's sudden distress over seeing his first wife here, and especially not when she hoped Hrald would overcome it. To protect both men she hid the source of her concern.

"Only tiredness, from travelling." She smiled at him, and he lifted her hands in his.

"I hesitate to add to it with my news . . ."

She was all alertness, and he went on.

"It was Edwin, Lord of Kilton, who the King had in mind for Ealhswith. We met with him earlier, with an outcome contrary to the King's objective."

Ælfwyn did not need to hear more; she saw at once the near impossible position the young Lord had been placed in. She saw this, yet she herself had been forced to wed Yrling, who had wrought such destruction upon the folk of Cirenceaster. Such things were expected of young women, in the service of peace.

Raedwulf went on, with reassurance. "Ealhswith will not hear of this; there is no reason for her to."

The girl's mother could only nod. To learn of such a rejection, however understandable, would be painful to the girl, who was tender-hearted almost to a fault.

"And Ealhswith still has opportunity to impress both King and potential suitors," he added. "She will be noticed not only by the men here in Witanceaster, but word of her carried to other families."

Ælfwyn gave a hopeful nod at these words. He tucked her arm into his as they prepared to leave.

"It is a great advantage to Ealhswith that she can be seen with her mother, so that any man wishing to wed her takes heart to see that her beauty will only keep unfolding."

This was a pretty speech, which despite Ælfwyn's disappointment about her daughter, and worry about her son, made her smile. It was a smile which earned her a kiss.

Those from Defenas would be joining Hrald at the high table that evening. Raedwulf, in his role as bailiff, had ever sat there, but now at his side would be his wife and stepdaughter. At Raedwulf's direction they entered rather late, when most of the folk were already seated, the better for Ealhswith to be seen. Burginde and Cerd went to a near women's table, where as soon as they had gained the bench, Cerd climbed upon the table with an exultant squeal. Burginde quickly restrained the boy with the distraction of a bread loaf, and pulled him upon her ample lap.

Hrald was already seated, and to reach him the bailiff, Ælfwyn, and her daughter must pass all those seated at the right of the King's oak chair. This was the first time the esteemed bailiff of Defenas appeared with his new Lady, and many noticed the arrival of such a striking couple, and the lovely maid, with her mother's colouring, who trailed behind. Ealhswith, in a pale blue gown, a delicate silver chain and cross about her neck, and a short head-wrap that showed off her flowing pale hair, felt the force of inquiring eyes upon her.

She kept her own eyes demurely down, lifting them only enough to glimpse those seated at the high table as they processed down its length. She saw many clerics, and older men of distinction, perhaps thegns like Raedwulf. But one young man was there, and her eyes fell on his face as he watched their progress. His hair was a dark reddish gold, and his gaze fixed and unmoving. His expression was serious, even stern, but it did not affect his handsomeness. She had seen a few folk at the table nod and smile in welcome; this man regarded her without reaction.

Yet as she sat down between Hrald and the bailiff, Ealhswith whispered into her step-father's ear, as she imagined he might know all who sat there that evening.

"That man in the green tunic . . . is he kin to the King?"

Raedwulf leant forward, turning his head sharply so he might see down the line of those seated. It was Edwin.

The girl went on, in unwitting truth. "I saw him, but he did not seem to see me."

Edwin had in fact seen the girl arriving with the bailiff, and knew her to be she he had been brought to meet.

PRIDE MISSPENT

ARLY the next morning Hrald was walking across the forecourt in front of Ælfred's hall. To its left was a smaller hall, the door of which now opened. A warrior stepped out, followed by two others, who fell into easy position flanking the first. All three were well dressed, and bearing seaxes of worth. The one in the centre had deep coppery hair, and a build familiar to Hrald. The hair was darker, but the face and form close enough to Ceric of Kilton that Hrald stopped in his tracks. The man he looked at paused as well. His two companions, body-guards by their actions, stood at alert.

The Jarl of Four Stones approached.

"I am Hrald."

Edwin looked up. Hrald was as impressively tall as Edwin had heard.

"I am Edwin, Lord of Kilton.

"I cannot wed your sister," was what Edwin said next.

"I did not ask you to," came Hrald's steady answer.

Edwin gave a short laugh.

"My King asked me, and I said no."

Hrald spoke. "It was to make up for the loss of Ashild. When nothing can."

"And I will not, because of your father," Edwin countered.

Hrald keep silent.

"Ceric and Ashild – that was another matter," Edwin went on. "Ashild's father was not your own." It was all he could say on this, without provoking insult.

There was nothing Hrald could add. Ceric had watched Hrald's father kill Godwin, uncle and lord to both brothers. Yet it was Edwin who remained aggrieved.

Both young men, Lords of their respective halls, eyed the other. Yet this exchange, terse as it was, cleared the air for them.

Hrald gave a nod of his head. "Yes. I would not have thought of such a match, myself. I was summoned by Ælfred not knowing who he had in mind for Ealhswith."

Edwin could not help a hollow laugh at their shared expense. "He is the King in the centre of the tæfel board, and we but the game pieces which move about him."

Hrald turned next to what he wished to know. "Your brother – is he with you?"

"He is at Kilton, in command in my absence."

Hrald was heartened to hear he was there, and no longer mad in the woods. Yet it was nothing he could overtly say.

"He has wed," Edwin added. "A maid of Wales, niece to King Elidon of Ceredigion."

This news was startling. Ceric had considered himself wed to Ashild, but if that were so, he was then widowed of her. Hrald's words were nonetheless heartfelt. "I am glad for him. For you all."

A wry smile passed over the Lord of Kilton's face.

Hrald studied that face, similar and yet different from his friend's. He made his request. "I would like to see Ceric."

Edwin considered. "You are half-way to Kilton now. The bailiff has asked me to stay a day or two more. If you like, you can ride back with me."

"I thank you. I will do that."

Later that day Ealhswith again saw the handsome man she had noted at the King's table. He rode through the gate on a big dark bay stallion, with two men flanking him. Ealhswith was walking through the forecourt before the hall, with her mother, stepfather, and Burginde and Cerd. Cerd cried out at the tossing heads and prancing feet of the heated beasts, and reached his arms up toward them.

It was Cerd's yelp of happiness that made Edwin turn his head and see them all, standing there. Raedwulf was foremost, and Edwin could not cut so old and valued a friend to the hall of Kilton as was the bailiff. He shortened his horse's rein and pulled up. Ælfwyn had not seen Edwin last night, but Raedwulf had told her of the episode of her daughter asking after him. The young man she looked up to was surely the brother of Ceric.

Ealhswith saw this not. In the clear light of day she only saw the young man to be even more handsome than she had imagined last night. Her heart was pounding, and she was glad she had donned her gown of light yellow, which she felt suited her almost as well as the blue she had worn last night. Her hands smoothed her skirt as she stood, waiting for her stepfather to address the young man.

Raedwulf lifted his hand to the rider. "Lord Edwin of Kilton, this is my wife, Ælfwyn of Cirenceaster. And her daughter, Ealhswith."

It was what Edwin had hoped to avoid, this meeting. The girl was looking at him, and in her modesty trying not to smile. It only added to his discomfiture.

"Bailiff," Edwin said. "And my Ladies." He spent a moment glancing at Raedwulf's wife, but averted his eyes almost at once after a quick nod to her daughter.

The shrill whinnying of his stallion gave cause for him to excuse himself to the waiting paddock, and with another nod, he and his companions trotted off.

Ealhswith stood there, flanked by her mother and the bailiff. A terrible realisation stole over her. Her face began to contort in hurt. She turned to her mother with tears in her eyes.

"He is the man I was brought to meet. It was him, the brother of Ceric. But he does not want me."

⚜ ⚜ ⚜ ⚜ ⚜ ⚜ ⚜ ⚜

It was only later that Edwin realised the child with Raedwulf was his own nephew. It made him put his hands to his brow. Here was the son of his brother Ceric, and in Edwin's haste to distance himself from the maid Ælfred had selected for him, he had ignored the child.

An oath fell from Edwin's lips. He had no way of knowing when he left Kilton that he would be brought face to face with Ashild's kin. Now he had invited Hrald to return home with him to see Ceric. Would he want to bring his son to him, he wondered. For better or worse Edwin was entangled with these folk, and he felt a surge of resentment that again it was Ceric and his interests which seemed to be foremost.

It was Ælfwyn who sought out Edwin. She sent word that she would like to speak to him of Ceric's son, and would the Lord of Kilton come, before the evening meal, to the bower she and the bailiff were staying in?

Edwin arrived to find bailiff and wife alone. He did not wish to see the girl again, but at least if she were present she could not be a topic of questioning.

He had nothing to fear on that account. The Lady Ælfwyn smiled upon him, and was far more courteous than Edwin knew his earlier conduct warranted. She went straight to the subject of Edwin's brother.

"We have had the happy news that Ceric is returned, and wed."

This was quietly stated, but with a warmth that Edwin must read as sincere. She looked to Raedwulf before she continued. "In future we would like to bring Cerd to Kilton, that he might see his father, and will await his message, bidding us come."

Edwin was forced to admire her; she was speaking of the man who killed her elder daughter.

"I will tell him this."

She smiled, and gave a nod of her head; perhaps, Edwin thought, in dismissal.

He found he must speak.

"Your younger daughter – I am sorry."

He felt his face flame, and regretted it the moment it passed his lips.

But Ælfwyn's smile, gentle and anchored in some distant sadness, only deepened.

"It was not your choice," she affirmed.

Jari sat in the kitchen-yard, off to one side of the active, working area of clay and brick ovens, fire-pits hung with soapstone pots dangling from iron tripods, and the many scarred work tables at which the staff laboured. The cooks of a burh such as Witanceaster must be ready with provender at all hours, and on short notice. The eyes of the Tyr-hand roamed with idle interest over those moving about him. Riders and messengers appeared at odd hours, needing food and drink, and often, their food bags replenished for the return trip. Those who lived within the confines of the burh, and those who were its guests, might grow hungered during the long stretch between the morning breaking of the fast, and the abundant evening supper enjoyed in the hall. Children were always about, and at Witanceaster they were many, begging for buttered bread, small cakes, dried fruits, and nuts. Men and women athirst would stop by, seeking a draught of ale. Bread and cheese and a bowl of oat or barley browis was always offered. Jari, large as he was, was possessed of an appetite second to few. During the three days of their stay at the royal burh he had spent a fair amount of time at these tables, with leisure to watch, and think.

At times some of the men from Four Stones joined him here; it was as good a place as any for dice. He and Hrald had chosen their escort with care. The ten men riding with them were older, wed, and settled, needing little or no oversight. They knew to take no liberties with the serving women of their host. Their stay would not be long enough for them to grow restless; Jari would not need to call for sparring or other training to keep them sharp. Instead, after the long journey south, they were met by a few days of rest, gaming, and wandering the confines of the royal burh.

Jari's eyes lifted beyond the kitchen yard and to a rank of timber buildings beyond, extending without seeming limit to the eye. This place had a different flavour from Turcesig or other large garrisons. It was more akin to Weogornaceastre, where Hrald had wooed and wed the Lady Pega. The King's burh had not as many stone buildings as remained in that Mercian town, but the enclosing stone walls were equally impressive. Walking the perimeter of the walls, both stone and timber palisade, or pacing along the paved streets, so regularly spaced that one might stand where another bisected it and look down a long expanse of buildings in all four directions, was more than ample proof of the burh's wealth and importance. Jari had good memory of his homeland and knew there was nothing in Dane-mark to rival it. The distance he had travelled since he left there felt far greater than the mere measured leagues. Now he was within the doubled walls of Witanceaster, the seat of the mighty Kings of Wessex, whom he and his brothers had come very close to overthrowing.

He was here, a guest of the King who had survived their predation, outwitted and out maneuvered and outspent the war-chiefs of the Danes who had arrived in waves to claim all. Jari had now been welcomed inside that King's hall, handed a deep cup into which mead and ale and wine had been poured, sat upon benches with Ælfred's own men and jested with them. Sidroc rose to his mind, and what he would say if he were now at Jari's side; and he pondered the same of Yrling. The Tyr-hand looked down at the stumps of his first two fingers, and thought of his older brother Une, and of how great would be his disbelief. You died, Une, he told himself, and the man who killed you as well, so that one day I could sit here and drink the King's ale. He thought too of his youngest brother Gunnulf, and of how he would have enjoyed himself here.

Sitting alone upon his bench, grasping his cup, Jari laughed aloud at his musing. "I am getting old, old and thoughtful," he admitted. He touched the hilt of his knife, that daily and silent companion, to bring himself back to the here and now. His sword, like those of all the men, was back in his alcove, safe and waiting for the open road.

Despite the satisfaction, even wonder, he felt, Jari found himself heaving a sigh. The royal burh, however welcoming it had seemed, proved to be full of hazards. Nothing had turned out as hoped. The woman Dagmar was here, and Hrald, against all reason, had gone to speak with her. Then it was learnt that the man the King of Wessex had in mind for Ealhswith refused the girl. Last night Hrald had told Jari they would not return forth-with to Lindisse, but instead head north and west to Kilton, that Hrald might see Ceric. Despite Edwin's rejec-tion of Ealhswith, Hrald had accepted his invitation. Jari understood this; they were separate issues and must not be conflated. It brought the prospect of venturing even deeper across Wessex, in peace and with an escort of their own. Jari had already sent two of their ten men back to Kjeld with this message, that they would be delayed by this visit. He had been grateful for rest, but Jari was now eager to leave the royal burh, and eager to get Hrald away from Dagmar.

When Raedwulf again met with Ælfred, the issue of the Lord of Kilton was the last broached. There was a revision of the old trading treaty between Wessex and Anglia to review, and the thorny question of making any such agreement with a former Kingdom which remained, following Guthrum's death nearly seven years ago, without a King. Ælfred wished to send a gift to Elidon of Ceredigion in recognition of that monarch's niece wedding his godson, Ceric, and wished advice on both this and the bridal gift to be sent directly to Kilton for the couple. And there were points of law and justice to be discussed throughout Wessex. The Lord of each burh throughout the Kingdom held responsibility to uphold and execute Ælfred's laws amongst his own folk, but there were always more difficult cases in which direct appeal to the King was recourse.

When the subject of Edwin of Kilton was taken up, it was Raedwulf who took the part of advocate for the young man.

"His regret is real, my Lord. And he is far from insistent that a union be made with certain known halls of Wessex or Mercia. His openness to consider a widow or foreign bride is gratifying."

Ælfred had kept his own counsel since their meeting with Edwin, and was now pleased, if not surprised, that Raedwulf had proposed this with the young man. The King's thoughts had leapt onward on this topic, across the tempestuous channel of water beyond which lay Frankland. His own father, late in life, had wed a Carolingian princess, Judith of Flanders. But since then all royal unions had been of a more domestic nature. This was a chance to unite Kilton with a foreign power in an advantageous pairing.

The King had a ready proposal. "In your absence this Summer I received a missive from a Count in Frisia. It was carried to me by a merchant I had sent. This Count, Gerolf, has been blest with six daughters, by two wives. In the Church," the King added. "He was widowed of his first.

"The four younger ones are yet unwed. He wishes further alliance with Wessex."

Raedwulf took this in. The King had already made use of his alliances with Frisia, whose skilled seamen had not long past helped Wessex fend off attacks by maraud-ing Danes on the southern coast. Mishaps in this action had been many. Rough weather caused twenty of Ælfred's newly-built fleet to flounder and sink. Several more went aground. Yet together his ships and those of the Frisians rebuffed the Danes, crippling several of their war-ships, and capturing the crews of two, who Ælfred had marched here to Witanceaster to be hanged. The bailiff was there-fore not surprised that a Frisian Count figured in Ælfred's considerations moving forward.

The King paused. "My merchant, Fremund, has seen the girls, and they are comely enough, and will bring with them estimable riches."

Raedwulf gave thought, and then answered. "Such a match will appeal to Edwin, I believe.

"He would like to feel of greater importance to you, my Lord, and to Wessex. He had sought to make alliance with Wales. To make one with such as the Count of Frisia would be, I think, most appealing to the young Lord of Kilton."

"Then we will present this," Ælfred agreed. "He must return to Kilton now, but there is still fair weather for sailing ahead. If he is amenable, I will send a courier to Gerolf and tell him to await the Lord of Kilton. He can take ship at Swanawic and be there in little more than a week."

"As you wish, my Lord."

Ealhswith was not easily consoled. Though Edwin of Kilton had not so much as uttered a single word to the girl, his refusal cut her as if he had broken troth. "Or I am not pretty enough," she cried to her mother. "If I were, I would overcome his objections."

Ælfwyn addressed her daughter's pain with patient loving kindness. Foremost was her hope that Ealhswith be granted a marriage issuing from mutual interest and affection, not just one dictated by the demands, imagined or otherwise, of affairs of state. "I would see you wed as I am now, and not to fulfil some desired end," her mother stressed, holding both of Ealhswith's hands in her own.

Burginde, watching this, and having fallen asleep to the fitful weeping of the girl, went to fetch Hrald. She found him in the stable yard, leaning against the paddock rail, staring at his bay, lost in thought.

"Your sister be needing you, Master Hrald. Her little heart is like to break, or so she thinks. `Tis a time only a man can help."

This spurred Hrald. Burginde, as she hurried by his side to keep up, was prompted by the grimness of his face to append an admonition.

"Only promise me no blood will flow. For the sake of Ashild you must not harm the pup's uncle."

Hrald could have laughed. The two sisters could not be more different. If Ashild were alive she would have understood that it was Sidroc being spurned, not Ealhswith. Hrald no more wanted to come to blows with Edwin than he wanted Ealhswith to mourn the loss of a union ill-considered from the start.

When they entered the bower Ealhswith was seated on the edge of a box bed, their mother's arm about her. The girl leapt up and ran to Hrald and hugged him. As soon as his arms were about her she began to cry. She kept her face pressed against his tunic, but her words tumbled forth. "Did you choose him, as well? Edwin?"

He shook his head, and gently held her away from him so they could see each other. "I knew nothing of it. The letter I received from the King asked only that I come, on the matter of your future."

"Mother says it is because of Sidroc." Ealhswith did not use the term father here; indeed she scarcely knew the man.

"Yes."

"Lord Edwin must have been against Ceric and Ashild, in that case."

"That I do not know. At any rate, Ceric has the right to wed who he wishes."

"But Edwin did not want me, for that reason."

"Yes. None other than that. And I leave tomorrow with Edwin, that I may go to Kilton, and Ceric. But Ælfred asks that you stay, that he may know you more, and that others may see you. This is high honour. Do not forget that."

The girl brightened at this; she had to, at such a reminder of esteem. It emboldened her to say the next.

"And . . . If you find someone you think I should wed, of course I will do so. If he wants me."

Hrald nodded.

It left Ealhswith free to tell herself: Let me marry to make you proud, Hrald, or I should bury myself in a nunnery – in Oundle, just as Ashild is buried there.

Ealhswith, hot-faced and dishevelled, betook herself to the bathing shed shortly after this. On the women's side she was offered a basin in which to wash face and hands, a deeper one for the hair, or a wooden tub in which to fully bathe. As Ealhswith straightened up from bending over her basin, face and hands streaming, she saw a familiar face across the room, near to the cauldron kept bubbling for hot water. It was Dagmar, fully dressed, but combing out her long damp hair. Ealhswith spluttered out her name. She reached for her towel; some of the soft soap had run into her eyes, and she must splash them again. When she looked up a second time she saw only the skirt of Dagmar's blue dress as she swept through the door.

It took no effort to find a serving woman and ask where lodged Dagmar. A few moments later Ealhswith stood outside the door of a small house, fast against the timber palisade, as if room had just been made for it. She tapped upon the door, then leant in and called softly.

"Dagmar! It is me, Ealhswith."

The door opened. There stood Dagmar, tall, as majestic as Ealhswith always recalled her. The comb was still in Dagmar's hand, and her brown hair not yet dried. Ealhswith gave a squeal of gladness, and at once placed her arms about her former sister-in-law.

All Dagmar could do was usher the girl within. She set down her comb, and closed the door behind them. Ealhswith stood, beaming at her with glistening eyes.

"Hrald is here as well. I will not tell him I saw you, unless you would like me to."

Dagmar shook her head. She gestured they sit; there was a tiny table with two chairs.

"How are you here?" Ealhswith asked. "And with the King!"

Dagmar's mouth felt dry. She answered as simply as she could; anything more would be beyond her.

"I am – a widow. I left Dane-mark, and travelled with some of Witanceaster's nuns to here. Ælfred and his wife sheltered me, a generous act." She paused a moment trying to sum up all that had occurred. "And so I remain."

The girl accepted this without further questioning. She turned to that she thought Dagmar would be glad to hear.

"Hrald is married. Her name is Pega. She is of Mercia, the ward of Lady Æthelflaed. She brought him much gold."

"I am sure they know happiness," Dagmar murmured.

"I think so. The day Ælfgiva, their daughter was born, he gave her a golden ring."

A moment passed before Dagmar spoke. "One of twisted metal?"

"Yes," came the answer. Ealhswith smiled as if she were surprised Dagmar had guessed this. "He put it on her finger, and she has worn it henceforth." The girl looked down into the hands in her lap before saying more. It gave Dagmar a moment to fight for her own composure.

The girl went on, in full memory of what she had witnessed. "How he grieved for you, Dagmar. His pain was terrible to watch. Ashild – " she stopped.

"I know your sister is at Oundle," Dagmar said.

"Yes." Tears had fully sprung into the girl's eyes. "I think she will become as famed as Judith, slayer of Holofernes."

Dagmar gave a nod. "It is a fitting tribute to her courage."

"Courage is what I lack," Ealhswith declared. "I was brought here to meet a man. The Lord of Kilton. His name is Edwin. As it turns out, he does not want me. They say he refused me before he ever saw me, because of my father." Again, her eyes dropped to her lap. "Now I am to remain some days, so other men might see me."

Dagmar drew a slow inhalation of breath. She considered she who sat before her, a girl somehow even more tender than her years might indicate.

"Ealhswith, you are young. And so lovely. You have the King's favour. You will find a match as good – perhaps better."

The girl's response was slower this time, and far more thoughtful. "Thank you.

"But I saw him, Dagmar."

Ealhswith's voice was catching in her throat, and the tears she had been blinking back now escaped her eyes, and rolled across her rounded cheek. She lifted a hand to brush them away.

"I saw Edwin. And I – liked him."

Such pain was in these last words that Dagmar gave a squeeze to the girl's hand.

"I liked him."

NO OTHER MAN

THIS would be Hrald's last night in Ælfred's hall. On the morrow he would ride away with Edwin and their joint escort. He knew Dagmar would once again keep herself from the hall, and resolved he must see her a final time before they parted forever.

He went to the King's stable. His own bay stallion was being kept there, and he had glimpsed the boy Ultan who had summoned him to meet Dagmar. Now he walked to the broad doors and stepped into the darkness within.

A man was at work at the table there, affixing a new buckle to a bridle. He glanced up and nodded at Hrald, awaiting orders. Hrald did not call for his horse.

"The boy Ultan – I will speak to him," he said.

A moment later the boy was at his side, blinking in the bright Sun.

"I would see the daughter of Guthrum. Ask her when, and where." Hrald opened the pouch at his belt and gave the boy a whole silver coin.

The child gaped, then bobbed his head and was off. Hrald went to stand at the paddock rail, waiting. He heard the boy's footfall behind him. Ultan came up, out of breath from running, but gulping to keep his voice low.

"The Lady's house is the little one, nearest the north
tower, against the wall. She will expect you there when
the King retires."

At the end of the night. All would be dark, and most
heavy from drink and ready to sleep. Hrald gave the boy a
nod of additional thanks, and turned away.

That night Hrald entered the royal hall with Ealhswith
at his side. They walked together, their mother and the
bailiff following. Hrald wished all to see this lithe yellow-
haired maid was his sister, that they would know a generous share of the treasure of Four Stones would accom-
pany the girl to her new home. Ealhswith felt herself
swelling with pride. She held her head high, and though
she kept her eyes demurely cast downwards, saw enough
to know that others remarked at her entrance at the side
of so powerful a Jarl. Only when she neared where Edwin
sat did she raise her eyes. She looked at him, as piercing
a glance as she could beckon. His own eyes widened, and
then he gave, she thought, the slightest of nods to her, an
inclination of his chin in acknowledgment.

It made her heart race. He had seen her, been forced
to see her. She could no longer be dismissed without a
glance; he had given her at least that.

Hrald ate and drank, spoke to the bailiff, his mother,
and sister. He did so aware only of the passage of time.
Salvers and platters came and went, his cup was filled
and refilled, two men and two women came forth with
cymbals and drums and sang. At last the King rose, his
Lady at his side. His mother and Raedwulf rose, along
with many others of the guests. Hrald kissed his mother
and told her he would see them in the morning before he
rode. Her final words were whispered near his ear.

"I know Pega prays for your safety, every night. As do I."

Hrald was unaware of any eyes upon him as he walked from the hall. Jari and several of his men were absorbed playing counters, and throwing dice. Hrald moved as if directed, out into a cool and cloudy night. He had earlier marked the north tower, seen the small house in which Dagmar dwelt. The noise of the hall tailed off as he moved further from it, and as he pressed deeper into the burh he saw fewer and fewer folk.

The torch lights in their iron baskets flared over his head, beating back the dark, casting him in small pools of light as he passed them. There was Dagmar's house, ahead. He would stand in her doorway, wish her well, and then part.

As he neared he saw the shutters were closed, but a thin line of light at their edges showed that tapers or cressets burned within. He stopped before the door.

Dagmar had to have been just within, listening for him, for she opened before he could lay hand on the planked wood. She stood at the door edge, the light behind her illuminating her hair and form. In the low light her face was pale, the dark eyebrows all the more distinctive.

Her lips began to move, but no sound followed. She stepped back, and into the small house. He must follow her in; the light from her door would attract the attention of any passing.

Hrald entered a room, spare but well furnished. A round firepit, cold now in the warmth of Summer, sat in

the middle. Near it stood a small table with two cushioned chairs, set with two lit oil cressets. Also upon the
table sat a beaker holding some form of drink, and two
bronze cups. Against one wall was the bed, built into a
deep alcove. The alcove curtain was drawn back, revealing a featherbed neatly dressed with cushions and pillows. A low shelf was in the alcove, with a single taper,
the light of which flickered against the snowy linen of the
bedclothes. Dagmar remained standing, near the table.

They both were silent for a long moment.

"How is all with Ealhswith," she finally asked. She
had no way of knowing if the girl had in fact told him of
seeing her.

He gave a shake of his head. "She was brought here to
meet Edwin, the younger brother of my friend Ceric, and
Edwin is Lord. But Edwin does not want her."

Not want her. Dagmar knew this, yet these words,
softly spoken as they were, echoed in her ears.

"Nonetheless, I want to see Ceric, and will travel
with Edwin to Kilton. We leave on the morrow." A further
moment went by, one in which he fixed Dagmar with his
eyes.

"When I leave Ceric I will head east, back to Anglia."
It was said evenly, and with firm decision. Hrald would
not be turning his stallion's head south, to Witanceaster.

Then this was it; their fare-well. She could do nothing but offer a mute nod of her head.

He went on. "My mother and sister may remain a few
more days."

Dagmar lowered her chin. "I shall keep well away
from the hall. There is no pressing reason for me to go
there." She lifted her face. "You need fear nothing."

"My mother knows you are here. I told her."

Dagmar had always known of their closeness, and could not be surprised. Still, she asked the next almost unwilling to hear the answer.

"What . . . did she say?"

Hrald must repeat the truth of his mother's warning. "That no good could come of it."

Dagmar tipped back her head, as a low gasp escaped her lips. "Yes," she offered, in admission. "No good has ever come from me."

Hrald closed his eyes against this. She would never know the joy he had found in her.

There was one thing he found he must ask before they parted.

"Were you happy with him?"

She gave a sharp exclamation of pain. "No. I tried to be, but I could not." She slowed her words. "He was so angry. And he was – not you."

Hrald's exhalation of breath was his only response. The silence went on until she broke it, with a shake of her head.

"I am a poor hostess," she admitted, in attempt to move on from what she had just said. "I have wine. Will you take a cup, that we may toast the past?"

She waited, watching his face, for a sign of assent before reaching for the beaker. He gave it by taking a step nearer the table.

The bronze cups were placed between the cressets, and Hrald saw the golden liquid as it fell from the beaker's mouth. She handed him a cup, then took up her own.

Their eyes met, and both lifted their cups in a small gesture. She took a sip, and he a swallow. They remained standing, holding the bronze cups, looking at each other.

"Will you sit," she offered, inclining her head to the table and its cushioned chairs. He saw that she had done the thread-work on the covers, it was near to a design with which she had embellished a tunic of his. He had laid aside that tunic, and not worn it since their parting.

"I will leave soon," he said in refusal. "I have an early start."

She nodded in acquiescence, but herself sat, as if she could barely keep her feet.

Hrald took another swallow of wine, and she too lifted her cup. The contents were of rare savour, but then, he was in a King's burh.

Dagmar looked up at him, standing there in the thrown light, cup in hand.

Hrald's impassioned declaration that he would never have cast her off had not ceased sounding in her head. She had used the faultiness of her womb as her own shield, certain he would have been forced to sunder their marriage when that was proved. His anguished claim that they would have found a child, made a family to over-come her barrenness gave the lie to this.

For all his steely coolness before her now, it was that voice, that face, from two nights ago, that she had clung to. They were together once more, sharing drink, as they had so many times in the treasure room. His near pres-ence now summoned every one of those nights, both memory and emotion.

He would not even sit down with her; soon he would walk out of that door and her life. But his insistence that they could have overcome all obstacles felt a goad in her side. Even young Ealhswith's telling her how much he had suffered at their parting urged her on. She must learn while she could if there was still hope for some kind of life with him, a shred of happiness, a single vein to nourish and sustain her.

She must try; she had nothing to lose, and perhaps everything she yearned for to gain. He might leave in disgust, but there was nothing more she could forfeit; she had lost all.

Dagmar looked as though she might speak, but Hrald asked of her a question. He could refrain no longer, since she had uttered those words at their first meeting.

"You said you loved me."

He knew it to be a fatal question. He knew it would lead to greater pain in future. But in order to absolve the past he must hear it again.

Dagmar lifted her face and answered. "I do love you. Yes."

He stared at her. It had been terrible to hear the other night. Yet if this knowledge were a cruel and slow poison, there was also sweetest balm mixed with it. Nothing could temper the single and profound sensation of being again in Dagmar's presence. To look on her was to again feel the connection, talon-like, anchoring him to her.

The movement of his face allowed her to rise. She took a step nearer, and spoke.

"I could come to Four Stones, and live as your woman," she whispered.

As a thought it had come, unbidden; but she gave it voice. It needed as well, a form; she saw it must be outside the place proper. She went on, in a near-urgent whisper.

"I know it could not be near, not even at the valley of horses. But all that forest ground between Four Stones and Oundle . . ."

Hrald had not so much as touched her hand, and she was speaking thus. It made him squeeze his eyes shut. "That is land I have given to Pega."

Dagmar saw the mistake this was, the insult to both Hrald and his wife.

If Hrald adhered to the ways of the Danes, she would be content to become his second wife, or even his third, so glad would she be to be brought again within his sphere. But his was a different world, with different mores, and she had not been up to those he followed. Still, he listened, and she was not able to stay her words.

"What would be the harm," she asked, "if I were near, and you could come and see me, at times?"

"The harm? It could be untold, for both of us."

"Not to me, Hrald. Not to me," she pleaded.

He began again. "The harm would be to my soul. And my heart. It would become cloven, split in two."

"Is it not thus, already?"

Hrald made a sound, low, struggling, as he tried to refute this claim.

Dagmar saw his pained struggle, and felt her own the sharper. She must not debase herself, yet her lonely desperation was real.

"I could live anywhere. Anywhere you grant me. I will cost you nothing. I will build a house. I can live modestly. I have been forced to, much of my life. I will never venture to Four Stones."

"No – no."

"Haward – he is my cousin. He will grant me land. I will build a house there." She seized upon this hope. "You have rightful dealings with him, giving you cause to come to see me without suspicion . . .

"As I am barren, you would have no fear of conflicts with your wife's children."

She meant it, meant it all. Hrald saw she had been left as devastated as he had been. But now he felt fear as well, the fear of her desire, and even stronger, his fear of the desire rising in him for her. He was at an utter loss.

He could bar her from returning to any part of his own lands, but not keep her from returning to Haward's, where they had met.

"You must not do that, Dagmar," he said. He was scolding her, and himself. He would tell her why.

"I never stopped loving you. Even when I tried to hate you.

"I am wed. I will not utter her name again in your presence. I am not worthy of it, while having the thoughts I am having. I will never see you again in this life."

Yes, I know, Dagmar said to herself. Nor shall we see the other in the next. You shall go to the Christian Heaven, and I will go either to the realm of the Goddess Hel, or the Christian Hell itself. But now I will go knowing you love me still.

Though her eyes were wet with gathering tears, a smile began to form upon her lips. Her answer was tragic in its recklessness.

"I have tried to rebuild my life as a respectable widow. Now I am utterly lost and damned. And I do not care. All I care is that you still love me – that you are mine as I am yours.

"God is merciful," she went on. "Loki, the Trickster, is not. And it is he who seems to sit upon my shoulder. Our meeting has caused you yet more pain. Forgive me. Again."

She used the back of her hand to brush away a tear rolling down her cheek.

It was time he must go; past time. He drank the final swallow of wine from his cup, and set it down.

"You asked for a single kiss, one of Peace," he said, stepping toward her. "After that we will part."

Hrald moved to her. He dare not place his arms about her, but she moved in against his chest nonetheless. He lowered his lips to hers. It was as chaste and as gentle as such a kiss should be. But their lips lingered an instant, and the firmer pressure of Hrald's increased against hers. Her own responded.

He was first to pull back.

"I will go now," he told her.

"Yes," she answered, barely able to form the word. Her eyes brimmed with tears, and the smile she had forced to her lips was one that revealed her pain. "Please go. Quickly."

Hrald gave a single nod of his head, turned to the door, and let himself out into the night. He felt as if on fire. His step was not quick enough to keep him from hearing Dagmar's deep intake of breath, followed by a low and raw sob of desolation.

Hrald stopped. She had not latched her door behind him, and the light within shone along the edge of the jamb. He pushed it open. Dagmar was on the floor, on her knees, her face in her hands. Her shoulders shook with the force of her grief.

His arms were around her in a moment, lifting her, pulling her to him.

No shared night could surpass this one. Hrald knew it. The heated, rippling anticipation of pursuing and then wedding Dagmar, his delight in her during their half year together, the depths he had been cast into at her loss – all was now melded into the rapture of her recovery. It was both recovery and discovery, for now she had revealed herself, and her love for him, wholly and without guard or reservation. She told him, in almost endless torrent, that she loved him, words uttered to him as he lifted her from the floor, and kissed away the tears from her eyes. Only when his mouth covered hers did she stop repeating these words he had most longed to hear. In the long and word-less silence of their coupling her eyes spoke it, her hands spoke it, just as his did to her. Each remembered action of their past love-making was expressed anew, more potent and powerful than even memory had served. But it was knowing her heart was his which returned him to a sense of wholeness, or rather, took him to a before unglimpsed pinnacle of completeness. It felt a supreme expression of his love and desire for her, one now at last met and returned by the only woman he had fully given himself to.

Dagmar thought her heart would burst. There would be no sweeter sensation, no richer awareness, none with more depth or import than that she now possessed in the arms of Hrald. For the first time in her life Dagmar felt herself completely free, unburdened, and entirely honest. She gave of her body and her heart without dissembling, knowing deep peace in his arms.

At last they slept, their bodies echoing the other's as if they had not passed a single night apart.

Near dawn they stirred. The night was exquisite in its first half, and for Hrald deeply troubled in the second.

His life of living a lie had begun; he had crossed that line. He had chosen duplicity and deceit. Even if he never saw Dagmar again this stain would be upon his soul, and be carried by his conscience.

Dagmar was still in his arms, but she too was now awake. She felt a kind of retreat in Hrald's body. His eyes were closed, but she knew he did not sleep. She whispered her question to him.

"Do you regret it?"

In answer he turned his head.

"I do not," she affirmed in a soft voice. "Never will I regret this. Only if it brings you harm, could I.

"For me, I know that you love me, and always have. And you know I love you, and always will. And I know there is much sweetness ahead of us."

Hrald did not answer. The sting of his conscience was already smarting. Here, in Dagmar's bed he found again that transporting elation he knew to be theirs alone. And he had pledged to another, and had a child.

He thought of Pega, and of how, on their first and only meeting in which they would decide if they would wed, she had told Hrald she was a woman formed for one man, only. He had thought himself formed for one woman, Dagmar. It had taken immense pain and great effort to move beyond that, and allow himself to welcome another into his life.

Hrald turned over, so that he supported himself on his forearms, and looked at Dagmar. Her hair, loose and dark and richly abundant, fell cascading over her shoulders. She had never looked as beautiful to his eyes as she did at this moment. His next words were difficult for him to say, but far less than they were for her to hear.

"You have begged pardon for harms done me. Now I must do the same, to you."

It was a death-knell to her hopes. He felt regret, or shame, or both for his feelings, and perhaps scorn for their act.

Dagmar, sovereign and whole at last, answered with quiet courage.

"Fate has treated us cruelly. Must we do the same to each other?"

He had no answer, not in words. But there was no hiding the water which had formed in his eyes. He stood, began to gather his clothing which he had pulled off in such heat.

As he buckled on his knife belt he spoke.

"You must wed, Dagmar."

These were the most brutal words he had ever uttered. They felt a deep injury to he who spoke them, lash-like, and she to whom they were directed. He wanted to add, "Go to Paris and wed," but after what they had just shared, could not further wound either of them.

Dagmar looked at him. "There is no other man for me, Hrald."

She gave her head a gentle shake. Her voice, still calm and low, made claim. "I will remain here, in Witanceaster, under the King's protection. I will live under his protection, or under yours. No other man."

Hrald fastened the toggles of his boots. He straightened up. His wrong was trebled: Dagmar, the innocent Pega, and his own soul. He could only speak of the first. "Again, I ask your pardon."

Somehow, she could smile. "I cannot grant pardon for a gift so great."

It was too hard to hear; he turned away from her. She went on, looking at his back, that remembered form she had so missed. She had final words for him, a promise for them both.

"Know this. I will remain here until you call for me, or come yourself."

The last of your voice, thought Hrald. As he stood there, his hand on the latch, that low tone filled him.

Hrald opened the door and stepped out into the dawn. It mattered not how many leagues he rode today, nothing could distance him from the woman he now walked away from. And nothing could undo what he had done.

He moved fitfully forward. All was still cast in the gray grasp of a new day. Across from him a figure jolted awake, one who had been seated upon the ground, slumped against a building. The man lumbered to his feet, and moved out of the gloom to meet him. Jari. The Tyr-hand said nothing, just fell into step with Hrald. But the older man's arm rose, and his hand rested a moment on Hrald's shoulder.

AT MY SIDE NOW

Kilton

THE combined party leaving Witanceaster moved off in near silence. Edwin, as ever, was flanked by his two chief body-guards, Alwin and Wystan. He had brought only five additional men beyond them, and three packhorses. Edwin's captain, Alwin, rode with a golden dragon banner springing from his saddle, a smaller echo of the many war-flags dotting the royal burh. Hrald, having come a far longer distance, and through more unsettled terrain, had Jari, the remaining eight members of his guard, and their five horses for pack.

Edwin was eager to depart the royal burh, and Hrald felt compelled to leave as quickly as they might. His parting with his family was as brief as he could make it. Yet it took Ælfwyn but a single long look at her son's troubled face to know the truth. Raedwulf, with his own skills of observation, scanned the face of his wife, and then Hrald's. He had no knowledge that Hrald and Dagmar had spotted each other, for Ælfwyn would betray neither, even though her silence on the matter denied her the comfort confiding in him would bring. The bailiff was thus more than aware of Hrald's unease, though not its root. Only Hrald's little sister Ealhswith, concerned with her own immediate future, seemed not to notice his distraction. The awkwardness of her brother riding off with the Lord who had refused her was foremost in her thoughts. She did not want Hrald to fight over it, but she wondered if he took Edwin's refusal as the insult she felt it to be. Yet Edwin had nodded at her, had he not? Her effusive parting words, and embrace of her brother, stemmed from this half-hope, half-fear, that Hrald would somehow punish Edwin for it.

Hrald's near final words were directed to all, but meant for his mother. He need repeat to her what he had told Dagmar.

"When I leave Ceric, I will head straight for Four Stones."

Last was Hrald's fare-well to Cerd. The boy, having been parted from his uncle for three months, now understood another parting was at hand. His small face, always open and laughing, began to change, his eyes shifting as if he foresaw the coming loss. He screwed up those eyes and began to bawl. Burginde picked him up, bouncing him in her arms as Hrald pulled himself up into his saddle.

Out they trotted, Edwin and his men in the lead, heading north. As the troop placed distance between them and the walls of the burh, their strict formation eased. The ranks and files of the horsemen loosened enough so that men from each camp fell into talking to each other as they rode, side by side. The day wore on. Following a break in which they watered their horses, and availed themselves of bread and cheese from their saddle bags, Hrald found himself riding in tandem with Edwin.

Edwin felt he must say something about all they had left behind. Hrald was brooding on it, he felt sure.

"Your sister," Edwin began. "She is quite pretty. And many will want alliance with you, and Anglia."

It was as much as he could say.

"There will be another for her," Hrald agreed. "Ælfred and Raedwulf will make sure of that."

This now behind them, the men again fell into silence, but one with more ease. The new landscape afforded Hrald needed distraction from the dark recess where his own thoughts dwelt.

He countered with a reference to Edwin's own sibling. "Your brother," he said. "Ceric often spoke to me about my coming to Kilton. I never thought it possible, and never so much as after Guthrum died." That event had thrown Anglia into such disarray to render travel for all but urgent matters unlikely.

Edwin thought back. "He was with you, at Four Stones, I remember." Edwin was little more than a boy, but the death of the King of the Danes in Angle-land was of such import it had left firm impress upon him. The safe return of Ceric had been cause for true thanksgiving, which he well recalled.

"It is to be regretted you cannot meet our grandmother, Lady Modwynn," Edwin added, after a pause. He must do the woman, and her memory, justice, and in his next few words hoped to pour oil upon the waters that roiled between himself and this Jarl. "She did all she could to further the union of Ceric and Ashild. I know she looked forward to welcoming her."

Hrald looked down into the dark mane of his bay. There was no reason to tell Edwin that Ashild would never have gone to Kilton.

Edwin went on. "Your Lady-mother would like to bring the boy to Kilton, and said she would await Ceric calling for him."

Hrald gave a nod. "I hope they will meet again, soon. When Cerd is older, perhaps Ceric will want him there to stay."

Edwin could not but recall Lord Æthelred's injunction, "You must get the boy." But happily the boy was no longer his to get. Edwin planned to wed soon, and have a son of his own.

This thought made Edwin give a short laugh. "I too await orders. The King and the bailiff are conjuring a woman for me. Perhaps one of Frisia, or Frankland. I am to expect they might call for me to go there, while there is still good sailing this season."

Hrald looked over at him. "I wish you luck in your pursuit." After a moment he added, "I know that sort of mission. My own wife is of Mercia, conjured, as you say, by Ælfred and Raedwulf."

"Of what hall is she?"

"She was the direct ward of the King's daughter, Lady Æthelflaed. She is of an old hall of Mercia. Her name is Pega."

Hrald was now looking straight ahead, and did not see the change in Edwin's countenance. For the young Lord of Kilton to admit that he had glimpsed the Lady in question, but had been refused out of hand by Ælfred's daughter was a bridge too far to cross. Hrald had already won her, and after discarding a woman as desirable as

Guthrum's daughter, as well. It took all of Edwin's restraint not to react, but whether it would have been a howl of insult, or bitter laughter at his luck he could not tell.

Each revelation revealed a twisted path in a labyrinth of chance and calculation. Lady Pega had been placed aside for Hrald. Edwin's own King had done so. Kilton had, for three generations, been the staunchest supporter of the royal house of Æthelwulf, yet this prize had been awarded not to Edwin, but to Four Stones. Edwin knew all matches were strategic. He knew Four Stones had more men than Kilton; Ceric had told him. But he doubted Hrald was richer. And the debt of honour owed to Kilton was first forged between Godwulf and Æthelwulf, with the Lord of Kilton's forgoing any run to the crown for himself, and supporting his friend. A surge of envy for the favour shown by the King, and jealousy for the lost maid of Mercia, surged up within Edwin's breast. He gave a quick and sideways glance at Hrald, sitting so erect in his saddle.

And this man's father had killed his own.

They found water again at the end of the day, a stream winding in and out through rowans and hawthorns. The camp they made lay behind a sheltering knoll, out of view from the road. It was nearly the same place Edwin had camped his final night down, and added to his sense of returning to the familiar. The Danes he escorted were far from their home in Lindisse, but Edwin reminded himself that some of these men were old enough to have ravaged through this part of Wessex before Ælfred and Guthrum struck the Peace of Wedmore. He had to quickly dismiss that dead Danish war-lord from his mind, as his name summoned that of his dark-haired daughter. Save for the hope the King would soon send him to Frisia, Edwin regretted every part of this trip.

It was not cold; the fire they built need do little but cook their browis and shed some light upon them as they sat, propped against their saddles, to spoon it into their mouths. Yet the mood around the campfire was subdued. Edwin, invited by his King, had ridden off from Kilton in confident expectation, and was now returning with hope dashed and a darkened brow. Hrald, quiet by nature, was thoughtful enough that even his most garrulous men noted his silence. For more than a few his pensiveness placed them more fully on their guard. To be within the royal burh of Witanceaster was one thing; they were privileged by the King of Wessex himself. Out in the wilds, far from those sheltering walls, and led by a young Lord who looked a hot-head or worse gave little cause for comfort. Still, they were ten to the Lord of Kilton's eight. This side trip would add at least a fortnight to their absence, and they assumed the seeing of Kilton would be worth it.

In this single day the combined troop had put many leagues between themselves and the flurry of Witanceaster, with many more to come. The skies darkened, and they banked the fire down to coals. As Hrald took to the tent he shared with Jari, even the calling of perching chaffinches in the overhead trees was not enough to quell his thoughts of that royal burh.

The Jarl of Four Stones, spent from lack of sleep and the long day in the saddle, should have at once fallen into a deep slumber. He did not. Jari, tired as well, could not himself find the refuge of needed rest. As they lay there side by side looking up into the oiled peak of the pitched roof tent, Jari had cause to reflect on his own dealings with women.

The Tyr-hand had enjoyed a long and enduring marriage with Inga. She had been his sweetheart when he had sailed with Yrling and Sidroc, and had come over, with her aged mother, in the first shipload of waiting women in Dane-mark. Inga had cried into her apron over Jari's lost fingers, then brightened up, blew her nose, and told him it mattered not a whit. Inga had made him a good wife ever since. She gave him two hearty girls, which he secretly did not regret. Watching his own brother be killed in front of him had been enough. Inga was full-breasted and cheerful of nature, and had been steadfast, hardworking, and as placid as any wise man could ever hope. He had just parted with some silver to bring her a few things from Witanceaster, a small, artfully crafted round copper box and lid, a new pair of shears for her sewing, inlaid with silver wire in the loops for her capable thumb and fingers, and a whole handful of pierced silver beads that she might string herself with those of glass and amber she already owned. She would welcome him home with a smile, make a hot compress for the small of his back which would be aching after so many days spent in the saddle, and hold onto him during the first night in their box bed. He felt himself a lucky man.

Jari had never been torn between two women, never had cause to wish for a second or third wife. Now lying there next to Hrald, a thought came to him, that perhaps at times, the old ways were better.

It was thinking of this, and of Sidroc, that made Jari finally speak into the darkness between them.

"Your father. He would have done the same."

Hrald stiffened. He would not accept this as excuse for his own actions.

"I am not my father, Jari.

"I am bound – or so I thought – by a higher stricture. A line which I have now crossed, and a bond which I have broken."

"You are too hard," Jari grumbled. "It was one night. A single night can lay the ghost of such a woman."

Hrald could not answer. The night just spent with Dagmar ended nothing.

∾∾∾∾∾∾∾∾∾∾∾

They were four days on the road. Two of the nights were spent at farms, where folk were glad to welcome them, and their silver. Edwin, with Alwin at his side, rode first into these farmyards, the golden dragon fluttering behind the captain reassurance that these were not marauders.

The men of Four Stones had ample reason to admire the landscape they rode through. The dense hardwood forests coursing with streams were in themselves impressive. Settlements were few, but each farmstead, in its late Summer abundance, spoke of the richness of the land. Fields of rippling, bearded barley shown golden brown as they rode by, and orchards and vineyards sagged under the weight of ripening fruit.

The night before their arrival at Kilton, Edwin sent Wystan on ahead, to tell of his near arrival, and the tidings that the Jarl of Four Stones was with him. They would ride in by late morning, and Edwin hoped he might spend no more than a few days at Kilton until a messenger came from Witanceaster, bidding him ride for Swanawic and set sail for Frisia.

Hrald was eager to see Ceric, eager for the demands on his attention being with his friend and at Kilton would bring. Every hoof fall of his bay stallion took him farther from the woman who dominated his thoughts. Despite the distance gained he could not keep his mind far from Dagmar, nor the night he had spent with her. What was more, he did not wish to. Recounting it was his only solace. Their reunion had reshaped him, re-formed something within him unseen to any eyes but hers. It felt both gift and bitter forfeit.

To not have seen her was to go to his grave without knowing she had ever loved him. That precious knowledge exacted just as high a price; Dagmar did love him, and they could not be man and wife.

Hrald could not think beyond this; the circle began and ended there.

As they neared Kilton the vast pasturelands appeared first, dotted with black-legged sheep in cream and grey fleece. Beyond the rolling orchards of apples, cherries, pears, and medlars the village began. Hrald saw crofts of trim neatness, the many mounded thatched roofs of houses and animal sheds penned round by wattle fences, behind which preening fowl strutted. A number of crofters had stopped in their work and watched their approach, leaning on hoes, and straightening up from their wash tubs. Ahead the palisade of the place proper rose up. Its broad gates were open, but two men, come to meet them, sat their horses just without the village confines, awaiting their approach. Even from a distance Hrald saw the coppery hair of Ceric, astride the horse he had given him six years ago. A touch of his heels urged Hrald's own animal forward, and a few moments later both men had flung themselves from their mounts.

Their embrace, so briefly shared, was heartfelt. It had been not much more than a year since Ashild's death and their parting at Four Stones, yet both lives had profoundly changed. They had a moment to regard the other, faces marked by struggle, loss, and triumph.

Worr was the second horseman, and as Jari cantered up the two body-guards shared their own greeting. Then Edwin was upon them, and Ceric and Hrald gained their saddles and fell in behind him.

A cluster of folk awaited at the open gates. A woman of solemn nobility stood amongst them; Hrald knew it must be Edgyth, the Lady of Kilton. At her side stood a young maid, brightly attired, and no more than a girl. A third figure was a dark clad priest; Ceric had told Hrald of Dunnere, a cleric of Wales who had served Kilton long decades. As the horsemen neared Lady Edgyth raised her hands in welcome to them, and the troop passed through the gates. The Lady moved forward to embrace Edwin, now off his horse. He need utter no word to tell his mother the trip had not proved fruitful; it was written on his brow.

Ceric stood now before her, and at his side the young man Edgyth had heard much of over the years. Hrald had none of the ungainliness which sometimes paired with extreme height, and in his leanness there was a suppleness of ease and attention, which struck Edgyth almost as much as Ceric's apparent pleasure in his presence.

"How glad we are to welcome you at last, Jarl Hrald," she told him. "May this be but the first of many visits to Kilton."

Hrald had only finished murmuring his thanks when another female claimed his attention. Edgyth now had turned again to Edwin, and Hrald, standing with Ceric, saw the young maid who had been at Lady Edgyth's side as they rode in. She was gowned in crimson, with a filmy veil of pale blue anchored to her hair of light brown; hair that Hrald now saw fell down her back and to her knees.

The girl was smiling at Hrald, beaming, and he could not help his own smile in return. She began walking, in short but rapid steps, right to him. In her excitement to greet him, Hrald thought she was just keeping herself from breaking into a run. She stopped before him, her small mouth open in delight.

"You are the tallest tree in the forest, my Jarl."

Hrald must laugh at her words, her pertness, her wide and shining eyes.

"I am Dwynwen," she added. She let her gaze travel up to the top of his head. "I know that many shelter under your strength. Ceric has told me of Four Stones."

He named was also laughing at his young wife's words. Ceric made the introduction as formal as he might, while smiling at them both.

"Lady Dwynwen of Ceredigion, this is Hrald, Jarl of Four Stones. My friend."

Hrald bowed his head, and Dwynwen gave a deep curtsey, still beaming. The three of them turned to

Edgyth, who gestured all to the open door of the hall, and the welcome ale awaiting.

Basins were presented, that the new arrivals might wash hands and if desired, faces, before partaking; and these were filled with water scented with crushed cost-mary, fresh and bracing to the nose. Bronze and silver cups were brought, and bright ale poured by Edgyth into each cup held forth to the lip of her ewer. As a sign of honour it was Modwynn's glass ewer she held, a distinc-tion not lost upon Edwin and Ceric.

After the taking of ale, Edwin and Lady Edgyth excused themselves. Hrald watched them, with the priest Dunnere, go to the door behind the high table, which Edwin unlocked, and vanish within. The bulk of the men retired to the kitchen yard, where food awaited. Worr, content to see some new spark which seemed to shine within the eyes of Ceric, took himself off to other duties; and Dwynwen, with her ready smile, went out the side door, her blue veil streaming behind her, a serving girl in tow hastening to catch up.

Hrald, now seated alone at the high table with Ceric, looked up and around the nearly empty hall. All pro-claimed wealth, old and noble: the heft of oaken trestles and benches, the high-backed chairs upon which Edwin and Edgyth had sat, the sinuous carvings on rafters and posts, the lofty recesses of the lime-washed walls. Even the very alcoves were curtained with woollens of dense weave and striking hue. Four Stones, though possessing more size, was crude indeed before Kilton.

"I went to the great hall of the Mercian Kings, at Weogornaceastre," Hrald told his friend. "I was there with the Bailiff of Defenas, and had never seen a hall so fine. I asked Raedwulf how it compared to Kilton. It is as he told me. The Mercian hall was larger, but Kilton every bit as grand."

Ceric too looked about, as if with fresh eyes. "Now you have seen Witanceaster, to put us all to shame," he reminded. "Come instead to my own domain," he invited. "If Dwynwen is there we will claim the pavilion in the garden."

As they walked away Hrald thought on this, that Ceric, the elder of the brothers, was not Lord, and it was Edwin with right to both hall and the bulk of the riches within. They walked through the stable yard, and past the kitchen yards and the many store houses there. Ceric pointed out the small church, notable for being built of stone, but they did not enter. The beech hedges surrounding the pleasure garden were ahead, and they ducked within the opening. There at the pavilion sat Dwynwen, bent over a length of fabric upon her lap. Hrald saw the serving maid she had at her side when they rode in holding one end of it. Ceric nodded his head at this, and they doubled back, without disturbing her. They stopped before a round bower house. Ceric waved down a passing serving woman and asked for food and drink, and after he unlocked the door, the two men stepped inside. Ceric left the door open to the warmth of the day, and the sunlight which streamed in.

The bower was remarkable for two things. First was the dragon bed which so dominated it. Hrald must let out a low whistle upon seeing it, and found himself moving the nearer to view the four posts which rose at each corner, crowned with the carved heads of dragons. From each gaping mouth a spiked tongue of painted wood shot forth, in suggestion of fire. It was as a bed magnificent, but he knew some might question if a peaceful night of rest could be granted beneath the bulging eyes and fearsome visage of the beasts.

Hanging from a peg on the wall next the bed was the second thing Hrald's eyes fastened upon. It was Ceric's gold-enriched sword. He wore the seax he had always worn, that which had become known as the seax of Merewala of Four Stones, and an estimable blade it was. But the sword had no equal.

Ceric saw Hrald regarding it, and remembered something.

"Not long ago I walked in, and Dwynwen was wearing it. Or trying to."

Ceric was smiling as he recounted this, and it made Hrald give a laugh as well, so unexpected an action was it. He could not imagine Pega ever doing such a thing. Even Ashild had never belted on a sword, not even in play.

Mention of this gave Hrald an opening to speak of Dwynwen. His eyes had fallen on a few items of feminine nature, including a jewel casket or work-box of rosewood and silver. Several chests, highly decorated and all sporting dragons in iron-work or paint, also suggested they belonged to the Welsh princess.

"Your wife," Hrald began. He could not help the fact that his eyebrows had lifted, naming her thus.

"Yes," said Ceric, though he was still smiling. "Dwynwen." His smile softened into tender thoughtfulness. "My child-wife. She is fourteen."

"Fourteen." Hrald blew out a breath. He shook his head in wonder. "I thought her ten. I thought her some young kin of Lady Edgyth's, or a child in her care."

Ceric nodded, but with more gravity. "Yet she is far older, at the same time. It is the woman she was raised with, her step-mother. Dwynwen calls her a wise-woman."

Now his smile returned, thinking of what Dwynwen had told him. "She promises she will grow."

"And she is of Wales," Hrald went on.

"She is." Ceric glanced up at the bed posts. "Fire-drakes. She is as fond of them as if they were living beasts, doing her bidding."

Hrald's eyes again rested on the painted heads, crested, wild-eyed, each different, each somehow with their own tale to tell. "But – how did you meet?"

Ceric paused. "Edwin carried her from Ceredigion. He went there seeking a wife, on suggestion of Dunnere. But when she arrived here . . ."

He was silent so long Hrald attempted to finish the thought. "You saw her," he offered.

Ceric drew a long and low breath. "She saw me," he countered. "And yes, I saw her."

Several moments passed before Ceric again spoke. "Next day we exchanged vows, in the chantry."

The terseness of this telling was enough; Hrald asked no more. And in fact it was Ceric, eyeing him as they stood there, who made comment.

"Your own sword. It is new to me."

Hrald no longer bore the sword his father had named a good one from the store of Four Stones; one nearly good enough to become Sidroc's own. It was a fine blade Hrald had always worn. Yet even the best forged weapons could be chipped or broken in action.

Hrald looked down at the scabbard at his hip, and what it held.

"A gift from Ælfred."

"The King gave you a sword?"

"Yes. For my killing the Dane Haesten."

Either statement was remarkable; in tandem almost incredible. They were near the table, and hearing these tidings Ceric sank down into one of the chairs there.

"Haesten, dead." Ceric lowered his eyes to the worn table top. The Dane had destroyed so much, disrupted so many lives. Ceric felt a personal grievance against the war-lord, one almost as great as did Hrald. He looked now to his friend. "And you killed him . . ."

Hrald told the tale. After hearing all, Ceric spoke.

"Haesten's sword – where is it?"

Hrald was not surprised Ceric asked the same question Ælfred had. It was the greatest possible trophy from a defeated foe.

"Lying in pieces, at the Place of Offering at Four Stones."

Ceric gave a nod. "A just end."

He gestured with his head that Hrald should show the blade of the King's gift. He did so, pulling it from the sheath and laying the naked steel upon the table. Ceric studied it, the many layers of which seemed to writhe like serpents under the force of the sunlight pouring through the door. "What a blade you have in its stead, and one given by the King."

"He said it was owned by his brother Æthelred, King before him." Hrald considered the blade. "Which Dane dropped it we cannot know."

"It is the gift of a King," Ceric summed. There was a certain fitness in this, that now both their swords were thus.

It led his thoughts on, to ask his friend of Ælfred.

"The King," Ceric began. "Did he look hale?"

Hrald considered. He had been in that monarch's company three times. The first was years ago at Saltfleet, when he had witnessed Ælfred's appeal to his father that he forsake Gotland and return to Four Stones. The second, when he and the King were both guests of the Lord and Lady of Mercia at Weogornaceastre. The last had been this Fate-ful visit to Witanceaster.

"He shows his weariness, now," Hrald must allow. "His is a life, I think, of constant engagement, if not in war, then with his books and laws. But when graver matters are set aside, he will raise a cup heartily enough, and to me at least, has always shown fellowship and good cheer."

Ceric took this in. "My grandmother had concerns for his health, always," he conceded. Indeed, at times the King had suffered so greatly from his bleeding disease that all near enough to know of it feared for him.

"And Wessex will be a changed Kingdom under Eadward," Hrald offered.

Ceric gave a nod, both unable and unwilling to conjecture further.

A shadow appeared in the doorway, two serving women carrying refreshment. It arrived in the form of a jug of ale, oatcakes, and a bowl of apples and pears.

They ate, and drank, but of the former neither with their prior relish.

"You are very spare," Hrald noted, looking at the chiseled planes of his friend's face, and the collar bones so prominent at the opening of his tunic.

"I am eating," Ceric answered, regarding the cores of apple and pear he had left behind. Indeed, Hrald himself had eaten not much more.

After the silence extended many minutes Ceric spoke again.

"I have been mad, Hrald. Did you know this?"

If Ceric could speak of this so openly, Hrald would not dissemble. "The Bailiff of Defenas visited, and told us you had taken to the forest."

Ceric gave a slow nod. "It was the only place I was fit for. I stayed there a year."

Given what the two had shared as boys on Gotland, Hrald must ask the next.

"Was it . . . like Tindr?"

"At times, it was. I remembered him, and us together, with him. But much of the time I was out of my head, living by instinct."

"And it kept you alive," Hrald noted.

Ceric gave a low laugh. "Worr kept me alive. He carried in food, other supplies as well, for all those months."

He paused, remembering how sparingly he partook of all that was offered.

"I built a weir, and began to catch fish. Knowing I could do that – it helped.

"It passed, gradually. Slowly. Then Worr brought a woman to see me. Her name was Begu." He paused, as he tried to find the right words to describe her. "She was a woman the thegns used to visit. She was a widow, and barren. So there was no risk.

"Worr had brought me to her years ago." A smile of remembrance crossed his lips. "After he and I returned from Four Stones."

Hrald was fifteen at the time, and with the clear memory of Ceric telling him that when he returned to Kilton, he would lie with a woman.

"She was more than welcoming," Ceric said. "I began spending more and more nights with her. Then when I knew I would wed Ashild, I broke off with her. I passed her on to Edwin, to keep him from the same trouble I was kept from.

"After I had been in the forest a twelvemonth, Begu asked Worr to bring her to my cave. He left her. I was wandering the greenwood, but I heard her singing when I walked back. Seeing her, hearing what she had to say to me, helped connect me to more than my own misery.

"Worr returned. It was the first time I did not run from him. It was Worr who then told me what really happened when I threw the spear. For all those months I rode the worst night-mare, ever darker. In it Ashild turned, and saw my spear coming toward her. I dreamt it so many times that I believed it. Worr made me see the truth of her death."

Hrald had closed his eyes during this, closed them against the awe-ful vision Ceric had suffered under.

"I left with them, that day; came back to the hall. Begu, a true friend to me, departed Kilton. She had wed a childhood friend in her old village.

"Then Dwynwen came . . ."

Hrald watched his friend's face light at the name. No one deserved happiness more, he thought.

"I am glad for you," Hrald told him. He waited a moment before he said the next. "Ashild . . . she would be gladdened, as well."

Ceric's answer was little more than a murmur. "Lady Edgyth says God sent Dwynwen to me. I think Ashild did."

There was no answer to this supposition, just a quiet moment in which Hrald nodded his head in agreement.

It prompted him to speak.

"I – I am wed, as well. To Lady Pega of Mercia. It was a match made by Ælfred and Raedwulf. But it was the King's daughter, Æthelflaed, who gave her to me."

Hrald told of his travelling to the royal court of Mercia, and of his pursuit and wedding of the maid. The contrast in how the two friends had spent the year could not have been greater.

"We have a daughter, Ælfgiva." Hrald thought again of his wife, and her grave grey eyes.

His marriage, their daughter, these were matters of fact, and Hrald saw the interest with which Ceric heard them. Yet the dryness in his mouth as he reported his news made him take a deep swallow of ale.

"Is that why you were at Witanceaster," Ceric asked, "on behalf of your wife?"

Hrald shook his head. "I was there for the same reason Edwin was called. My little sister, Ealhswith. My mother is now wed to Raedwulf of Defenas, and Ealhswith went with them there."

Ceric recalled the girl, most memorably when he sat with Hrald at the high table of Four Stones, after bringing Ashild home. Ealhswith carried to him a little copper-haired boy, his son with Ashild. But he remembered Ealhswith for herself as well; her slenderness, long yellow hair, and questioning eyes.

Hrald went on. "Ælfred thought that Edwin and she might wed."

Ceric could not hide his startle at this notion. Hrald answered for him.

"It was a plan that pleased no one." He thought a moment, then corrected himself. "No one but Ealhswith. She cried, thinking she was not pretty enough."

Ceric shook his head. "It was perhaps . . . ill-considered. I am sorry that your sister was hurt."

"She will mend. I left her there at the royal burh; my mother and Raedwulf would have had much opportunity to show her off to others seeking a bride."

"And alliance with you," Ceric added.

Hrald just nodded.

"My mother wishes to bring Cerd to you, when you are ready, so that he might know you." Hrald thought of how the boy had grown and changed in the past year. "He is a sturdy fellow, fearless, and loves horses as did Ashild."

Hrald went on, speaking of the boy's mother; Ceric must hear these things. "I will tell you of Oundle," he began. "Women and girls come to Ashild's tomb."

Ceric gave a slight shake of his head at this, wondering at his meaning. Hrald told the simple truth. "They come to make offering . . . and I think, to pray, for themselves, and for Ashild.

"Not only women have done homage. Ælfred sent a nugget of gold in her name, half the size of my fist.

"Noble women have arrived at Oundle, taken off their gems, and passed them into the hands of the prioress or Sigewif herself. Some have, without being seen, draped jewellery on the outstretched arms of the statue of St Mary, then left."

Hrald, looking on his friend's puzzled face, gave a low and solemn laugh. "For Ashild."

"The Abbess Sigewif," Ceric wondered. "What does she think of this?"

"Sigewif has ever compared Ashild to Judith, slayer of Holofernes. She believes the visits to her tomb helpful to those who come, and has written a Life of Ashild, so that she may guide the manner in which she is recalled." Hrald need add one more detail, one not without merit. "Certainly the gems and silver arriving in Ashild's name aid Oundle in its work."

It took Ceric a moment to ask Hrald the next. "Where . . . where is her hammer of Thor?"

It was the silver that led him to turn over her body.

"I have it. Sigewif gave it me, that night. I will give it to Cerd when he is older, and can understand."

"Cerd . . ." His father's voice trailed off.

"You will see him soon," Hrald assured him. "As soon as you call for him. He looks much like you. But he is his mother's son, in temperament."

Ceric was more than aware that Hrald knew and loved this child. Though Hrald was Cerd's uncle, he had served more as father to him. His next words acknowledged this. "He must miss you, now that he is in Defenas."

Hrald could not disavow this fact; the boy had cried at their parting. He downplayed it with another fact. "It is my mother, and Burginde, to whom he is most attached."

Hrald let his eyes lift to where lay the silver and rosewood box. "But such as your young wife will be good company for him."

Ceric also looked to it, and remembered aloud her words to him concerning his son. "She promised to welcome him, when he comes." He must smile at the thought. "And yes, they can grow up together."

⁂

Within the treasure room Edwin could not wait for his mother or Dunnere to be seated before he spoke.

"The maid the King called me to meet. It was none other than Jarl Hrald's young sister, Ealhswith."

Edgyth blinked. Even the priest was open-mouthed.

Edgyth's hand reached for the back of a chair pulled up to the table. This was the match that Ælfred had tried to work? All knew of the girl's parentage, a mother, Ælfwyn of Cirenceaster, wholly honourable, and a father who had slain Godwin, Lord of Kilton. Her husband. She must sit down.

"I begged his indulgence, but told him I could not wed the daughter of the man who had killed my Lord."

How badly Ælfred wants union with Anglia, Edgyth thought. Her blue-veined hand rose to her breast, to rest there a moment.

"The King meant no insult," she said, when she was able to respond. She forced a smile at her son, and reminded him of their guest.

"I have just received Hrald in sincere welcome. The maid is no more guilty of their father's act than he who is Ceric's good friend."

Edwin tried to mask his impatience. "Mother. But to wed the girl – bring her here, under our roof – that I cannot do." He might have said more, broach the topic of fathering children, but his own sense of decency spared his mother from hearing the disgust he would attach to it.

Edgyth looked up to where Edwin stood, a resolute and aggrieved pride marking his young face. He had ridden so far, and with such high hopes. Neither Dunnere nor her own efforts had availed Edwin in his quest for a wife.

Her son's next words opened a new path.

"I spoke openly with the Bailiff of Defenas. The King has good report of the daughters of a Frisian count, Gerolf. I am to expect that a messenger will arrive soon, bidding me ride for Swanawic, and then take ship to the coast of Frisia."

That night Hrald sat at the high table, honoured guest of the hall of Kilton. He had ridden in, at invitation of Edwin, and in keeping with those of high estate, the steward had placed a silver cup for Hrald, next to the Lord of Kilton's own. Thus Hrald sat between the two brothers. Jari was shown to a bench at the table of Ceric's own picked men, the rest of his escort placed at the trestles of the men of the hall. The kitchen yard had been prepared to serve up a welcome feast for their Lord, and though Edwin was returned without cause to celebrate, their labours served in good stead for their guest, the Jarl of Four Stones. Late Summer bounty brought both variety and abundance to the table, and Lady Edgyth made full use of a score of Dwynwen's black peppercorns to flavour a smoking roast of tender young pig flesh surrounded with baked apples, sage leaves, handfuls of green orache gathered from the sandy beaches, and rue.

The talents of Garrulf the scop were brought into full play. Mindful that not one but two Lords of halls of renown were present, Garrulf placed the art of the scop in its rightful place as witness and celebrant of great deeds. His tale that night was of the singer of songs Widsith, and of that scop's wanderings between the halls of ancient heroes of many tribes. The harp resting in Garrulf's lap was of age-dark wood, and its bridge of yellow amber; but it became as a living thing when the strings trembled under his stroking hands. The lay of Widsith and of the war-chiefs he praised was not a story Hrald had heard sung, and he listened with appreciative ears to the aged harpist.

There was a special alcove in the hall, kept for guests of note, one both longer and deeper than was ordinary, but Hrald did not sleep there. Lady Edgyth had a serving man escort him to a bower of his own, one which Dwynwen had used upon her arrival. Hrald was grateful for the solitude it provided, grateful even for the fact that here, under the friendliest of roofs, his old friend Jari could remain behind in the hall. Hrald craved time and quiet as much as he needed the presence of Ceric. After what occurred at Witanceaster Hrald could not have returned forthwith to his home, and he trusted the few days spent in this excursion would provide the distance his knotted feelings needed.

He slept that night, deeply and dreamlessly, worn out by his thoughts and the weary travelling. If a hall such as Kilton itself was an ideal never to be achieved, at least he was once again with Ceric, and for the first time could partake of this aspect of his friend's life, as Ceric had shared in his own at Four Stones.

Early the next morning, before the hall met to break its fast, Hrald sought out Dunnere. Ceric had pointed out the priest's small abode near the stone chantry, and Hrald tapped on the door almost as soon as the cleric had opened the shutters over his windows. Dunnere, accustomed to being roused at all hours to attend to the spiritual needs of the hall and its guests, welcomed Hrald with a nod and opening of his hands. They moved within, the priest shutting the door behind them. Despite the opened windows the room was, at this early hour, still dim. Dunnere struck sharp fire from a flint and steel, let the thrown sparks smoulder in a pan of tin, and wordlessly lit a bronze cresset upon his writing table. He turned to his guest, his own countenance open, mild, and with the patience of his calling upon it. He could guess from the young man's face what he sought. Dunnere crossed himself, and murmured his welcome.

"I am here for you, my son. May the Spirit of the Holy Ghost move you. Speak as you will."

Hrald drew breath. "I would confess a sin, Father," he told him.

Dunnere at once sat upon the bench which served as confessional, and turned his face away from he who stood before him. Hrald knelt down upon the wood planking of the floor, crossed himself, and began.

"I have known a woman not my wife. My lawful wife," he must add, for Hrald had never stopped thinking of Dagmar as his first wife.

This was all he said.

Adultery was a grave sin; Dunnere took time and care in explaining the hurt Hrald had wreaked upon his soul. Even if his sin remained secret, damage had been done to his lawful wife; the avowed bond frayed from his act. Hrald listened with bowed head, and with an expectation he feared would not be fulfilled, regardless of demanded expiation. And in fact, every word from the priest, however sincere, took Hrald further from any consolation.

His was a flawed confession. It must be so, for Hrald was not truly contrite. He regretted his action for the sake of others, but not for himself; never for himself. The doling out of penance, the priest's assurance he was absolved, brought no comfort in the face of this truth.

Hrald regretted the deception, regretted deeply the potential for pain to Pega, any hurt to his own mother, even his baby daughter. But his inability to feel full contrition for his act with Dagmar gave him further misery. As he arose from his knees he felt outside the church as well, denied that comfort of being shriven. Hrald did not regret his night with Dagmar. It would be a lie to claim he did.

The Jarl of Four Stones had four days of rest in the company of Ceric. The two saddled horses and rode out together, along coastal heights and to the edges of woodland. They took long walks through Kilton's orchards, where they might pluck ripe plums from those hanging about them, and eat them out of hand, dripping and sweet. Ceric took Hrald to look over the hall's great flocks of sheep, and herd of spotted cattle, the latter slowly being rebuilt from the murrain which had felled so many. One morning with Dwynwen and Worr they took the small boat and sailed together down the coast. Worr let the two young men handle the craft, while he, in the second with a few of Ceric's thegns, skirted the shore in their wake. Hrald had sailed to and back from Gotland, but in a ship

of many oars. To man the sail while Ceric held the steering-beam in his hand was a new pleasure, one made the
greater by the joyful cries of Dwynwen as she gripped the
gunwales in the prow. They skimmed along the surface of
the blue-green water like a great sea bird, and with nearly
as much freedom.

When they climbed back up to the pleasure garden,
wind-blown and red-cheeked with Sun and air, the three
sat in the pavilion as refreshment was brought. Dwynwen
revealed a wicker basket from beneath the table, and from
it unfurled a length of cream-coloured fabric. She held it
up for them to see her handiwork. It was a flag with two
dragons, worked in coloured yarn upon the light ground.
One scaly beast was of reddish hue, the other yellow-
gold. In their action they seemed to be soaring overhead.
They faced the other, tails coiling, claws extended. Their
jaws were open, but no flames issued forth.

"Fire-drakes at play," Dwynwen told them. Ceric had
seen the flag before, but now it looked near completion.
The webbed wings of the beasts were veined, as the back
of a leaf is veined, making the beating action as they hovered the more real. She was just laying down these veins,
in dark yarn, and considered her work.

"Lady Edgyth helped me with the dragons, though
she said she has yet to see one appear." Dwynwen thought
of the sail snapping behind her on the boat they had just
quitted. "When I finish it I will carry it to the boat, for the
fun of having it flap and wave over our heads."

She looked to their guest. "Ceric and I have dragons.
And you, my Jarl – what does your pennon carry?"

Hrald had in fact no battle-flag in his possession; the
only one he had ever owned now lay folded, stiff with the

blood of Ashild, in a silver casket on the Mary altar at Oundle. Still, he answered.

"A raven is most used by the Danes." He looked again at her two dragons, sporting freely in open air. "But we use a pennon or flag only in war-time."

Dwynwen returned her eyes to her handiwork. "They play, but they are ready with fire if danger nears," she assured them.

Hrald at last determined to tell Ceric of Dagmar. He had thought long and hard of it, reluctant to present a quandary unsolvable, resistant to troubling a friend, who, though now knowing happiness, was recovering still from great sorrow and strain.

Jari knew; yet his body-guard's views were not Hrald's. No one, he thought, could listen with the understanding with which Ceric could receive his news. The day before Hrald had set to leave, he and Ceric descended the stone steps to the beach below the garden. There, sitting athwart the bench in the boat they had sailed together with a laughing Dwynwen, Hrald drew a long breath, and broached the subject.

"There is something I would tell you." He hesitated, questioning his motives, asking himself if he must share these tidings just to hear himself speak aloud of Dagmar. He shook his head at himself in impatience, then went on. "There is in fact no one I can tell, save you."

Ceric looked up at him, alert. If his face clouded with caution it was for his friend's sake, not his own. After what he had lived through he did not think Hrald could shock him with news of any action he had taken. Hrald seemed to read this, for he went on.

"I want no secrets between us – ever. Yet to burden you with it . . ."

Ceric thought of Begu, telling him of holding her husband as he died. "Sorrows shared . . . for the teller they may be lessened, yes. But such also take the hearer out of their own griefs."

Despite these words Ceric felt some unease at what was coming, but managed a smile at his friend.

Hrald took another long breath, and began.

"I was wed, before Pega. Not long after you and Ashild were man and wife, I met a daughter of Guthrum. Her name is Dagmar. I saw her, and knew she must be my wife.

"We had six months together. Then one day I came without warning to the treasure room. She was there with a strange warrior, a Dane, one come as a messenger, who was holding her in his arms. He had been her lover years earlier. He had been outlawed by Guthrum; she thought him dead.

"I cast them both from the hall, though she begged me, in front of him, to forgive her.

"It was a wound so deep I thought I should not recover. Our priest Wilgot expunged her from all records; it was as if Dagmar had never come to Four Stones.

"Yet I must wed again; my mother could not continue doing all. Four Stones must have a mistress to run it. And – I needed a wife.

"It was Ælfred and Raedwulf who stepped in, as I have told you."

Here Hrald must pause, as he repeated the truth of she who was now his lawful wife. "Pega is wholly good. Pure of heart, and kind to all. Devoted to me, the hall, and now our child. Yet – "

He stopped another moment, before going on.

"Just now, in Witanceaster, I found Dagmar there. She had travelled to Dane-mark with the man. He was killed there, along with the King he followed. Dagmar returned here, to Witanceaster, and for memory of her father, or out of Ælfred's own beneficence, was welcomed at his royal hall."

Hrald's voice dropped. "We spent a night together. It was – "

He had no words for it, but Ceric read on his face it had been a source of sublime joy, as well as deep and confused remorse.

"I told Dagmar I will not see her again. She in turn told me she will remain there at Witanceaster, awaiting me, or my call.

"She thinks she could live at her cousin's hall, not far from Four Stones, and that I might visit her there."

His pain, in saying this, was all too apparent, that she he still regarded as his true wife would become such a woman.

Hrald fell silent; there was no more he could say. Ceric asked the one question he felt mattered most.

"If you were not wed, you would take her back?"

Hrald let go a breath. His reply spilled forth, in urgent strength. Behind his exclamation was great pain, which he could not allow to surface. "She would be at my side now. We would return to Four Stones, marry again in the eyes of the Church, and go on with our lives.

"But Pega – and our child. I cannot break with Pega. For reasons of state-craft, and for my own regard for her. And . . . it would truly damn my soul to Hell, to so cruelly injure her."

Ceric gave thought. He would not steer Hrald amiss, but he must repeat what all knew. "Many men have women to whom they turn, in private," he offered.

Ceric himself had had Begu. Yet he had readily surrendered her to make way for Ashild. His friend would have no such clarity in his own dealings.

Hrald had full answer. "Women who they thereby force to live in shame. Themselves as well."

Ceric was ready to counter this. "If Dagmar made offer, I do not think it appeared to her a life of shame. Rather a way to have what she could of your former happiness."

Hrald was forced to nod his head at this. "Would I could do that, Ceric."

"I can subject neither woman to that, nor my own soul. The one night I spent with her was transgression enough." His chin dropped. "I would only want more.

"Pega would learn of it, she must. Just as my own mother already knows. She read it all on my face, the morning after.

"No. It is over, fully over, with Dagmar. It must be. Our night was a gift, a form of un-looked for reparation for us both. But that must be the end of it."

Hrald's efforts to convince himself of this were nothing short of heroic. Ceric, watching his friend's face, gave a grave nod of his own.

"I made confession to your priest," Hrald went on. To come was the worst admission of all. "It was wholly flawed. I do not regret what I did."

He gave a hollow laugh. "There are charms of forgetfulness, runes to be written on the body. My father told me of them. Perhaps they are my only recourse."

FALSE HARVEST

LADY Edgyth sat sewing with Dwynwen in the pavilion of the pleasure garden. Hrald had ridden away that morning, and all were mindful of his going. Edgyth had enjoyed Hrald's company, and was more than grateful for the good his visit had done Ceric. Looking on Dwynwen she recalled the young Jarl's bemused reaction to the girl. Hrald's kindness to her was especially meaningful to Ceric, she knew.

The two were at work at the table, stitching the finishing touches on Dwynwen's dragon flag. Edgyth had proposed a border for it, in yellow and red. "It will both strengthen it, and add to its handsomeness," she promised. Edgyth had cut thin strips of dyed linen in those two shades, and was sewing them on. She sat at the table, while Dwynwen rose to stand at its edge, holding the fabric taut for her. Glancing up at her Edgyth was again struck by the girl's small stature.

"Your birth mother, Dwynwen – are you very much like her?"

Dwynwen's eyes narrowed in thought. "I was so little when she left . . ."

Her brown-flecked blue eyes fell pensive, but the corners of her mouth curled in a smile as she found answer. "In size, I think so. We Cymry are not a big folk, we women certainly not. Not like the folk of Wessex." Her smile widened. "And not like Jarl Hrald!" A remembrance came to her, and she said it aloud. "It is the Faery in us. That is what my mother used to say."

Edgyth smiled, not only to herself, but broadly, to Dwynwen. "Your Faeries must always be of good cheer, in that case, for this is what you have brought to us." Dwynwen gave a delighted laugh at this.

The serving woman Mindred now appeared, with the slave Tegwedd behind her. Mindred had taken the girl in hand, and was teaching her every skill a good serving woman tasked with caring for a Lady need possess, beginning with the care of clothing. Tegwedd, who had scrubbed scorched pots with handfuls of wood ashes in Elidon's kitchen-yards, now was taught by Mindred how to launder Dwynwen's gowns in soft lye soap. She learnt to fold them and press the water from them between boards without wringing, and how to lay them out on a table and ease the wrinkles with a bone smoother before hanging them to dry. Mindred had brought the girl out so both the Lady of Kilton and Lady Dwynwen might see her progress. Tegwedd had begun to speak the tongue of Wessex, but was as yet abashed to do so with any but Mindred. Likewise, the girl stood unmoving as well as mute before her two mistresses. Mindred gave the girl a look, and bobbed her head at her, which made Tegwedd remember to curtsey. She held out part of her morning's labour so both women might see. It was a blue linen gown of Dwynwen's, folded in half lengthwise, and then in thirds.

"Your gown, my Lady," Mindred began. "Washed and shaped by Tegwedd, and ready for wear."

Dwynwen clapped her hands together in approval, but it was Edgyth who examined the hem of the gown, wordlessly teaching her to check for this telling detail of cleanliness. Edgyth too was pleased, which left Tegwedd red-cheeked. The girl clutched the gown tightly to her, risking the smoothing she had spent much effort on.

After the two had left, Edgyth felt moved to speak of the Welsh slave. She had nearly affixed the whole of the red stripe to the dragon flag border, and now run out of thread. Edgyth rose, the better to hold two skeins of similar shade to the clear daylight, to make the choice.

"You might free Tegwedd, Dwynwen," she posed. As a prod it could not have been voiced more gently. Edgyth turned to look at her, to better gauge her response to what she would next say. "She is safe here at Kilton, of course. But a freedwoman has more rights, with more recourse to the law if she is harmed. And – Tegwedd will grow, just as you shall, and may wish to wed. Her children will be free at birth, should you free her now."

Dwynwen looked struck at this idea, but could not help her smile. "I wonder who she will wed," she mused aloud.

Edgyth considered a moment. Tegwedd was as plain as a hay-rick; there was no denying that. Yet every woman could find a husband, if she was skilled, good-tempered, and sound of body. Edgyth, and Dwynwen, could help her to become just that.

The Lady of Kilton made suggestion. "A serving man, one of the crofter's boys, a stable man, perhaps even one of the boys who aid the smiths . . . There are many who would welcome her.

"And remember, Tegwedd is attached to you. It gives her a special – lustre."

Dwynwen seemed to find true delight in this last. "Tegwedd, a gem. I like that."

All of this gave scope to Dwynwen's active mind. "Yes, of course I will free her! I will do so, now.

"What need I do?"

"You must provide the freed with the means to make her own way. Also a weapon, a knife, which she already wears, as she is trustworthy."

Indeed, as Tegwedd carried her own small knife for meals and hand tasks, this was not needed.

"Make her own way . . . Will silver do?"

Edgyth smiled. "Silver always does."

"I will give her a handful."

"A handful is too much," Edgyth cautioned. "Give her – five pieces, and promise her that she will be kept by you, and well kept, until she is ready to leave your service, should she ever wish. Though I doubt she ever will."

The girl looked ready to run after Tegwedd, and Edgyth smiled and stayed her with a raised hand. "Let us get another witness," Edgyth advised. "There must be at least three. Ask Mindred to bring Dunnere as well."

In truth, no one could be more appropriate than he, as he had taken early interest in Tegwedd. Dunnere had asked the slave girl upon their departure from Ceredigion if she were Christian, and in response she had quickly crossed herself. He could now record her manumission in Kilton's archives.

"And Ceric!" Dwynwen proposed. "I have never freed a slave before. I would like him there."

Edgyth agreed. "And I think perhaps Edwin should witness as well. He is after all, Lord of us all here at Kilton."

Dwynwen nodded. "I will find them and bring them."

She went first to the bower, where Ceric sat over the open Boethius. She went to his side and took his hand.

"Do not be mournful Hrald is gone. Good friends are not long parted. And now I need you to witness, for Lady Edgyth has thought it a fine thing if I free Tegwedd."

Ceric was forced to smile. It was just like Dwynwen, to move at once on any task that caught her fancy. Nearly anything novel was of interest to her quick spirit. She had never freed a slave before, thus she would do so the moment Edgyth suggested it. He closed the volume and rose. Dwynwen had flitted off, and was opening one of her chests, fishing about with her hand inside. Finding what she sought, she closed it.

"I must find Edwin. Then we are almost ready."

"Shall I go with you?" Ceric offered, lest she be unsure of approaching him. Edwin had hardly spoken to Dwynwen since she had joined hands with his older brother.

"I brought her from Ceredigion, and I should be the one to ask," she decided. "You keep none as slaves here, so he will be happy," she further reasoned.

"Shall we meet in the garden?" she asked.

Ceric had been present at several such occasions, and spoke from his own remembrance. "Such freeings are traditionally made at a crossroad, so that they who are freed understand they may now go their own way."

Dwynwen clapped her hands. "I like that; what good sense it holds. Where shall we go?"

"There is a kind of crossroad just outside the gate. The main road through the village meets the path circling the palisade. Both are free of the confines of the hall."

"Then we shall meet there," Dwynwen pronounced. "I will bring Edwin, and you gather the others."

Dwynwen readily found Edwin, standing with Alwin at one of the armourer's stalls. She went up to him with a smile, and blurted out her request.

"Please Lord Edwin, will you come outside the gates? I am going to free Tegwedd, my slave, and Lady Edgyth thought that you might be there, as Tegwedd is now of Kilton. As am I."

His presence was not at all required; any who owned one enslaved could enact a binding manumission with three witnesses of any estate. Yet the Welsh girl's shining face showed she thought Kilton's Lord looking on as witness added importance to the act.

Edwin could not refuse. There was no reason for him to demur, and with the girl's unsparing frankness she had likely told either his mother or his brother that she would ask it of him.

Looking down at her he found himself nodding assent. At least she had a sense of fitness about things of small moment; he must credit her that.

They turned from the stall to see Lady Edgyth, Dunnere, Ceric, Mindred, and Tegwedd making for the open palisade gates. They paused in their motion when they saw Dwynwen and Edwin, and all walked out together.

Tegwedd had not been outside the palisade since arriving, and was at once alarmed to find herself so. Having gained the road, her mistress Dwynwen was more than ready. None knew what she was about to say, least of all she most concerned.

She lifted her hands to the girl.

"You are free, Tegwedd," she sang out. She said it twice, first in the tongue of Cymru, and then in that of Wessex.

Tegwedd blinked. Dwynwen turned back to Edgyth, as if she expected some changed state in the girl.

"What more must I do?"

"I think perhaps suggest she should stay on in the role Mindred and I are training her for, to be of help to you."

Dwynwen spoke in rapid Welsh to the girl, whose eyes continued to widen.

Edgyth went on. "Now you might give her the means by which she can make her own way."

Dwynwen took the five coins from the tiny purse at her waist. She handed the girl the silver with becoming gravity. Yet Dwynwen's smile, quick and warm, said even more. Tegwedd's eyes opened the wider, and her mouth gaped as her eyes fell on the coins in her palm.

Dwynwen looked first to Ceric, then to Edwin. "It is silver, that of Cymru. Coins my grand-sire minted, when he was King." She smiled at the brothers. "They are not as pretty as yours."

Edgyth's heart was swelling in her breast. The girl's effortless grace was foremost, always; that, and her dis-arming honesty. No spit-fire she, despite her proclivity for fire-drakes. The Lady of Kilton's thoughts went on, in private reflection, but as clear to her as if she had uttered them aloud: How grateful I am that you have come. You have wrought health and happiness in Ceric; and though you cannot be Lady here, you have brought joy to my own heart.

Dunnere led the party back through the gates and toward his house, where he would register the freeing of Tegwedd so that none could refute it. The brothers fell in together behind them. As they approached the wall, Ceric could not help but think of his bidding fare-well to Hrald just that morning. He looked to Edwin.

"I thank you for welcoming Hrald as you did."

His brother gave a slight shrug. "We met by chance, after I had told the King I would not wed Ealhswith. Hrald told me he wished to see you. Having refused the girl it seemed a slight act to bring him." Their pace had slowed, and Edwin waited a moment before saying the next. "But to wed his full sister – after what their father had done . . ."

Ceric stopped. He looked down the edge of the palisade, its timbers upright, its face stalwart and blank. He took a quiet moment of his own before answering.

"It was a fair fight, Edwin. More than a fair fight. Our uncle was given several chances to withdraw, and leave in peace."

Edwin's answer was akin to a growl. "That Dane stole our mother."

Ceric contested this, and with speed. "She was by then wed to the Dane. She was happy with him, living a contented life, and with two babes granted them. She had a right to remain, and begged Godwin to let her do so."

"You defend her?" Edwin could not allow this affront to pass unremarked. "She cannot be held up as a model of propriety!"

Ceric had strong remembrances of his mother, both here at Kilton and on Gotland; and a strong and adverse memory of his uncle's behaviour when he caught up to her on that island. In fact, the inside of his lip still bore a slight raised scar, from where his uncle's seax hilt had caught him. Ceric could feel it now. He gave of his head a single shake. Edwin had not witnessed the ugliness of that incident, and scarcely knew their uncle. Ceric saw his younger brother still revered Godwin, whereas his own belief in him had been utterly shaken.

As brothers they must collide on this; Ceric knew it. He said what he could.

"You were not there. Hrald and I were. We were forced to watch it all."

Another witnessed, one here at Kilton. Ceric spoke of him now. "Worr was there. Our uncle was in the wrong. Worr must have told you."

Edwin could scarce hold his tongue, yet did. Yes, Worr had been there. And Worr had told him something about their mother Ceric would not believe.

That night, after Edgyth had knelt to say her prayers, she lay abed as she often did, awaiting the wash of sleep to cleanse away the cares of her day. This day had been a good one; Dwynwen's freeing of a simple girl had helped balance the loss of Hrald. Edgyth took no credit for Dwynwen's act, which might not have happened for months or perhaps years without her suggestion. She trusted that Dunnere, or Ceric or Edwin, would have prompted her to do so. Still, life was uncertain and often cut short; and she was gladdened that Dwynwen had so seized upon this task. As she lay in her bed, one hand resting on her breast, Edgyth felt the quiet movement of her breath, and murmured additional thanks for having seen this day.

Edgyth had long known of the inconstancy of her heart's workings. She had been made aware of it while still a young girl, when her heart would seem to flutter within her chest, to pound from activity of childish games, and even at times to seemingly skip beats, so that she sometimes feared it might stop.

It did not keep her unduly from a normal girlhood. She would sometimes faint, but the spell passed quickly. It was after her marriage to Godwin that the faultiness of her heart became more apparent. The loss of so many babes in the womb took a toll on every part of her slight person, but the greater toll seemed to be her heart.

During those fallow years Edgyth was overwhelmed with grief enough to forever still it. But the loss of blood, strain of many early and fruitless labours, and debility of ceaseless bodily disappointment sapped what natural vigour her heart possessed.

This weakness of her heart was not widely known. It had been important to her to hide the irregular and wearisome activity of that organ from Godwin. She might faint, but some folk were prone to such. It was only her mother-in-law Modwynn who Edgyth confided in. That good woman, always solicitous of Edgyth, searched for healing herbs to abet her daughter-in-law's delicate health.

The dried leaves of foxglove could be used to strengthen a faintly-beating heart. But a tincture made thereof had proven fatal to some, Modwynn knew,

causing the heart to race itself to death. She must there-
fore stay her hand at its use. Vale-lily was milder, but the
old tale that it grew only where dragons had once bled
gave her pause; it could be unlucky to one of Wessex and
its golden dragon. Modwynn decided on the flowers and
seeds of pansies. These were used much in love-charms,
and its second name, hearts-ease, the proof of this.

But no tincture gave surcease to the irregularity of
Edgyth's heart. Still, she lived, was productive to a high
degree, and accepted each day granted her as the gift it
was. She would not allow this weakness to become an
impediment.

Some could not be deceived. Worr, acute of observation, had intuited this well-concealed infirmity, as had a
few others. It was never spoken of, save between the two
women.

But when those about her saw Edgyth lay her hand
on her heart, then smile, it was not only from a surfeit of
emotion.

Lady Edgyth had need of her strength, for the yearly
harvest fest, hosted by the hall, was upon them. The fest
was a thank-offering to the village folk of Kilton for their
hard work within fields and pasturelands. It was the last
celebration of Summer-tide, and a full day off from all but
the most necessary of chores. And as at all such gather-
ings, it was chance for young people, finally at leisure, to
laugh, to game, to drink, and dance.

As befit a harvest festival, abundant food and great
quantities of ale were consumed. Apples were coming

ripe; pears and plums already so, and grapevines hung heavy with juicy orbs of yellow and purple. It was above all a celebration of barley, that most-used grain that swayed golden and bearded under the late Summer Sun. Barley was esteemed for its role in the browis all spooned into their mouths, and once malted, in the mellow ale they drank.

It took close to a full day to set up for the feast, carrying trestles and benches to the field by the orchards, laying out the cooking ring with tripods and cauldrons, readying waggons to transport the many scores of loaves the ovens of the kitchen yard would begin baking at dawn. Perhaps most vital to the spirit of the occasion itself was the hauling out of the casks of ale.

When the Sun was overhead on the appointed day, all of hall and village gathered. The last stand of dry barley was cut with due ceremony, six men with scythes working inwards in a circle, until a final tuft, enough for a single sheaf, remained standing. This was then tied round with a plaited cord and cut, and the sheaf placed into the arms of one of the reapers' daughters. She selected for this honour was always a pretty maid, and few who had served as such remained unwed for another harvest. The priest Dunnere would make blessing, and the girl take a handful of the ripe grain and place the cluster on every table, where men and women would choose a stem to weave in their hair, or tuck into their belts.

The dark wooden casks of ale, standing stoutly in the backs of waggons, were tapped, and jugs carried by the crofters from their own homes filled and carried off to the tables at which they sat. Foodstuffs trundled from the hall followed. Crocks of creamy cheese upon which moisture beaded were set out, along with deep tubs of sweet and grassy butter. Baskets of crusted loaves were passed, and at the cauldrons barley browis bright with carrots was ladled. Bushels of pears, apples, and plums awaited, as did bowls of ripe and red cherries, still held fast by their green stems, which the courting young would dangle as they fed each other. There would be music in the form of drums, cymbals, flutes and whistles; with those thegns of the hall skilled in the blowing of the brass horn embellishing this as they pleased, more and more it seemed as the day wore on. And there was song.

The role of the family of Kilton was to preside over this, and as Lady Modwynn had always asserted, to mingle fully with the crofters. At each feast Modwynn moved table to table so that her folk might know her, and she them, the better. She had ever insisted that her sons do the same, and from a young age Godwin and Gyric had in fact taken ale at this table or that; eaten a loaf at a second, tasted browis at the next, and so on. The late and revered Lady of Kilton had raised her grandsons to do the same. Now Ceric had the added attraction at his side of his young wife. Lady Dwynwen went with him to every table, where her laughing, girlish countenance was most welcome.

Edwin as Lord must do so as well, and eschewing the shadowing of Alwin and Wystan, undertook the task of making himself known to those he protected. As Modwynn had before her, Lady Edgyth focused her attention on those who were older, crippled, or bereaved, sitting with them, touching their hands, listening to their woes. It left Edwin free to move amongst the tables in company more congenial to a young and active man, and in fact any youth he noticed and spoke to, or any maid he chose to sit down next to, received it as a special favour.

All sated, the music resumed, and the afternoon wore on. A fire was kindled, to lend its cheer against the coming dusk, and benches dragged near it so songs and stories could be shared by those skilled in tales. The aged might be led to their own crofts by the younger members of the family, that they might sleep off so rich a feast and its surfeit of ale, but as always the young were only fuelled by what they had partaken.

It was not only the denizens of hall and village who attended. Folk came from Kilton's furthest hamlets, as well as those families, such as charcoal burners and tar-makers, who lived in the near-seclusion their trades demanded, with nought but the forest for their company. It was custom to welcome any upon the road as well, those merchants or farmers or tradesmen who might be travelling, and by the stream of folk heading to the burh of Kilton, many such were tempted to join them.

So it was that late in the afternoon two strange waggons rolled in, hooped over with tarpaulins and clattering with snipped and cast metal. Tinkers they looked, judging from the worked metal hanging from their conveyances, pans, rush light holders, griddles, and small pots.

"Cornish," Ceric told Dwynwen, after studying the new arrivals. "Their kind have been here before. They mend bronze and copperware, also tin iron against rust." He looked over to the cooking ring, where browis was still being ladled up. "Their timing is good. They will be fed, as well as have a chance to show their wares."

Dwynwen stood up a moment, and regarded them with care. She had met no one from Cornwall before.

Most of them were fair-skinned and sandy-haired. The men who had been driving the waggons were now better revealed, as they used their upraised forearms to wipe the dust of the road from their faces.

The two waggons held not only the tinkers' metal goods, but a range of folk; older women, grey of hair, sitting in the back, who had in their care babes and small children, men and women of a middle age, and two young and pretty women.

Edwin too had seen them roll near, and as was meet and right, rose to welcome the strangers. The young Lord had held an ale cup in his hand much of the day, and held one still. The sweet potency of mead had also been passed in jugs amongst the younger folk, and Edwin had lifted such a jug more than a few times to his lips. A few of the Cornishmen jumped from the waggons grinning, raising their hands in greeting, and after the exchange of a few words with their host, made for the ale casks. Others remained with the waggons and awaited the approach of the young man with the gold chain about his neck, and the fine seax spanning his belly. Edwin was not alone; both his captains Alwin and Wystan came, as did a number of the crofters, expansive with ale, who would hazard a peek at the tinkers' goods.

A movement on the second waggon caught the eye of the Lord of Kilton. This conveyance held both younger women. One moved to the rear and seemed to check on a babe being held by an old woman. She then looked up, and was caught by Edwin's gaze. She smiled at him, and he smiled back. Both of the young women were pretty, and this one, perhaps the elder, possessed a head of curling auburn hair. Her figure was trim, snug in a dress of verdant green, with many necklaces of tiny dark stones resting upon a bosom of appealing fullness. She was not afraid to smile in a way which showed her fine teeth, even and white. Edwin, warmed by drink, was entranced. It had been one thing to smile at the village girls surrounding him, and allow himself to look at them as they smiled back, when he had Begu he could later turn to. Now she had left him, and the allure of village women one more frustration he must suffer.

He moved nearer, and one of the Cornishmen, bronze salvers in hand, began to approach Edwin to show him their wares. He was arrested in this action by an old tinker, who gave him a sharp nudge, so he might let Edwin proceed to the object of his interest. Alwin, who had not been far from Edwin's side all day, trailed in his wake, trying to conceal his own smile.

The woman who had caught Edwin's eye climbed down from the waggon, and moved behind it, away from the crowd still clustered at trestles and benches. Edwin followed. They stood, looking at the other, she with a smile which had not changed. The russet hair curling upon her shoulders lent a softness to her face, a softness in contrast to her narrowed eyes. Stones of jet spilled like minute black beads of water from the strands about her neck, to rise and fall with each breath she took. Edwin took a step nearer. In a quick action she lifted one shoulder, so that her gown slipped down, revealing the creamy flesh of her upper arm. He needed no further invitation.

Yet she paused a long moment, first looking at him, and then about her. She sighted a thicket fronting a grove of trees at the edge of the orchard, and turned and made for it. Edwin glanced back to see Alwin emerge from around the waggon, and gestured him come.

Once at the thicket Edwin and the woman half circled it, looking for a track in. He had taken her by the hand as they pushed their way through, to the hollow that often times stands in such growth. Having gained it, her smile had faded, and the skittish action of her eyes told of her unease.

"There is nothing to fear," Edwin assured her. "My man is there, as guard. No one will trouble us." He reached out and cupped her bare shoulder, then pulled her to him. He had silver to give her and was ready to part with it.

At the feasting grounds folk were moving, some to refill their ale jugs a final time, others to make a concluding circuit about the tables where small cakes dotted with raisins and fennel seeds had lately appeared. Worr had left to take Wilgyfu and the boys, the two younger sleepy from missing their naps, to the hall. Ceric had seen Edwin rise and go to the tinkers, then turned back to the crofter family who had asked him to take their part in petitioning Edwin for an expansion of the sheep pasturelands. Dwynwen was now sitting with Edgyth by the fire, amongst a cluster of younger folk. When Ceric looked again at the waggons he saw neither his brother nor Alwin. Wystan was there, though, and Ceric rose and walked to him.

"Where is Edwin?"

"Off with one of the Cornish women. Alwin is with him."

Ceric did not hesitate. He moved past the waggons, and looked beyond the last of the apples to the tree cover. He saw Alwin at a distance, standing alone. He went back to Wystan. "We are going," Ceric decided. "Come with me." Wystan fell in with him.

Behind them the Cornishmen began to shut up their waggons as if they wished to place a few leagues upon the road before nightfall. Dusk was coming on, but Ceric was aware of a certain abruptness in their actions. From long habit his hand rose to the grip of his seax, just touched it, and returned to his side in readiness. He neared Alwin, standing some lengths outside a thicket. Ceric looked to the man, clearly standing as sentry, and in a low tone, voiced his question.

"Edwin?"

Alwin lifted his hand to the shrubby growth. "There. With one of their women. I am waiting for him."

Ceric was forced to shake his head. He understood all too well, but liked none of it. The woman was willing, but her people unknown. Edwin had drunk much and might well be the worst for it; surely his judgement was off. Ceric made a move forward.

Alwin hesitated. "He just went in," he said in protest.

Ceric repressed a sigh. "Then we will make sure no one else joins them. You two stay here. I will circle to the back, to make sure they are not surprised."

Within the thicket the woman spent some time toying with Edwin, allowing him a kiss, then breaking away, treading upon the long grasses they stood upon as if to ready their bed, and then at last sinking to her knees. She laid down, and began lifting the skirts of her gown in short increments, past her shoes and ankles, up her pale stockings to her knees, and then revealing the naked flesh of her thighs.

Edwin, on his feet before her, was just unbuckling his seax when another hand grabbed its belt from behind. The surprise was such he twisted sharply away from the thief. At nearly the same moment a jarring blow hit him on his right shoulder, brushing his ear and scarcely missing his head. It staggered him, allowing him but a muffled cry. He fell on the ground, clutching his shoulder, and rolled, to see one of the Cornishmen brandishing a spear over him. A second held a piece of firewood, used as a club.

The woman had scrambled to her feet, and made as if she would quit the place, but the man with the spear stopped her with a movement of its shaft. He turned in disgust to the one who had clubbed Edwin.

"Missed," he accused, with a grunt. "Now we have to kill him."

The other shook his head in violent objection. "Tie him; stuff his mouth. It will be morning before they find him." He was already reaching to the woman, gesturing for her head-wrap.

The circuit Ceric had taken had placed him far from where Edwin had been struck, yet he had heard some utterance, indistinct but surely from a human throat. He took a step nearer, straining his ears. Now there was rustling, and low voices, more than two. Ceric gauged the nearest point to these sounds, and picked his way in. Through the leaves he glimpsed a woman, holding what was surely a seax and belt in her hands. At her feet Ceric then spotted his brother, lying on his back. Edwin was attempting to prop himself up on his elbows, while a man with a spear advanced, to hold the spear point at Edwin's throat. A second man dropped down to kneel at his side, a length of cloth in his hands.

The tinker holding the spear had his back fully to Ceric. There was nothing Ceric could use as missile save his seax, and he could not part with that. But at his feet were a few rocks, and he grasped at one fist-sized now. He flung it with force at the small of the man's back. The man dropped, doubling over with a low groan. The spear from his fists fell within easy reach of Edwin, who at once closed his hand over it. But the second man had jumped up, and now bent for the spear shaft as well. Edwin lurched forward on one knee, shoving the man away. Ceric had hurled himself through the remaining brush-wood to gain the slight clearing. The spear shaft had been pushed closer to where he now stood, and Edwin called out over it to his brother.

"The spear – get the spear!"

A spear was a most effective threat, and also goad. Without touching the opponent one could drive him off. One of the Cornishmen was disabled upon the ground, felled by the thrown rock. The second assailant, and the woman, were on their feet and ready to fight their way out.

Yet Ceric could not reach for the contested weapon.

Edwin watched in near-disbelief, and yet with sudden understanding. From the way his brother avoided it, the spear might have been red-hot steel, or a venomous serpent. Ceric could not close his hand around it.

What Ceric could and would do was kill to protect his brother. He drew his seax instead, the length of the raw blade so immediate, so deadly, that the woman gave a low cry of startle at seeing it.

The second tinker, desperate now, had drawn his own knife, a puny weapon held against the long seax in the grip of Ceric. The Cornishman was perhaps a few years older than his opponent, and no trained warrior. Even the way he wielded his knife proved that. Ceric could kill him with little risk to himself.

Ceric lunged toward him, blade foremost, signalling his readiness to plant its steel in the tinker's body. The tinker was forced to jump back.

Ceric gestured him to kneel, and he did so.

The sound of breaking branches and leaves being thrust aside told him Alwin and Wystan moved from the other side. They emerged, their seaxes at the ready. Alwin fairly leapt to Edwin. Wystan took up the spear which Ceric had so purposely ignored, and now held it upright in his hand, as Ceric had already forced both Cornishmen to the ground.

The woman was trapped, caught between men blocking both passages. She stood there, holding both Edwin's seax belt and the gold chain from his neck. Her clutching hands opened and they fell to the trampled grasses. A moment later it looked as if she would scream, but Alwin turned to her, seax drawn, warning her to silence. She had been the lure, clear and simple, and Edwin's captain would not allow a cry of rape to be sounded now.

Ceric sheathed his blade. He picked up the seax and gold chain, and took them to his brother. Edwin was standing, and it was clear from his pinched brow he was not only abashed but in pain. This was as nought to the Cornishman on the ground, whose whitened face and upward rolled eyes told Ceric he bled within.

The wind shifted enough to hear the faint strains of music, coming from the feasting grounds. Ceric moved his gaze to Edwin. Full justice could not be served without the truth being known of the Lord of Kilton's lustful intentions with the woman. The assault was against Edwin himself; he could not judge the penalty, but need appeal to the King. The crime would be made public, and the miscreants must be transported to Witanceaster. Both of the tinkers would likely be condemned to death, and the woman enslaved. And this, when Ælfred was trying to help Edwin to a good marriage.

Ceric looked again at the tinker on the ground. The man was unmoving, his face blanched, and like to die; this was grave punishment to his kind. All could be kept quiet, and none but those who had witnessed it ever know.

Ceric gave a nod of his head to Edwin, and a gesture, slight but perceptible, that he tell his attackers to go. Edwin was more than ready to comply. His head, addled from mead, had cleared in an instant from the surge of energy which had shot from the pit of his belly when he was attacked. His shoulder ached, but other than his pride he had suffered no real hurt.

Edwin straightened up. "Go," he ordered. "If you are ever found on Kilton's lands again there will be mercy for none of you."

The man and woman tried to pull the other tinker to his feet. He injured could not aid them, and the second man was forced to stoop, load him on his shoulders, and carry him out with difficulty through the undergrowth. Wystan still held the Cornish spear, and now offered it to Ceric. It was rightly his, for downing the man. But Ceric gave a single shake of his head; Wystan would add it to his own battle-gain.

Ceric and Edwin and his two captains followed the tinkers out. They looked down the road. Their two

waggons had left the fireside and were at a distance, waiting. The woman ran to them; the man carrying the dying
tinker hobbled behind. As he neared, men jumped from
the rear waggon to help them board.

The four from Kilton turned their backs on them.
All had happened so quickly, and with such violence
of intent, to leave them largely silent. Ceric could only
think of himself at Edwin's age. He had said nothing to
his brother's two captains; they were not in a position
to challenge the will of the Lord of Kilton. Worr would
have, but Worr was different. Still, the worst had been
averted, and the tale remained theirs to keep.

"Where were you hit," Ceric asked his brother.

"They got my shoulder, when I turned."

"They meant to knock you out, leave you senseless."

Though his tone was low, Edwin must admit the fullest extent of the harm he could have suffered.

"Or dead."

Edwin put his left hand on his shoulder and shrugged
it up and down. "The bone is bruised, nothing worse."

As they approached the gathering Ceric placed his
arm around his brother's shoulders, to steady and reassure him. Those who sat round the fire were brightly
illumined in the blue dusk. Across the fire ring they saw
the face, all unsuspecting, of Lady Edgyth turning toward
them, with a smile of greeting. Dwynwen was with her,
and she jumped up at the sight of them. Ceric hoped she
would remain with Edgyth; with the girl's high sensitiv-
ity she would know something was amiss, and with her
habit of saying the unexpected he could not assume she
would leave it unremarked.

But Dwynwen, after looking at them fixedly for a moment, came straight to the four men, her red gown snapping and fluttering like a flown pennon over her quick steps. There was the slight, almost shy smile on her lips which often marked her countenance, but the round eyes had perhaps an extra gleam, which she partially concealed by the lowering of her lids. It was as if she discerned something had gone awry, something regarding the quickly departing tinkers. Though it was clear she noted it, she did not let her eyes rest overlong on the new spear, held by Wystan. She came to Ceric. It made him relinquish his hold on his brother, and also made her speak. She looked down into the growing gloom of approaching night. The tinkers' waggons were now far enough away that their rattling and clanging could not be heard. Yet Dwynwen stopped and stared at them, making the men pause also. They stood with her as she looked after them.

"They will break down before night is full upon them," she predicted.

There was such surety in her words that both brothers were forced to move their eyes from the retreating waggons to her.

Edwin thought one thing only: Was she then a witch, or a seer of some kind, like the strange old woman who had fostered her? Had she even thrown a curse, with her very look?

Ceric, knowing little of Lady Luned, but having seen much which was good and generous in his young wife, did not rush to such conjecture. Yet in a hushed voice he posed to Dwynwen a question.

"What makes you say this?"

She looked him full in the face, her puzzlement clear. "The left rear wheel on the first waggon had two mended spokes, and the iron rim bounding it was sheared."

※※※※※※※※※

When Worr and Ceric took up weapons practice a day later, the horse-thegn saw a new drive and directness in his sparring partner. If not yet returned to the warrior of yore, Ceric took far more initiative, using his blade in a way that suggested his past skill. They used only swords and shields; Worr did not feel he could propose more. Yet the improvement was real. Worr had nothing to attribute this to, save returning strength of both body and mind. Perhaps the festival just passed had also worked for good.

Ceric, wielding the gold-trimmed weapon, was aware of it too, and felt something of the old energy stirring in his grip. Whether it was the urgent summons to defend his brother from the tinkers, or the knowledge Edwin would soon depart, leaving him as guardian of Kilton, even Ceric himself did not know. But it was another step on the journey to returning prowess at arms.

※※※※※※※※※

If Edwin's mishap at the harvest fest increased his restlessness, he did not have long to wait for a release. The overmorrow brought two riders from the King to Kilton's borders. They were met first by Ceric and Worr, who with two others of the watch-guards had been making daily forays to the boundaries of the burh, to gauge if the markers needed mending or renewing. Some of these were tall tripods of peeled logs, which however stout were liable to eventual rot. Others were stone cairns which had stood generations, but could under force of wind or frost shift and topple. To survey these was work both pleasant and needful, and in most instances could be accomplished in a single day, or for the furthest markers, an overnight spent under the stars.

The four from Kilton were in fact approaching the tripod marking the southern track when the King's riders appeared. Both sported the golden dragon of Wessex springing from their saddle cantles, and Ceric and Worr reined up to welcome them. Like most men chosen for such duty, the arrivals were tough and wiry youths, expert riders, good trackers, and more than able to run long distances should the service of their mounts be lost to them.

Ceric lifted his hand and called as they neared. "I am Ceric of Kilton."

They had been coming at a good trot, and slowed their animals. The older of them bobbed his head at Ceric and spoke. "We are from Witanceaster, with letters for Edwin, Lord of Kilton."

"You are near. Further on, nearing the fields of an outer hamlet, you will meet ward-corns; they will call for an escort for you."

The messengers having been sent on their way, Worr turned to Ceric. The horse-thegn had been made privy of Edwin's expectation by Edgyth herself. "We will trust this Frisian Count can indeed provide a Lady for Kilton," Worr offered.

After the adventure at the harvest feast, one a secret to the horse-thegn, Ceric felt certain Edwin was more than ever set on marriage. "He wants to wed," he said of his brother.

"And Kilton wants a Lady," Worr summed. "Lady Edgyth cannot continue doing all."

It was true, since the death of the brothers' grandmother, the entire burden of running Kilton rested on Edgyth's slight shoulders. Ceric felt a twinge, realising this, for he had wed the maid intended to fulfil that role.

As if Worr was privy to his thoughts, he addressed them. "Not Lady Dwynwen," he told Ceric. "She – she was formed for other labours."

In truth, Worr could not name these, other than the bringing of joy to Ceric. Yet if that was all that was accomplished by the Welsh princess, in his eyes it was enough.

Late in the day Ceric and Worr trotted through the gates of Kilton. They saw the horses of the King's couriers in the paddock, reminder that Edwin had news. And indeed, Lady Edgyth appeared, to tell Ceric that the summons had arrived, and Edwin awaited his brother in the treasure room.

Edwin was alone in the room and opened the door as soon as Ceric spoke his name. He gestured to an open parchment on the table, and confirmed the expected. "Ælfred has called for me. He has given me a letter to Gerolf, Count of Frisia."

There was in fact a second missive, impressively folded and sealed with the King's own stamp. It would be the King's endorsement of Edwin to the Count, and thus of inestimable value.

Ceric knew nothing of Frisia, save that it was a watery place, one of endless marshes and meres, hard to penetrate to those uncertain of its water routes. Of its famed trading centre of Dorestad, he had heard; it had been built by the men of Caesar, just as so many great towns here had been formed by their hands.

Edwin was ready with his plan. "I will in fact ride back with the couriers, taking Alwin and Wystan with me. Then we will break for Swanawic. I will find further escort along the way, the King assures me."

Edwin would leave three days hence, enough time for him to gather all needful, and for the horses and men of the King to rest for the return to the road. The distance Edwin need travel called for a significant absence, a month at least. Some of Summer's warmth still hung in the air; when he rode through the gates on his return the orchard trees might all be bare.

Ceric had a few days earlier perhaps saved his younger brother's life, and certainly his pride. Edwin felt gratitude for this. If it had happened with Worr present Edwin did not think he could live down the shame. But Edwin had no fear that the incident, as tawdry as it had been, would ever find its way to the ears of either Worr or Lady Edgyth. Ceric would reveal nothing of it, Edwin knew. Yet the lingering awkwardness surrounding Dwynwen made it hard for him to seek his brother's help in considering a bride-price for a Frisian wife. Ceric almost inquired about it, then, determining from his brother's reticence he should not, remained silent. And Edwin could not bring himself to ask. After all, his older brother had never so bargained. Though Ceric had set aside treasure with which to win Ashild of Four Stones, that pursuit had never reached a stage of active discussion; and concerning the Welsh maid, Edwin had unwittingly done the bargaining for Ceric. He would rely on himself to again do the same.

Edwin alone decided what to offer, driven by the fact that he had the King's letter to a rich and powerful Count, and the sum proffered must be worthy of the daughter of such a man. The second factor was the journey itself, by land and by sea. For ease of travel he needed portable treasure with scant mass. This meant not silver, but gold, the value of the latter ten times that of the former. And he would not repeat the casual stance he had assumed for his trip to Wales. He would not be bringing items in troth or in trust, but rather the outright bride-price; he must have it with him so he might conclude the bargain and sail off with his bride.

The treasure the young Lord of Kilton assembled was culled from the deepest recesses of the iron-bound chests he slept amongst. This he divided into three parcels. The first was a single ingot of gold, a little longer than a man's pointing finger, and even thicker. The second was comprised of a few gold coins and a number of small ornaments: rings, pendants, and hair pins of red and yellow gold. The third held a single golden neck chain, similar to that which Edwin himself wore at high feasts.

His mother Edgyth readied this, wrapping each bundle in a narrow tube of linen, sewing it shut, then rolling each separately in oblongs of soft tawed leather, the whiteness of the skin acting to proclaim at once that something of unusual quality was concealed within. Edgyth cut thin strips from the tawed hide to use as lacings, and wrapped each small parcel in an intricate pattern. One of the shoe-makers of Kilton was then called for. He arrived with brass thimble and leathern palm-guard, and a range of curved iron needles and sinew thread. He sewed the lacing firmly to the tawed sleeve, making of it almost a web. The contents of each parcel could not be accessed without cutting through this webbing. The bride-price was thus secured.

Edwin would carry one of these sleeves, and Alwin and Wystan each the others. The finished pieces were small enough to rest inside a man's tunic without detection, and the final act was the stringing of a leathern thong from which to wear it.

It was not only for safety's sake Edwin prepared the bride-price in three portions. Separating the treasure had a further advantage. They could be presented one by one. Edwin had no way of knowing the requirements or expectations of the Count of Frisia, or of his circumstances. With many daughters to wed Edwin might be able to carry one off by surrendering only a third of what he brought. If this was found wanting, he could offer a second, and even a third.

Edgyth voiced aloud the next issue to be addressed. "And if more is needed?" she posed, then added in hopeful tone, "and you like the girl well enough . . ."

Edwin gave thought. "I can offer her land." It would be onerous for her father the Count to collect rent from a land so distant, but he might be content in knowing his daughter was being further enriched in her new homeland.

Edgyth smiled. "With treasure so great, I expect nothing more shall be asked of you," she told him.

Her son gave a nod. He intended to bring back a prize. Each day he was confronted with the Welsh girl, and must face as well the happiness she was bringing to his brother. Edwin would fetch a woman from Frisia to become the pride and staff of the hall, as he knew Lady

Edgyth had been regarded upon her marriage. Dwynwen and her childish sporting would be rightfully regarded as a fanciful indulgence, and his pursuit of her recede in memory. That effort had been misguided. He was glad now her caprice had spared him.

On the morning of the leave-taking, Ceric reported to the treasure room, where Edwin handed him the key to the oaken door. The brothers had but a few moments alone together, but Edwin watched as Ceric slid the key into the slit in the inside of his belt. Alwin and Wystan and the King's riders were already outside and horsed; the family of Kilton and folk of the hall were in the forecourt, waiting to see their Lord off.

Ceric would stay his brother a moment longer. He must repeat something he had clear memory of his Uncle Godwin telling him, when he and his mother left for Four Stones. It had only been later that he understood the depth of his uncle's misgivings about the impending stay under the roof of the Dane Ceric's mother was now wed to. Yet the advice was ever good, and as a nine-year old boy Ceric had taken it to heart.

"Stay alert," Godwin had ordered him.

After the incident with the tinkers, perhaps such a reminder to Edwin was not amiss. His was no warning, but rather wish.

"I know you will stay alert," Ceric said, and placed his hand on his brother's shoulder.

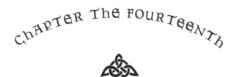

THE SHADOW OF DUTY

Four Stones in Lindisse

HRALD had been gone little more than three weeks, yet he felt years older. Once again on the lands comprising Four Stones, Jari kept up what passed for lively banter for the taciturn Tyr-hand. He sensed the difficulty of return for the young Jarl.

As they neared the turnoff to the Abbey of Oundle Hrald felt a calling to rein his bay's head toward it. He was of a sudden seized with the hopeless and wrenching desire for Ashild. If his sister still lived, he would tell her of his quandary. Ashild's fury at Dagmar's betrayal was no impediment; as harshly as she had judged Dagmar for her actions, she would not judge him for his feelings. As different as they were, Oundle's nearness gave rise to thoughts of both women, far beyond his reach.

The distance to both was unbridgeable. Ashild would never leave Oundle, but the abbey was as well tied part and parcel to Dagmar, from his desire for Abbess Sigewif to meet her, their subsequent wedding at the portal of the stone church his mother's silver had built, and his despairing escape to the then-bleak gardens following his casting her from his hall. What comfort could he find there now? Only these past echoes. He could carry nothing new to those hallowed walls. Seeking solace there would only compound his wrong. He must press forward; the hall awaited him.

Gaining the road proper to Four Stones Hrald drew a deep breath, that of a man about to plunge under water. His own watch-men posted along the route had already greeted him, and one had ridden ahead to let all know he was returned. Approaching the village he watched as cottars stood up from their labours, shielding their eyes against the rays of a lowering Sun, and squinted at the troop he fronted. He heard the cries of welcome.

The road of pounded red clay drove through the village. At its end Hrald could see his wife by the opened gates. Pega was easy to pick out, yellow-haired, gowned in pale blue, and holding their babe cradled in her arms. The look on her face was one of joyful expectancy, yet she remained at her place, awaiting him, as was her role. Mealla stood next her, and his Aunt Æthelthryth as well. Yrling was grinning, off to one side, holding the leads of Frost and Myrkri, the hounds prancing and excited by the swirl of arriving horses. A wide-eyed Bork was stationed with Mul and his sons in the opening to the stable doors, ready to take the horses. They rode in, road-weary, dusty, and nearly to a man glad to be home.

Once alone with Pega in the treasure room, Hrald turned to his saddle bags and began to unpack them upon the table. He felt a nervous energy to be at some task, despite his exhaustion. Pega, still holding a sleeping

Ælfgiva, now laid her down in her cradle, and stroked the child's brow. She looked up with a smile to Hrald.

"She has changed," she said, a claim that held true for the babe's father as well.

The afternoon was far gone. He had brought her nothing from Witanceaster, had no gift to bear. Yet hearing his news she expected none. The trip had not been a success. Hrald had the pleasure of again seeing his mother and sister and the bailiff, and seeing them well. Pega understood that after the disappointment the family had suffered, Hrald would be in no mind to look for trinkets to bring back.

She turned her attention instead to his trip to Kilton, asking much of Ceric and his new bride, and now knowing of Edwin's refusal of Ealhswith, enough of that man to satisfy her curiosity about him.

Hrald had only time to wash before the evening meal was laid. He had a few needed words with Kjeld, who had, as Hrald trusted he would, kept all in good order in his absence. Jari, reunited with his wife Inga and his bench companions, looked relieved to be back. Wilgot the priest greeted him, bringing to Hrald's mind the memory of his short time with the cleric of Kilton. He knew he would not repeat that rite here.

Hrald ate with appetite, and drank rather more than was his custom. Pega noticed this. When she excused herself to join Ælfgiva in the treasure room, Hrald stayed on to talk and game, as he often did. His men who had travelled with him were full of tales of Witanceaster, the great hall of the King, and then of the second, seaside hall of Kilton, which those who had stayed behind were more than eager to hear. Hrald need do little but listen and nod.

One by one the men took themselves off to their slumber, the younger of them going to the second hall where they slept. Most of the torches were rubbed out, and oil cressets snuffed. The coals in the fire-pit were raked into two small piles, one at either end, for easy rekindling in the morning. And Hrald turned his back to the hall to face the treasure room.

The torch light behind him cast Hrald's long shadow on the wall. It loomed above him. He recalled something he had heard years before; whether it was from the Sagas or the Holy Book he could not recall. How cold is the shadow of duty, it went.

The door was locked from within; Pega would have rightly locked it, and he used his key to release the catch. He let himself in. The room looked different from their prior nights together. There were two cressets, rather than one, left burning for him. And Pega was not abed. As he turned from locking the door behind him he saw her standing past the foot of the bed. She was cloaked, holding the soft wool about her with both hands, but a smile played upon her lips. He took a step nearer, wondering. Then she allowed the cloak to fall free from her shoulders. She stood there, naked before him, save for the fine silver strands of the body jewellery he had given her.

Hrald fell back into the routines of his Jarl-ship of Four Stones; its demands were many and he had little choice. If Pega sensed his distraction she felt it due to concerns about his young sister. She had been at Four Stones long enough to see Ealhswith's innocent adulation of her brother, and sensed the girl's unusual dedication to being of service to him. Pega was astute enough to surmise that the Lord of Kilton's refusal of Ealhswith had stung, both as a rejection of herself, and of her brother.

As they were readying to sup one night, Hrald seemed particularly thoughtful. Pega touched his shoulder. "She will meet her match," she promised, thinking of Ealhswith. The words, soft-spoken as they were, jarred him.

His head was full of Dagmar, standing before him, proclaiming that she would live under the King's protection, or his own.

"Yes," he mumbled. "She will meet her match."

A night later Hrald awakened in the dark, again thinking of Dagmar. He could not remain there, next to the sleeping Pega, with his mind fixed on his first wife. He pulled back the bedclothes, feeling under his palm the coarse fur of the wolfskin spread, recalling the memory of making love to Dagmar upon it. He stood up and went to the table. He sat a time in the dark, and then with his back to the bed to shelter the light he would kindle, struck out sparks and lit a single oil cresset.

The knowledge that she was there, now, in Witanceaster gave him no rest. In the years following their separation Dagmar had arisen frequently as a memory, one which, shrouded in grief as the remembrance had been, he had fought. But now the recent physical sensations so powerfully experienced with her anchored him with searing directness to the everyday. Dagmar was become a presence, at his side as she had never been during their brief marriage. He was now possessed of her in the way he had always wanted. And at one and the same time, she was completely lost to him.

Hrald wished for more than one reason that he had thought to give her silver, even force it upon her if need be. Silver as emblem of his regard, to allow her freedom to quit that place, journey to Paris or any other town as rich, where she could make a new start. A half dozen of times he had thought he could still do so; take a quantity of silver, wrap it carefully, and entrust it to one of his men. He would have him take it to one of the priests at the cathedral of Witanceaster. No one would know its true destination. When the priest unwrapped the bundle he would see his directions, that the parcel was the property of the daughter of Guthrum, Dagmar, and need be given her post haste.

Yet he realised he must not do this. He wished to enrich Dagmar so she might leave, and place herself even further from him. But he saw how such a gesture of concern could be misread. To send her silver would only bring her hope, when there was none. It would only strengthen the tie between them.

Hrald forced himself to make decision. He thought of Ceric, who having lost Ashild in the cruellest way, was yet able to begin again with his new wife. He must put Dagmar out of his mind. It would take every particle of mastery he could summon, but he would do so.

The demands of events made fair claim on Hrald. Almost the whole of the Danelaw was unsettled, with a growing and general unease. While Guthrum lived, the halls and war-chiefs were aligned under his leadership. There were squabbles between chiefs, but under the great war-lord these were as mere quillets, settled by him with a word or two of warning. His death had brought an extended period of confusion; the steering-oar dropped from the hand of a now absent steers-man. Guthrum's eldest son Agmund, aware perhaps he lacked his father's strength of will, and with no taste for governing, seemed content to clasp firmly to those immediate holdings his father had left him. The arrival of the vast flotilla of massed Danes at the mouth of the Thames, and the eighty-five war-ships which Haesten led from Frankland to Middeltun created an uproar, both in Wessex and Anglia. But Haesten found rallying support for his efforts to conquer what remained of Mercia and all of Wessex more difficult than he had gauged. Long-settled Danes, many of whom had taken wives of local folk and begun to farm their new homeland, were hesitant to join in an effort which might lose them both land and lives.

Then Haesten vanished, seemingly gone to ground. When he resurfaced he had the misfortune to do so on Hrald's own holdings. Hrald's men had witnessed his downing of the old warrior, yet Hrald had not bruited this fact about. Too many of the other Jarls had remained unmoved during much of the turmoil. Hrald was uncertain as to which side their loyalties fell.

It was well-known that Hrald upheld the Peace struck long ago by Ælfred and Guthrum. He had been driven to kill Thorfast, the chief of Turcesig, as result. In the aftermath Hrald had witnessed the divided loyalties of Turcesig's men himself. He had made appeal to its warriors to accept him, or quit the place, and some few had, rather than follow him.

Now word was current that Ælfred was in decline. It could embolden those Danes who might seize a final chance to overrun the one Kingdom they had never conquered. Hrald and Ceric had spoken long about it. Eadward was almost certain to succeed his father without real challenge within Wessex. Ceric had served hard campaigns with the Prince, and knew him ruthless in his dealings, and less governed by the rules of mercy his father attempted to hold to. Hrald's adherence to the Peace of Wedmore would, Ceric trusted, stand his friend in good stead, for he felt certain Eadward as King would attempt nothing less than to redraw the map of Angle-land.

Yrling had spent much time at Turcesig. He went back and forth, duly escorted, between the two halls, but even with Lady Ælfwyn's removal to Defenas it was at Guthrum's old garrison he felt the greatest freedom. His father's great good friend and battle-companion Asberg commanded Turcesig, and Asberg's two boys, Ulf and Abi, though a few years older than Yrling, treated him as kin. Yrling had grown so that he was nearing their height, if still far from their skill level in the arts of war. The boy had much to master and knew it.

Given this, he had as yet better than average ability with shield and spear. And Yrling was doubly skilled, for he had proven talent as a bowman. Tindr had guided him since the time the child could pull back a bow-string. Archery in battle was often relegated to those neither large enough nor strong enough to fight hand-to-hand, or those lacking the war-kit to do so. Yet a good bowman was of immense value. A single well-placed arrow could take out the leader of any war-band. It was not therefore a skill to scorn, and Asberg and Yrling both had reason to be proud of the accuracy the boy achieved.

Still, shield and spear were the basic tools of the warrior, and those most needful for his survival. One day it was Asberg himself who escorted the boy back to Four Stones, for every other month he checked in on the spear training of the young there. Yrling was happy to return, for the new coursing hound Myrkri was about to whelp, and Yrling wished to be there to greet the coming pups, one of which he hoped Hrald would give to him.

Jari too looked forward to the pups. He knew dogs; his father on their Jutland farm had kept a kennel of hunting animals. Together Jari and Yrling had made fitting preparation to house the newcomers. Frost, it is true, was nearly always with Lady Pega and thus slept in the treasure room, and Myrkri and her pups deserved better than a pile of hay in an unused corner of a barn. Jari commandeered a small outbuilding, once kept for excess grain, to serve as kennel. A wattle-woven pen was built outside its door, adding to its utility. There Myrkri could whelp in peace, and the pups be safely confined. Judging by her growing girth it could only be a matter of days before they came.

This gave Yrling two events to look forward to, the pups, and sparring with the boys of Four Stones under the attentive eye of Asberg. Yrling thought he had made great strides during his last visit to Turcesig, and with his newly gained height was no longer shorter than other boys of his years. On the appointed morning he gathered with the other youths, nearly two score in number, on the strip of practice ground on the other side of the large paddock.

In the main barn, Bork was at work. He saw the boys coming in twos and threes across the stable yard, holding blunt staffs as practice spears, and carrying their shields, either strung on their backs or already in their hands. He could not join them. It was a changeover day, in which the horses kept at Four Stones were largely changed for those out in the valley of horses. Mul the stableman, his sons, and Bork were all readying to lead a long string of horses out there, and return with fresh mounts.

It was Hrald who stopped Bork. Asberg had told him of the coming sparring match, and that Hrald should witness it, so he could gauge himself how the boys were doing. He was thus crossing the stable yard to join them when he saw Bork saddling the horse he would ride. Hrald walked over to him; Bork still had the girth strap in hand, and had been looking over his mount's back past the paddock at the gathering boys. Anyone could read the wistfulness in his eyes. Hrald appeared between the horse and the scene Bork looked at.

"Nej," he told Bork, and inclined his head toward the open doors of the barn. "Get your kit."

Bork grinned in answer. Mul was already horsed and took in the exchange, and nodded at the eager boy. Bork was good with horses, as able as were Mul's own sons. But Mul knew he would not long have the boy's services. The Jarl had marked him out, and Bork's own proclivity confirmed it. He was destined to join the fighting ranks.

Bork emerged from the barn with his shield and staff, both of which Hrald had furnished. They thus rounded the paddock corner together, Bork, tall and lanky, bearing his weapons and looking as though he were already protecting the Jarl of Four Stones. Yrling, standing in line, was one who saw, and thought this.

Bork left Hrald's side and joined the others. Hrald gave a nod at Asberg, standing before them, then looked at the line of boys. He was struck by the resolve in their faces, and by their youth. A few, like Yrling and perhaps Bork, had not yet reached fourteen years. Who would those shields be raised against, in earnest, he wondered. Once Eadward was King of Wessex, would he ride against Guthrum's old holdings in Anglia? Where would Hrald and Four Stones figure in his strategy? Ceric knew the man, but would Ceric have the new King's ear, enough to ensure that those who remained faithful to that old pact forged by his father Ælfred and the Danish war-lord would remain unmolested?

Something else was foremost, looking at the rounded cheeks and youthful faces before him. There was always a new generation coming up. Dane-mark could send more waves of invaders, just as his father and great-uncle had been part of an earlier one. The men of Norway had headed further west, to Éireann and beyond, to the fabled islands of the setting Sun. The Svear were always known to seek to the east, and the treasures of gold, silk, and spice found there. Yet this huge island with its vast tracts of forest on which Hrald had been born remained a prime target for the Danes. Protecting what had been won was the role fallen to the warriors of Four Stones.

The practice match got underway. Asberg began by pairing each boy with another, so that he might watch them spar one on one with shields and staffs. With no protective kit but their shields, striking at the head was forbidden. None of the youths had a sharp terminus to the iron bosses of their shields, so none could be punctured by this common feature of a larger shield. And though their wooden staffs lacked any iron point, a blow from one could leave a deep and painful welt, and a jab to an organ prove fatal. Only a touch was allowed with the blunt end.

Asberg walked amongst the sparring pairs, silently assessing, and as warranted, lustily calling out approval or disparaging insults to the efforts displayed. He then took up shield and staff himself, and in turn faced the bigger of the boys as they came at him, eager to try and get a touch in on the old warrior's leg or spear arm. Some attempts were occasion for laughter, as Asberg feinted with his shield so effectively that the youth ran almost beneath it as he raised it, or were spun around on their heels by a well placed push with its broad wooden face.

To end the session, he split the boys into two groups, each a mixture of younger and older, taller and shorter. They would face each other as a shield-wall. It happened that Yrling and Bork were sorted into the same line, and thus must spar to protect both themselves and their brothers in arms to the left and right of them. The two lines were set but a few strides apart, and the boys raised shields and hefted staffs, ready to collide. Holding the line was foremost in this sort of drill; keeping an unbroken chain of defence while advancing or standing firm, the goal. In the shield-wall working in threes was key, the men flanking the one in the middle providing cover so his own spear could dart out and find home in the flesh of the man diagonally across from him.

The boys were winded, and each engagement as brief as the time it took to register any meaningful touch to shield, shield edge, or body. After this the young fighters swapped position, the third in the grouping of three becoming the first, the first the second, the second the third. After the first swap, and another touch being made, the initial three took places between the new set of three to their left, providing an ever changing lineup, each boy taking turns being to the left or right of the man in the middle, or in the middle itself.

Asberg scanned the lines, calling out the change. This was the culmination of their sparring, and a chance to display not only one's own skill, but the ability to fight as a unit. As the boys switched position, Yrling and Bork grew closer in their line; one more switch and Yrling would be next to Bork, with Yrling in the middle. Any fighter so positioned was charged with keeping his spear widely active, flicking it to distract not that man facing him but those flanking that opponent, giving his own brethren a better chance to land a thrust on leg or spear-arm of those they faced.

Yrling had played this part well in all prior matchings, but now, with Bork at his left, provided little cover for him, giving far more protection to the boy on his right. Bork was opened to several sharp jabs, forcing him to parry strongly with his shield, as Yrling ignored him. None of these were punishing blows; they were but mere strikes to his shield, knocking it askew, but Yrling's neglect was clear. By the time one of their opponents landed a firm blow on Bork's staff arm, several of those near voiced snickering condemnation of Yrling's neglect.

The next switch was the final one, and placed Bork in the middle of Yrling and another boy. Bork was steaming, yet did as he had been taught and protected Yrling equally as the boy on his right. One facing them was an older youth, Ingvar, well-set, and while having had no complaint with the young Gotlander in past, had taken note of Yrling's failure in this final test, and would not let it slip. He went fixedly for Yrling with his staff, with his bigger size and longer practice overruling Bork's protective actions. After an onslaught of rapid but slight blows on Yrling's shield Ingvar stepped forward and with good weight behind him planted the butt of his staff on the Gotlander's shield, knocking him down with rather more violence than needed. Yrling sprawled on his backside, losing his staff as he fell, but keeping hold of his shield, which he pulled to his body. Ingvar stood over him, staff held just at Yrling's upper chest as if it were a true spear. All eyes were now upon them, and the older boy made the most of it.

"Now for the kill," said the staff holder, ready to make the touch at Yrling's chest.

"Let Bork do it," called out another.

Those who had witnessed the hits Bork had been subject to whistled and laughed in agreement.

Bork, standing now with the butt of his own staff resting on the hard soil, just shrugged.

"He is yours," he said to Ingvar, dismissing Yrling as simply as that.

Yrling sprang to his feet in defiance. He picked up his staff, but assumed no defensive posture. His sparring mates had sided with Bork. He felt his face flame; he had been made a fool of.

Asberg, having watched the speedy end of the sparring drill, said nothing. The final lesson was given by those he trained. He turned his back on Yrling, and gave a few closing words of tempered encouragement to all he faced.

At this dismissal, Bork did not try to walk back with the Jarl. He knew Yrling had never liked him, though he did not know why. Bork understood that things were now far worse between him and the Jarl's brother. Yet a few of the boys who had never paid him any mind were now walking with him, a couple chortling in remembrance of Yrling's treatment at the hands of Ingvar. Bork must leave them at the great lead-roofed barn; Mul and his sons were gone, but there was one more stall to muck out, and he would have it ready when they returned.

Yrling was left, nearly alone on the sparring ground. Only his brother stood there, awaiting him. Hrald said nothing; he thought Yrling was well beyond needing it. But they turned and walked back toward the hall together. Yrling, when he was at Four Stones, slept in Jari's house, and he did not wish to enter within; Jari's wife Inga might be there. He kicked at a random stone in his path, then muttered something to Hrald about being hungry, and peeled off to the kitchen yard.

After Bork finished his mucking, he determined to run the white stallion, which had not left the paddock for a few days. That great horse of Ashild, the lost daughter of the hall, was Bork's special charge, just as the Jarl's own bay stallion was. Tied to a neck line the animal could get a good leg stretch, and as Bork would take him out toward the valley of horses he might even meet Mul and his boys coming back with the fresh horses.

So it was that when Yrling walked back from the kitchen yard again he saw Bork, seated on the dark horse Mul had assigned to him, and leading the magnificent white stallion, a horse he himself was not allowed to touch.

Kjeld had little chance to see Mealla alone. The woman of Éireann with the snapping eyes and black hair spent many of her hours up in the weaving room at the top of the stairs of the hall. When not at work up there, Mealla was either with Lady Pega, or when alone, tending to that Lady's babe. So she was when Kjeld spotted her later that day, the babe upon her shoulder, walking slowly to the bower garden. Kjeld was returning from the cooper's stall, where he was checking the progress on the making of small casks to house knives. Without seeming to try, he hastened his step toward her before she reached that low gate.

Mealla heard the crunch of his booted feet behind her and turned. He cleared his throat.

She regarded him, waiting. The line of her narrow nose made her look always as if she was expecting something, a sense of impending demand that Kjeld took secret pleasure in guessing the source of.

Mealla had her right hand on little Ælfgiva's back, her long fingers covering most of it. The babe, resting upright on her shoulder as she was, had fallen into sleep. When Mealla removed her hand from the child's back Kjeld saw she wore the silver bird pin he had given her to close her shawl across her breast.

Seeing his pin there, knowing she favoured it enough to wear it, and her holding a babe made him blurt out his first words.

"Suits you," he said.

Mealla's eyes opened wider. Kjeld had decided what to name. If he mentioned the costly pin she might think he sought thanks for it.

"The babe," he went on. "She suits you."

Mealla gave a small laugh. She reached her hand out, to place it on the gate and allow herself entry to the garden and the bower it held.

"Makes me want to know if you cared for siblings," Kjeld offered.

Mealla hesitated, but made answer.

"My mother had one before me, and three after, when she wed again," Mealla summed.

It was more than Kjeld had so far heard about Mealla's life. And it explained something, why Mealla had left her mother. There were siblings enough. Even if she were again widowed, Mealla's mother would be cared for in her old age.

Kjeld had heard the troubled beginnings of Mealla's life, but he had no idea of the circumstances thereafter. How a child born in Dubh Linn could have ended as a young woman with a noble Lady of Mercia was beyond his ken. This was his chance.

"How did you come to be with the Lady Pega?"

She paused. For all the attraction Kjeld felt toward her, there was a sharpness to Mealla as well, as if he were admiring a honed blade, which one must always handle with care. In her response she proved this yet again.

"That has nothing to do with anything," she answered. She seemed at once to think the better of this, for she continued with a claim. "And I know nothing of you!"

Kjeld thought back. There were certain events in his life he did not wish to dwell on. But if there was ever a time to air the chests of the past, it might be now.

"My mother," he began. "I think what happened to your own, happened to mine. My father would never speak of it. I think he was away. When he came back, somehow she was just – gone. Taken. I was left behind."

He let this hang in the air for a few moments as he considered how to go on.

"Later my father moved on, and came here, when I was still small. I do not recall our arriving. It was during the years when Hrald's father Sidroc was Jarl. We had one horse, and little more. I was mounted on the saddle before my father; he told me this. The horse was a nag, but my father had a good sword, which he had earned the hard way. We were stopped at the borderlands on our way here. My father told the watch-guards he wanted the chance to prove himself to the Jarl. They might have roughed him up right then as a test, save for me on the saddle with him. Instead they brought us to the hall. My father was one of the men Sidroc accepted, just as there were those he drove off.

"I was too little to live in the hall. A few of the village women, the older ones, were glad to take in those young needing to be reared. My father left me with one."

Mealla considered this. "So you were more of the village than of the hall."

"I was. But knowing all the time I would earn my place here."

"And your father?"

"He fell years ago."

"Against the warriors of Wessex? Or other men?"

"The men of Mercia," Kjeld admitted.

Mealla nodded, and a sigh escaped her lips. It was no bond, but somehow connection nonetheless, between them.

He paused a moment, trying, and failing, to gauge her thoughts.

"Now you know my story," he went on.

"And yours?" Kjeld invited. He stopped himself from appending the words, my beauty, to this. He knew too well she chafed when he praised her person. Yet studying her curling black locks and milky skin, how worthy she was of them.

Mealla remained quiet. It prompted him to go on. "Will you not share with me, as I have shared with you? We are here now; the Gods – " he checked himself and went on – "and God has brought us together."

He glanced again at her shawl. And you wear the pin I bought for you, he told himself.

Mealla straightened up even more. Her words came out with a shrillness which did not conceal the possibilities. "I can do nothing without my Lady's consent."

This gave Kjeld further hope; it seemed little barrier. Both Lady Ælfwyn and Burginde had favoured his pursuit, and must have spoken to Lady Pega of it. Burginde had even sewn him a new suit of clothes, to appear more favourably before both Mealla and her mistress. And he felt sure Hrald would speak up for him.

"'Twas Pega's father who brought us to Mercia. He came to Dubh Linn on behalf of Lord Æthelred, buying iron weaponry with silver. He fell ill – the spotted fever – and my mother and step-father, who kept the stable where his horse was housed, took him in and cared for him. When he was well again he offered to take the two oldest with him, back to Weogornaceastre, to serve his household.

"I was one," Mealla went on. "My brother, the other. He had fifteen years, and me, twelve."

"Your brother," Kjeld repeated.

"He is dead. Through soldiering," she added, looking pointedly at Kjeld.

"Against – Danes?"

"And would I be speaking to you now, if that were true?" was the tart response.

She shook her head. "Against a wild tribe from Cymru."

"Ah. The Welsh." Kjeld nodded, not a little relieved. He did not need yet another offence laid at his door; being Dane seemed crime enough.

"So you were then in Lady Pega's household?"

"That I was. There were many maids there, the hall was large. But Pega – she was never the silly sort. I suited her as companion."

"Já," thought Kjeld aloud. None could judge you as silly, even as a girl.

"She took to me. Of course 'twas a blessing to me, and I slept in her chamber, cared for her clothing, spun and wove with her and her sainted mother." She stopped here, as if there was nothing more to add.

"We will never be parted," she now declared.

Kjeld was surprised at the firmness, one close to vehemence, of these last words. "Why should you be?" he asked, aware too of her note of warning there.

"I know your ways," she returned, in decided fashion. "You are second here. As soon as you have enough followers, you will quit Four Stones. To ride off and conquer on your own. And you will expect your wife to follow."

She paused, and her tone became lighter. "So. Perhaps she will. But it will not be me."

Kjeld's relief was so great he almost wanted to laugh.

"Mealla. That was once true. But now, less and less so. There is little left to claim for a small war-band. And it would be a doubled effort, for it would mean carving out land, and gathering men, from another chief's domain."

She pursed her lips, and by the small furrow that appeared in her brow, looked to be attending well to his words. It emboldened him to go on.

"I am not so different than you. I find myself second here, in service to the Jarl, something I had never thought could be. Why would I want more?"

The babe on her shoulder had begun to stir, and now to whimper.

"'Tis not what I want that matters now," Mealla decided, craning her neck to the restive child. "Ælfgiva needs her mother, having a lie-down in the bower house."

But as she let herself into the garden, Kjeld thought he had at last made a real stride in closing the distance between himself and the maid of Éireann.

That night in the hall Yrling looked about him. Bork was sitting at the very table he sat at, that set apart for the young who had lately begun their training. Bork always sat at the end of the bench, furthest from the high table where sat Hrald and his wife and Jari. Asberg was there that night at the high table as well, seated next to Jari, as he would spend a day or two before returning to Turcesig. At first Yrling thought he would go back with him, but the shame he felt at being laughed at before all the other boys made him feel that if Asberg said but one word to him he could not bear it.

Yrling brought his eyes back to his own table. Ingvar was staring at him, a pointed look that suggested the older boy hoped Yrling had learnt his lesson. Yrling dropped his eyes to his bowl. The browis seemed tasteless, or maybe it was the bitterness of the ridicule he had suffered. His head dropped lower over his wooden bowl, but he was not seeing the contents.

He saw instead a new way for himself, a new life. He had wanted to leave Gotland and see the hall his father had claimed, and which his brother now was Jarl over. Well, he had seen it. But there was much else of the land he had not seen. He recalled standing at the steering-beam with the dwarf Aszur as they neared the dark green mass which was Angle-land, and how he had whistled at its bulk, filling the whole horizon before them. Yrling had seen Saltfleet and Four Stones and Turcesig and nothing more.

This was his chance. He had been given a horse by his brother. It was not perhaps his outright, but the under-standing was the animal was Yrling's for the duration of his time here. Well, he thought, I am still here, and I am taking him with me. Wherever I am going, I will not walk.

He began that moment to plan his leaving. He did so with the close intent that only his own mother might have recognised, along with nearly the same innocence she had held about what might be in store for her.

Over the course of the next two days Yrling began stockpiling food, gathering kit with which to make his camp upon the road, and all other needful things. These he carried in small parcels out beyond the kitchen yard door, and past the old Place of Offering. It was an unknown echo of his mother's determination as a maid, in quitting the priory. On the third day he saddled his horse as if he were just riding out for a spell before the evening meal. He circled round to the back of the palisade where his traps awaited him. Upon his back he placed his shield, a red zigzag of lightning on a dark ground. He had a real spear, a shorter one meant for throwing, which suited his height. At his side, as it was each day, was the long knife Hrald had taken from his own waist on Gotland and given him.

Yrling headed along the same path Ceridwen had guided two horses down, so long ago. He would not show up in the hall for the meal, but soon it would be dark, too dark to track him. And he did not care.

IT WAS FORETOLD

Kilton, and The Fold

RAEDWULF had saddled his black mare and headed north from his hall in Defenas. The animal was both fast and thrifty, and travelling alone as he was, it would take him but two days to reach the burh of Kilton. His visit was not an official one, though it concerned the King and his interests, which the bailiff worked always to further. This trip, undertaken on the bailiff's volition, was equally rooted in Raedwulf's own personal considerations.

As a man lately married, invested anew in his own future, and knowing the time could not be long when his own sworn duty to King Ælfred came to its close, he was placed in mind of another man lately wed. This was one years younger, who Raedwulf had always taken unfeigned interest in – Ceric. The bailiff's warm friendship with the young man's grandmother would allow nothing less.

His son-in-law Worr had long since informed him via a letter that Ceric had both returned to the hall of Kilton, and had wed. As cheering as this news had been,

367

Raedwulf wished to gauge the fitness of the man with his own eyes. He had not seen Ceric for more than a year, in the small stone church of Kilton where Lady Modwynn was being laid to rest.

Raedwulf had left from Defenas; the King was away in Witanceaster. He had not sent message there of his impending visit to Kilton. It was not only for reasons of delicacy the bailiff had not approached Ælfred about this, for it concerned the time following the King's own demise. He had reason to suspect Ceric would be a changed man, and must judge what that change had wrought before mentioning it to Ælfred.

The bailiff entered the boundary of the village with an escort of two of Kilton's watch-men, one of whom, when within sounding distance, signalled with his horn of a King's envoy arriving. Raedwulf would have been happy to canter up alone and unannounced, leaving it to the men walking the ramparts of the palisade to alert those within of his coming. But the man was of such standing that every ward-corn and watchman would have seen him in, and the bailiff, always alert to the duties of others, would not have these final two accused of the slightest dereliction of duty.

Ceric came away from the bower house and his Boethius; Lady Edgyth from her own bower and her loom. It was late afternoon, that time which granted an hour or two of private pursuits to both, before the hall gathered to sup. Dwynwen was out of earshot of horn and welcome, down at the water's edge with Tegwedd, alone but under the watchful eyes of the guards stationed above. The Welsh princess walked there, combing through the beach detritus for sea shells.

Within the palisade Raedwulf had ridden through the opened gates, to be met by Ceric and Edgyth, who called out his name in happy surprise. Once off his mare he greeted the Lady of Kilton first, glad to be the object of her gentle smile. The welcoming party was small, and after their embrace Ceric told the bailiff why.

"Worr is out at Sceaftesburh, but due back today," he assured him.

"I am glad I will not miss him, then," Raedwulf returned, pulling off the gloves he wore while riding. His mare nosed him from the back, making both men laugh. As a stable-boy took the reins from his mount in hand, the bailiff's daughter appeared. Wilgyfu was laughing with happiness to see her father, as were her three boys. He soon had a boy in either arm, while she kept the youngest in her own. Holding them in his arms he was more than ever aware that his investment in Kilton only grew with the years. He put the boys down; there would be time enough for them to clamber into his lap, and he would sit next to Wilgyfu tonight at the high table, and have all the long evening with her at his side.

Edgyth's acute nature was such that she posed the next. "It will not be long before we gather in the hall," she began. "Would you two take ale together in your bower, Ceric?"

So it was that a few minutes later bailiff and Ceric sat alone at the small table within the bower. The arrival of the serving man bringing cups and ale gave Raedwulf's appraising eyes time to note numerous chests, richly embellished with rampant dragons, now sharing space with the more sober furnishings of Kilton.

The first sip of ale made Raedwulf close his eyes in pleasure. This was Kilton ale, a recipe devised and perfected years ago by its former Lady, Modwynn. It varied in weight from season to season, as all drink from living grains must, but kept always the creamy savour and pleasing bite which proclaimed it Kilton ale.

His first words were of the goodness of the ale, and of the woman who had excelled in establishing its brewing.

"The Lady Modwynn," he said, lifting his cup again in salute. He said it, recalling again that it was at that Lady's funeral Mass he had last seen the haunted face of her grandson. Ceric nodded his head at this toast, his own eyes closing briefly in tribute.

Ceric looked to Raedwulf spare in form, but with a visage which spoke of returning health. Grief, and a year of rough living in the wilds of Kilton's woodland had sorely tried him, imposing a sinewy strength to his face and form; but the golden-green eyes, Raedwulf was glad to see, were still bright.

Those eyes now looked inquiringly at Raedwulf. Ceric would of course be wondering what had brought him here.

"I am on my way to Witanceaster," the bailiff announced.

"By way of Kilton?"

Raedwulf gave a conceding laugh, and answered. "I wished to speak to you," he admitted.

Ceric made a movement of his hands, and the question in his eyes grew the greater. The bailiff read the concern there; Ceric must think he was being called forth to the fyrd. Raedwulf made haste to correct this.

"Your leave continues, of course. There will be no immediate call to duty for you, nor any at Kilton. Unless the need is urgent," he qualified. "Ælfred would not have sent Edwin to Frisia if he had cause to expect otherwise."

Ceric nodded, and briefly closed his eyes. Though he knew that day must soon come, he was glad it was not yet at hand.

"Nonetheless I am here to speak of your future, both here at Kilton, and in Wessex. I will begin by telling you my Lady-wife sends you her warmest greetings, and the first matter I must speak of is one dear to her. Your son, Cerd."

Ceric lifted his head. Concern for himself had been replaced by a higher alertness, and Raedwulf's smile allayed any fear he harboured for the child's health.

"He grows well. A handsome little fellow, happy, and active in every way. Ælfwyn takes great joy in him. Yet this is balanced by her eagerness that you might see your son again. When you are ready, we will come with the boy, that you might know him more."

Edwin had told him of this intention on behalf of the bailiff and Ashild's mother, and as much as Ceric wished to see the child, it felt hard to initiate such a meeting. His belief that Cerd was all that remained of Ashild had never allowed him to progress further with his own desire toward the boy. Raedwulf's next words offered a pathway forward.

"He is too young to be parted from those who have cared for him most closely since the loss of his mother. But that you should see him at intervals will place you firmly in his mind, to prepare for that coming day when you might wish him fully here."

Ceric found himself nodding his head, as well as blinking back the water forming in his eyes. He stood for a moment to compose himself, using it to fetch the ale jug, which the serving man had left on its tray on a nearby chest. He refilled both their cups, and sat down again.

"The second matter I am here for more directly concerns your return to service. And what form that service might take."

Raedwulf paused here, as he studied the young man's reaction. As the great Godwulf's first grandson Ceric should have been put forward as Lord of Kilton after the death of both his father Gyric and his uncle, Godwin. Yet Godwin had made Edwin his son, bypassing Ceric. Despite this he had gone on to distinguish himself at the highest levels as a warrior, and as a leader. A return to fighting service, and one even closer to the right hand of Prince Eadward would be expected. Yet after what Ceric had suffered, Raedwulf was not at all certain this would be what he desired, or was even capable of. The bailiff, kept apprised of the year of his absence, had even feared Ceric might never return from the greenwood, or if he did, might speedily dedicate himself at Glastunburh as did numerous men who had seen too much bloodshed and loss.

The bailiff remained silent, wishing Ceric to respond openly and without being led.

Indeed, Ceric had given thought to his future; now that he was returned to Kilton he could do nothing less. Yet the fact that he had wed a week after his return had greatly altered the landscape of his life. And he knew it was not only that he wed, but whom he had wed. Dwynwen had changed him – was changing him – far more than he and life here was changing her. If she had not come to Kilton, he would, he imagined, return to the service of Prince Eadward as soon as he was fit. Yet he could not imagine that service being what it had been in the past. And Raedwulf's next words suggested he did not, either.

"I would not have you return again to the ranks, Ceric," is what he said.

It startled the hearer, and for a wild moment he wondered if Worr had told his father-in-law about his inability to use a spear. He took a breath, and dismissed the thought as unworthy of so great a friend and mentor as was the horse-thegn. And that alone would not disqualify any warrior, unless it was symptom of a greater reticence on the field. Yet he must ask the next, without knowing if shame, fear, or relief would rise in his breast as result of the answer. He did so as steadily as he could.

"Do you wish to remove me from direct combat?"

Raedwulf paused at this. "I wish instead to propose a role more fitting for your experience, and perhaps your inclination. That you join the few men at the side of your King, privy to his thoughts. To act as sounding-board, advisor, and yes, in diplomacy. And act even in the meting out of justice."

When Ceric had considered what path might open before him, he had given thought to the bailiff. Now the man himself broached the topic.

He knew Raedwulf's own life had greatly changed; he was now wed to the mother of Ashild and Hrald. Raedwulf would wish more ease as he grew older; he had served Ælfred long and well. The admiration Ceric held for the man had coupled with his inner inquiry as to his own prospects. Ceric had in unvoiced wondering felt he might perhaps pattern himself after Raedwulf, and aspire to become to the King what the bailiff had been. Serving as bailiff took judgement and wisdom; it required study; he must know the law codes by heart, and be able to apply them to a wide variety of circumstances. Perhaps he could serve as a help to Raedwulf, become in effect his second, and learn from the man who had served Wessex so well.

The bailiff went on, in further answer to the question Ceric had asked.

"You would serve, I am sure, as part of the King's own body-guard, as I have. At times it would place you at extreme risk.

"But yes, you would be out of the shield-wall, and guarding – and advising – the new King."

"The new King," Ceric asked. "You mean Eadward, after the death of his father."

Raedwulf nodded his agreement.

"I am bound to Ælfred," the bailiff went on, "as is Edwin, as Lord. Your allegiance has been pledged to the Prince, and you have served him well. I have been in the King's presence and heard Eadward speak highly of you. One day – a day which may arrive sooner than any of us wish – Ælfred will go to his well-earned reward. My influence with him, slight as it has been, will close. My service to him will also be at an end, and at this age, while my sword will always be in service to Wessex, I will welcome a retirement to private life. On the day of Ælfred's death, Eadward will become King. You may perhaps serve him as I have served his father."

It was much to take in. There were many aspects Ceric had yet to consider, but it was clear Raedwulf would support him should he wish for such advancement. What Raedwulf said next underscored this, and yet removed the pressure of immediate decision.

"May God grant Ælfred more years, and no move on your own part need be made now. What is important is that you have heard me out, and will bear this in mind. When Eadward becomes King, he will need the best of men about him. And you are one."

Their eyes met. The bailiff lowered his just a moment, then returned his gaze to the searching eyes of Ceric. He saw something of Lady Modwynn there, and it made him say the next, words unbidden but which he must speak.

"Kilton must not lose you," is what he said.

Such words would never ordinarily drop from the bailiff's mouth; they could be read as a discounting of Edwin's ability. Yet he could trust Ceric with such a confidence as this. This elder son of the hall had proven his loyalty to his brother as Lord. Raedwulf need not fear that overweening pride nor bitterness would grow in the soul of the man before him, and overthrow his evident and many better qualities.

And Ceric had of late acquired an asset to serve both Kilton and Wessex. Raedwulf spoke of this now.

"Your Lady-wife is a princess of Cymru," he began.

The smile that broke upon the face of Ceric was broad and warm. "Dwynwen of Ceredigion," he agreed. "My child-wife," he added, to prepare the bailiff for her youth.

He turned his head to the window. "She has gone down to the shore-line, but I will go and call her up."

They rose together and quitted the bower. They entered the garden, now past its final profusion of late flowering as the mellowness of the last of harvest-tide grew deeper.

The Lady Dwynwen was in fact just emerging from the stone steps cut into the cliff face, her clothing splashed with sea water, but smiling at the prize she and Tegwedd bore. Both Lady and serving maid had stripped off their shoes and stockings when Dwynwen spotted a goodly cluster of red dulse bobbing in the rippling incoming tide. They had claimed it and were wading back with the dripping thing in their arms before the guards in the lookout above could fully react. This seaweed was a favourite of Dwynwen's, one she had not enjoyed since coming here. Chopped, the kitchen yard could add it to broths and browis, where its mineral saltiness enhanced the savour of all other vegetables. But she liked it best crisped on the griddle in oil, where its smoky qualities made it nearly like cured bacon. She and Tegwedd had a basket with them, heavy now with both shells and seaweed. They made their way, holding it each with one hand, step by step up the hewn rock to the pleasure garden.

At the top the two young Welshwomen straightened up, and set down their burden. Dwynwen gave a little cry of happiness at seeing Ceric, walking toward her with a nobly dressed older man at his side. As to Raedwulf, upon sight of Dwynwen he thought how apt was the endearment Ceric had appended to her. She wore an undyed linen pinafore, as little girls wore in play, which had afforded scant protection to the blue gown beneath it. In her smallness of person and mobility of face she might have looked a true child, save for the marked intelligence of expression, and a searching depth to the round eyes. Her composure too marked her. Most Ladies of her rank, having been found before a stranger in a gown wet at hem and sleeves, would have blushed with discomfiture.

This Princess of Ceredigion stood and allowed the two men before her to approach as if she stood on a dais in resplendent array.

Ceric spoke first, and formally, as was meet for the occasion.

"My Lady Dwynwen of Ceredigion, this is Raedwulf of Defenas, Bailiff of Wessex. A true friend to all here at Kilton," he must add.

Upon presentation to the bride, Raedwulf gave a deep bow. After he straightened up, he addressed King Elidon's niece in the tongue of Wales.

She beamed, clapped her hands in delight, and answered him.

Ceric turned to the bailiff, his astonishment clear. "What did you say," he demanded with a laugh.

"Nothing of import. I only gave formal greeting to a Princess of Ceredigion, and your Lady returned my good wishes with a kind word of her own."

The serving woman Mindred had appeared. She clasped her hands over Dwynwen's appearance, but took up the heavy basket of dulse with Tegwedd and made for the kitchen-yard.

It left the three alone. Both men assumed Dwynwen would excuse herself to the bower and a dry gown, but instead she led them to the pavilion.

"It is so pleasant in the Sun," she began, "and warm days like this will not be with us much longer." She claimed a chair and with her small hands spread the damp fabric across her lap, as if to dry in the last rays of the afternoon sunlight. She seemed to read their amusement, for she assured them, "My name means wave. I cannot be harmed by water. But I will wear another gown tonight at table."

Her charming directness was such that it prompted Raedwulf to speak plainly. He could not linger at Kilton, and so good a chance to continue the discourse he had opened with Ceric might not readily present itself.

"I must congratulate you both on your union," he began. Indeed, Raedwulf's observant eye gleaned at once the effect the bridal couple had on each other. It revealed itself in an almost animal vigour in Ceric, and for her, the kind of bright ardency which accompanies deep attachment. Nothing will sunder these two, the bailiff found himself thinking, and woe betide any who attempt to do so.

"May I convey the greeting of the King," Raedwulf went on, "and assure you, my Lady, he is well pleased that King Elidon and the Kingdom of Ceredigion has entered into happy confederation with Wessex through your marriage."

Her answering words surprised the bailiff, but not Ceric. "It was foretold by Lady Luned, who raised me. Elidon had nothing to do with it." This was so simply and sweetly stated that Raedwulf must repress a smile, until he saw she herself was smiling.

He must meet her on her own high ground, and was pleased to join her there. "I look forward to meeting such a remarkable woman as must be Lady Luned."

"I will see her face again, she promised," Dwynwen replied. "As you are such a friend to Ceric, I hope you may know her as well."

This opened for Raedwulf another portal, one he stepped through.

"Lady Luned raised you to fulfil the high estate into which you were born, and assume any role that marriage might thrust upon you."

The pointed chin gave a nod of assent. "This is true. I was Fated to save the life of Ceric."

Raedwulf could only nod in acceptance to this extraordinary speech. Yet it seemingly was true, and Ceric not disquieted before him while he was being told this.

"You are an exceptional woman, my Lady," he went on, though the term woman was hardly appropriate. Yet she responded to it, and as a compliment, sitting the taller in her chair.

He went on. "I think Kilton will long bless the day you arrived."

She smiled as she addressed the bailiff.

"I am blood to every Kingdom of Cymru, through the lines of my grand-sires and grandmothers. Rhodri Mawr is my grand-sire, over-King who killed the Dane Gorm long before my birth. Though he could not see which brother I should wed, King Elidon took pride in my marrying into the hall of Kilton. It adds to his standing amongst the manifold Kingdoms of we Cymry. They are all kin to me."

It was a simple and factual telling, free from pride; merely the facts of this young bride's life. Raedwulf gave a small bow and responded in kind. "You will be an asset in every way, my Lady, to both halls. To both Kingdoms," he predicted.

Indeed, standing before this slight girl, hearing her speak, Raedwulf felt that Ceric had taken to wife not a noblewoman of a single Kingdom, but wed all of Wales. The Lady Dwynwen could be of immeasurable value in forging alliance throughout that vast terrain.

Should Ceric travel with his bride to Cymru, and Ceric be presented to the other Welsh Kings and Princes of the various Kingdoms, it could go far in aligning support for Wessex against the Danes, and all other interlopers. With his bride's directness it would not be subtle diplomacy, but yet could be high in aim, and accomplishment.

⁂

Worr returned in early evening, in time to sup with all. Sceaftesburh had entrusted a number of yearling horses to him two years ago, and he had returned them, as well-grown as they were now well-schooled. Sceaftesburh had a small but fine stud which he had helped build, and this dependency of Kilton's was not the only hall and burh he had so aided. Raedwulf had before this thought of how his son-in-law's skill with the animals would be valued at Witanceaster. If in fact Ceric grew closer to Eadward in service, it would demand time spent there at the royal burh. Though the bailiff did not like to think of Kilton left without either Ceric or Worr, he felt certain the horse-thegn would insist on accompanying him. Raedwulf glanced to his left, where sat his daughter. It would mean uprooting the family, and two households to maintain, or long periods of separation for Worr from his wife and boys. None of these were things Raedwulf wished to contemplate tonight. Lady Edgyth had poured more brown ale in his outstretched silver cup, and now, over honeyed sweetmeats, they were drinking mead. He would enjoy long and raucous sport with his grandsons in Worr and Wilgyfu's house; they were now seated at one of the children's tables with a serving woman. Wilgyfu had claimed much of his attention at table, eager to hear of Lady Ælfwyn, and her father assured her that she and

Worr were welcome anytime at The Fold so they might finally meet.

In Edwin's absence Ceric sat in the Lord's carved chair, with Edgyth, Lady of Kilton at his right, and Dwynwen at his left. Ceric would have preferred a bench, drawn up to the same spot in the centre of the high table; but the folk of the hall must look at that high-backed chair and see one of the sons of Kilton. His sitting there was eased by the presence of his young wife, whose nearness brought to Ceric an inner comfort and confidence unknown to him before her arrival here. The presence of the bailiff also brought succour. He was most aware that Raedwulf was akin to a living emissary from his lost grandmother, and felt he could trust the man almost to the extent he had Lady Modwynn.

That night as they readied for bed, Dwynwen asked Ceric about the scar on his arm. He had just pulled off his tunic, and his right shoulder was toward the table, upon which the cresset burnt, and stood out in the flickering light. The scar was as long as her pointing finger, reaching at an angle near the top of his arm, at the thickest part of the muscle there. She knew it was some years old; the dull red of its hue told her that, and had seen as well that it had been sewn, as the gash was too broad and deep to heal well on its own. She had known of this scar from their first night together, and felt it before she had seen it. But he had never told her of its origin, nor had she asked.

"Every scar has a story to tell, my father said," she began. "But not every story need be told," she added, should he wish not to tell of it.

He looked at her, standing there in her white shift, her long and straight hair a cascade of light brown about her shoulders. On her lips was the slightest of smiles, that quizzical half-smile which often seemed to others to indicate some private understanding, or a jest too rare and subtle to be shared. In this light, dressed as simply as she was, she looked more than ever from the world of Faery.

"There is a story," he told her. It was as if she had placed a key in a lock, but allowed him to open the chest it secured. "Of Hrald and me. And also – Ashild."

He went on to relate of that long-ago day at Four Stones when they sparred together, alone and unattended, and of the leather blade-guard on Hrald's sword failing. Much was attached to that wound, and to that day. Image followed image in Ceric's mind, and he told Dwynwen all: Hrald slicing his own arm with his knife and having them stand shoulder-to-shoulder, their blood mingling; a fretful Burginde and an impatient Ashild, inspecting the cuts, and stitching them; the burning, stinging pain of the angry slice. He told her how he and Hrald had later used a silvered disc so they might see the wounds as they healed. He fell silent then, as memory and emotion rose and fell away.

There was one thing only he did not speak of. It was the memory of Ashild holding his arm in that dim store house, and his feeling that her tenderness was that of a wife. He had been wrong. She had never considered herself that. He understood this now. Ashild had been to him as much as she could have been, and he had been grateful for it all. So much was passing across his face that Dwynwen took a step closer to him and laid her hand upon his cheek.

This was of his past. Raedwulf, so lately at table with them, had presented a version of what might be his future.

He reached for her hand and held it to his lips a moment, and still holding it, spoke.

"Raedwulf – he asked today if he might bring my child here, to see me." He searched her face, as open and fresh as always, as she looked up at him. "He fears the boy will not know me. I fear that, as well . . ."

She delighted in hearing this, just as she had promised him. "Let us ask that he be brought, as soon as you feel ready," she urged. "Those dear to our hearts – we do not know if they shall be with us only a short time."

That night he whispered a question to Dwynwen as she lay in his arms. He felt free with her to ask or say anything; she seemed impossible to disconcert or distress. He was on the threshold of sleep, warmed by drink and the feeling of well-being the bailiff had instilled in him; and bathed still in the glow of the embrace he had just shared with her.

Still, his voice was low enough that one might have thought he feared being overheard.

"The Faery folk of Cymru . . . do the Ladies thereof ever take mortal men as their lovers?"

He almost stopped there, but knew he must ask the next.

"And – if they do, can a babe be born of such a union?"

He spoke thus, near to sleep, hardly knowing what he asked, or why, or if some unknown danger might be attached to either question or answer.

She answered with quiet significance.

"Yes, and no. A Faery will sometimes risk lying with a man. And nay, she cannot bear his child. That is why Faeries will steal the babes of folk."

"When will a Faery risk such a union?" he whispered next.

It took her a moment to answer this, but answer she did, and with the same quiet and sober tone.

"Only if he is beautiful enough," she assured him. "As you are."

She lifted herself on her elbow, and brushed his lips with her own as he fell into sleep.

The bailiff of Defenas stayed a second day at Kilton, and left the third. On the morning of his departure he paid a private visit to the stone chantry. There he stood before the resting place of Godwulf and Modwynn, bade them greeting, and asked their blessing on their grandsons and their affairs. He had not known the old Lord of Kilton well, having seen him but once or twice, on campaign with King Æthelred, when Raedwulf was young, but felt strongly that Lady Modwynn's benevolent nature would take pleasure in the burh he would quit today.

He had a parting word for Edgyth, taking hold of her offered hand, and reminding her of a destination he thought she must yearn for.

"Glastunburh, my Lady?"

She smiled, the mild grey eyes creasing with pleasure at the thought of a life of prayer and study. "One day. When Edwin is wed and his wife, Lady. Then, yes, Glastunburh."

"We will hope he returns with a Frisian bride," he countered.

Then he was off, on a southerly track, toward Witanceaster. He arrived four days later, slowed by rain, wet through, his mare's long mane plastered to her neck as was Raedwulf's own hair under his sopping hood. He would not quit the animal upon arrival, even though she was led to Ælfred's own stable, but remained with her, rubbing her down, and murmuring endearments to her furred ears for her uncomplaining service.

Dry clothes, hot food, and good ale restored him, and when he was called to the King's private bower Raedwulf was much refreshed. The King was hard at work at his translations from the Latin, but set the pile of parchments aside. The two had not seen each other since the attempt to present Ealhswith to Edwin, and they spoke as old friends do of the bailiff's new and unfolding life at his hall in Defenas. The King then turned to refinements to the law code which had occupied Ælfred for the past several years. He had worked upon it as time allowed with Raedwulf, gathering all known law codes of prior Kings of Wessex, and of Mercia too, to serve as guidance. This was augmented by their own records of cases brought before the hall-moots of various burhs, and how when no suitable solution could be sought, they had been sent on to the King. It was a large undertaking, one Ælfred was intent on committing to parchment, so that it could be readily copied and dispersed throughout the Kingdom.

There was time though, for the bailiff to assure the King of the appropriateness of Ceric's marriage, and to assure himself that Ælfred was well enough. After two days, his mare and his own body rested, Raedwulf headed west for Defenas and The Fold. The weather was clement, no rain fell, though the coolness of the nights spoke more and more insistently of hard weather to come. He had no need to spur his pretty mare as they neared home; her nostrils flared with the scent of it and her own stable.

That night of arrival, in Ælfwyn's arms, she told of a discovery she had made in his absence. She must not tarry; the meal was ready, and though he had been given a moment to greet the household, all awaited them to welcome him more fully.

She was wearing the pink gown which she had donned the day they had made vows and been blest as man and wife. Its colour suited her, and her glowing cheeks, as she spoke.

"I am with child."

His lips parted in joy, as if he would let loose a whoop of glee, yet but a puff of wind escaped. He clasped her to him, and heard her say in his ear, "I am almost too happy."

"For you there should be no such thing," he told her.

He held her by the shoulders, looking into her face. She smiled back at him. "Thank you. I know I will store this up, and count on it in times to come."

He could only nod, and felt at that moment unable to speak further. He knew happiness; it was what he truly wished for, but for a man who had lost his first wife in child-bed, it was a shadowed joy. She read this.

"It will be my fourth child," she reminded. A woman who had been safely delivered in the past could look forward with greater confidence to the next.

"And our first," he answered, with a touch of his lips on her own.

They held this sacred secret between them a few days, though every time little Cerd came running through the hall, chased by Blida or Burginde, Raedwulf had cause to smile the deeper, knowing that such a one as this might be coming to them next year. Burginde of course knew already, but Ælfwyn had waited to tell Ealhswith until he arrived. When she did so, she told the girl alone, as they walked the confines of the nascent garden Ælfwyn was planning.

"I must leave room enough for rough play, a place where Cerd will feel he can romp and not be chided for doing so," she began, as they passed near the beech tree at the garden's heart.

Ealhswith gave a laugh. "Cerd, and the dogs, and his pony when it arrives," she agreed.

"And – and a new little one. My coming child," her mother told her.

Ealhswith stopped. Her young face betrayed the confusion she felt, and also something akin to startle, if not shock.

Ælfwyn took her hand and gave it a squeeze. "I am not perhaps as old as you think, my darling girl." She would not say more, for the sake of delicacy, and the real surprise in Ealhswith's face. There was, Ælfwyn knew, many a mother who was still bearing babes when her own daughter began doing so; early marriages made it so, even though to the young such felt unseemly. At least the girl before her was not also a bride.

She leant forward and kissed her daughter on the cheek. "Please to tell me you are happy for us, my dear girl. Happy for us all."

Ealhswith found her tongue at last. "Of course – of course I am happy," she managed.

A moment later she dissolved in tears. "You are newly wed – and happy – and have a coming babe – and no man wants me," she stammered. She was biting her lip, trying to stop her tears. It was but a weak reminder of the real pain within her breast, that pain of loneliness.

THE CHANNEL

THE first thing that impressed Edwin was the ship itself. Tied as it was to the long wooden pier, he could readily compare it with the others there at Swanawic. Though destined to carry goods for trade, it had been built along the lines of the new war-ships Ælfred had commissioned. The dragon-ships of the Danes were long, low, and flexible, their shallow draught enabling them to sail or row up streams and rivers and strike deep within the heartland. The low sides of their hulls allowed warriors on board to jump down into shallow water upon landing. The vessel Edwin studied was a merchant ship, but one built to withstand a battle at sea. It had a deeper draw and wider breadth, and the sides were much higher. These provided not only greater protection for those aboard, but for the goods they carried, lashed upon the wooden deck.

Dawn was breaking, and in answer, a sliver of Moon slipped toward the sea. The sky at the horizon paled to a rosy hue, casting the wood planking in a pinkish light, though that above was still the same deep blue as the water. Lading was underway, and Edwin took in those men carrying goods aboard. They were seamen all, toughened from wind, salt, and weather, strong of back and shoulder, their leathery hands having spent, when needed, much time at the oars. And they were impressively armed. Along the keelson, and stowed under the pine planks before the mast was the same amount of war-kit as would be found on any ship preparing to make a strike. Spears were tightly secured; shields were hanging from the inside of the gunwale, and Edwin would not have been surprised if the sea chests which held their goods, and the men would sit upon when rowing, yielded up iron-rimmed war-caps.

One thing more made impress, and it was the evident number of archers amongst the crew. Along the high sides of the ship, just beneath the gunwale, leathern quivers had been fixed, ready with fletched arrows. The bows, he saw, were stowed in the stern, behind the oak steering-oar, where they would be safe and out of the way.

The hour of departure was at hand. Edwin was already aboard, with his two chief body-guards Alwin and Wystan. They had ridden south to Swanawic, arriving just yestere'en. Their escort had been six men, who now would return with all their horses to Kilton.

The three from Kilton were laden enough, having packed full war-kit. They were thus each equipped with spear, shield, sword, and seax, and had their helmets and ring-shirts at the ready as well, in their packs. They had been given a tent-like flap in the stern under which to sleep, where their kit was stowed. Before them was the steering-oar to starboard; and at the port side of the stern, a small dinghy lay empty on the deck. Edwin and his captains stood, the sole passengers, as the crew readied to cast off. The tide had been at its slack when they crossed over the gangplank; now it had turned, the gathering water beneath them making the ship creak as she rubbed against the stanchions of the pier.

Wulgan, the ship-master, had last night told Edwin that Dorestad in Frisia was his destination, for from there Edwin and his party would be met and taken to Count Gerolf. The ship would discharge its goods at that great trading town, and linger a few days replenishing supplies and taking on the items requested by those awaiting them in Wessex.

"You have been to Frisia many times," Edwin offered.

"I have. Dorestad's treasures have always been worthy of my efforts."

"I have been told that I will be met by a merchant known to the King," Edwin continued.

The ship-master nodded. The man had hair the colour of steel, and eyes nearly so. "Fremund. I too know him well; I have ferried him many times with goods, and restored him to Wessex."

Edwin had a concern of which Wulgan might relieve him.

"I have once been to Wales," he told the ship-master, "and could understand nothing of their speech. Will it be the same for me, there in Frisia?"

The older man grinned. "You need have little worry of that. Their speech is close to ours; the words less distinct to our ears, but recognisable still. There will be a word or two you will not catch, but much of it will be no different than if you spoke to a countryman hailing some leagues distant from your own hall."

"I am glad to hear this."

"I know you go seeking a bride, and wish you well. May I carry both of you back."

Edwin had to smile, and gave a nod at this.

Now, with the Sun stretching bright fingers across the ripples of the dark sea, they cast off. The steers-man was at his great oar, rudder to their progress. He called out. Two men on the port side, where she had been tied up, took up oars and pushed her away from the pier. Her slow movement as she slid from the freed tethers was almost imperceptible beneath their feet. All others swung into easy position on their sea chests, took oar in hand, and dipped them into the water at Wulgan's command. They would row but a short distance, until the protective bay of Swanawic was left behind, then unfurl their sail and catch the wind driving them east.

Wulgan stood before the steers-man, a fellow as burly and strong-armed as any smith. To port stood the dark landscape, to starboard, the open water of the broad channel, beyond which lay Frankland. Edwin had sailed all his life in the small boats Kilton kept, but the greater heave and swell of a large ship under his feet was new to him. He had never been sea-sick and was glad of it, for the roll from starboard to port, combined with the dipping of the prow as she took on the waves, would have tested a weaker belly. Yet there was in the very movement of the deck beneath him a kind of vital aliveness, even a sense of mastery over the watery element through which they ploughed.

Edwin watched Wulgan's eyes as they scanned first his own ship, and then rose over the gunwales to sea and sky. He went to his side. The ship-master had shown no hesitation in speaking with Edwin last night, and today he would learn more. Edwin began with an observation which would make glad the heart of any war-chief.

"Your men are well-armed, and look more than able."

"That they are. And in the last two sailing seasons we have rarely seen more than two drekars together, hunting for game. We might spot a single ship, most of which we can stand up to, well enough. They have passed us by when they see our size, and the number of men we carry."

It was not the full tale, and Wulgan did not spare it.

"I have lost two ships, and once nearly my life," he admitted.

"By storm, or capture?" Edwin wished to know.

"Capture, both times by Danes. The first happened as our ship sat at anchor, while coasting. My crew and I were left stranded, impoverished, but unhurt. The second time was direct attack, outnumbered three ships to one. We were taken prisoner, but having made the Danes understand we could be ransomed, I was allowed to send a man ashore and to Ælfred to do just that. For our return they gave us something little better than a river barge to sail back. It was four months of hardship, but we returned alive."

"Yet you have persisted," Edwin noted.

The ship-master lifted his chin a moment, and gave a low laugh. "There is no surer way to build riches than through trade. No surer way that does not include the killing of other men. Yes, I persisted.

"I have been of service to the King, and before that, my father, to his Kingly brothers. We have rarely failed in bringing them those goods they asked for, nor in delivering those they entrusted to us. Thus I have persisted, to our mutual gain."

On this sail to Frisia they would be doing little coasting, but rather sailing through the night when they

could. Deeper waters brought safety. The draught of
the ship made the vessel liable to run aground on shallow shores, and her heavy construction took much tide
water to refloat her. They would land only at those ports
of call needful to the trading mission, all of which sported
wooden piers in water deep enough to keep her out of
danger. The weather at harvest time was often clear at
night, allowing the steers-man unhindered view of the
stars. And Wulgan himself was a star-reader. At night,
with the coast of Wessex obscured by darkness, he and
the steers-man both could pilot onward.

On the second day they had passed the Isle of Wiht.
They were headed due east, the coast of Wessex remaining in sight, when they saw the war-ship.

The man stationed in the prow as look-out saw her
first, and whistled out warning. All eyes rose to him, his
arm straight before him, off to starboard, his pointing
finger as rigid as a wind-vane.

All were silent. The ship was yet a single form, a
smudge upon a light, noon-day sea. She was broadside
to them as they drove forward. Edwin stood motionless
in the stern, wanting to pick his way forward to the look-
out, and yet in the freighted silence unable to move. He
was aware Alwin had turned and vanished under the tar-
paulin which served as their tent. He heard the sounds of
their packs being pulled open.

The sail over their heads held steady; the steers-
man gave no order, his hands gripping the oar as it had
moments before. Wulgan too held silence. Their sail was
undyed linen and wool, a colour which vanished against
a cloudy sky. The sail of the ship they watched was dark
with dye. All stood, straining their eyes to it.

The current was swift here, past the Isle of Wiht, and driving back for its shelter would be costly in time and effort. They must see who and what this other ship was before acting.

Alwin was now at Edwin's side, Wystan as well. Alwin had helmet and sword in hand, Wystan, Edwin's shield and spear. No others of the men had armed, and Edwin was loath to take them, but Alwin's eyes told him he must. The man at once returned for his own war-kit, as did Wystan. Tunics of leather were pulled on, and over them, their ring-shirts. They belted on their swords, slung their shields on their backs, and took up their spears. Their helmets remained at their feet, awaiting that extreme.

They stood to a man watching the dark ship. They kept on their course, a merchant ship on a trading mission, letting nothing daunt them. They neared enough so that some details of the strange ship became known to them. She had not tacked, and was still lying broadside and ahull to their view.

A low murmuring growl arose from the throats of a few of Wulgan's men. Edwin felt himself lifting almost on tiptoe, straining to see more of the ship. The wind was fresh enough for salt spray, and some mist from it seemed to hang in the air. Then Edwin saw the vessel for what she was. A war-ship, and likely a drekar of the Danes. Even from this distance, he could number the painted shields hanging outside the hull from the gunwale. Eighteen, he counted, which meant thirty-six at the oars, and the possibility of more, aboard just to fight. The assurance of Wulgan's words of last night, concerning the scarcity of Danish pursuers, vanished as quickly as the mist he peered through.

"To starboard!" called the steers-man. Prow-on as they were, the drekar could see their breadth. He would tack, turn the ship so the drekar might fully see the length of her. Her size was such it might deter them from thoughts of attack.

It did not. All aboard the merchant ship knew the war-chief on the Danish ship was making the same calculation. It was hastily made, for she was at once off, beating her way to them.

Wulgan made quick decision, and had brought forth a small iron cauldron in which he set about kindling fire. Fire-making upon most ships was strictly forbidden. Of all the ways a seaman might die, fire at sea was greatly feared. But Wulgan and others like him must seek recourse where they could. He began soaking linen strips in oil to use as large wicks, the source of fuel the wick itself. One each of these would be tied just behind the flare of an iron arrow head, and when the bowman was ready, lit. As soon as the drekar was within striking range it would be met with a barrage of flaming arrows.

Yet it was not a simple, burnable linen strip the ship-master prepared. He had not traded in the waters of Sicily, Pisa, and Rhodes in his youth without hearing of their own sea-raiders, and the great military battles fought at sea in ages past. He had learnt enough of the making of war-fire to combine pine resin, quicklime, and sulfur in his mix. Once lit it became a sticky, white-hot source of flame, one difficult to extinguish. Water was of no avail, it must be thoroughly smothered. These were the arrows which would greet the drekar.

Most flaming arrows hitting a ship would be at once snatched up and flung overboard. It was a weapon which could not be returned to them from the enemy's own bows. Nearly all Wulgan's crew were good bowmen, and many arrows could find home in some flammable substance. A number might strike sail and deck at once, and lodge in the upraised shields held in the fists of the men who stood under them. Straw might be aboard, oft used as packing material to cushion goods. And coils of hempen rope, rich in natural oil, were vulnerable to flame, and the shredded remains of such used as tinder. The war-fire Wulgan mixed to anoint the linen could be far more deadly than the arrows themselves.

Wulgan's crew knew these things; the men of Kilton guessed only that the ship-master sought to dress his arrows with fire. The intent with which Wulgan worked, cauldron and open chest of materials before him, made Edwin hesitate to trouble him. Yet he squatted down next to where the ship-master knelt. Wulgan's eyes shifted to him, taking in how the young Lord had armed himself, then back to what he worked with.

"If we are boarded your skill will be welcome," was all Wulgan said.

His archers were his first line of attack. If they failed, all hands would be required to repel, and hopefully overcome, the foe. And indeed, letting fly an arrow on a rolling ship was far different from on land. The bowman must adjust for the swell of the waves, watching and timing his release so he neither over or under shot.

Edwin arose; the look-out had again whistled. The nearing drekar had tacked so that they now had full view of her starboard side. The curl of the prow was crowned with the carved head of a beast, mouth agape. Each swell the merchant ship rode lifted her, giving her a glimpse within the enemy ship.

The shields were there, the men seemingly were not. Six-and-thirty painted wooden discs hung outside the gunwales. But a scan over the starboard rail showed far fewer of those who could wield them. Unless men remained somehow hidden until the actual assault, the display of hanging shields was there in attempt to cow their targets. Wulgan had a crew of two-and-twenty men, all warrior-seamen. He and the steers-man must remain in their vital roles, but with the three from Kilton they numbered twenty-five fighting men with whom to rebuff the attack.

The ship-master rose from his efforts a moment, calling out that the dinghy they carried in their stern be lowered. It was a launch which could fit five or six men, and used for going ashore in shallow water. Wulgan ordered it overboard with its oars, so that if any of his men found themselves in the sea they could be retrieved.

The crew of the merchantman could see the war-chief leading the band of Danes, standing starboard next the steers-man. His shield, painted with circles of black and green, was in hand, but he had yet to lift it. Every man on Wulgan's ship who had attained thirty Summers judged the same: this captain looked a young hot-blood, hungry for winnings, hasty in judgement. He had given chase, exhorted his men, and now must live up to the promise of booty. He would be the first target.

Now nearing their quarry, the drekar tacked again. The merchant ship was so high-hulled that the Danes' standard tactic for boarding gave them pause. Thrown grappling hooks to pull the victim ship alongside were of little use. The merchant ship's higher gunwales made it more difficult to land a hook, and even if the two hulls should touch, the attackers would be left at grave disadvantage. Instead of leaping gunwale to gunwale, they must clamber up and over, making them prime targets for the thrust of a spear.

Wulgan and his steers-man did not slow. They had become aggressors, bearing down on the dragon-ship as if they might ram her. The ship-master had his preparation at the ready, and those men not needed in the handling of the sail took up bows and quivers. Three men squatted by Wulgan, tying the soaked linen strips to the arrows. A fourth had lit a cresset, its flame steady even in the breeze which swept across the deck. They would grow closer, tack again broadside of the drekar, light the wicks, and the archers let fly. First they would see if they could kill the Danish captain.

The two best of the merchantman's archers took up position amidship. Their bows were in hand, arrows at the ready, but both were lowered to their knees, and out of sight of the approaching Danes. No fire would flame from these arrow heads; this they would save for the greater assault. It was not unknown that the sudden death of a war-chief could halt an attack then and there, as those senior most amongst their followers fought to assume command. It was worth sparing the war-fire to see what would happen if Wulgan's two best shots could remove the attacking chief first. The man stood, spear upright in hand, shield held before his chest, just before his steers-man. He had donned no helmet, whether from personal dislike of its weight, or his ignorance that archers were aboard his chosen quarry.

The Danes he led had begun their war-chant, a rowdy mix of metal clanging on iron shield rims, taunts, and boasts. Those aboard Wulgan's ship remained quiet.

When his two bowmen deemed their target within range, they glanced at the other, then raised their bows and nocked their arrows. They let fly at nearly the same instant, their target the head of the Danish war-chief.

One arrow found home there. It hit the man above his right eyebrow. A moment later and the ship would have dropped enough in the sea swell to have missed him entirely. As it was the arrow ploughed upward into the crown of the skull, and he fell back, almost hitting the steers-man.

Cheers erupted from the throats of Wulgan's men, the three from Kilton joining in hoots of jubilant acclaim. Bellows of dismayed anger followed from the drekar, and the rush of men to where their captain had fallen obscured the downed body. Now shouting voices arose, as some aboard vied to assert themselves as leader. If any claimed that mantle the steers-man remained undeterred, and drove steadily for the ship which had now claimed their war-chief.

The drekar neared, its prow to the merchantman's stern.

A barrage of flaming arrows greeted the dragon-ship. Some fell short, others overshot. Those aiming for the broad face of the sail fared best, the arrows themselves puncturing the linsey-woolsey, the soaked, flaming linen tied behind the iron head forming smouldering, and growing, dark wounds on the billowing fabric. Others fell on the deck, and even lodged in the hull. The Danes snatched the flaming arrows up and threw them overboard, yet in many cases a strip of the sticky fabric remained behind, burning still. They stepped on them with booted feet, threw dippers-full of rationed fresh water, and then buckets-full of sea water upon the fiery mess. The Danes who had taken up grappling hooks were left scrambling for cover. Still, the drekar neared.

More arrows, both aflame with fired linen and those of simple, deadly iron were let fly. Danes fell, some of them overboard.

Edwin looked to Alwin. Wulgan and his steers-man were well defended. The prow and stern of both ships rose higher, and were thus more difficult of access. They must move amidship; it was that part of the merchantman least protected. And it was the point at which the Danes would try their grappling hooks, in attempt to board. Edwin had never fought at sea, nor, he knew, had Alwin or Wystan. It seemed now he would. He who had taken command of the drekar seemed resolved to risk all to board; indeed, now in danger of losing the dragon-ship to fire, there was little else to do.

One thrown hook made it aloft, but the distance and upward angle was too great for the Dane's strong arm to overcome. It raked the outside of the merchantman's hull a moment, then splashed into the water. He had no chance to pull it up, for in the time it took to fling the hook and see it fly, an arrow from Wulgan's ship found home in his breast.

Upon the drekar one of the hemp lines controlling the sail caught fire, small licking flames travelling up to the heavy spar to which the bottom end of the sail was tethered. The sail, already pocked with fire, was now fur-ther weakened. A faulty line meant one easily snapped under the stress of wind and handling. Amongst the Danes were those who must lay down their weapons and take up any bucket or basin of water which could be used in attempt to quench the many small fires. Yet anything touched by the actual war-fire would not yield to water; it must be smothered. And if remnants of the sulfurous substance touched flesh, the resulting burn made men howl in agony of pain.

The dragon-ship would not relent. It carried no archers, but as it came within range of the merchantman it unleashed a volley of throwing spears. Two found home in the bodies of the undefended bowmen. The hunter had become prey, but was still able to inflict a toll.

Aboard Wulgan's ship all effort was placed on driving off the drekar, and removing itself from its range. But the wind had slackened, and the drekar's sail was further impediment, cutting off needed breeze. Setting men to the oars meant no chance to keep on with their offensive barrage. The small launch had been lowered off the port side into the water by two lines, one fore and aft, and it remained there, further drag to their escape. Wulgan called out that it be hauled up, and with his own men giving needed cover to the ship-master and steers-man, Edwin and his body-guard crossed the deck to haul. They looked down into the water swirling along the hull. Hanging to the side of the dinghy was not one but two Danes. A third had closed his hands upon the bow-line securing the small craft and, feet braced against the hull of the ship, was in the act of pulling himself up, scaling the straked planks as he came.

Edwin had his spear in his fist. Alwin was right at his side. Their surprise was such that not a single oath fell from their lips. He scaling the hull was less than a man's length below them. Both men from Kilton jolted forward, leaning over the gunwale, spear-points foremost. The Dane's face, straining from exertion as he walked up the side, contorted further at the sight of them. They hit the Dane nearly as one, strong two-handed thrusts in the chest and belly of the invader. His clenched fists opened from the hempen line; his feet dropped from the wood of the hull. He fell, splashing back into the sea from whence he had come.

Wystan had whistled sharply to the nearest bowman, who now joined them, arrow nocked, and more in his quiver. The two Danes who had been clinging to the dinghy had surrendered their holds and were swimming away. They did not get far.

The four grasped the lines to the launch and began hauling it up. It came with difficulty, bumping the side of the hull until it could be steadied, then grasped by the rail, and pulled up and over.

All during this the clamour from the deck had grown, a riot of shouts, oaths, and war-cries mixed with the clang of metal and the scrape of wood. Edwin and his two captains turned back to see the drekar, overcome with many small fires, gybing, and almost upon them. The Danes' hope of survival lay in the merchantman, and their determined steers-man would do his utmost to bring her alongside.

Wulgan's men must circumvent that. Not many of the drekar's men remained standing, but a cluster still fronted the steers-man in his relentless effort.

The nearness of the afflicted ship had become hazard. Bits of flaming sail cloth came loose from near the top of its mast, and began to float down, a slow and fiery rain, into the water, onto its own deck, and onto that of the merchantman. They dropped their own sail to spare it. Its men stood, their oars in their hands, in attempt to push the much lighter drekar away when it came within range. Edwin stood, heart pounding, as the action unfolded. His spear was clenched, upright, in his right hand. With it he had taken part in the killing of one man, but now must stand and wait. A burning ship neared, its warriors doomed to a man if they could not take the merchant-man. Failing that, it would try to take its quarry with them to the cold depths.

In the stern Wulgan and his picked men made ready. They had grabbed any fabric at hand, clothing, towelling, pieces of sail cloth used for patching, and soaked them in sea water. As flaming clumps landed, they smothered them with these.

The only remaining offence for the Danes lay in ram-ming the merchantman, though it might be the sinking of both ships. Undaunted it approached, smoking like an oily torch.

The crew of the merchantmen had seen enough. The outrage of attack was now surpassed by the sheer need to survive. The senior most of them, glaring down at the dragon-ship began to yell. "Board! Board!"

These men of Wulgan's would now jump down and fight their way to where the steers-man stood, and stop his resolute progress with their steel.

Edwin saw this; saw too he must be part of it. Wulgan's men had their war-caps on; hardened leather strapped over with thin bands of iron. They had no ring-shirts, no leathern tunics to protect their bodies; but they doused themselves with buckets of sea water as protection from the flaming pieces of sail wafting down.

He looked to Alwin at his right. The man's jaw was set, and the glint of his eyes through the holes in his helmet told of his readiness. Wystan too looked eager, and by the motion of his eyes Edwin thought he counted each enemy they must overcome. Given the men that must remain aboard, both to handle the ship and to prevent direct ramming from the drekar, they would slightly outnumber the Danes. Yet the men they would face aboard that burning vessel were desperate.

For a moment Edwin found himself thinking of the treasure of gold hanging about his neck, and the same about the necks of Alwin and Wystan. If they risked their lives they must risk the gold. There was not time enough to pull them out from under leather and ring-tunics, and entrust them to Wulgan. He found himself thinking a moment of Ceric, and his telling him how glad he had been, not to have been forced to fight upon a rolling deck. Now Edwin could return to Kilton having done so. He knew his father had fought at sea; he would, as well.

Alwin was speaking, snapping Edwin back to confronting the burning ship into which they would now jump.

"Stay alive," he told Edwin.

Yes, thought Edwin. Stay alive; a dead man cannot fight. But he knew Alwin meant more than this. They would fight, the three of them, as a unit, and just as it was his two captains' roles to try and ensure his survival, he must not place himself at unnecessary risk. Kilton depended on his return.

Wulgan had his steers-man ease his prow nearer to that of the dragon-ship. The lines from the stripped mast would allow a few men to swing over in quick order, while others leapt down to the drekar's deck. Those clustered there to protect the steers-man must divide, if they were to meet the crew of the merchantman as they began their assault.

The chief amongst Wulgan's warriors was first over, swinging from a mast line to land just before the spar. An instant later a second followed, taking time to fling both lines back within range of reaching arms awaiting them on the deck of the merchantman. For the Danes the action of their landing was partially obscured by the drekar's tattered sail. Despite burnt patches across its face, it still was catching wind.

Two more from Wulgan's ship took line in hand and swung out over the shrinking distance between hulls. This had closed enough to meet outstretched oar tips, blunting its approach, turning the drekar's prow to bump a moment against the sturdy oaken planks of the merchantman. The gape-mouthed monster on its prow no longer bore down on them, but was turned toward their stern, the distance between the two gunwales at times no greater than a single ell.

It was their chance. Ten men leapt down from deck to deck, shields on their backs, fists clenching spear shafts. They dropped in groups of twos and threes, trying to time their leaps, their knees folding under them as they absorbed the greater or lesser shock as the deck rose and fell beneath them. Some staggered to all fours, but all straightened, freeing their shields and closing their left hands behind iron bosses.

The grunt issuing from Edwin's mouth as his feet hit the deck was echoed by Alwin and Wystan. The drop of the sea-swell had carried the drekar down, and they hit the planked surface hard. All three pitched forward, stumbling a long unsteady moment before regaining footing, scrambling to get out of the path of those now leaping after them.

It was a hellish scene to jump into. Two Danes lay sprawled in death, arrows in their chests, nearly under the wooden spar. One had been hit by an arrow anointed with the war-fire, and his torso was become a smouldering torch, repellent to the eye and repugnant to the nose. The spar itself was afire, blackening under tiny licking flames crawling across its length. A store of controlling hempen line which had been hit by the war-fire lay in a neat coil of ghostly, fibrous cinders. The arrow which had found it was burnt to powder, but the long iron head stood rigidly fixed at a slight angle near the heart of that grey ash.

The last of the fourteen men from Wulgan's ship were in the act of leaping down when the sky seemed to fall. It was dark red, and eaten by fire; the dragon-ship's sail. The Danes, seeing their chance, took up axes with violent hacks at the hauling lines. The sail collapsed in a billowing heap upon the spar and deck, forming instant barrier between the opposing warriors. A few of Wulgan's men were caught under, and their brethren leapt to free them. But the spar lines, compromised as they were by fire, snapped on the port side, dropping the spar at a shallow angle on the deck, one end wedged under the starboard gunwale.

The Danes had few throwing spears left, but now with free view of the boarding party, used them. Two of

Wulgan's men, clambering over the wreckage of sail and spar, fell. The bellows of those who rushed onward to the stern were the greater for their loss. It was spear to spear, Wulgan's men trying to align themselves as a moving shield-wall as they dodged patches of burning deck, lashed casks and goods, and the bodies of fallen Danes.

The defending Danes split into three groups, one shielding the steers-man, with two, in fanning out to the starboard and port gunwales, attempting to defeat the makeshift shield-wall. There was no sail to catch the freshening wind, but the ruffling sea gave uncertain footing for all. Wulgan's men must split as well, to keep from being flanked by the parted Danes. A moment's hesitation found Edwin having to choose to turn to port with the men just before him, or continue ahead to the stern, where Wulgan's two head warriors had stormed. He took a breath and plunged forward, hearing in his right ear Alwin's oath against his choice. The fighting at the steering-oar was bound to be the fiercest. Stay alive, his captain had warned him, yet the knowledge that he might play a decisive part in ending this threat spurred Edwin on. And he knew Wulgan was looking down upon the action.

There were fewer obstacles here, all sea chests and goods having been cleared away, and though he heard the clang of metal and calls of men as they fought to either side along the gunwales, those Danes standing firm before the steering-oar braced themselves for the onslaught. One thing littered the deck before their feet. It was the body of their captain, he who had fallen first. The arrow had been pulled from his brow, but the wound, and his black and green shield, gave proof of identity. Edwin looked down at him, veering to avoid the body. The man had known no more than five-and-twenty years, he gauged. About his neck, and resting on his tunic, lay a triangular amulet of silver. A few strides more and Edwin and the five men with him clashed with the waiting Danes.

The pitch and roll of the ship made Edwin feel he fought two adversaries – those men before him, and the deck itself, ready to make faulty his spear thrust, or open his shield arm to a body hit. Yet as engagement it did not last long. He did as he had been trained, moving his spear to threaten the heads and shoulders of those he faced, giving with his shield both cover to himself, and with a shift of stance, to Alwin at his left. Unbalanced as he sometimes felt, his foe faced the same handicap. The Dane across from him was taken out by Wystan with a sudden, lucky jab to the thigh, after which Alwin's point ended it. Edwin made a touch at a second man, a hit at the right shoulder which made him lower his spear. One of Wulgan's men finished him. The way ahead opened; the view cleared as Wulgan's two picked men dropped three more. Edwin caught a glimpse at last of the steersman. He was an older man, resolute, hands still agrip on that oaken steering-beam. His was become a death ship, but he would not relent. Wulgan's chief man took him down with a drawn seax. As he fell, Edwin saw the same silver triangular amulet about the neck of the steers-man. Father and son, or uncle and nephew, Edwin knew, to wear the same amulet. They could go to Asgard or to Hell now, wearing them.

A cry went up, in loud and urgent demand. All the Danes who had defended the steering-oar were dead. Those few who remained along the gunwales had thrown down their spears in surrender. There were six of them, two at starboard, four at port. Wulgan could be heard, shouting down orders from the deck of his ship. The drekar was beyond claiming, a piece of floating wreckage upon which crept small but steadily spreading fires. The battle won, at once attention turned to the hasty gathering of booty. Men stripped the dead of their weaponry, and took up any leathern packs easy to shoulder.

Cargo nets were thrown onto the drekar's deck, into which the captured Danes and the victors heaved sea chests. The three of Kilton joined Wulgan's two men in hastening to the recess of the curved stern, behind the now-abandoned steering-oar. This was where the sea chests and packs of both the captain and the steers-man would be stowed, the two most likely to hold treasure. Any goods quickly laid hands on were seized and added to the battle-gain. The prisoners were forced up rope ladders to the deck of the merchantman, and the cargo nets hauled up. As a final sign of its vanquishment, one of Wulgan's men scaled the inside of the prow, and knocked out the wooden pins holding the gape-mouth figurehead. It was the last thing loaded in the final cargo net as trophy.

Wulgan wasted no time in placing distance between his ship and the despoiled drekar. Indeed, that ill-Fated vessel seemed to trail in their wake, wandering ghost-like, attempting to catch them. The merchantman's sail was hauled up, and she tacked away from the drifting wreck. Wulgan had lost four men, with two more taking injuries, both flesh wounds. The surviving Danes were made to sit upon the deck while Wulgan addressed them.

After the affront the merchantman had suffered, it would have been meet to cast these Danes overboard, or leave them upon the burning ship, where they might try to claim any bit of flotsam to float on, hoping the tide would carry them to some shore. It would be meet and just, but it would not be merciful.

"I will set you to the oar until our next port of call here along our coast," Wulgan told them. "If you serve well, you will remain aboard. If not, I will march you off, and into the hands of the King's Reeve, who will undoubtedly hang you straightaway. Or you can continue to serve me, and when we reach Frankland I will sell you in the market. The silver you bring will be taken back to Swanawic and given to the families of those you have killed."

He spoke slowly and loudly, and scanned their faces, grimy with oily smoke and sweat, as he did. As a choice it was simple: certain death at the hands of the King's law in Wessex, or life and the uncertainties of slavery in Frankland. At least some recompense might come to those whose men did not return.

Wulgan's eyes fell on a Dane no older than eighteen years, who looked back at him.

"Do you understand," he demanded. His question was met by nods.

One of the Danes was gripping his forearm, just below the elbow. The tunic sleeve was gone, ripped away, and a dark rent in his skin showed where the war-fire had eaten at his flesh. Indeed, fragments of the fiery mixture were like tiny living coals within the wound, even now. Wulgan took pity on the man. Going to the same chest from which he had taken the makings of the deadly stuff, he brought forth a pottery crock. A soft salve of beeswax, honey, the crushed seeds of both nettle and hemp, and a few drops of rose oil was within. Wulgan stirred this with a wooden spoon, and smeared a bit over the charred and blackened flesh. It melted at once, filling the cavity, smothering the burning effect. The war-fire had not reached the bone, and though the arm would be scarred, he should not lose it.

He and his men turned now to the hard-won battle-gain. Those who had downed men had claim to all they carried, but the contents of sea chests, leathern packs, and goods aboard the drekar were shared out in equal measure amongst all. There was the standard gain of extra weaponry, clothing, small stores of silver, and jew-ellery. Surprises were there as well. One chest yielded a rich set of horse trappings, a bridle and reins of dark tanned leather set with small lozenges of bright brass. A small cask held eight tall pale green Rhenish glass bea-kers, carefully swathed in straw, perfect and whole in the grasp. Bolts of blue woollen cloth awaited the skilled hands of wives at home, from which to fashion mantles and Winter tunics. There were two bales of long-fleeced white sheep skin, and a rare sealskin cape, proof against the rain, which single item Wulgan set aside for himself. The gape-mouthed figurehead he would take to Ælfred. The rest he parcelled out to his men and guests, who in many cases set about trading with each other.

The men from Kilton were equally enriched, and for ease of transport nearly all awarded to them they traded for silver. There was fitness and satisfaction in this for Edwin. He had been part of a band of warriors, fighting for an urgent and common end. All were rewarded for their success, accepting the spoils of the battle from the hands of Wulgan. It gave Edwin unexpected insight into what the thegns of Kilton had ever experienced. His own brother knew this, having been awarded booty by Prince Eadward. Now Edwin entered into this brotherhood.

After all had stowed their battle-gain, eyes rose, almost as one, across the water. It was late afternoon, the Sun still hot and bright above them. But as they sailed onward they saw the plundered drekar fully engulfed, right to the waterline, a flaming beacon and funeral pyre both.

FRISIAN WASTES

FRISIA was a place of water. The mouth of the River Rhine was the only distinct thing about it, a broad open flow snaking through endless tidal marshes and mud flats. The river was immense; what surrounded it a thing almost of sorcery. What looked sodden land one hour was in flood the next. Folk went about in shallow, flat bottomed boats to cross these reed-dotted expanses; large ships hewed to the deep waters of the Rhine to reach the trading centre of Dorestad. As they sailed down, Edwin saw the occasional croft set above the mud flats. These small farms were green with verdure, and well fenced to keep livestock from wandering. He was astonished to learn the earthen berms these crofts sat upon were man-made, painstakingly dug from the mud, and thus built up beyond the tidal reach.

Dorestad sat at a fork on the Rhine, and had been built by the men of Caesar. The old fortress of stone was still extant, and wooden walkways led from the landing stages through the gates. It had once been a trading centre to rival Jorvik or Haithabu or Ribe, but lying as it did upon a river difficult of defence, Danes had, in recent generations found it a ready target. They had been at last beaten back by the forces of local war-lords, and as reward the King of East Francia had granted additional lands to the leader who had become known as Count Gerolf. It was Gerolf Edwin had come to see.

At Dorestad Wulgan placed Edwin and his party into the hands of Fremund the merchant. This trader, trusted by Ælfred, and the source of no little profit to the Kingdom of Wessex, had been alerted to Edwin's arrival. Wulgan would remain at Dorestad four days, and as he was charged with returning the Lord of Kilton to Swanawic, let him know that if his wooing required it, he would be prepared to wait another day or two.

Fremund was a man of Wessex, one in his fifth decade, and one who travelled always with a body-guard at his side. He was slight of frame, with a quick and searching eye, but a slowness of speech becoming to his dealings with the rich.

Rhenish wine and objects of glass formed the greater part of the goods passing through Dorestad, and it had as well a mint, stamping molten silver from the sale of these into coins. Yet evidence was there the town was in decline; the structures just behind the sheltering wall being kept in service as workshops, warehouses, and dwellings. Beyond this timber buildings and some of stone too were crumbing from disuse. Cows roamed here, sticking their heads from the doorways of roofless buildings which had once housed folk; and numberless cats sauntered along empty lanes.

As they had tied up late in the afternoon, Edwin and his men were taken to a timber house kept by Fremund within the walls, for with the mud flats waiting to snag any boat, there was no safe travelling down the Rhine after dark. This household was run by a buxom woman and her daughters, who did not join them at table, and whose exact relationship to Fremund remained unexplained. The women were fine hostesses though, and amply skilled as cooks. That night Edwin, Alwin, and Wystan drank the strongest ale they had ever tasted, a musky brew so potent that a single mouthful was felt in the head. This was offered in flared beakers of bubbled clear glass such as those found on the drekar, and made fine show for them. Their meal was a pottage of duck served with firm loaves of rye flour, an admirable pairing after days of ship's rations.

In the morning they were off, five men in a flat-bottomed craft, oared by two boatmen in Fremund's employ. It was not long past dawn, and the mist arising from the grey waters of the Rhine was thick enough to bead as drops of moisture along the surfaces of the open boat, and upon the men within. There was that smell of living river water common to all such flows, a scent of cool rain steaming up in mists from the still surface. They headed south down the broad river, where a certain inlet would lead them to the hall kept by Count Gerolf. The two boatmen began by oaring, sitting side by side, one thick paddle in the hands of each as they pushed them down stream, slicing into the heavy brown face of the Rhine. But at the inlet they at times stood and punted for lack of water, the tide running to ebb just then.

"All your journeyings must be carefully timed," Edwin observed to Fremund. He sat in the stern with the man, the three body-guards sitting one in the bow, and two behind the boatmen.

"The river and her tides rules all," the merchant admitted. He grinned and added, "And the sea rules the river, and the Moon, the sea."

This ordering of the natural world was familiar to Edwin, and at this moment, acting under the advice of his own Earthly King, felt apt reflection of the spheres of power and influence. When they had set out this morning, the Moon, at its tender crescent, was just setting. It prompted Edwin's question.

"And what rules the Moon," he pondered aloud.

Fremund had been beholden to this shining orb's movements, and effects upon his sailing ventures his entire life, and made thoughtful answer. "It follows us, the Moon, circling round, as does the Sun."

"Are we then such objects of fascination?"

It was an unusually thoughtful question for a young man, and Edwin almost surprised himself by uttering it.

"Only to ourselves," Fremund allowed, with a low laugh. He looked across the sodden marshlands they pushed through. "Yet the Eternal King in Heaven gives care, and has sent it all spinning."

Edwin nodded. The man would be devout; Ælfred would deal with no less, and Edwin knew enough in his nineteenth year to understand the comforts of a creed. As brutish and short as life could be, more awaited, either grandeur or punishment. And there was comfort in knowing life went on when we had left; his grandmother Lady Modwynn had often reminded him of this. Even these barren mud flats and brackish meres sheltered birds to whom they offered succour.

They fell back into silence. Edwin had of yet not broached the topic of Gerolf's daughters to the merchant.

The man had shown no proclivity last night to undertake the subject, possibly deeming it unseemly to do so at table. Yet the young Lord of Kilton knew so little; only that the Count had, through Fremund, made known his willingness to entertain Edwin and present the maids. Propelled by the steady punting of the two standing men, Edwin was aware he glided toward a woman who very likely would become his wife. It was an unsteadying thought, far more so than the approach to Elidon's keep had been on the coast of Ceredigion. Then he had cantered through that monarch's gates full of confidence. Once within he had seen a winsome girl he admired, and wanted. Then, at Kilton, she had spurned him.

Well-wrapped as Edwin was in his wool mantle, the fog rising from the water chilled him. As if his innermost thoughts were known, a crake cried out in seeming complaint, flapping over his head, seeking more than these watery wastes.

It took the better part of the morning to reach Gerolf's hall. The narrow inlet they punted upon was joined by another, allowing the boatmen to sit and row in its deeper waters. An odour arose from the waters wherever they rowed or poled, a fusty and fetid vegetal scent of decaying marsh plants lifting from the ooze. The Sun had burnt through the mist and was nearly overhead when they sighted their goal. It looked to Edwin's eye a small island sitting above the marsh, and was in fact man-made, laboriously dug from mud trenched out of the marsh to form a surrounding moat. Behind a stockade fence cattle grazed on still-lush grass, and beyond the herd lay a small timber fortress.

Near the landing stage stood a simple wooden tower, the height of two men giving view enough over such a low landscape. A watcher within that tower sighted them and placed a brass horn to his lips. As they oared up, a man, richly dressed, came hustling out to greet them. His face was creased with care, and Fremund clambered to the bow and was on the landing stage first. As his boatmen tied the craft up, Fremund remained speaking in low tones to the man, who looked some high ranking functionary in the household, judging by the chain of silver reaching from shoulder to shoulder upon his tunic.

Edwin and his men disembarked and stood waiting at a respectful distance. Fremund turned to them, and all could read the dashed hope upon his furrowed brow.

"My Lord Edwin of Kilton," he began, and gestured to the functionary. "This is Eberhard, the steward of Count Gerolf." Eberhard nodded to Edwin, but the bleak expression on the steward's face warned Edwin of bad tidings to come.

Edwin was not kept in suspense. Eberhard addressed him directly, and Edwin found that he could, as promised, understand his speech. It was much like his own, but with a decidedly softer, more slurred tone.

"The Count has just died," Eberhard began, "gone to his Redeemer under cover of night.

"All is in turmoil," Eberhard went on. "Though Count Gerolf was aged, the death was quite unexpected."

Edwin stood, slack-jawed at this news. He had never imagined he would not be given chance to present himself. He looked helplessly to Fremund.

It was the steward who spoke, distress and apology both in his tone. "The hall is in mourning. I invite you nonetheless to come in, and take refreshment, before you return to Dorestad."

Edwin must remind himself a man had died; a man who could have been his father-in-law. The effort and time to reach here was irrecoverable, but a man was dead. He uttered his condolences to Eberhard, barely able to form the words through his shock.

The steward excused himself, asking the arrivals to await his return, and made for the hall.

When he was out of earshot Fremund spoke.

"I grieve for your timing, my Lord. The Count has a son and successor, Dirk, who is on his way, but I doubt anything could be decided with the speed in which you prefer. Also in a time of mourning . . ."

The trader's pause was an extended one.

"And – I have had dealings with Dirk," he continued. "His desired ends for his sisters may be quite different from those of their father's."

There was something ill-omened about this, and Edwin's face prompted the man to say more.

"A father wishes to see his daughters wed. A brother, with daughters of his own, may be just as happy to see his sisters closeted in a nunnery, to save him the effort and silver of marrying them to advantage. Especially when his sisters are many."

Edwin said what he must. "So I have come all this way, to return without a bride."

"It sorrows me to say this is likely the case."

Eberhard was approaching now, and they followed him up the planked walkway, past the herd of browsing brown cattle, and through the waiting gates.

They were led not to the main hall, but to one ancillary, stoutly built of upright timbers and highly decorated in paint of red and blue. It was in fact a separate feasting hall, kept for high occasions. It was deserted, but two serving men followed them within, to whom Eberhard gave quiet instruction.

"You will be brought food and drink, and I will return shortly," he promised.

The steward left, and from the doorway they watched him as he entered the main hall. The opening of that door allowed a discord of lamentation to escape; the wailing of women, and more poignantly, muffled and heaving sobs. The Count's body had perhaps been brought out, to be laid upon a table before those grieving.

Edwin turned from this, back to the empty feasting hall which had known many a joyous gathering. He might have been wed here, he told himself. He must curse Fate for his timing. Could he somehow remain in Dorestad a while, and then be presented to the orphaned daughters? And with whom would he deal, for bride-price and dowry?

He tried to temper his impatience in his next words to Fremund. He must, for the sake of civility, and the fact that Alwin and Wystan were with him.

"Tell me the truth. The daughters – you have seen them. Are they worth waiting for?"

"They – are sturdy of make," Fremund offered, as if they were articles of utility.

"Sturdy of make," Edwin repeated. "Are they then stout?"

"They are of comfortable aspect, yes."

"Are they fair of face?'

"They are not displeasing to the eye."

If this was all the girls had to recommend themselves, it was little enough. He found himself looking to Alwin, who gave a shrug.

"And of their fortunes?" Edwin asked next.

"Ah. Unless the late Count has made separate allowance for them in his will, his truest heir is his son."

Gerolf had been willing to offer generous dowries for his unwed daughters, but like many men had left them little on their own account.

Edwin stifled his sigh, and nodded instead. "I thank you," he said.

Fremund went on. "There are of course other families here in Frisia to provide a Lady for your hall. But that the match be one approved, even encouraged by Ælfred . . . of this I could give you no assurance."

Again, Edwin could only nod in agreement. It was better to wait, to wed with the King's blessing, than grasp at a union without it.

Eberhard appeared, leading several tray-bearing men and women. One look at their faces told them Gerolf's death pained them, or perhaps it was the uncertainty of their own futures Edwin read there.

Fremund spoke again, while there was still time for privacy.

"At any rate, with the hall in such disarray . . ."

Edwin need answer. They must eat, convey their condolences once more to the steward, and leave. "Yes. I am
an intrusion, and will withdraw."

◊◊◊◊◊◊◊◊◊◊◊

After the return to Dorestad, Edwin betook himself to the long walkway fronting the town. He needed
to clear his head, and with no mount to ride out on, and
indeed few places not mired in mud, a walk there was
the best he could hope for. Alwin and Wystan were with
him, as they must be, but he trusted that like all trading
places Dorestad punished crime with due severity, and
thus suffered little from it. Edwin could do nothing now,
but walk, and think.

A myriad of wooden piers jutted a short way into
the water, and at one Edwin could plainly see Wulgan's
ship. The man would not leave for another three days.
The thought galled him, that he must be soon upon that
ship, returning to Wessex with nothing to show for his
efforts save the battle-gain from an unintended engagement. I have sailed so far – for what, he asked himself.
His thoughts travelled on. He was in fact not sure where
he was in this watery land, and had no good conception
of where Dorestad lay, save that knowledge that he now
walked in the further eastern reaches along the North Sea.

The ships tied up before him were in various stages
of lading and unlading. Many of the smaller were clearly
fishing vessels, from whose nets the silvery bodies of
catch streamed water. Others were merchantmen of
every stripe, packed, some of them, with casks, chests,

and roped bundled goods. One even looked a war-ship, today on a mission of trade, and not raiding.

As Edwin walked he caught the eye of not a few of the men working on and about the ships. He was dressed soberly for travel, with no show about him, but his bearing, youth, and handsome aspect spoke for him, as did the quality of the weaponry he bore. And it was all too plain that the two slightly older men flanking him were there on duty. Aboard one smaller knorr was a man coiling line. The end was attached to a long forked iron anchor, which stood upright against the inside of the hull. The man so engaged was of perhaps thirty years, with an alert but easy attitude about him, and well dressed enough that he looked no common seaman, but perhaps the captain himself. His was a trim little craft, and that costly anchor and a furled sail which looked almost new gave voice to his success with it. His hair was light brown, worn short for working ease, and balanced by a beard the same hue and length. The eyes were quick and amber brown, and sat above a blunt but not ill-shaped nose, and mouth that readily enough curved into a grin. It was a face plain, and without guile.

He bore at his waist a long curved knife in an ornate and equally curved leathern scabbard, capped with a chape of gold; a weapon new to Edwin. The grip of the blade was of pure white horn, or even ivory, and the whole looked like a prize indeed.

"It is from Constantinople," the man told Edwin, in answer to his glance. He took him in, and the two at his side, as well. "I have been there three times, for spice of cardamom, pepper, and cloves."

It made Edwin approach nearer, and make himself known. "I am of Wessex."

The man thought a moment. "Lundenwic," he answered, naming that port on the banks of the Thames. "It is near, is it not? I hear the trading there to be nearly as good as Jorvik."

Edwin shook his head, but was forced to smile. "I have seen neither place. I am Edwin of Kilton, on the far western coast."

"I am Ruddick, Frisia-born, but my ship is my true home."

There was a glint in his eye as he said this, and Edwin found himself with a twinge of envy at this life. He went on.

"I came in hopes of wedding a daughter of Count Gerolf. But the Count is dead."

Ruddick shook his head. "The news was brought, this noon-tide."

"What will happen now?" Edwin wished to know.

Ruddick again gave his head a shake. "His son Dirk will come. Gerolf has another, at least, a foster-son. But Dirk will be Count."

"Will he give his sisters in marriage?"

He gave a laugh. "I think he hardly knows them. They are half-sisters, far younger than he."

From what Edwin had gleaned about the maids from Fremund, he did not think pursuing the matter worthwhile. He would find out more about where he really was, though.

"I sailed from Swanawic in Wessex with Wulgan," he said, pointing out the ship moored at a distance from them. "But where are we, now, here in Dorestad?"

Ruddick gave another laugh, but rattled off the answer readily enough.

"We are three days out from Hunefleth. That is the trading post at the mouth of the Seine, from which I just came, trading Frankish wine for Rhenish. Six days sail north will bring us to Aros in Dane-mark, five south and east to the Baltic trading posts of the Pomeranie. Then, with good winds, a crossing of two days more to Gotland."

The final word had effect on Edwin, one quiet but unmistakable. He felt his head lifting, and his stance changed, as if he leant gravely into the name and what it represented.

"Gotland?"

The sea captain nodded. "Paviken, on the west of the island. There are good ship-wrights there. Salt and silk and gems flow through Paviken; rare oils, whalebone, many furs, and amber too."

"I would go to Gotland."

The moment the words were out of his mouth Edwin felt it a vow.

He heard a noise issue from the throats of both his men, but did not turn to them.

"I can take you, if you can leave on the dawn tide. It is my last stop, before I turn to set sail to the Pomeranie posts again, before they close for Winter."

Alwin spoke. "And the return to Swanawic?" The query was voiced to Ruddick, but meant, Edwin knew, for him.

The sea captain gave a steady exhale. "You will find coasters enough, even now. It will mean changing ships, but traders you will find. Once you reach Hunefleth, there will be merchants of Wessex to carry you back to your shores." Ruddick gave thought to what he had seen at this burgeoning port. "Even a ship of your King, I have seen there, readying to sail down the Seine to Paris to parley with their King."

Edwin needed no assurance; his mind was made up. But he was glad Ruddick said it for the sake of his men. It was not too late in the season to sail further east, then return to Wessex. He would go to Wulgan forthwith and tell him of the change.

"My men and I will join you," he decided.

The young Lord of Kilton must move on this chance. Nothing had worked out for him, nor would it as long as he was content to only follow the guidance of others, those who thought they knew what was best for him. He must be the one to decide, he must take control, strike out and make his own choices.

Ruddick craned his neck to take another look at the big merchantman which had carried them here. "You must travel rough, as my own men do, and I myself," he cautioned.

If this was a challenge, Edwin felt more than up to it. In service to his King he had been in the field for weeks of riding, and had just endured the long voyage, and even sea attack, on Wulgan's ship, with no adverse effect. He turned his own neck to the row of stalls behind him; most were still open.

"We will gather our provender now, and see you at dawn."

Late the following day Alwin and Wystan sat side by side on the deck, knees drawn up, backs against the hull, in the stern of Ruddick's knorr. The Lord of Kilton was standing with Ruddick at the steering-oar; the Frisian was his own steers-man, though any of his crew could spell him as he needed. All day they had passed endless pale sand beaches, wave-lapped, on their starboard side, and open water on their port.

"Why does he do this?" Wystan asked. His eyes had not moved from Edwin's back, as if he watched him still, with no apparent threat to his charge.

Alwin gave a low grunt of puzzlement. Worr would know, he felt certain, but Worr was away at Kilton. He recalled once Eorconbeald mentioning something about Gotland, but he was not sure it was more than what he himself had always known. Ceric, while still a boy, had been taken there by his uncle, the late Lord Godwin, and there Godwin had been killed in single combat with the Dane who had wed the mother of Ceric and Edwin. Both Alwin and Wystan knew Edwin had almost no memory of his birth mother. Was he now seeking her out?

He must be; there was no other answer.

"His mother – the Lady Ceridwen. He is in mind to see her, as he is near to being wed."

It was as good a reason as Alwin could conjure, and had more than a grain of truth in it. Those who wed and brought forth offspring were often moved to revisit their own folk; all knew this.

It was not, as answer, wholly satisfying to either man. Edwin's very stance had changed at the word Gotland, and not in tender remembrance, either. Yet it could not be the

Dane – the man had even given Worr Godwin's war-kit. And boys as they had been at the time, they knew that not a single pledged man of Godwin's had sworn vengeance for his death. His end had been told in a way that none could justly be sought. Worr was Godwin's chief man, he had witnessed all, and his word had sealed it. Perhaps Edwin, finding himself nearer than he had expected, was going just to see his mother.

As an adventure the foray had its attractions; there was no man save Worr at Kilton who had gone so far east as Gotland, and now they too would see it. There would be trading posts along the way, great trading towns as well, with brew-houses and gaming and women too. Neither man had any complaint with Wulgan; he had handled the attacking Danes with cool composure and showed them the wonder of war-fire as well. But Wulgan was near to the King, and had special care and concern for the young Lord of Kilton. Now they all three would be free of that.

Ruddick carried a crew of eight. Like all who plied the seas in trade they were highly armed, and of interest to the three from Kilton was that only one other was of Frisia. Ruddick numbered crew from Frankland, from Iberia, from Dane-mark, and the land of the Svear. The two from Iberia were of special interest, swarthy, and each with a single gold earring puncturing their right ear lobes. Those of Kilton, born and raised there, pledged to stay there, felt they too had slipped some invisible bonds in taking ship with such.

Their first days of sailing were untroubled, the creak and heave of the small vessel more pronounced than the big merchantman they had quitted. They saw other ships, none of which gave chase. Ruddick told them many fishing boats were out, beginning final hauls before shoals of herring and cod drifted further north. From the second day they had open water to cross, beating their way up the long coast of Dane-mark. As they neared its low and pine-dotted beaches Edwin bethought him of the choice he had made, and the route it was taking him. They went on, coasting up the western side of Dane-mark, dropping anchor in deserted coves at dusk, keeping good watch out for any approaching ships. When they crested the top of the great landmass and headed south, they would land at Aros. The knowledge that Edwin would be willingly walking into a trading town of the Danes now gave him pause. All his life, and the life of his father and even that of his grand-sire, had been lived under the shadow of Danish attack. Now he was willingly placing himself in their midst. Yet all Frankland and Frisia had also suffered their incursions, and here was Ruddick, like any trader, making use of the safeguards afforded those who entered at designated ports to buy and sell. They would be under the Danish King's protection, whoever he was. Ruddick told them there had been seven different men claiming title in the past ten years. Despite the mayhem without the walls of trading towns, the order within was inviolate.

Aros was set upon a river for shelter, and had two long piers of wood to welcome trading ships. The same river was generous with yielding fish, caught in upstream weirs, salted and smoked and sold by the cask-full as provision for departing ships. It was the largest trading town on the eastern coast of Dane-mark, and saw the transfer of its share of goods from west to east. An official of the King met each ship, exacting a tax to land and trade, and those arriving overland to buy or sell were likewise subject to a toll at its gates.

They spent but a night there, while Ruddick shifted goods. The trading stalls were still crowded with folk, some, like the Frisian, preparing for final trading runs before cooling nights brought stormier seas. Folk from many lands were about, and while even still upon his ship Ruddick had pointed out rough and ready traders in loosely gathered leggings who were Rus, those with yellow-white hair and rosy cheeks from the Polonie, and numbers with rich garments and reserved mien he pegged as hailing from Paris. There were also scores of Danish warriors, spears in hand, shields slung on their backs, active on their dragon-ships, and sitting at brewhouse tables from which laughter rang. Given this, Edwin and his men walked about with a certain reserve. Any number of lewd women were there, lingering enticingly as they strolled; indeed, three or four of them, sighting their landing ship, came to meet it. A pretty display they made, in their bright gowns and contrasting shawls, and they noticed Edwin and his men at once and smiled over at them. But mindful of the tinkers at the harvest feast, none of the three men were willing to vanish with the women into the small huts at the end of the trading road.

The next day began the most dangerous leg of the journey, the sail south down through the straits of Jutland and Scania. This was ofttimes patrolled by drekars large and small, sailing slowly or lying in ambush. So great was the danger that Ruddick had rarely hazarded the passage alone, and indeed, those aboard his trim knorr were glad to find a small flotilla of traders clustered in a cove of an island the next day. These were at anchor or beached just at the commencement of the narrows, and when Ruddick's billowing sail appeared from round a slight promontory it was met by a lusty chorus of welcome. His knorr would round their numbers up to six. An hour later all were off, challenge enough to any two drekars.

Such numbers were warranted, for twice they passed single drekars laid up in shallow water, as if in wait. The flotilla had benefit of not only numbers, but steady wind at their backs, and sailed smartly on.

"If you had been alone through that first cove before the narrows . . ." Edwin posed to Ruddick. He was again standing next the captain at the steering-oar. On either side green shores slipped away.

Ruddick laughed. "I would be there still, at anchor, waiting for another trader to join me. As I have in the past."

The captain glanced over at him. "And – I am not sure who you are, but I know of Wulgan, and his King. When you return to him in Wessex you will tell him what care Ruddick of Frisia took with you."

It was said as a jest, but like most jests had at its kernel a truth. Edwin thought a moment, then was prompted to speak.

"You said your ship was your home. Do you in fact have no wife, no fixed place at which you live?"

Ruddick, hand steady on the steering-beam, again looked at Edwin.

"No wife. A couple of women, good ones, whom I see; one in Frisia, one in Frankland. I over-Winter with one or the other of them, whichever wants me more. They have each had silver brooches and gem-set pendants from me. Come Spring and sailing I ready my ship and am off."

It sounded a free and enviable life to Edwin, and he gave himself up to imagining himself in it. Ruddick must have guessed this, for he answered with the next.

"You are rich, rich enough to win a daughter of Gerolf if you like. And these two men you lead are, I wager, two of many more back at your hall in Wessex."

Edwin nodded. This all was true, and what he had been born into and raised for. But now, far from Kilton and even Wessex, he glimpsed the liberty and challenges of a life lived for oneself, and not as Lord of a burh in a Kingdom which needed constant defending.

Ruddick's next words shook him from his reverie.

"What do you seek in Gotland?"

For a moment Edwin could not answer.

"Something there seeks me," he said at last. Or someone, he thought.

Ruddick asked for no silver to ferry Edwin and his men to Gotland. The three provided their own provisions, and as a gesture of good will when they had first boarded, had arrived with a small cask of brown ale to be shared out amongst all. For the duration of their voyaging the knorr captain was gaining three able warriors to defend his ship, if trouble arose. Beyond this was Ruddick's own interest in other men, their lands and ways. Hampered by endless war, the Frisian had never ventured to Angle-land, but a part of it had come to him, in the form of these men of Wessex.

They landed twice along the southern shores of the Baltic. The first trading post was of little account, save that Ruddick was due there with a large sandstone grinding stone he had carried from Hunefleth. It had sat long weeks in the prow of his ship, lashed flat to a pallet of wood, awaiting being passed into the hands of the blade-smith who had ordered it. It took four brawny men to hoist it, the smith himself and Ruddick's three strongest crew. A small crowd gathered, watching this; the thing was costly and heavy, a dangerous combination. Once it was upon the pier the smith freed it to general acclaim, and wheeled it carefully and with help to his forge by inserting a peeled sapling in its centring hole. This accomplished, the smith was happy to stand ale for Ruddick and all who had sailed with him.

The second post was one of the larger of the Pomeranie, where they were greeted by the sight of over a score of stalls and workshops, animal pens, and warehouses. After this post the final stop would be Paviken, on Gotland, a mere two days hence. Edwin was more than aware of this as they filed down the gangplank. He forced it from his mind, intent instead on relishing what awaited here amongst the Pomeranie.

There were two brew-houses crowded with cheerful, fair-haired folk, and at one of them Edwin had a small pile of silver taken from him by Ruddick over dice. They drank a strong and sour brew, ale mixed with kvas, brought to them by a jocular brewer with long, pale moustaches. Edwin sat laughing with Ruddick, Alwin, and Wystan, soon joined by four young women, yellow-haired, smiling, and plump as partridges, whose gaily dyed gowns were so tight through the bodice that the cleavage of their breasts was revealed. Edwin dropped silver for all, round after round. The three from Kilton could understand none of the girls' speech, though Ruddick made way with them, but talking was beside the point. Their friendliness was such that they readily sat close enough to the men so that their shoulders touched, and when the ladies leant forward, laughing, over the table, those opposite them could not help but peer down into the dim crack between their milky bosoms.

At length Wystan stood and left with one of the yellow-haired charmers, who was at this point clinging to his arm. Edwin, having drained another flagon of the cloudy drink, was not sure when Wystan returned, but when he did, and alone, Alwin nodded at him, and left with the girl who had been sitting next him. By and by Alwin returned, and the two remaining women raised their eyebrows at Edwin and Ruddick. Edwin began rising, none too steadily, to his feet, at which both women jumped up to claim him. But the ship captain pulled Edwin back down.

"You would remember nothing of it," Ruddick told him. He drew a few fragments of silver from his belt and pushed them to the disappointed beauties. Then he stood, hauling Edwin with him, and made for his ship.

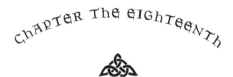

THE CHALLENGE

Gotland

EDWIN awoke with the ship underway beneath him. He was bundled in his blankets in the stern of Ruddick's knorr, the swell of the sea carrying it high before dropping into staggering troughs. Over his blinking eyes the sky showed brilliant blue. His head ached, and his mouth felt furred, as though he had swallowed a caterpillar. He got to his knees, and a grinning Alwin bent near, handing him a dipper of water.

Edwin took a deep swallow and dashed the rest on his face. He stood, feet apart, bracing himself against the pitch of the deck. Nothing but open sea was about them, blue-green and frothed with foam. The knorr's billowing sail was the only white in the empty sky. He raised his eyes above the boundless horizon, squinting against the brightness of the Sun. It was not yet overhead. On the morrow they should reach Paviken, and Gotland.

They spent the day like this, propelled by fresh winds, seeing nothing but the waves that crested, to part about the sturdy prow of the knorr. The next morning

437

they sighted other ships ahead, all making as they were for the dark smudge of green which had appeared before them. It was, Ruddick told Edwin, the southern tip of Gotland, and narrow enough it looked, but beyond it the land flared out, steadily wider, high, and verdant.

As they neared that shore it was the sea-stacks that Edwin stared at, jagged limestone towers rising into the air, solitary upon beaches just above the water line, and many in groups as well.

"Rauks, they call them," Ruddick said. There were wind-and wave-carved caves and grottoes which Edwin had seen in Wessex, but nothing like these great single-stone cairns. They sat upon pebbled beaches of blin-dingly white limestone chips, and rose behind shores of pale golden sand. He saw them standing on cliffs amongst pines, looking like the bleached spine of some vast beast; and in some places, with the base of the rauks in water, as if they had been caught walking from it into deep sea.

Paviken lay half way up the western coast of this island, and it was late in that second day when they sailed up the inlet into the lagoon on which it sat. Edwin knew when they neared it, for a ship within sight ahead of them suddenly vanished from view after tacking. They did the same, veering to starboard into an inlet which looked like many others they had passed.

It was not like the others, leading to the habitations of water fowl and little else. This unmarked channel, narrow as it was, led to one of the most valued of all anchorages to a sea-faring folk, a place free of tolls and tax to trade, offering fresh water with which to refill one's barrels, and access to some of the innumerable riches flowing from distant eastern lands.

But it did not give up its secret easily. When the inlet widened to a lagoon, the sight of any human habitation came almost as a shock.

Ruddick lifted his hand to the small settlement before them.

"Here is Paviken."

Compared to Aros or the posts of the Pomeranie there was little enough to see. The ship-wrights on the facing bank sported the largest and most impressive of any of its structures, and even now, late in the sailing season, were hives of activity. At one a new ship was being completed, and made ready to receive its mast, which still lay alongside. Other wrights laboured at repairing vessels battered by storms or languishing from neglect. Yet trading stalls were there, though it was clear much was transacted right from the decks of ships, or upon the wooden planking running along the inlet shore. A small cluster of tidy wooden homes stood on one bank, showing that folk remained here year round; indeed, the ship-wrights worked through Winter. Long rows of wooden frames held the flayed bodies of stockfish up to the drying Sun. Nearer to where they stood, two brew-houses were open and doing brisk custom, offering those arriving Gotland after long travelling welcome food and drink before venturing further on.

Ruddick looked to Edwin, whose eyes had completed a sweep of the place. "You will have doings here," he suggested.

"Not here," Edwin admitted. "But if this is the largest of the trading posts, I will learn what I seek."

The ship captain tilted his head to the nearest brew-house. These were ever a likely source of information, and this young Lord should glean what he wanted there. "I have trade, there," he said, pointing to a stall selling bees-wax, before which was stacked a myriad of barrels and smaller casks. "Go take ale, and I will join you later. The Norse spoken here is odd, but I can make myself known."

Edwin and his men did just that. One of the brew-houses offered a washing shed, with wooden tubs and hot water, which the three from Kilton made full use of, such baths having been in short supply on their travels. The knorr's crew had their own small trades to attend to, but began drifting to the brew-houses themselves. An hour later Edwin sat outside at a brew-house table with Alwin and Wystan, holding a deep pottery cup of rye ale, redolent of that ripened grain. He was on his second cup when the ship captain appeared, his face flush from suc-cess at his trading venture.

Edwin rose and went to him. Together they approached the brewer, standing at attention at a long table near his door. The man readied to refill Edwin's cup, still in his hand. Edwin lifted his free hand in gesture to wave this off, and spoke.

"I am looking for a Dane, one called Sidroc. He lives here on Gotland."

The brewer cocked his head at most of what had come out of Edwin's mouth. It was not easy to read the man's expression, and Edwin felt it best to qualify his request.

"I seek to trade with him," he added, with a nod at Ruddick, standing next him.

Ruddick took over, repeating in words more or less unintelligible to Edwin, what he had just said. The brewer gave thought, then replied in a long and steady stream. Ruddick listened, nodding his head, stopping the man with a raised hand at times to ask him to repeat, but seeming to ken the response.

"The one you seek is a wealthy trader. He lives on the east coast," Ruddick began.

The brewer went on, with the ship captain listening with attention. He learnt enough to turn back to Edwin.

"I can drop you at the bay on which he lives. But I cannot stay." Ruddick inclined his head to the brewer, and went on. "He tells me there is a small trading road there, and ships will be making stops, come from the east and the Rus ports to trade and re-provision before heading here to Paviken. You can return here with one of them. And," he added, with a glance to the right at the long racks of flayed, drying fish, "lacking that, fisher folk are many, and can bring you down in stages."

Ruddick looked along the line of vessels tied and waiting. "When you leave here you will need to travel in several ships until you reach Hunefleth, at the mouth of the Seine. But once there you will find merchants enough to sail you across the channel. One might be able to take you right to your King, if he has goods fine enough to show him."

They set off at dawn. It would take a day to round the tip of the island, and then beat their way up to the bay where sat the hall of Sidroc the Dane. They glimpsed few habitations from the deck; forested country or barren wind-swept beaches met their eyes. Yet they were not alone. The limestone sea stacks gave the look of wary sentinels as they sailed down and rounded the south-ern-most tip. The knorr was overtaken by dusk short of Edwin's goal, but dropped anchor for the night in one of many small bays.

In the morning as they began the sail up the eastern coast, Edwin changed his clothes. He opened his pack and unrolled the same new tunic and leggings he had brought for his presentation to a prospective bride. He had not occasion to change into them at Gerolf's mourning hall. They were the finest he had with him, the tunic of russet-dyed linen embellished with narrow tablet woven trim in blue and green. The leggings were dark brown, with brown leathern calf wrappings. Both tunic and leggings were from the hands of his mother Lady Edgyth, and he would don them now. He remembered her face when he had tried the tunic; she had smiled, telling him how its shade became his dark coppery hair. As a final touch he unwrapped something from within the toe of his second pair of boots, and placed it on his right wrist. It was a bracelet of yellow and red gold which had been his father's. Lord Godwin never wore it during Edwin's lifetime, but Edgyth told him it was a prized possession, one he had given to Lady Ceridwen as reward for bringing Gyric home alive. She had in turn presented it to Edwin as a babe, at his christening. That was all Edwin knew of it, and that it was the most costly single object of gold he owned.

Alwin and Wystan took good note of his adorning himself so, yet said nothing. Ruddick, looking over his shoulder from where he held his steering-beam, also saw him. The Frisian thought to chaff him, until he noted Edwin's face, grave and unsmiling. He knew Edwin had gone to Frisia to woo a woman, but despite his finery it was clear this stop on Gotland had nothing to do with winning a bride.

Edwin's thoughts were fixed at what lay ahead of him, but as they rounded the southern-most tip of the island, and the great rauk there, he found himself brooding upon his brother. Here he was following in the wake of Ceric, as he so often had; Ceric had made this voyage years ago. He had scarcely given thought to his brother during this absence. Now he pictured him there back at the hall, acting in his stead as Lord of Kilton, and with a wife at his side. He had not forgotten Dwynwen's words, the morning he had first found them together, and she offered to return to Wales. If Ceric will come with me, Elidon will make of him a Prince, she promised. It had shocked Edwin then, so much that he accused his brother of contemplating deserting him, a charge at once denied, and vehemently, by Ceric.

Yet it could have happened, could still happen now; his brother could gather his abundant treasure and decamp for Ceredigion, where Edwin had no doubt Dwynwen and Elidon would make good on her claim. As threat it had not lost its power, for having only once been voiced.

He forced his thoughts from this unhappy prospect, lowering his eyes to the waters they parted. It was of curious hue, its clarity shading from rich and deep blue to a vital blue-green over the submerged limestone shelf below them. At least here he could see the danger he skimmed above.

As they pressed on up the eastern coast they passed a few small farms, but nothing like the bay and trading road they sought. Then in late morning they were there. The bay was a shallow one. Behind it was a short trading road set with stalls and workshops, with a wooden pier jutting from a white shingle beach. A small trading knorr was tied up on one side of the pier, and two or three fishing boats had been hauled up onto the beach, out of the reach of the tide. On one side lay a drekar, beached, but well-tarred and looking fit for service. Above all this was the hill they had been told of, and crowning it, a narrow hall with a stone front and steeply gabled timber roof.

Folk were about, both at the stalls, and lingering on the pier. Ruddick dropped sail and eased the knorr in, and one of the old men who had watched her approach stood ready to catch the thrown line.

This done, Ruddick called out a question to the man, who answered by pointing up the hill.

"You are here," the Frisian told Edwin. "Just as the brewer told us."

Now that he had brought his passengers to their goal, the ship captain seemed almost hesitant to relinquish them. "I can stay here until the tide turns," he suggested to Edwin.

"No. You should go now. And I thank you." Edwin said this, and then his eyes shifted to the gable-roofed hall.

"I might see you when you pass through Dorestad," Ruddick went on.

Edwin only nodded. Dorestad was the last thing on his mind.

He shouldered his packs; Alwin and Wystan stood by the gangplank, awaiting him.

Edwin took a last glance at the knorr, and he who captained her. "Again, I thank you," he added.

Ruddick could not guess what mission had brought this young Lord of Wessex so far, but he must trust that with his two men and the riches he carried, all would be well. Despite the gold circling his wrist, Ruddick did not envy Edwin.

The three made their way down the gangplank, turning to lift their hands to the knorr. Captain and crew looked back, then at a word from Ruddick, freed themselves from the line which had tethered them so briefly to the pier. Oars were set down to push away, and the sail hoisted.

Edwin, fronting his men, walked on. At the end of the pier head and to its right sat a series of small buildings, with house, work sheds, and a garden overrun with herbs. The closest structure to them had the look of a place where ale might be served. Two sides of it were composed of short wooden walls, above which fabric awnings had been furled. Tables and benches stood within, as well as tables for serving, one set with stacks of pottery cups. No one was about.

"An ale house." This was Alwin.

Edwin nodded. "Wait for me here."

The door was open, and they stepped inside. Edwin put down his packs against a wall and laid his spear next them. His shield was on his back; his baldric held his sword at his chest, and as ever, his seax spanned his belly. He had ring-shirt and helmet in one of his packs, which he left behind; he was heavily armed enough. As a final act he reached into his tunic and pulled from over his head the linen pouch with the golden ingot. He handed it to Alwin.

"Keep this for me."

His captain could not hide his alarm. "I am going with you. We both are."

"No. You are not. I do not need you." Without further direction he turned on his heel, and left.

Rannveig the brewster was not that morning at her trade. She was in fact at her son Tindr and his wife Šeará's forest house. Gudfrid, the cook at the brew-house, also missed the landing of the knorr, being at work in the brew shed. One who did see the ship was the Mistress of Tyrsborg, Ceridwen, who was on the trading road, her basket over her wrist. She saw nothing unusual in a small knorr oaring up to land, and after a glance went back to scooping into her little pottery jar the crystals of sea salt she was buying. Asfrid, the salt seller, had weighed the empty jar first, and now that Ceridwen had filled it, she again placed it into one of her scale plates, adding pellets of lead to the other to calculate the difference. Ceridwen was this day alone at her errand; her two daughters Eirian and Rodiaud were also at the forest house, with Gunnvor their cook, gathering late berries and early mushrooms with Rannveig, and Tindr and Šeará's boy and girl.

Edwin did not know the name of the hall he approached, only the name of the man who lived there. He walked up the hill alone, his eyes fixed on the stone front. Helga the serving woman was within, out of sight of the young man approaching. Opposite the hall was a large stable or barn, and beyond it a paddock in which horses stood. The kitchen yard sat to one side behind the hall, and beyond it loomed the dark green of a spruce forest.

Sidroc was in the stable, its broad doors open to the morning light. Nonetheless the dimness within was such that he blinked when he passed through those doors to see the man walking up toward him.

Sidroc froze. He stood there, framed by the darkness behind him.

The young stranger kept coming. His fine raiment, suitable for a feast, drew a striking contrast to his fixed blankness of expression. The stranger stopped a man's length before the Dane.

Sidroc took him in. Another Kilton, he thought. And here, in my stable yard.

This Kilton looked impossibly young, a boy in a man's body. What was he – eighteen or twenty years, Sidroc gauged. Yet the face, for all its youthfulness, was telling, angered and tense, the jaw set. The eyes, greenish-blue, almost glittered with the strain of the meeting as he stared back. There was about the boy the sense of the over-tightened strings of a harp, ready to snap at the touch of a finger.

The visitor was the first to speak.

"I am the son of Godwin of Kilton."

Sidroc eyed his sword hilt. He gave the slightest of nods. "I know your sword."

He knew, Sidroc thought. Somehow another knew or surmised, and had told this boy of his true father, or he had intuited it himself.

Edwin made answer. "It is why I came, this sword. To have you spar with me, sword-to-sword."

He continued to study the Dane. He saw a tall and lean man, past youth, in a sweat-stained tunic of dark blue. He was unarmed save for the seax he wore. It was a weapon fit for a nobleman, one set with gems of red and blue in the hilt. Edwin did not expect this, and the fact that this Dane wore the prized weapon of the Saxons made his eyes flare the wider.

Sidroc looked down the hill. A ship was sailing away, and no one else was in sight.

"Where is your brother Ceric," he wanted to know.

"Away at Kilton. He has nothing to do with this, and does not know I am here."

A note of impatience now crept into Edwin's voice. "Will you spar with me?" The young Lord's hand made a gesture, as if he just restrained himself from pulling his sword from its scabbard.

"I have no sparring covers for our blades."

"That does not matter," Edwin answered. He well remembered the scar from the bad cut his older brother had taken when one of the covers had split while sparring with this Dane's son, Hrald. In truth Edwin did not care; he wanted to test his skill against this man; find out why his father had fallen.

"We are only sparring," he added.

"I will not," Sidroc answered.

It enraged Edwin. Not only the rejection, but the calmness with which it had been delivered.

"I have come a long way," Edwin countered. "You would deny me. Why?"

"It will serve no end," Sidroc replied.

Edwin looked down at the ground on which they stood, then back to him he would face. The Dane was tall, far taller than he, but the streaks of grey in his dark hair betrayed his age. And the ugly scar on his cheek proved he could be bested.

You are old, thought Edwin. I am young and fast. I will best you, too.

If Edwin must taunt this old warrior to make him fight, he would do so.

"In Paviken they told me you were a wealthy trader. Years, and silver, have made you soft. Other men fight for you, while you amass riches.

"You fear me," Edwin went on. "You can no longer hold your own against one like me."

Sidroc threw back his head and gave a laugh.

Edwin tried a final time, summoning a truth the Dane's reluctance hinted at. It took something to say it, for it was about he himself. He could not hide the edge, one sharp as a honed blade, in his voice.

"You think me unworthy. And I have come, openly, and alone, to face you."

At this Sidroc paused. There was something almost shimmering off the boy, resentment, or an anger which simmered just below his surface. Or was it just the need to prove himself, a need that propelled so many to rash and deadly acts.

Sidroc drew breath. The boy was right. The challenge he carried with him was worthy of respect.

"You have travelled a long way. And you are now my guest. I will spar with you."

He turned to the stone and timber hall behind him. Tyrsborg he had named it, in honour of that God of Justice he had given himself to when he was young.

Sidroc was back moments later. His sword was hanging where it always hung, in the treasure room, and he had buckled it on. His shield was there in the body of the hall next to the spears he kept. He emerged, armed as Edwin was, with sword and shield, even down to the seax at his waist.

It had might as well be here, Sidroc thought, right where we stand.

Edwin had already taken his shield from his back and had it on his left arm. He had used several shields painted in differing colours and patterns, and not yet resolved upon one. This one was painted in wedges of green and yellow.

Sidroc threaded his own left arm through his shield. It was painted in tight spirals of black and white, mesmerizing to the eyes if one looked too long at it.

He would set no boundaries for their contest, no hazel wands marking the duelling ground. It was not a duel, no life would be forfeit.

Without a word they began. Sidroc drew his sword and made the single gesture of lifting the blade upright before him. It was both salute and occasion to steady one's thoughts. In the Dane's mind were two truths, as divided as was the view beyond the blade he held before his face: The son of a man he had killed was here, challenging him with a sword. And – this boy was the son of his shield-maiden.

Edwin attacked. There was no trying an opening feint to see how his opponent would react, no subtle shift nor gradual play with shield nor blade. He sprang at Sidroc with an earnestness belying his stated intent.

Sidroc's shield was active, repulsing the initial blows. The serving woman Helga emerged from the side door of the hall, summoned by the clanging of metal. Her mouth opened in soundless terror. She looked down the road leading to the trading road, then bethought her that no one was more needed than Tindr. She picked up her

skirts and ran as quickly as she could along the outside
of the hall, past the cooking-ring and to the forest path.

The steeliness of his opponent surprised Edwin. At
times the Dane scarcely seemed to move, yet blocked
his blade, tracking each swing with his shield. The ease
with which he did this made Edwin think despairingly of
the training ground, and facing Eorconbeald or Worr or
Ceric, overcoming all of his efforts when he was yet a boy.
Edwin drew back, already panting from his onslaught, to
catch his breath, only to lunge again, hoping to catch the
Dane with his guard down. To be repelled over and again
served to further anger him; that and the knowledge that
Sidroc had made very few offensive strikes, only fended
off his own.

Edwin's frustration grew, sharp and hot as was the
forged iron in his hand. At one point he got in close with
his sword tip, nearly enough to make a hit, only to have
the Dane's own blade intercept it. An instant later that
piece of polished steel had slipped down the blade to the
guard, and nicked Edwin's hand. He cried out, an angry
howl, but kept hold of the weapon. A smear of blood,
that reminder of mortality, shown on the meaty part of
Edwin's right thumb, and the look of it served to further
enrage him.

Tangled in his anger, Edwin redoubled his efforts. In
sparring there was no end more desirable than depriving
your opponent of his weapon. He had wanted to knock
the sword from the Dane's hand, and now his blade had
nearly been knocked from his own. He began lashing
out in unbridled frenzy, forcing the Dane to give ground
under his speed.

Sidroc ceded a few strides to the boy, staring him in the eye as he did so. As Edwin made a lunge, aiming for the Dane's forward knee, Sidroc lowered his shield a moment and forcefully thrust it toward his young opponent. Edwin's sword tip hit the great iron boss in the middle of the black and white disc. An instant later Edwin had been knocked flat upon his back on the hard ground by that shield.

Sidroc had had enough. His patience was wearing thin, and he would not belabour this boy's humbling.

"Stop now. It is over," he declared. He trusted this would end the contest.

It did not. Edwin jumped up, and stood at his guard, hand bleeding but still gripping his sword hilt.

Edwin's next words were uttered through gritted teeth. He was out of range of the Dane's sword and turned his head, looking with wild eyes at hall, stable, and the ground they fought upon.

"Where did you fight? Where did you kill him?"

The Dane was slightly winded as well, but his voice was grave.

"Here, just where we fight." His next words were solemn warning.

"Do not end as he did, Edwin, his broken body on the straw in my stable."

The young Lord of Kilton glanced there, into that dim opening, and gave a howl. In answer he raised his sword and again leapt at his father's killer.

Sidroc would have none of it, and while fending the boy off, gave him an order. "Edwin, stop. Do not make me hurt you."

"I am no boy," Edwin panted out.

"No. You are a man. But your anger is that of a boy. It is misplaced, unjust. And you know that.

"That boy, that anger, is what keeps you from besting me. Who is it, who so angers you?

"I could disable you. I could kill you. But I will not."

The coolness of these statements only added to Edwin's frustrated efforts. But he did not aim more than two more blows when a woman's shriek rang out.

Ceridwen had come walking up the hill, basket in hand. She hurried her steps, for at Rannveig's brew-house she had spotted two young men, sitting on benches with a disconsolate air. They were neither men of Gotland nor of the Danes; she saw at once they were of Angle-land by the seaxes at their waists. She hurried past, and as she neared Tyrsborg began to hear the awe-ful sound of sharpened steel striking steel.

She dropped her basket and ran the last few lengths until she could see the stable yard.

It was a hideous vision. Two men stood at battle, swords in hand. Sidroc was facing her; the other had his back to her. She saw Edwin's hair and was transported back to Sidroc's duel with Godwin. A cry fell from her lips, one cut short by the action of her picking up her skirts and running as fast as she could toward them.

Sidroc saw her approach. Edwin turned to look, and beheld his birth mother for the first time in fifteen years.

Ceridwen's shock could have been no greater. Edwin, sword still extended, glared at her. The hand that held that sword was reddening with blood. Upon that hand sat a broad bracelet of red and yellow gold, the very same that Godwin had once pressed upon her own wrist. It was now borne by their son. A chill shot through her, one of fear at the memory of this boy's father, and a raw but real tenderness for the boy himself.

"Edwin . . ." she whispered. Her eyes went again to his bloodied hand and she lifted her own, as if she would come to him. "My boy . . ."

Edwin spat out his next words.

"You are not my mother. You gave birth to me, yes. But you are not my mother. That woman is Edgyth, at Kilton. A good woman.

"You are little more than a whore!"

The savagery of these words spurred all of them. She to whom they had been hurled lifted her hands to her mouth in horror. Sidroc was more direct. He slapped his blade down along Edwin's sword arm, the tip at his elbow. Edwin yelled. A seam of bright blood opened, from elbow to wrist. The bracelet of gold stopped it from extending further.

"I could have taken your hand," Sidroc told him. "But you will leave with it, and a scar to remind you."

Still, Edwin clutched his sword. Ceridwen, tears running from her eyes, began to move to him. Sidroc raised his shield to stop her.

She felt at that moment heartbroken; crushed. Yet she forced words from her throat, an admission of her guilt, and a plea to her child.

"What I did was wrong. I must live with it for the rest of my days. Yet, you resulted. You can condemn me, but the act is what led to you."

At last Edwin's hand opened, and his bloodied sword fell to the ground. He shook off his shield, and gripped the bleeding arm in his left. His mother was there, pulling off her linen head-wrap to staunch the flow of blood.

The next motions were compressed in time and space; the sensation of holding Edwin in her arms was what Ceridwen would most remember. She clutched her son to her, kissing him, tears running from both their eyes. His upheld arm was pressed between them, the wound thereupon that price exacted for a hurt anger he could not repress. Together they moved to the table there by the side of the hall. She saw Sidroc, standing to one side, watching, saw too when he bent to wipe his sword blade in the long grass growing by the stable. She held her son, kissing his face, murmuring to him, their hot tears of grief and shame mingling.

Then came a flurry of activity, which parted them by degrees. First was the arrival of Tindr, bow in hand, filled quiver at his hip. Helga had gestured to him the action going on at Tyrsborg, and with every pelting footstep down the path Tindr knew he must be ready to use his bow against another human. Now he stood gaping at the sight of Bright Hair and this strange warrior whom she embraced. By his face and hair he knew him for a son of Bright Hair, and knew him too as kin to the warrior he had watched Scar kill. He turned to Scar, whole and unbloodied, who only nodded to him. All was well, well enough that he might go and tell Deer of this. Then Scar turned and left, to return from the hall with the Simples chest.

Next to arrive was Tindr's mother; Tindr greeted her on the pathway, but gestured her onward to the hall. Šeará had kept all the children, but Rannveig had followed after her son, as fast as her sturdy form could make haste. She emerged from the forest, her cluster of bronze keys jingling mightily at her waist with every step. She took in what awaited her quick eyes, and assumed command.

She placed her hand on Ceridwen's shoulder to part the two who huddled together, her eyes widening at the blood spotting the bodice of Ceridwen's gown, which had soaked through the linen she had pulled from her head. Rannveig pulled free the cloth from the wound. Opening the Simples chest she brought out shears, and cut away the remnants of the tunic arm, which had been sliced open from elbow to wrist. Ceridwen stood up, returning with a jar. She sat down at Edwin's side, holding his left hand. The boy's mother had brought wine with which to wash the wound. Rannveig did so, and daubed the arm with fresh linen. The cut was an echo of the blade that caused it, long and straight.

"I must take a few stitches at the top, the gap is large there. For the rest, tight wrapping will do; it needs no stitching," Rannveig decided.

She spoke in Norse, but Edwin scarcely heard. Sitting there on the bench before the table, he was overcome with competing emotions. The shock of his own fury, the incredulity of being hurt, and the brutal fact that he might have lost his hand, or his life, was still with him. Most demanding of all was his response to this woman, an utter stranger to him, and of her manifest love for him. His damning words had not deflected that. She had loved him; she had suffered for him. The fever pitch of this meeting threw his disordered inner landscape into sharp relief, one shadowless and brilliantly clear. He had not come to challenge the man who had killed his father. He had come to challenge this woman who had given him life.

He was nearly silent, yet kept hold of her hand.

Ceridwen too could barely speak. Her son was here, bleeding from a wound given by Sidroc, just as Sidroc had sat here years ago, bleeding from a wound driven by the hand of this boy's father. She saw the length of the wound as Rannveig unwrapped and washed it. It was a gash angry and red, one that would mark the arm evermore. Her gratitude to the brewster for her calm presence was never deeper, and she watched her leech-work with an attention that helped carry some of that calm certainty to her own breast.

Rannveig had gone to work, knowing nothing for sure, but filling a pressing need. The task underway, she must ask of Ceridwen that which seemed all too certain. "Is this your boy?"

"He is," she admitted. "The younger brother of Ceric. But . . . his father – he was the man who came here, long ago."

The brewster bit her lip in remembrance of that awe-ful day, and kept working. Whatever had happened between this son and the Dane, at least the boy had ended alive.

There was a small square of linen in the chest, with steel needles ready charged with red silk thread. Rannveig chose one. It prompted Ceridwen to take up the jug, and hold the unwatered contents to the lips of her son.

"Drink this wine, Edwin. It will help the pain."

He took a sip, and the tart pungency of the wine warmed his throat enough to open for a deep swallow.

Rannveig pierced the skin and drew the needle through four times, a crossing track of red silk pulling the flesh close along the muscle of the forearm. She cut the silk and knotted it. Then she smeared the cut with a spoonful of Tindr's honey, and using ready cut rolls of linen, began to wrap it. When she reached the golden cuff, she pulled it off and laid it on the wooden surface of the table. It would need a scrubbing; blood running from the deep nick on the thumb was already drying in the intricate grooves there. Rannveig kept unspooling the linen, until the cut on the thumb was wrapped as well.

Eirian had appeared. She had not been able to stay away, and had slipped down the path not long after Rannveig. Now she stood taking in the scene at the outdoor table. Her mother's hair was loose, and bloodied linen lay at her feet. Rannveig was bent over the arm of a man with chestnut coloured hair, one whose other hand her mother held fast to. Eirian could see her mother had been crying. She moved to her father, looking up at him with eyes both fearful and questioning. He was wearing his sword, which he rarely did.

"He is your mother's son, the brother of Ceric," he told her.

"Did you – did you cut him?"

A moment passed before he made answer.

"Yes. I did not want to. But like his father, he could not stop himself from fighting."

They looked over.

"He will have a scar, that is all."

It was to be the outward mark. Sidroc surmised more than this would change for the young Lord of Kilton.

He looked back to his daughter. The girl was frightened, but able to both give and receive comfort. He spoke softly to her.

"Go to your mother; go."

Eirian went. She came to her mother's side and put her arms around her neck. Ceridwen's hand went to her, pulling her close.

The girl, still holding to her mother, spoke to the young man.

"My name is Eirian. I am oldest." She never forgot that she had been born before Yrling.

Edwin gave a nod.

"You are my brother," she told him. "Like Hrald."

The realisation would have startled him, if Edwin was not at this point beyond startle.

"Do you have a sister, away in Angle-land?" she wished to know.

He shook his head.

"Now you have me," she assured him.

Rannveig went down to her brew-house and to the two men waiting there. She waved them up. They could not understand what she was saying, but followed; the fact that an older woman was messenger seemed to offer a safe-conduct. Nonetheless they had their shields on their arms as they walked into the stable yard.

The first person they saw was a tall and dark-haired warrior, standing alone. As he turned to them the tip of his sword, hanging there in its scabbard from his left hip, moved as well. The warrior had no shield; but one was set along the base of the timber wall to a barn. He made no move to it as they approached. Both Alwin and Wystan had been ready to pull their swords and fight, to the death if called for. Instead, the warrior gave a nod of his head, admitting them. By this big Dane's manner, fighting might not be called for.

A naked sword lay on the hard and bare earth; Edwin's. A thin sheen of blood filmed the hilt. The man himself was sitting on a bench, flanked by females, one who they knew at once must be the Lady Ceridwen, the other, just a girl.

Alwin moved to the sword. He bent to retrieve it, then stopped. Whatever had occurred, Edwin had lost the blade. It might be forfeit.

"Take it," Sidroc told him, in a low voice.

Edwin, watching this, pushed himself up to his feet. His tunic sleeve was gone, and his sword arm bandaged from elbow to knuckles. His brown tunic was badly blood-ied at the chest, but his two captains understood all the blood had come from his arm. The older of the females rose with him. Edwin had let go her hand so he could stand, but she stood at his very side. The little girl stood as well, wanting to help, and risked placing her hand on Edwin's back a moment, as if to help steady him.

"My Lord," Alwin said.

"We were sparring," Edwin answered. There was no need to indicate who had been his partner.

Both Alwin and Wystan stood silent. Their eyes moved, taking in the Lord of Kilton and the two females at his side.

The silence extended many moments. Edwin broke it. "Lady Ceridwen. This is Alwin and Wystan," he said.

Rannveig, who had trailed behind, had not yet fin-ished with her patient. She stepped forward and spoke. "Let me tie the arm. It will throb less if held up." She moved to the pile of linen from the Simples chest and folded a square of it on an angle. Edwin and his men did not understand her words, but the gesture was clear. Edwin sat down again while the brewster threaded the cloth around arm and neck in a supporting sling.

That night in the treasure room Ceridwen and Sidroc were at last alone. Edwin was asleep in the alcove that his older brother had used the year he lived here. His mother and Rannveig had made up a sleeping draught of cowslip to ease his way to rest. His two men had been given alcoves head to toe to Edwin's. All had supped; all had drunk both ale and mead.

The spotted dog Flekkr had settled, as he often did, outside the curtained alcove of Eirian. He had emerged from the woodland with the rest of the household, and after a sniff at each of the men, curled tail thumping, had accepted them as no threat to hearth and home.

Little Rodiaud was shy of the sudden strangers at first, but during the meal had been happy to climb down from the bench next her mother and go from man to man. Edwin was nearest. She squatted down to touch the silver toggle of Edwin's boot, then giggling, arose to pat him on the face. She repeated this with Alwin and Wystan. To do this they must lower their heads so she could reach. After so winning a greeting the child lost all reserve, and crowing, climbed back to her mother's lap to swing her spoon in the air.

The meal was yet a quiet one. Sidroc said almost nothing to the men at his board, but when his shield-maiden had poured out the first cup of ale, he offered the welcoming toast of Skål, memory of the common ale bowl from which brothers-in-arms would share. Custom dictated that all lifting a cup together must pause a moment and allow their eyes to meet, proof against treachery. All old enough to hoist such a cup did so.

It was Eirian who carried on the role of mistress of the hall, relieving her shaken mother from pouring out further libation, walking with young grace and admirable skill around the table to offer ale and then mead. She asked her guests news of Kilton, and of Ceric, and in this way all heard that Ceric was not only well, but had wed, quite lately, a princess from Wales.

"Wales! I have Cymry blood," Eirian chimed. "Mother is half Cymry."

By the time Rannveig rose to leave, Edwin too stood. The family had spoken Norse to her, but it was clear the brewster kenned a few words of the speech of Angle-land as well.

His right arm, pinned up to his chest, was throbbing with a searing heat, and it had not been easy feeding himself with his left. His weariness was such that the act of standing up made him light-headed. Yet no man raised by Modwynn and Edgyth would fail to thank this woman for her leech-work.

"For your help – I thank you," he began, glancing down at his arm.

The brewster beamed, yet waved this praise away. She gestured to the little cup he was to down before climbing into his alcove.

Edwin nodded. It was all strained, and strange. He now knew the fair-haired archer who had run from the forest was her son, and so understood Tindr had been ready to kill him if needed. As he wanted, for a moment at least, to kill this man who headed the table. Or thought he wanted to.

Just now he needed rest. He had come in anger and found it impossible to sustain. He was certain of so little, just now. He drank the potion, gritty with something granular but slightly sweet, laid his head on the cushion in the alcove and fell almost instantly into needed sleep.

The hall quieting, Sidroc made certain the fire was banked, and the outer doors locked. When the treasure room door closed behind him, he turned to see his shield-maiden sitting on their bed. Though her woollen night shoes were off she had not yet undressed, and looked as if she lacked the strength to do so.

A single cresset threw enough light for him to see her face, and he watched it as he spoke to her.

"I could do nothing less."

She was more than aware he could have done a great deal more; this was understood.

She gave a nod of assent.

"It is his father," she allowed.

Would I could lay that ghost, once and for all, Sidroc thought. But blood was blood. This prompted his next thought, to which he gave voice.

"He is of your blood as well; half. That is his hope."

Weak and worn as she felt, it struck her as praise to cherish. Her chin had been lowered, now she raised it.

He came to her. He took her hand and lifted her to her feet. The hand was cool, and he placed the back of his own on her cheek. Cool as well, as those who have suffered great shock oftentimes felt. He pulled down the coverlet of their bed, in this season a linen sheet topped with a light blanket of creamy wool. She had woven it, and they had spent many nights under it.

"You need warmth. And sleep," he told her. In a single gesture, one he was well practised at, he pulled off her gown and under shift. He guided her into that bed he had carved for them, then pulled off his own clothes, snuffed the cresset, and slipped in next her. She was shivering, and he pulled her close.

He murmured into the darkness over her head. "We have built this life. Our young will do the same, with theirs. The fluttering of their wings cannot knock you from our sky."

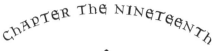

THE TELLING

"**H**OW did you learn?"

Edwin and his mother sat alone at the table in the hall. All had met here to break their fast, and then as one accord, left mother and son alone and together. It was a question Ceridwen must ask, for the secret had been guarded so long.

"Worr told me."

"He felt forced to," Edwin added, in defence of the man. "He did it to help me understand I deserved to be Lord."

"Ceric, and Worr," Ceridwen posed next. "They do not know you are here?"

"They do not. My goal was no further than Frisia."

She gave a murmur of understanding, and assent.

He had another thought.

"Lady Edgyth will never learn. That is one thing you need not fear."

She nodded at this, her gratitude plain upon her face. "And your brother?"

"I would never tell him." Saying this, Edwin felt the truth of it. Ceric had never contested the fact that Edwin had been raised to be Lord of Kilton.

This promise held deep meaning to his mother; he could see this on her face.

"Ceric . . . he remembers Gyric, his father. As I do. I would want nothing to besmirch that memory."

A stillness settled between them, each in their own thoughts. Hers were of both her older son, and his lost father, a man she had loved first, and truly. Edwin's were of his brother, one who for as many months as Ceric had returned from the greenwood he had tried not to think of. He had yearned for Ceric's return, but the man was so changed. And Edwin had changed toward him. He could not think of his brother without a roil of pain, rooted in the hurt of his dealings with his own intended bride, and the dark shame Edwin felt at having struck him.

He let out a breath to try and clear his head. He had a question of his own, concerning his origins.

"But . . . why?"

His mother's brow creased in thought, but a wary smile bowed her lips.

"Yes – why. From this distance it is hard to comprehend. Even for me." Especially for me, she thought.

She drew breath and began.

"We lived in such danger that year. War was ever present. Each time Godwin rode out we feared he would not return. He – he felt he might not return. The hall of Kilton needed an heir. Ælfred could have taken the hall at any time; it was a royal granting, long ago, through his family. You know this. There was nothing to stop him from claiming it, if he felt it could not be well-ruled. I knew this as well.

"Your father . . . convinced me of the need."

To revisit those days was a most unwelcome task. Yet Edwin deserved to understand.

"And Gyric . . . he was so unhappy."

Edwin closed his eyes a moment, eyes so like those of Godwin. He looked at his mother. His voice when he spoke was low, but the sense of assurance, and perhaps relief, was clear.

"I think somehow I always knew; knew something perhaps. Why it was me and not Ceric you gave away. Why the King, and others, said I looked like Godwin."

She wished to answer this, so he might more fully understand. "It was four nights," she murmured. She did not add the word, only, to frame her wrong-doing, to limit it. It was the simplest possible telling.

Edwin must ask the next. "Did you care for him?" He thought further, and spoke again. "Did you love him?"

Ceridwen gave a single shake of her head. "I loved Gyric."

For her sake as well, more needed to be said. "I cared for Godwin, of course. He was . . . impossible to ignore." Here she had almost said to escape, but stopped herself. "His admirable qualities were many. But he was covetous . . ."

He was selfish and rash, she could have ended. "It was Gyric I loved. But Godwin wanted me.

"Amongst brothers there can be, I think, a bond, painfully deep and strong. There was, I think, one such bond there. Godwin wanted what his brother had. Me. And I was too young, too weak, too confused, to resist. And Gyric too agreed to it."

A long silence followed this, during which both lowered their heads in thought. Edwin broke it.

"Godwin – my father. He sounds a monster."

She was quick to counter this appraisal. "He was not. He took the greatest care of Edgyth. She was greatly weakened by the loss of so many babes. He wanted her life, more than an heir. Then I appeared. And a way to have both, an honourable wife whom he loved – Lady Edgyth – and a child."

Edwin's thoughts turned for a moment to Ceric, and the maid who had come between them. The comparison ended there. Ceric had not been covetous, Edwin knew this. The Welsh girl, small as she was, was a force of Nature. She had wrought this; she had admitted it upon discovery that first morning.

His mother was speaking again, forcing his thoughts back to the here and now, and the painful talk of his origins. There was true tenderness in her tone.

"You have memory of him, Edwin; I know you must. You were young when he left you – but perhaps his voice, the sense of his presence . . ."

She did not expect his answer, made in form of demand quiet but real.

"Tell me of my father's death."

She took thought; steadied herself. There must be something he had been told, by Ceric and as well by Worr. She began there.

"Ceric would have told you of Godwin's arrival here.

"I was a free woman. Godwin came to drag me back, by force. I had given him what he most wanted, something precious to me – you. But he wanted more. He was obsessed. The longer I was gone, the greater the obsession grew. He was used to getting all he demanded. But he could not have me, not again. I was wed to Sidroc, was happy, had babes of our own . . ."

Edwin tilted his chin in the direction of the side door, that leading to the stable yard.

"And so they fought," he summed.

"Yes. In front of Worr, and Ceric and Hrald, and Tindr. And in front of me,"

She shook her head, slowly, as if seeing figures rising up from the past.

Nothing could expunge the memory of that morning; nothing. But this was perhaps the final telling of it, and that allowed her to go on.

"I was here alone with our serving women; Eirian and our son Yrling were yet toddling babes. To see Ceric again, and Hrald – I was overwhelmed. But at once Godwin made it clear he had brought them only to tempt me. He demanded I return with him, that instant, abandon my little children and husband. He laid hands on me, twisted my arm as I fought against him. Only Worr's presence kept him from doing worse to me.

"But Tindr was in secret watching. He ran for Sidroc, on a forest path, and brought him back. Words . . . were spoken. Sidroc offered to let Godwin leave unhindered, despite the insult. But Godwin refused."

She could not keep the pitch of her tremulous voice from rising. "Sidroc warned Godwin he would kill him. They fought, with knives. And that . . . is what happened."

Ceridwen must stop here, a break for both her and he who listened. When she resumed her words were steadier.

"Afterwards some of the townsfolk came, to hear of the matter, and judge if any wrongdoing had occurred. Even Worr would not speak against Sidroc.

"Ceric and Hrald could have returned with Worr, but both chose to remain with us over Winter. And Worr brought your father's weapons back to Kilton."

Edwin's left hand touched his seax at these words. He gave a nod, unable to do more.

Ceridwen placed her own hand over his for a moment, a presence warm and tender.

She must ask of her other son.

"Tell me of your brother. I yearn to see him."

He hardly knew where to start. She helped him with her next words.

"Hrald came here, after Ashild's death. He told us of it, of Ashild's burial, and Worr taking Ceric back to Kilton." She reached to a shelf near the table, where a small clay imprint of a child's hands was kept. "And he told us of Cerd."

Edwin nodded. "Yes. He has a child. I have seen him, briefly. The boy is living with the Lady Ælfwyn, who is now wed to the Bailiff of Defenas, and lives with him there."

"Ælfwyn, wed? And to Raedwulf?" Her surprised happiness was there upon her face. Edwin's next words pricked her eyes again with tears.

"After our grandmother's death, Ceric spent a full year in the forest."

"Lady Modwynn – dead?"

Edwin nodded. "She died the night of Cadmar's memorial feast. During her own funeral Ceric slipped from the chantry and stole away, into the wood. He ended living in a cave.

"Worr brought him food and supplies, little of which Ceric availed himself. He foraged. And starved. But he was coaxed out by a village woman." This was as much as Edwin could say of Begu; his mother need not know more.

"I was not at Kilton when he emerged. I had gone to Wales with Dunnere, to seek a wife. I brought a maid, from Ceredigion, the niece of King Elidon. She would not wed me there, but desired to see Kilton first, and then decide."

The next was not easy to say.

"She saw Ceric. And wed him."

Ceridwen was taken aback; the pain on her son's face was clear. But he would not let her speak of it.

"It matters not," he insisted. "She would not have suited me. She is only a child, and . . . a kind of sprite, I think."

The Welsh girl's step-mother came sharply to his mind. "She was raised by a woman who is a witch. And Dwynwen herself is odd."

Ceridwen's ears almost hummed. Edwin's voice and judgements were harsh, but they were not what filled her head. "Dwynwen," she repeated, as to herself. Was ever a name as lovely, she wondered.

She looked at him full in the face. "But Ceric – he is happy with her?"

"He is," Edwin admitted. "All are. Lady Edgyth formed an almost instant attachment to the girl."

This held true meaning, as Ceridwen trusted Edgyth's discernment in all things. Yet she felt at a loss. The joy she felt at hearing both Ælfwyn and Ceric were wed was countered by this boy's loneliness. For she knew him to be lonely.

"And you, Edwin? Have you any bride in mind?"

He heaved a sigh, and gave a single, rueful laugh. "Ælfred sent me to Frisia to court the daughters of a Count. When I arrived, his hall was in mourning, as he had lately died." He looked down the length of the table. "It was then I learnt Gotland was not far."

"And you determined to come," she said for him. She asked the next with both calmness and courage. "Did you find what you sought?"

It was not an easy question to answer. He could not say he came searching for the truth about his father's end; he had no reason to doubt either Ceric or Worr about the circumstances of his death. Was it just his anger that drove him, he now wondered.

She moved to offer the next. "Things are ofttimes not what they seem."

He gave a nod. There was more he must do, and he named it.

"Godwin – he is buried here. Ceric told me of it."

Her answering voice was as gentle as a whispered breath. "He is. I will take you soon, if you would like to visit."

"Yes," he returned. His head was lowered as he said this, but he raised it now. "I am glad to have seen you, mother," he ended.

In answer she pressed him to her, then drew back and kissed his brow. "And seeing you has answered a long held wish," she told him.

Later that day Rannveig walked back up the hill, wanting to check Edwin's wound, and her leech-work. Alwin and Wystan were down at the trading road, while Edwin sat at the same table outside at which she had first attended him. It gave a clear view into the stable, and he had spent some little time looking into that dimness. Looking, but not entering. After shedding his own blood on the hard soil without the stable, he imagined all too well his father's body lying therein on a heap of straw.

Ceridwen had just brought out the Simples chest when a light rain began to fall, and the three of them moved inside the hall. Helga the serving woman lit one cresset while Ceridwen lit the second. They would lend enough light for Rannveig's scrutiny. She untied the knot of the sling holding his arm to his chest, and stretched the bandaged limb out upon the tabletop. No blood showed through the linen, at least these outer layers. She unwrapped the arm fully. Dried blood was there, crusted along the borders of the slice, but the honey she had smeared kept the wound itself moist. Most of what showed on the linen was the yellowish liquid that wept from such wounds. Its clarity, and the fact that no part of the gash was puckering, told them all the wound was free from putrefaction. The nick on the fleshy part of his thumb was deeper than he had thought, and pained him when he tried to close his hand. He would have a small divot there, one which he hoped would not hinder his ability to grip a weapon. And he would bear as well the long straight scar from elbow joint to wrist.

After careful study the brewster smeared a spoonful of honey over both, and rewrapped arm and hand in fresh linen.

Edwin was not wearing his broad bracelet of braided gold; he had last night restored it to its travel place in the toe of his boot. The bracelet had been bloodied; his birth mother had scrubbed it clean. His fine tunic, crafted by the mother who raised him, had been spoiled, and rent and blood-spattered as it was, he had this morning asked that it be thrown in the fire. He wondered what was in his effort to impress, wearing both. To signal his estate as Lord of Kilton? He hardly could name it now.

He only knew he felt tired, though he had slept long, and that, as much as he wished to ignore it, and to dismiss the injury as a trifle, the arm felt stiff and hot.

The old brewster tending to him looked well satisfied, and again tied the arm up in the sling of linen. When she spoke to him in loud and slow words as if he might understand, his mother repeated them for him.

"Rannveig says to wear the sling for one more day, and if the arm does not trouble you, leave it off. The cut is still angry, and holding it up will ease it."

"Again, I thank you," he told the brewster. This was close enough to her Norse that she understood both words and intent, and grinned at him.

Edwin returned to his alcove after this, desiring sleep, needing to be alone. When he walked out later that day the rain, which had not been more than a drizzling mist, had ceased. The sky was the same watery hue as the sea he looked down at. The wooden pier at which they had docked was empty of any craft. He had stepped out the front door of the hall, and now turned his head to the voices coming from his left. There were Alwin and Wystan, standing with the Dane at the paddock rail, looking over the horses within. It was common enough for men to discuss the animals, and entirely apt that his captains, guests in this Dane's hall, would enter into converse with him. His men need never learn the truth of their contest. He had told them they had sparred; that was all they need know. Yet the ease with which they spoke to the Dane discomfited Edwin.

Sidroc had noticed him, and Edwin could do nothing but join them. He walked over, seeing penned behind them a black stallion, a dun mare with striking markings, and three other horses, all worthy animals.

As Edwin stopped before the three, Sidroc looked down at him and gave a nod. He had watched the boy approach, his hurt arm held up close to his chest in a sling, and seen Edwin's attempt to master the uncertainty on his face. There was no pretence of a swagger, rather the sense of one coming late to some gathering he had heretofore been excluded from. The nod Sidroc had given Edwin was a considered one, one of the same acceptance he had granted to Edwin's men when they entered the confines of his hall yard.

Talk had ceased upon Edwin's arrival, and to mask his awkwardness, he said what he had awakened thinking of.

"I should leave soon. I was told the voyage back must be made in stages."

Sidroc gave thought. "I will speak to my captain, Runulv. He has ventured to Paris many times for me, and to reach there he must pass Hunefleth. If he will make the trip he can take you there. Unless you wish to go on with him to see Paris."

Paris was indeed a place Edwin would like to see, but he shook his head. "If he can take us to Hunefleth, it would save much time and effort."

"I will go and see him tomorrow, and ask," the Dane responded.

Edwin uttered a word of thanks for this offer.

Sidroc considered the boy, and what he had been through. A secret kept could be a powerful force in one's life, especially if that secret might grant benefits otherwise denied the bearer. Sidroc being told by his father that Ingirith was not his mother was one of the most freeing moments of his life. Boy that he was, it reframed all else for him. He thought perhaps the secret truth this young Kilton had carried about his true father had done the same. But rather than free Edwin it had bound him to the actions and manner of a man mad with passion. Perhaps he could now be released of the burden.

There was further kinship shared with Edwin, Sidroc knew. Just as he had been left alone by his father's disappearance at sea, Edwin had few friends. Cadmar, his councillor, was gone, his grandmother too. His brother Ceric was there, but the inversion of roles must be awkward for the younger Edwin. And Ceric had Worr, the kind of man Edwin sorely needed at his own side. To complicate matters, his shield-maiden had told him that the bride Edwin had chosen had instead wed his brother. The way ahead would not be easy for this Kilton. At least he had rid himself of the bile of revenge for his father's death. Sidroc could see that much in the young man's troubled eyes.

The next day Sidroc returned from Runulv's farm to say the ship-master welcomed the chance for a late trip to Paris. Runulv had taken possession of a quantity of lapis and agates after meeting some Rus at a Polanie trading post, and wanted a rich market to realise the greatest gain. He had resolved to set the stones away until next Spring, when Sidroc approached him with the offer to sail now.

"His ship is a good one," Sidroc assured the three who would venture forth on it. "I should know, having supplied sail, walrus-hide line, and new oars for it. It will take him a few days to ready for the voyage, but then you will be off. And all the way to Hunefleth. From there he will find you a ship heading to Wessex."

It was more than Edwin could expect, more than he could have hoped. He had been gone weeks longer than any generous estimate, and a speedy return would help salve his conscience for those who worried over him. For a moment the thought of asking to stop at Dorestad crossed Edwin's mind. He shook his head at this. He had no appetite just now for courting the grieving daughters of a dead Count. If Ælfred had not already learnt of the demise of Gerolf, Edwin could tell of it. Either way his returning without one of the Count's daughters would be understood.

It would take Runulv a few days to ready ship and crew. It gave Edwin time for further healing, though more would be needed before he could draw his sword from his baldric. But he and his men walked the trading road, viewing its surprising wealth of long-stapled fleece, woven goods, fine salt, and beeswax, and were hailed warmly by all. They hiked up the coast to a stand of rauks, and with Edwin's hurt arm, climbed but the shortest of them, marvelling at their time-worn, twisted strength. And they went down to the brew-house one night with Edwin's mother and the Dane, to drink deep of Rannveig's good ale. Edwin watched his men at dice; he could not flex his thumb enough to throw with his right hand, and throwing with the left was unlucky. But it gave him more time to take in the men and women about him, Gotlanders and visiting merchants alike, as they sat at ale or laughed and chaffed over dice or counters. They were a good-looking folk, these islanders, strong and forthright with their fresh and open faces; he must admit this. His eyes travelled more than once to families with pretty daughters in tow, girls who blushed and looked away as soon as he caught them staring at him.

Eirian was there with the family of Tyrsborg, that night. Though she began sitting at her mother's side she worked her way round to end at Edwin's. From there she advised him as to certain of the denizens crowding the brewster's establishment, telling him of the older girls who had caught his eye, while Rannveig herself, with her cook Gudfrid to aid her, stood planted at the broad table by the back wall. This held crock after crock of fresh brewed ale, and numberless pottery cups to serve it up in, which Rannveig unerringly tallied up in her head as she dipped. Eirian possessed their mother's warmth and her father's confidence, and slipped her arm readily through Edwin's left as the party made their way up the hill to Tyrsborg at the end of the night.

"I will come and visit you one day, brother," she promised.

There was such bright hope in her words Edwin must take them seriously.

He surprised himself with a warning. "You might not like it," he began. He turned his head over his shoulder. Behind them trailed Alwin and Wystan, but Edwin looked beyond them, down to the silent waters of the Baltic, and closer in, the mild merriment of the brewster's gathering place. A rutilant glow issued from the cressets inside the brew-house, suggestive of the warmth within. He was aware of the comely girls whose presence he had just left, and the relative peace and safety of this island. He exhaled a held breath. He had but arrived, and now must soon leave a place he would like to know better. This too he had not expected. "The village of Kilton is large," he told Eirian, "its folk number many score more than live here, or at Paviken, or any place I have seen on your island."

She had given his arm a little squeeze at this, and he looked down at her eyes, which danced as she imagined such numbers.

"Even within the hall itself many dwell. When my folk gather each night, the noise is such that it can be hard to be heard above the din."

Nothing deterred, Eirian asked a question. "And do you have a scop or skald, to sing and play for you?"

He nodded. "We do. A man, old and well-revered, greatly skilled with harp and song."

"I should like to hear him," she breathed.

Eirian had another thought, and shared it. "I have a yealing brother, my twin. He lives with our older brother Hrald, at a place called Four Stones. He is named for our grand-uncle, Yrling. Even though I was born first, I was not allowed to go there with him.

"But one day I should like to come to Kilton, where mother lived. Her own mother lives north of there . . . I am not certain just where. But I would find my grand-mother, as well."

Despite himself Edwin found himself thinking of Lady Edgyth and Dunnere the priest, and wondering if they knew of this woman Eirian asked after.

He again looked at the girl clinging to his arm. She was as slight as an arrow, and would as a woman be tall. The eyes which shined at him were dark blue, a less pierc-ing version of those of her father. Her hair was long, a brown like wet and fallen leaves, enriched with some of the russet which made their mother's hair catch the eye. And she was likely to be pretty, or at least, have the pres-ence to attract the attention of many. Edwin bethought him of a sudden that she might be the richest maid on the island of Gotland. If she came to Wessex, her parents would endow her with treasure enough for a good match. And she would bring more than silver with her. Though their mothers differed, this girl at his side was, after all, sister of a Jarl, just as the maid he had spurned was. There were rich thegns and noblemen enough through Wessex to welcome Eirian, and amongst the long-settled Danes of Anglia she could be a highly-sought bride.

"If you are given leave to come, I will welcome you at Kilton," he ended telling her. He thought, but did not say, that his brother's wife, only a year or two older than this maid, would also welcome her. And Dwynwen was of Wales, in which Eirian had ardent interest.

Eirian gave a little pull at his arm, enough to make him lower his head, so she could kiss his cheek.

The following morning Rannveig walked up to Tyrsborg to re-dress Edwin's wound. Young and hale as he was, he was a rapid healer, and it was with satisfaction that the brewster could find no trace of the cut going green. She re-wrapped the arm in fresh linen, and looked to the boy's mother when she finished.

"I think Tindr should take him out. To walk the woods."

Ceridwen considered the offer. She knew Edwin was growing restive. Even his two companions, chosen not only for their prowess in fighting, but their unwavering calm, would welcome a purposeful outing. It was too early for hunting, and Tindr did so always alone, companioned by his Goddess; but Rannveig understood the need her own boy might fulfil.

"He has seen Paviken, and our life here," Rannveig went on. "Tindr will show him some of what the island truly is."

Ceridwen's son was watching her, wondering of what they spoke, and she told him.

"Rannveig thinks that Tindr might take you into his forests. There is much he can show you there."

Edwin had seen Tindr emerge from the trees that morning, holding a brace of hare destined for Gunnvor's cauldron. He knew the man's skill at venery was such that he supplied both Tyrsborg and his own household with game, and Eirian had confided more to her brother, extolling Tindr's kindness, and her affection for his entire family. Edwin had only glimpsed his wife, a woman of pale, almost preternatural looks and bearing. But Tindr himself was of marked appearance, with his eyes of ice blue. They, and his deafness, were not the only things that set the man apart. Edwin could not name what was different about being in his presence, but he could feel it, as though Tindr appeared from some other realm. Now the man's mother, and his own, proposed an outing with the silent hunter.

Edwin's face showed his doubt. He had watched Rannveig sign to her son, seen the entire household of Tyrsborg do so, with rapid movements of hands and arms. It was its own speech, one he could not ken.

"Go with a deaf man?" he began, "to hunt?"

Ceridwen shook her head. "To Tindr hunting is no sport, but a sacred act. But he knows this part of Gotland as no one else. And as a tracker – well, you have been out with Worr, since your boyhood. Tindr is like that, sees things hidden to our eyes. You will not need speech. He will take you into his woods, and show you things."

Edwin gave a shrug, but also a nod of acceptance, clear to both women. Ceridwen turned to the brewster, who gave her own nod of satisfaction. "A day or two spent with Tindr will be good for them," she judged. "They can leave today; I saw Runulv this morning, and his ship needs more time."

So they made ready. Tindr was at that hour in the stable, and Rannveig went to him. Ceridwen and Gunnvor began gathering foodstuffs for an overnight trek. The four might take all the bread Gunnvor had baked for the day;

she had time for more to rise before the evening meal. There were cured cheeses, walnuts, early apples, and raisins dried from Ceridwen's own grape vine by the front door of the hall. And they might have one of the hares Tindr had earlier delivered; with the three guests away in the woodland, one would be enough for Tyrsborg's pot. Gunnvor had them already dressed, and now jointed one and fried it up in sizzling butter, adding savour to the leanness of its flesh.

The four gathered at noon, leathern packs across their shoulders. Tindr's grin as he greeted the three told of his pleasure in their interest. He had his knife at his hip, but had left his bow behind; he had already won their dinner from his snares, and they had provision aplenty on their backs. But before they started up the forest path behind the kitchen-yard, he pulled a tiny white object from a thong around his neck. He put it to his lips and blew out a shrill whistle, then pointed to the three.

"His way to call us," Alwin surmised, "should we be out of sight."

Edwin had a thought perhaps shared by his companions, that with eyes like Tindr's, he would never lose sight of them. When he directed his gaze your way, it was like being watched by a wolf.

They started up the path, Tindr first, then Edwin, then Alwin and Wystan, and entered the sudden dimness beneath the trees. Never was the contrast between coast and woodland so great. This island, with its clarity of air, and brilliant sunlight falling on barren and rocky beaches, had beyond its margins forests of unimagined depths. The transition was almost a curtain being pulled, admitting them to a gem-like richness of verdant growth and ruddy-brown bark and branches. They moved through the spruces, heavily-needled and dark, to a more diverse woodland, brightened with clearings in which hazels and aspen grew. After a short time the track diverged, offering a fork heading west. This they took, through pines under which tall and feathery ferns rose. At times they came across great boulders, moss-shrouded. These were nestled amongst the roots of nearby trees rising above the scant soil, like reaching feet, green with lichen.

They walked slowly, Tindr setting the pace. Though the men from Kilton had entered the forest remarking upon what their eyes met, they too soon fell into silence. Tindr would raise his hand, signalling a pause, so he might point out something to them. They first came to a run of un-set osier and sinew snares at the ends of barely perceivable animal trackways, leading to the path they trod. The deaf hunter gestured to their food pack, and they understood it was here he had collected this morning's catch. They continued on, at times pausing so they might admire an ash or beech or oak which had reached majestic girth over slow centuries of growth.

Tindr pointed out the scumber of foxes, and with a low grunt and point of his hand indicated that a den lay at the end of a faint trail which vanished into the undergrowth. He showed them a snag of spruce trees, downed by a wind storm, where boars came to rub their bristled backs against the rough bark, with channeled gouges against which they had driven their tusks to clean them. They followed the trodden path they had begun upon, to leave it often as he led them across tracks of his own making, to return again after another discovery to the same path, or one they could not recall. They skirted marshland thick with growing sedge, and Tindr steepled his fingers like a roof to indicate the thatching made from it. Long-legged cranes stood amongst the spiky growth, spearing small fish with their sharp bills. Overhead a goshawk appeared, earning a low yelp of happiness from the deaf man. Those from Kilton had already learnt that Sidroc had a steady trade in these raptors, raised and trained on Tyrsborg's upland farm. Twice Tindr, scanning the trees in a certain dale they crossed, pointed out tawny owls. These seemed to sleep, unseen, above them until the brown heads swiveled to watch the men progress.

As the light began to wane, they found themselves at a stand of slender white birches. Tindr scanned the bases of the trees, then led them to one. At its base a fungus grew, a blackened thickening on the white bark. Their guide pulled his knife and sliced a narrow section off. Tindr scraped away at this, to reveal a reddish-brown underside, which crumbled under his fingers. He dropped what he held in his palm into the leathern pouch at his belt.

Then he stood, and looked up, and with his finger described the arc of the setting Sun. It was time to seek water, and make up their shelter. The last rays of sunlight were slanting through the trees when they crossed over a narrow and free flowing beck, to arrive at a small camping ground. A fire-ring sat there, its scorched stones telling of many meals warmed thereupon. All set about gathering fallen wood as kindling, and both Edwin and Alwin reached within their packs for iron and flint. But Tindr had knelt by a small pile of dried lichen, and rubbed some of the ruddy crumbles from the birch tree upon it. Edwin offered his flint and striker, but Tindr gave a quick nod and smiled. He had his own, a piece of white quartz, and two flicks against his steel striker cast out spark enough to ignite the crumbled growth into instant and steady flame. Edwin saw Tindr look up at him then, look up and smile, as if at some memory which must remain unvoiced.

They built fire enough to toast some of the loaves they had brought, then tore them open to enfold slices of the sharp sheep's cheese they dug from one of the crocks. And there was the hare meat as well, shreds of which set off both cheese and bread with the kind of savour that only a meal taken out of doors can offer. Sitting there, none were surprised when a big hare appeared, hopping on the trunk of a downed tree. In the low light the bluish cast of its fur was even more pronounced. It looked at them, the dark eye catching the glitter of the fire, unknowing they supped upon one of its fellows, but seemingly curious. Tindr laid down his loaf, and raised both hands to the creature, palms facing it. Benediction, or apology, Edwin wondered.

They had no need to trench out hollows for their shoulders and hips so they might sleep the easier; moss grew in lush abundance but a few strides from their fire-ring, offering beds of a comfort rarely found in the wild.

Edwin was tired from the long ramble, and his hurt arm felt sore. Once wrapped in his blanket he fell with grateful readiness into sleep. As he did he reflected on these few hours spent in the deaf hunter's company. Tindr's silence was such that Edwin and his two captains had themselves spoken little. The young Lord of Kilton had not known a day like this one, nor he thought, had Alwin or Wystan. Each of them had slept out, underneath the stars, in the past. Each had walked woods and flushed game, purposely or by startle. But to move slowly through the trees and along marshes and meadowlands, to move with such intention and regard for all they encountered, as did their guide – this was unknown to them.

At dawn they rose, broke their fast with what remained of their rations, and set off, this time eastward. They neared soaring cliffs which were the haunts of sea eagles, for they saw the huge birds gliding in looping circles overhead, their broad white tails and white barred wings making fine show against the deepening blue of the morning sky. Edwin began to wonder when they would turn back, but Tindr led them onward with firm step. There was, the men from Kilton surmised, something more he wished to show them. They did not reach it until close to noon, but it proved well worth the effort spent in doing so.

The trees over their heads thinned, opening the sky and granting the welcome warmth of the Sun. The four climbed a rise greened with stunted scrub junipers and waving grasses, now drying in the late Summer winds.

A mound was there, a massive hill of round stones, rolled and carried there before men knew iron. It was the ancient burial mound of some great chieftain. Such dotted Wessex; but few had not been despoiled in the hunt for treasure buried deep within. The careful way in which Tindr approached this told them he felt it still a place of power, and awe. It was by far the largest such mound Edwin had ever encountered. At its apex it was the height of three or four men, and a gradual climb up, he judged, one easy if mindful of the placement of feet so as not to dislodge any of the stones. Edwin would have liked to climb it, for the look-out it would have given; he had done so on any number of such monuments at home. Here, before Tindr, he knew it would be sacrilege.

Still, as their eyes followed the contour of the heaped stones, Edwin could not help muttering a few words below his breath. "Imagine the treasure here," he breathed. "What he was buried with . . ." He felt he beheld the lair of dragons, and if Garrulf's lays be believed, that one might coil still at the heart of this piled rock, tail and claws encircling gold, and weapons of repute.

A number of smaller mounds sat at one end of the large one. Edwin now saw that four tall stones had been placed about the mound, as markers. Looking up toward the Sun he knew they must signal the four directions. These too were undisturbed, though their kind were coveted as building stones for upright portals. Nor had the smaller mounds been disrupted. Edwin looked at Alwin in wonder, who answered him with a few low words of agreement.

"His sons, or wives, perhaps; some folk wanting to lie near their war-chief."

Tindr, with a tilt of his head, gestured them to the tall stone marking the eastern point of the mound. It was no mound itself, but part of a small circle, ringed with low stones, with an oblong space of blackened rock lying within. Tindr gestured what had occurred there, holding his hands before his face, pulling them down to reveal closed eyes, and crossing his arms over his chest, as folk are oftentimes laid out at death. He squatted down as if he kindled fire, then lifted his hands as if to rising warmth.

"The pyre," Edwin murmured. "The dead were brought here, to be burnt." He turned his head to look up to the sky. "The Sun rises up from the east, as symbol of fire, and at dawn would strike this place first."

Tall spruce encircled this clearing, and from above their heads the three from Kilton now heard a raucous croaking. They raised their eyes as a mob of young ravens appeared, flashing, almost tumbling through the air above them as if in play. Tindr could not hear their approach, but now that the ravens were overhead, his ice-blue eyes tracked them as they sported above. The birds retreated to the boughs of the trees as quickly as they had appeared, though their rattling could still be heard.

Tindr grunted up at them, and turned to face his guests. He pointed to the trees where the birds rested, then using two fingers, pointed to his own piercing eyes. Then he pointed straight up, beyond the confines of the skies.

It was Wystan who spoke. "I think – I think he tells us that the ravens are watching us. Sent from the Gods."

Edwin nodded. "That we not dishonour the mounds."

The four circled the great hillock, aware of the watchers in the trees. A sense of awe hung about the place; Edwin could not gainsay this. They spent a long moment looking upon the mound, as if in fare-well, before turning their backs to it.

This great monument behind them, the men made start for Tyrsborg, a route direct and unbroken. As they moved through the forest Edwin thought of Ceric, and his long sojourn in the greenwood of Kilton. He might have died without Worr's supplies, but Edwin now thought his brother had found certain nourishment there, without the provender the horse-thegn carried to him.

THE CROSS

RUNULV had brought his ship over to the wooden pier before the brew-house. He had already heaved her out of the water for the season, and wanted her back in for a night or two, so the wooden strakes of her hull would swell. When they did, he would easily find and tar any leaks between. He laboured within with a few of his crew, busy with this, and early lading. Two of his men were at work in the stern rigging up a series of oiled tarpaulins to serve as shelter for Edwin and his captains. The three were aboard the knorr, as was Sidroc. The latter had a small selection of furs which Osku the Sámi had brought him last year, including two fox in their white Winter guise. These were so rare that Sidroc had held them back for a worthy market. Paris was one, and he knew Runulv would bring him a fat pouch of silver in return. Just now the ship captain stood with Sidroc and Edwin as the final lines securing the tented shelter were fixed. Such was a luxury to look forward to, afloat.

"I am light on cargo, and can afford the space," Runulv grinned. Indeed, as he meant to trade precious gems once in Paris, he was free of bulkier goods, though his men, taking advantage of this, were stowing bales of fleece they were bringing on their own account.

Runulv's wife Gyda had appeared at the mouth of the pier, their four children running ahead toward the ship. The oldest boy would be ready to sail with his father in another year or two. Runulv left the men to greet them, and Alwin and Wystan wandered to the prow.

Seeing his ship captain's family put Sidroc in mind of something his shield-maiden had shared with him. He and Edwin were now alone, standing just behind the steering-oar, positioned by its slot, but high and dry.

"My wife told me your brother has wed. But you have not."

Edwin gave a single shake of his head. "I have not. Ælfred had sent me to Frisia to meet the daughters of a Count. But the man had died, and the daughters in mourning."

So you came on to here, Sidroc thought.

Other women rose in Edwin's mind: the lovely maid of Mercia he had glimpsed at the cathedral in Gleaweceaster; the strikingly tall and dark-haired woman at the hall in Witanceaster. Both had been barred to him. One was destined to be bride of this Dane's son; the second was Hrald's discarded wife. It seemed an almost laughable doom, the tightness of the circuit his path had taken him down.

Edwin decided to say the next. "Before this, Ælfred had summoned me to Witanceaster. But the maid he meant to present to me was Ealhswith of Four Stones."

Sidroc did not expect this. His eyes lifted to the heavens, milky-blue above their heads, and he ran his hand through his hair. He had not seen the flaxen-haired

Ealhswith since his visit to Four Stones years ago. She was now of age, he knew.

"Ælfred always knew how to surprise us," was all he said.

Edwin's thoughts had taken a deeper turn. The trek with Tindr had removed him from his many concerns; such had been forced to the edges of his mind, as he took in the landmarks and secret fanes the hunter had shared with him. Now though he was heading back to Kilton, and must again confront his failed efforts. He was of a sudden awash with the fruitlessness of all he had attempted. Sea birds cried sharply over his head, making him lift his eyes a moment to the vastness of the otherwise empty sky. He glanced toward the road running alongside the beach. He took in the paltry buildings, the few houses, of this place which had beckoned to the dead Lord of Kilton, and to him. If he turned his head more fully he could see the roof of the hall in whose shadow Godwin had breathed his last. Edwin's answering words were touched by the bitterness in his young heart.

"It all came to nothing. Just as life does."

The Dane studied the young man before him. "You are not only of your father, Edwin. The limits of his life are not yours.

"You are half your mother. The best half."

Edwin's head had dropped, as if the truth contained in this judgement was beyond fully compassing.

Sidroc let a long breath escape. He had some counsel for this son of his shield-maiden, and because he had travelled an arduous path to win that woman, he felt honour-bound to offer it now.

"The woman you seek – you must pray to be led to her. Pray, and make sacrifice to the Gods. To your God," he corrected.

They were words of import, both in consequence and in tone.

Edwin drew a long and slow breath. Whether it was Fate or the Hand of God at work, he had felt called – nay, driven – to make this journey. It had been anger driving him, but he was no longer certain who that anger had been directed at. All he had was this present moment, and its quiet revelation. This Dane who could have easily taken his life a few days ago now gave him advice on winning a wife.

"And," the Dane went on, "prepare to make great choices, for you cannot have all. If it is demanded of you, be ready to abandon what you know."

The day before Runulv was to set sail, four rode out from Tyrsborg to the place of burial. They passed the ranks of trading stalls and workshops which those of Kilton had already visited, passed the large wooden statue of Freyr, at which the men stopped and stared, passed too the fish drying racks, now stacked high with the white bodies of cod. The Mistress of Tyrsborg led the way on her dun mare, stopping at the boundary of the burial place. Two stone piers had been built as entry, and though no fence extended from it, they served as portal to another realm. They all quitted their mounts and walked with her. Low hog-backed stones marked many graves; piles of smaller rounded beach stones others. Off to one side the firing place lay ready, a pile of massive logs topped with a mound of faggots. She moved on. It had been years since Ceridwen had come to the spot they sought, but she knew the wooden cross her older son had pounded in still stood; she had seen it from the tail of her eye on rare occasions.

She stopped behind it. The cross had weathered in the dry air to a deep silvery grey, the shade of certain driftwood which washed up on their shores. The name GODWIN OF KILTON which Ceridwen had burnt in with a fired poker had worn away, so that only a part of the first letter could be read. The crosspiece, notched and hammered in by Tindr all those years past, still held fast. She recalled how large the cross had seemed in the arms of Ceric, and how it had tired him to carry it, yet he would do it himself. It looked modest enough now, but striking for its Christian symbolism in this heathen place of fare-well.

No one spoke. The three men approached with due reverence, but his captains stopped and held back. Edwin passed his mother and turned to face the cross. He kept his eyes fixed upon it. His father lay here, in a grave unconsecrated save for this simple wooden cross, and the fact that the man beneath it had, for all his failings, considered himself a Christian.

Edwin looked down at the grave, no more than a grassy expanse under which the man lay. He knew of his father's great valour in battle from what Worr had told him, just as the horse-thegn had told of Godwin's selfish anger.

He could just see the skirts of his mother's gown beyond the base of the cross; she had withdrawn a few steps to allow him his privacy. Edwin let his eyes lift to her. She was looking away, out to the white-lapped sea. He looked back to the wooden cross.

No words fell from Edwin's lips, but he addressed his father just the same. You lost your life trying to get her back. My life, and that of Edgyth, was not enough for you. We were not enough. You wanted her, and Edgyth too. And so you fought, and lost. And we lost you.

It is you who so angered me.

Having found this truth, he need give it utterance, to shape it into sound. The sense of loss, resentment, and abandonment rose within his breast, and might have emerged as a wrathful howl. Yet the words passed his lips, low, and full of discovery.

"You, father, are the one who angered me."

It was a bald avowal, one painful to accept. Edwin allowed his eyes to leave the bleached wood marking the grave. His mother had shifted her gaze, and stood looking at him with eyes wet from tears. She had heard him, and was witness to this truth.

Edwin gave a single shake of his head, rousing himself from these thoughts. His father's mortal remains lay under his feet. The man's soul was far beyond Edwin's anger, or the hurt caused to any here, or at Kilton. But his son lifted his wounded right hand to his brow, and with it, crossed himself. Having spoken aloud, he could release his father, and he did. May you rest in peace, he soundlessly uttered.

The Mistress of Tyrsborg stood steadily by, to see her son cross himself. Their eyes again met, and despite the sombreness of the setting, despite the grief wrought through long ago actions, she smiled at him.

He nodded back, ready to leave. Ceridwen turned. There outside the stone piers that marked the burial ground another horse had appeared, a black one, the beast nodding its great head up and down as if eager to be off. Upon it sat Sidroc, her past, present, and future, awaiting her.

———

Here ends Book Ten of
The Circle of Ceridwen Saga.

———

Now that you have finished my book, won't you please go to Amazon.com or Amazon.co.uk and write a few words about it? Your review is the very best way new readers have of finding great books! Thank you so much.

The Circle of Ceridwen Saga:

Sidroc the Dane
The Circle of Ceridwen: Book One
Ceridwen of Kilton: Book Two
The Claiming: Book Three
The Hall of Tyr: Book Four
Tindr: Book Five
Silver Hammer, Golden Cross: Book Six
Wildswept: Book Seven
For Me Fate Wove This: Book Eight
Two Dragons: Book Nine

Also by Octavia Randolph:

Light, Descending
The Tale of Melkorka: A Novella
Ride: A Novella: The Story of Lady Godiva

FREE CIRCLE OF CERIDWEN COOKERY BOOK(LET)

You've read the books – now enjoy the food. Your free Circle of Ceridwen Cookery Book(let) is waiting for you at www.octavia.net.

Ten easy, delicious, and authentic recipes from the Saga, including Barley Browis, Roast Fowl, Baked Apples, Oat Griddle Cakes, Lavender-scented Pudding, and of course – Honey Cakes. Charmingly illustrated with medieval woodcuts and packed with fascinating facts about Anglo-Saxon and Viking cookery. Free when you join the Circle, my mailing list. Be the first to know of new novels, have the opportunity to become a First Reader, and more. Get your Cookery Book(let) now and get cooking!

THE WHEEL OF THE YEAR

Candlemas – 2 February

St Gregory's Day – 12 March

St Cuthbert's Day – The Spring Equinox, about 21 March

St Walpurga's (Walpurgisnacht) – 30 April

St Elgiva's Day – 18 May

St Helen's Day – 21 May

High Summer or Mid-Summer Day – 24 June

Sts Peter and Paul – 29 June

Hlafmesse (Lammas) – 1 August

St Mary's Day – 15 August

St Matthews' Day – The Fall Equinox, about 21 September

All Saints – 1 November

The month of Blót – November; the time of Offering for
followers of the Old Religions; also time of slaughter of
animals which could not be kept over the coming Winter

Martinmas (St Martin's) – 11 November

Yuletide – 25 December to Twelfthnight – 6 January

Winter's Nights – the Norse end of year rituals, ruled
by women, marked by feasting and ceremony

ANGLO-SAXON PLACE NAMES,
WITH MODERN EQUIVALENTS

Æscesdun = Ashdown

Æthelinga = Athelney

Apulder = Appledore

Basingas = Basing

Beamfleot = Benfleet

Beardan = Bardney

Bearruescir = Berkshire

Bryeg = Bridgenorth

Buttingtun = Buttington

Caeginesham = Keynsham

Cippenham = Chippenham

Cirenceaster = Cirencester

Colneceastre = Colchester

Cruland = Croyland

Defenas = Devon

Englafeld = Englefield

Ethandun = Edington

Exanceaster = Exeter

Fearnhamme = Farnham

Fullanham = Fulham

Geornaham = Irnham

Glastunburh = Glastonbury

Gleaweceaster = Gloucester

Hamtunscir = Hampshire

Headleage = Hadleigh

Hreopedun = Repton

Iglea = Leigh upon Mendip

Jorvik (Danish name for Eoforwic) = York

Legaceaster = Chester

Limenemutha = Lymington in Hampshire

Lindisse = Lindsey

Lundenwic = London

Meredune = Marton

Meresig = Mersea

Middeltun = Milton

Readingas = Reading

River Lyge = River Lea

Sceaftesburh = Shaftesbury

Scireburne = Sherborne

Snotingaham = Nottingham

Sumorsaet = Somerset

Swanawic = Swanage

Turcesig = Torksey

Wedmor = Wedmore

Welingaford = Wallingford

Weogornaceastre = Worcester

Isle of Wiht = Isle of Wight

Witanceaster (where the Witan, the
King's advisors, met) = Winchester

ADDITIONAL PLACE NAMES

Frankland = Much of modern day France and Germany

Haithabu = Hedeby (formerly Denmark;
now in modern day Germany)

Aros = Aarhus, Denmark

Laaland = the island of Lolland, Denmark

Land of the Svear = Sweden

Cymru = Wales

Dubh Linn = Dublin

Hunefleth = Honfleur, France

Frisia = modern Netherlands

Dorestad = former trading town on the
Rhine in modern Netherlands

GLOSSARY OF TERMS

Althing, and Thing: a regular gathering of citizens to settle disputes, engage in trade, and socialize. Gotland was divided into three administrative districts, each with their own "thing" or meeting, but the great thing, the Althing, was held at Roma, in the geographical centre of the island.

alvar: nearly barren stretches of limestone rock, typically supporting only tiny lichens and moss.

Asgard: Heavenly realm of the Gods.

brewster: the female form of brewer (and, interestingly enough, the female form of baker is baxter . . . so many common names are rooted in professions and trades . . .).

browis: a cereal-based stew, often made with fowl or pork.

chaff: the husks of grain after being separated from the usable kernel.

ceorl: ("churl") a free man ranking directly below a thegn, able to bear arms, own property, and improve his rank.

cottar: free agricultural worker; in later eras, a peasant.

cresset: stone, bronze, or iron lamp fitted with a wick that burnt oil.

cwm: Welsh name for a mountain hollow, or ravine.

drekar: "dragon-ship," a war-ship of the Danes.

ealdorman: a nobleman with jurisdiction over given lands; the rank was generally appointed by the King and not necessarily inherited from generation to generation. The modern derivative *alderman* in no way conveys the esteem and power of the Anglo-Saxon term.

ell: a measure of length corresponding to a man's forearm and outstretched fingers.

fey: possessing magical or supernatural powers; one belonging to the Land of Faery.

fulltrúi: the Norse deity patron that one felt called to dedicate oneself to.

fylgja: a Norse guardian spirit, always female, unique to each family.

fyrd: the massed forces of Wessex, comprising thegns – professional soldiers – and ceorls, trained freeman.

hack silver: broken silver jewellery, coils of unworked silver bars, fragments of cast ingots and other silver parcelled out by weight alone during trade.

hamingja: the Norse "luck-spirit" which each person is born with.

leech-book: compilation of healing recipes and practices for the treatment of human and animal illness and injury. Such books were a compendium of healing herbs and spiritual and magical practices. The *Leech Book of Bald*, recorded during Ælfred's reign, is a famed, and extant, example.

lur: a vertical (or curved) sounding horn fashioned of wood or brass, dating from the Bronze Age, and used in Nordic countries to rally folk from afar.

morgen-gyfu: literally, "morning-gift"; a gift given by a husband to his new wife the first morning they awake together.

nard: (also, spikenard) a rare and precious oil, highly aromatic, derived from the crushed rhizomes of a honeysuckle-like plant grown in the Himalayas, India, and China. Mary Magdalen was said to have anointed the feet of Christ with nard.

philtre: a potion to excite love or lust in another.

quern: a small hand-driven mill consisting of two grind stones, the top stone usually being domed and having a hole to insert a wooden handle for turning. The oats, wheat, or other grain is placed between the stones, and the handle turned until the desired fineness is attained.

rauk: the striking sea- and wind-formed limestone towers on the coast of Gotland.

seax: the angle-bladed dagger which gave its name to the Saxons; all freemen carried one.

scop: ("shope") a poet, saga-teller, or bard, responsible not only for entertainment but seen as a collective cultural historian. A talented scop would be greatly valued by his lord and receive land, gold and silver jewellery, costly clothing and other riches as his reward.

scrying: to divine the future by gazing into a looking glass, a crystal, or water.

shingle beach: a pebbly, rather than sandy, beach.

skeggox: steel battle-axe favoured by the Danes.

skirrets: a sweet root vegetable similar to carrots, but cream-coloured, and having several fingers on each plant.

skogkatt: "forest cat"; the ancestor of the modern Norwegian Forest Cat, known for its large size, climbing ability, and thick and water-shedding coat.

Skuld: the eldest of the three Norse Norns, determiners of men's destinies. Skuld cuts with shears the thread of life. See also Urd and Verdandi.

strakes: overlapping wooden planks, running horizontally, making up a ship's hull.

symbel: a ceremonial high occasion for the Anglo-Saxons, marked by the giving of gifts, making of oaths, swearing of fidelity, and (of course) drinking ale.

tæfl or Cyningtæfl ("King's table"): a "capture the King" strategy board game.

thegn: ("thane") a freeborn warrior-retainer of a lord; thegns were housed, fed and armed in exchange for complete fidelity to their sworn lord. Booty won in battle by a thegn was generally offered to their lord, and in return the lord was expected to bestow handsome gifts of arms, horses, arm-rings, and so on to his best champions.

treen: domestic objects fashioned of wood, especially tableware.

Tyr: the God of war, law, and justice. He voluntarily forfeited his sword-hand to allow the Gods to deceive, and bind, the gigantic wolf Fenrir.

Tyr-hand: in this Saga, any left-handed person, named so in honour of Tyr's sacrifice.

Urd: the youngest of the three Norse Norns, determiners of men's destinies. Urd makes decision as to one's calling and station in life. See also Skuld and Verdandi.

Verdandi: the middle of the three Norse Norns, determiners of men's destinies. Verdandi draws out the thread of life to appropriate length. See also Skuld and Urd.

wadmal: the Norse name for the coarse and durable woven woollen fabric that was a chief export in the Viking age.

wergild: Literally, man-gold; the amount of money each man's life was valued at. The Laws of Æthelbert, a 7th century King of Kent, for example, valued the life of a nobleman at 300 shillings (equivalent to 300 oxen), and a ceorl was valued at 100 shillings. By Ælfred's time (reigned 871–899) a nobleman was held at 1200 shillings and a ceorl at 200.

yealing: one the same age

NOTES

CHAPTER THE FIRST

Elf-shot, and early English healing and healers. The Old English term læce "leech" is the name for a healer, often coupled with the Latin term "medicus", doctor/physician. Wort-cunning is the knowledge of herbs, and all healers, whether a mother dressing a child's scraped knee, or a nun or monk attempting to stem plague, employed herbs in their efforts. Many recipes for remedies from the period have survived, primarily in three manuscripts: the Leech Book of Bald (Bald being a monk); the Lacnunga Manuscript, and the Old English Herbarium Manuscript. In addition to the use of herbal preparations – a number of which have been proven efficacious by modern science – many treatments include magical elements, such as singing into the wound, performing ritualized actions in the gathering and application of the remedy, and wearing or sleeping on certain charms and amulets. Many healing remedies combine early, heathen wort-cunning with Christian elements. Certain performative treatments include the participation of a priest, such as that known as Æcerbot ("Field-Remedy", also known as For Unfruitful Land), where representative sections of sod were cut from the soil, anointed with yeast, honey, milk, and herbs, carried to a church and laid upon the altar before being returned to the field. The cure for Elf-shot, for which Dwynwen and Edgyth treat Ceric, makes use of a healer's knife, a læceseax, to repel the power of a curse which renders him for periods in a near-catatonic state. The authoritative source in modern English on Anglo-Saxon medicine is *Leechcraft: Early English Charms, Plantlore and Healing*, by Stephen Pollington.

CHAPTER THE THIRD

Boethius and *The Consolations of Philosophy*. Born into a patrician Roman family about 480, Boethius rose to become a senator and consul as well as respected translator, commentator, and author. After revealing and condemning widespread corruption in the Ostrogothic Court in which he served, Boethius was imprisoned and sentenced to death. It was there, awaiting execution that he wrote his masterwork, *The Consolations of Philosophy*. The manuscript survived his execution at age 44 in 524, and went on to become one of the most popular treatises of the Middle Ages. It is not surprising that a man like Ælfred, plagued by poor health and beset by war over nearly the entire span of his reign, should have found solace and wisdom there. The King rendered the Latin of Boethius into Old English to make it widely available to all who could read, and embellished and enriched the text with glosses and anecdotes germane to his, and his countrymen's, lives. His translation exists in two manuscripts only, one in the Bodleian Library, Oxford; the other in the Cottonian Collection of the British Library (wherein also reside such masterworks as the sole manuscript of

Beowulf). A modern English version of Ælfred's translation by Walter John Sedgefield can be found online at the
University of Kentucky site.

CHAPTER THE TENTH

Gerolf, Count of Frisia. Gerolf (died 895 or 896), took
part in driving back repeated Viking attacks on Frisia
in modern day Netherlands. In 889 by the King of East
Francia rewarded him with a substantial land grant,
including valuable properties on the banks of the old
Rhine. He is known to have had at least two sons, Dirk
and Waldger (possibly nephews he named as sons); but of
Gerolf's daughters, if any, we know nothing. The Count's
wealth and the date of his death provides the novelist with
a likely candidate for a potential match between a daughter of Gerolf and Edwin, Lord of Kilton.

CHAPTER THE FIFTEENTH

Rhodri Mawr (in Welsh, "Rhodri the Great"). A renowned
war-chief against both the Saxons and Danes, Rhodri
Mawr was born Rhodri ap Merfyn about 820, and died
either 873 or 877/878. Rhodri became King of much of
Wales during his lifetime, and was famed for his defence
of Cymru against Viking invaders, killing the Danish
leader Gorm in 856. Rhodri was seemingly killed in battle
against the invading Mercian army, likely at the Battle of
Anglesey in 873. At his death four of his many sons each
helmed a different portion of those territories their father
had briefly unified.

The Law Code of Ælfred. Certainly one of the crowning achievements of the King's life was the effort he placed
in producing a more or less unified code of laws. In his
preface, Ælfred explains that he examined many existing
law codes, from the Old Testament to those of previous
Anglo-Saxon kings in neighbouring kingdoms:

> *Then I, King Ælfred, gathered them together and*
> *ordered to be written many of the ones that our*
> *forefathers observed – those that pleased me; and*
> *many of the ones that did not please me I rejected*
> *with the advice of my councillors, and com-*
> *manded them to be observed in a different way.*
> *For I dared not presume to set down in writing at*
> *all many of my own, since it was unknown to me*
> *what would please those who should come after us.*
> *But those which I found either in the days of Ine,*
> *my kinsman, or of Offa, king of the Mercians, or*
> *of Ælthelberht (who first among the English people*
> *received baptism), and which seemed to me most*
> *just, I collected herein, and omitted the others.*
> (*Alfred the Great: Asser's Life of King Alfred and*
> *Other Contemporary Sources*, translated by Simon
> Keynes and Michael Lapidge.)

The Laws outline a wide variety of crimes and appropriate punishments, from cattle-rustling to the rape of
a slave girl to cutting off a man's long hair without his
consent (short hair was often the sign of a slave, thus
to be forcibly shorn would be an insult to one's class).
Punishments, whether corporal or exacted by fines, varied
according to social class, but all classes were protected,

though in the case of enslaved persons the fine exacted for harming them was awarded to the owner.

Women enjoyed legal rights under the Laws of Ælfred, and earlier Anglo-Saxon law, that they were to lose after the Battle of Hastings (1066) and for many hundreds of years afterwards. Amongst them were the right to own land in her own name, and to sell such land or give it away without her father's or husband's consent; the right to defend herself in court; the right to act as compurgator in law suits; that is, to testify to another's truthfulness. She could freely manumit her slaves. And she could not be forced into an unwanted union.

Ælfred compiled his *Laws* in the last decade of his life. I have taken the novelist's liberty of having his faithful Bailiff of Defenas, Raedwulf, aid him in this task.

CHAPTER THE SIXTEENTH

The design of Ælfred's ships. Whether Ælfred can rightly be claimed the Father of the English Navy has been discussed amongst military scholars for over a hundred years. The pressing need to meet the onslaught of Danish war-ships with vessels approaching the speed, maneuverability, and flexibility of the famed and feared drekars – dragon-ships – certainly drove him to experiment with new designs. The Anglo-Saxon Chronicle notes, for the years 896/897 *". . . Then King Ælfred ordered warships to be built to meet the Danish ships: they were almost twice as long as the others, some had sixty oars; some more; they were both swifter, steadier, and with more freeboard than the others; they were built neither after the Frisian design, nor after the Danish, but as they seemed to himself that they could be most serviceable . . ."* (Translation G.N. Garmonsway, *The Anglo-Saxon Chronicle.*)

These seem not always to have proved successful – the Chronicle notes several mishaps with the ships; or nascent naval skills were far from what they would become when Britannia ruled the seas. At any rate Ælfred, ever the innovator, can be credited with greatly spurring efforts to mount a satisfying maritime defence, and several times as a younger man he himself fought at sea.

War-fire, also known as Greek Fire or sea-fire. One of the most fascinating – and deadly – weapons employed by the ancients at sea, this napalm-like substance has never been fully understood, though records of its use are widespread and credible. Its exact composition is still a mystery, but naptha (which could be made from distilling coal tar and peat) was likely mixed with sulphur, tree resins, and other substances, along with quicklime. It was dangerous and volatile to handle, and certain preparations could be smeared by night on the buildings and weapons of the enemy, to self-ignite in the Sun. Other forms used for sea battles, for which we have manuscript illuminations, show the fire being blown out of a metal pipe powered by a bellows, and the hapless enemy ship being met by a wall of fire.

CHAPTER THE NINETEENTH

Fire-starter fungus (inonotus obliquus), also known as tinder fungus or Chaga. A parasitical fungus which lives on birch, and sometimes other deciduous trees. Its use as a fire-starter was known in pre-history, and the powdered fungus is used as well in various herbal remedies.

ACKNOWLEDGEMENTS

The release of every new installment in The Circle of Ceridwen Saga is akin to the launch of a boat, and none more so than *Water Borne*. I was not always alone in this small vessel, but companioned by Beth Altchek and Libby Williams, who, when my prow touched shore at intervals, clambered aboard with provender in the way of warm enthusiasm and critical discernment. When I pushed off to sea again, their gifts remained, and the book you hold is the better for them. Beth and Libby, sustainers and compass-bearers, I salute you with heart and mind.

My invaluable First Readers continue to inspire me, and my gratitude to them for their unflagging care in reading and commenting on *Water Borne* is deep and sincere. Great thanks are due to Tony Allen, Lorraine Angelopoulos, Judy Boxer, Lyndall Buxton, Shani Goode, Mary Kelly, Elaine MacDonald, Kristen McEnaney, Jennifer L. Morris, Rebekah Paraskevas, Amanda Porath, Ellen Rudd, Linda Schultz, and Lorie Witt. Sharing the excitement of an additional Saga novel with you is a joy.

Janine Eitniear and Misi are Founder and Moderator respectively of The Circle of Ceridwen Discussion and Idea Group on Facebook. There members can discuss the novels, comment on new archeological findings about the Anglo-Saxon and Viking Age, explore period handcrafts, foodways and fashion, and find the kind of fellowship that springs from shared interests and mutual discovery. Janine and Misi, your dedication to the Saga and the interests of its followers have led you to create a happy and engaged on-line community which never ceases to delight me. You have my daily thanks for your creativity and effort.

ABOUT THE AUTHOR

Octavia Randolph has long been fascinated with the development, dominance, and decline of the Anglo-Saxon peoples. The path of her research has included disciplines as varied as the study of Anglo-Saxon and Norse runes, and learning to spin with a drop spindle. Her interests have led to extensive on-site research in England, Denmark, Sweden, and Gotland. In addition to the Circle Saga, she is the author of the novella *The Tale of Melkorka*, taken from the Icelandic Sagas; the novella *Ride*, a retelling of the story of Lady Godiva, first published in Narrative Magazine; and *Light, Descending*, a biographical novel about the great John Ruskin. She has been awarded Artistic Fellowships at the Ingmar Bergman Estate on Fårö, Sweden; MacDowell; Ledig House International; and Byrdcliffe.

She answers all fan mail and loves to stay in touch with her readers. Join her mailing list and read more on Anglo-Saxon and Viking life at www.octavia.net. Follow her on Facebook at Octavia Randolph Author, and for exclusive access and content join the spirited members of The Circle of Ceridwen Saga Discussion and Idea Group on Facebook.